CW01506778

Praise

A NOTE ON THE AUTHOR

Richard Mabb is fairly old and has come late to writing. His aesthetics were formed long ago before the myth of a common culture was exposed as a paternalistic, phallocentric construct with its roots in the European Middle Ages. Knowing what he doesn't know he is still questing after what he has been taught to believe is beauty.

He is currently working on a transposition of *Far From the Madding Crowd* into the 1970s featuring a transsexual hero/ine.

Manette is his first novel

Manette

Richard Mabb

writesideleft

2022

ISBN: TBP 978-1-7396993-0-7
ISBN HB 978-1-7396993-1-4
ISBN eBook 978-1-7396993-2-1

Compilation & Cover Design by S A Harrison
Cover Image: *The Achievement of the Grail (The Attainment: The Vision of the Holy Grail to Sir Galahad, Sir Bors & Sir Perceval)* - Edward Burne-Jones, 1891 - 1894

Published by WriteSideLeft UK
https://www.writesideleft.com

Manette

Richard Mabb

For
The Royal Masonic School for Boys, Bushey, Herts.

Contents

Rome, Via Labicana, August 1951

Bucatini all'Amatriciana

On a chopping board in the miniscule kitchen Percy unwrapped the parcel of brown paper tied up with string that had made its journey here downhill from the market in Piazza Vittorio Emmanuele along the via Foscolo and past the huge Post Office Savings Bank on Piazza Dante. Percy liked to recognise in that unlooked-after square with its smoke-blackened buildings a fellow survivor of recent events. Underneath the palazzo of a bank lay a warren of underground tunnels that had been sheltering Romans from bombs just a few years ago. During those years the square, too, had lost its identity for a while; changing from Dante to Leonardo da Vinci and back to Dante again when the Espozisione dropped its claim to the name. Like so many places, so many of us, thought Percy, it's had the grandiosity knocked out of it.

Percy and the parcel had continued along the Via Alfieri and out into the Via Merulana. It was here, almost on the turning into the Via Labicana that would take him home, that Percy today, as on every day he passed by, wished "buon giorno" to The Man in the Ironmongers, seller of the fine cook's knife he'd long coveted, had finally bought and that would soon be cutting into the piece of fat pig cheek in the bag.

Sweating a little now Percy had turned downhill again into the wide Via Labicana its plane trees providing shade to the gleaming tram tracks that lit a path down toward the Colosseum in the distance. Keeping to the South side of the street Percy had hugged the sides of the apartment buildings until he came to the little cobbled courtyard in front of his own block. Inside the door the hallway stretched dim and cool to the stairs.

Now, in his cramped monolocale, before him on the chopping board, beaded and moist after its journey, the piece of guanciale sat on its wrapper, the fat gleaming white and smooth as silk. Having washed his hands at the tap with cold water on the very last sliver of bergamot and lemon-scented Fields spermaceti soap Percy (who since the war had insisted on using only the finest of soaps) dried them on the knobbly blue Komtrust towel he'd bought in Bombay on the way home.

For so long a staple of Roman cuisine the guanciale had had a bad war in the City with pork being in short supply. For someone like him with no family, no connections in the countryside, no acre with a pig in Lazio, something as simple as this dish would then have been an unattainable luxury and was still something of an extravagance. Percy stared at the aromatic piece of pork on the chopping board then, giving thanks, raised the sharp knife and pressed it down into the fat and flesh. Small pieces, lardons, pezzetti are what he needs. He slices, dices with the Merulana knife until the entire 100 grammes is reduced to a faintly luminous sprawl over the board. Using the blade of the knife Percy sweeps the entire haul into his frying pan; the padella he'd picked up at the Porta Portese the day after he'd taken on this monolocale, its kitchen empty of everything other than the pre-War gas stove, sink and draining board.

Olio 1 cucchiao
To the frying pan he adds olive oil, one spoonful. Strange, he thinks, how other languages sometimes throw up stumbling blocks to comprehension. Here we have, he thinks, holding up the spoon, a spoon. Spoooon he says to himself; spoon, moon, June, loon, boon and remembering the country of his father's birth: Dunoon. Cucchiao. Cookie-I-owe. Cookie-I-owe, Cookie-I-owe. Dicula. That was what they'd been taught at school. Dicula mea lucida est. My spoon is shiny. This spoon wasn't shiny, of course. He looked again at the spoon in his hand, the no-longer-shiny spoon with its point, its head, worn down on one side so that it looked like a shovel. Nearly four years in Camp grating along the bottom of mess-tins, vats and kettles had done that until faithful Spoon could attract every single atom of every grain of rice, every green of potato into its bowl. Good old Spoon. Filched from the Cathay Hotel for a dare, Spoon had become his friend, his companion, an extension of his hand, his arm, conveying life-sustaining food, things that might not previously even have been thought edible, up to his ever-hungry gob.

Ah, but he thought; of course; cochlearium. Cucchiao. Spoonful, not spoon. Funny how a language sieves out the words it actually needs from those it doesn't. He pours the oil from the flask to the spoon to the pan. He then sucks Spoon clean. Waste not want not.

Passato pelati 350g

The pig in the pan starts to splutter and brown (rossolare) while he stares at it attending to its transformation. After a few minutes he takes the pan off the heat and, using Spoon, he scoops all the pezzetti into a shallow earthenware dish at the side of the stove. Then he picks up the jar of tomato passata, 350 grammes, that the Signora downstairs has given him. It comes from her family's farm on the outskirts of Vico Equense South of Naples where they grow, sieve and bottle enough tomatoes every year to supply their entire diaspora. Percy remembers attempting to impress the Signora by asking if the tomatoes were San Marzano and being rewarded by a withering look accompanied by a firm slap of the back of the Signora's hand to the underside of her back-tilted chin. "Mai," she had said, "Mai, mai, mai!" The fingers of her right hand came together into a point that thrust up toward his face like a dagger. "Ciliegini!" said the Signora before turning away an expression of disgust on her wizened old face.

Vino Bianco Secco 50ml

Sale, Pepe

Percy grapples with the lid of the jar until his hand hurts then finally with a suitably dramatic, even operatic pop the lid swivels open and the unused energy carries Percy forward into the rim of the sink with a collision that practically winds him. Still the jar is open and Spoon then dives inside to ladle the contents bit by bit into the cooking pan. Then Percy adds cold water to the jar, swirling it about till the water turns a faint pink and this too is added to the pan. The tomato mess begins to bubble, to form craters that ejaculate fiery red gobs that then subside back into the magma. Plop, plop, plop. The trick is to keep the heat at the point where the stuff plops away gently with as little adhering to the wall or scarring the forearm as possible. He reaches for a pretty, lidded majolica jar next to the stove. Salt, thinks Percy, the magic ingredient. Salt rationed. Rice cooked in seawater. Bloated stomachs, cramped muscles, dizziness all from the lack of salt. Salt once came up in conversation with the Other Signora downstairs who had family in the North. During the war they'd sent her packs of salt they'd collected from the railway tracks where it had been thrown to prevent the points from freezing up. Percy adds a little salt to the passata, a pinch of pepper and a splash of the tooth-enamel-stripping Frascati wine sold in flagons at the Alimentari over the road.

Peperoncino

That done he turns back to the chopping board and picks up his other market purchase; a small red peperoncino. Well not exactly a peperoncino (Italians are so specific when it comes to food ingredients) but a frigitello; nothing too hot. Reaching for the knife he swiftly decapitates it, splits it, deseeds it. Sharp, he thinks, always keep your knives sharp. The image of a blade comes into his mind as it does whenever he's chopping food in the kitchen. Up flashes a sword, a Japanese sword but not the real Tamahagane or simply not sharp enough. Hack goes the sword followed by a scream. Up it goes and hack it comes down again. Hack then hack then hack goes the sword but it can't cut the vertebrae through. Mercifully another officer steps forward with his revolver and delivers the coup de grace. From the watching ranks of prisoners resounds a deafening silence. The man at the ironmongers on Merulana keeps this knife honed to perfection for him. Tried to sell me a Japanese knife. Not a bad sort though, the ironmonger man. Now he adds the neatly beheaded and eviscerated chilli to the simmering sauce.

Next Percy reaches down under the console table that serves as his sideboard and pulls out the ancient, enamelled pan (another Porta Portese trophy) that holds five litres of water for cooking pasta. Filling it from the tap he lights the burner (the other burner) and places it on the heat. That done he turns away from the stove toward the window from which he can see down into a biggish courtyard inside a sort of barrack-block with a gate that gives onto the tiny Via di San Giovanni in Laterano. A Vespa motor-scooter buzzes along its canyon length. Ahead over the rooftops stands the Pontifical Irish College. Away Southward rises the Parco Ninfeo di Nerone on the Celio. "Ninfeo di Nerone," says Percy to himself conjuring a vision of Roman high jinks in a spectacular fountain. There would be a scene worth watching; a group of large-buttocked women (Roman female nudes are usually generously seated), uplifted breasts cleaving the torrents, invoking the spirits of the waters, welcoming them to their journey's end from springs in the Sabine Hills. He picks up an opened pack of Nazionali, taps it on the base, pulls out a cigarette from the sheaf and lights it. "Dreadful habit," he says, once again, then coughs. Moving closer to the open window he looks out and over to the basilica of San Giovanni. More buttocks, he thinks for there on the skyline are the rear sides of the twelve Apostles, decorously draped. Beneath their feet lie over two thousand years of recorded history from cavalry barracks to imperial palace, to chief basilica of the Christian world. Just a few years ago a congregation of Roman Jews and other refugees was sheltered here from the Fascists. Swallows dart from apartment block to yellow-gold apartment block. He jettisons the cigarette out of the window. There is a faint shout from down below.

Pecorino di Amatrice 75g

Behind him there come the sounds of water coming to the boil. Ebullition; one of his favourite words. Turning back to the sideboard he unwraps a paper packet of bucatinis and slips out of the wrapper just enough to fill the circle made by his thumb and forefinger. He drops this bundle into the pan and returns the remainder to its packet. Picking up Spoon he first stirs the boiling water and next scrapes the cooked cubetti of meat into the sauce before lifting out the peporinco. That done he unwraps another packet of cheese; not just any cheese but Pecorino and not just any Pecorino at that; this is the Pecorino di Amatrice brought to the market from the fertile farms around Rieti, site of that ancient lake drained by the Romans to provide superlative grazing land. Softer than the usual Pecorino Romano this cheese has been bathed in olive oil and vinegar to aid its six-month seasoning and is considered the best cheese to accompany the Amatriciana. What Percy has learnt about food since coming to Rome has mostly been extracted, tortuously at first and then more fluently as his Italian has improved, from the theatre shows that can be magicked into life at any market stall by uttering his stock phrases: "Come si cucina questo?" or "Come lo usi in cucina?" First answers the stall holder followed by the sharp-elbowed Roman matron, so tiny that Percy may not have noticed her. She is sharp-beaked like a Bantam hen, responding loudly and shrilly with quite a different cooking suggestion larded with all the traditions of the Roman table screeched out in a dialect he can barely understand. While Percy's Italian has improved his Roman is still patchy though from the tone of the matron's voice and the gesturing of her hands he infers that the lady would only, say in the case of choosing a cheese, buy the Pecorino Romano, the products of Lazio, such as the Pecorino d'Amatrice, being tainted with molecules of Fascism and a hatred of Rome that goes back to the Rape of the Sabine Women and probably beyond. Guided by these thespians Percy has bought thin fish with sword-like beaks, artichokes, oxtail, eel, tripes, fresh borlotti beans, Misticanza. He's cooked or dressed them according to methods he's half-grasped. Even today when buying the Pecorino the Matron del Giorno (they blend into one) had accosted him to ask if he were buying it for Amatriciana or was he some kind of tourist or heathen? Answering yes, for the Amatriciana, the Matron launched another attack demanding to know whether his intended sauce were to be rosso or bianco because, screeched the lady, as any real Roman knows the original sauce is alla Gricia, made with Guanciale but not tomatoes, never, mai. Same with pizza. Only a Southerner would eat pizza with that spew of tomato all over it! Gesturing at the stallholder who laughs uproariously she accuses him of polluting Roman kitchens with the cooking of Amatrice which as everyone knows is practically Abruzzi anyhow. Percy finds the Gricia a bit dry but not daring to say so, slips away thinking that you might as well add an egg and make a Carbonara. Pizza Bianca on the other hand he has a great fondness for, it being the nearest thing to cheese on toast he's encountered in Italy.

Bucatini 100g

While the pasta cooks Percy grates a little of the cheese and returns the rest to its wrapper. He lifts a colander from a hook on the wall and puts it in the square sink. Carefully, using Spoon, he lifts a strand of bucatini pasta from the roiling water and, resisting the temptation to throw it at the wall to test its doneness (if it sticks it's ready) he bites into it. It resists his teeth. It's al dente. Percy drains the pasta through the colander then tips the slithery, hot, still-squirming entity into a bowl (a terrina) and strews over it the cheese, then his sauce, amalgamates them and prepares to get stuck in. But he's forgotten the wine. Walking over to the tiny bathroom he lifts out from the basin of cold water a flask-shaped bottle. Tonight he will take a break from

Frascati and treat himself to Verdicchio.

He eats his early supper. "Then I shall go out for a walk," he says to himself before starting on the washing up, la vaisselle, il lavaggio, gazing out on the ochre and gold and listening to the keen cries of the swallows.

Rome, Piazza Navona, August 1951

Negroni
One part gin

Percy blamed that Orson Welles fellow for it. Once tasted, he knew, he would never abandon its charms or escape its oily embrace. The first little sip always delivers the vermouth. The second, the Campari. The third, the fourth, the fifth down to the bottom of the glass are spent hunting the elusive spirit of the gin that bypasses the tongue entirely and rises in a fume straight to the brain. The glass empty, Percy fishes with his fingers to the bottom and pulls out la scorza which he first sucks dry and then eats whole. Disgusting habit, he says to himself; never know where it's been. In a dozen other glasses, probably. No, no, that's not fair. You're sounding like an American tourist who looks for lack of hygiene everywhere. Like Orson Welles himself, probably, dragging around Rome with an assortment of local starlets. Not that he has any idea of Welles's views on Italian hygiene (the gin begins to let his thoughts flow in a gentle stream of consciousness) nor that he even saw Welles it being a couple of years ago at least that he was here making the film. Moreover it was unlikely that the actor and his entourage would have come over here to Piazza Navona to bar-crawl. They all went to Via Veneto, didn't they? He doesn't. All those starlings in the trees chattering as madly as the Cinecittà folk and that new style of rapacious news-photographer that follows them everywhere. Chatter, chatter, chatter and bird-droppings.

Actually, Percy admits, Navona's history is equally one of crowds and mess. The ancient Circus Agonalis then Navone now Navona: Gladiators, baying plebs, decline. Mock naval battles, cheering crowds, palazzi, show, decline. Fascism, war, decline. Now, though, this evening, it's peaceful, mostly empty. The children playing games have gone and the passeggiata seems to favour the Campo de Fiori. Navona is just too – public. Too grand, No nooks or crannies. Not enough places for Nonna to sit down and rest her feet. Or perhaps it's just the war, still. The huge, smooth paving slabs glisten in the rosy evening light as though they were ice. The tall windows are shuttered. Which was the one they used in that film with La Lollo? They all look just the same. You'd have to remember which was its nearest fountain. The fountains play with the waters filling the basins. "O fons Bandusiae, splendidior vitro," mutters Percy. Crikey the gin must be doing its work. Yes please, he thinks, I'll have one more for the road and he beckons to the little knot of Camerieri hanging around by the door hoping that the good-looking one will be the one to come over. No not this evening it seems. It's the too-thin lantern-jawed one, the one that always appears to sneer at tourists and foreigners. And he's not the only one. They all seem to. Percy doesn't mind in the least. He overhears their conversations and knows what they think. It's nothing to do with the customers, it's the owner who's as tight as a tick and keeps far too much of the tips. So they vent their ire on the foreigners which in turn keeps them from coming back and the tables mostly empty. Perfect. They don't mind him, in fact they've seen him often enough to be just disdainful rather than openly hostile. To them he's just the little finocchio inglese that comes here on his own. Fennel is one of Percy's favourite plants. He loves the feathery fronds whose gorgeous green when lit by the Spring sun appear as bright torches to light Her back from the underworld and the gloomy realm of Dis. He loves the tang of the seeds of the wild fennel, the finocchietti that flavour salume, the hint of it in a strega. He buys them by the etto at the market and puts them whole in a cabbage soup or a ragù with crumbled-up salsiccia. And that, he thinks, is just the seeds. Florence fennel he loves, too, sweet and cool like the arse-cheek of a marble putto. He makes a stew of them with onion and wine making sure they've been candied a little by letting them stick to the pan for a few moments. In Spring he slices them very finely with his mandolin and sets them out on a plate with salume and shavings of Pecorino Sardo. So no, he doesn't mind at all being called a Fennel.

Lantern-jaw, smirking, brings his second Negroni out on a tray and with an exaggerated sway of the hips and a leering smile puts the glass down in front of him. "Altro, Signore?" he asks, assuming the foreigner is immune to double entendre. It would spoil the fun thinks Percy to admit that he understands Italian. "Ah no," he says and then "Grazie," mangling the word into the stock American "Graze-eeh-yay." The waiter seems pleased and minces off back to his huddle of colleagues saying something mildly offensive that has them laughing together.

The only problem with this side of the Piazza was its being in shadow at this time of the evening but the reward was a delightful coolness and the sight of all the buildings on the East side of the Piazza bursting into bright orange as the sun flamed across them while the fountains began to recede into violet and the paving slabs to the colour of a bruise. The space was now nearly empty with all the grandeur of a huge stage set. Not even Hollywood or Cinecittà could come up with anything on this scale. And this was why Percy had trekked over from the Labicana along Mussolini's barbaric road across the Foro Romano, past the Vittorio Emanuele, through Piazza Venezia, along Plebiscito, Gesu, Santa Chiara, Sant' Eustachio, looping around Sediari and finally into di Pasquio so that he could emerge to take in the full length of Navona from Moro to Nettuno. It settled him. It settled his thoughts. It was a parade ground. He knew where he stood.

The quiet, the wonderful quiet that settles on busy places when their business is done was broken by a babble of shouts as though a covey of partridges had been flushed out from one of the alleyways opposite him. Looking across into that unearthly facade he saw a group of men burst out into the piazza. Five perhaps, or six? They staggered a little, some more than others. They walked in couples, arms around each other's shoulders. Taller than the average Italian and one or two of them blond or gingery. Dressed for the most part in... were they cricket trousers? They're wearing a kind of collective camouflage of off-white and dirty cream. One or two have cable-knit V-necked sweaters loosely draped over their shoulders and another one or two have belted their trousers with, good heavens, striped ties. As they staggered over towards this very bar Percy heard a scrappy but loud chorus that began "When Britain first..."

English. British. One was so used to Americans here in Rome you forgot that for almost a century Rome had been a kind of British colony. And then the cricketing whites. I suppose, he thinks, one would still call them whites even when they were beige with dirt. But cricket? In Rome, in August? Mad dogs, he thinks, mad dogs. The waiting staff behind him have closed together for safety like innocent sheep watching the progress of the pack after the fox. Yet as the cricketing group grew closer and distinguishable words began to emerge it was clear these were what his father would have called Harmless Drunks. "Never, never, never Shall Be Slaaaaaves!" Where on earth was the nearest cricket pitch? And. No. Could that tie round the waist of the tall, slim, blond man in early middle-age be MCC? Now they were near enough Percy could see that indeed it was. A toff. He'd thought they were extinct here but clearly not. He takes the last swig of his negroni (better not go for a third he thinks remembering that awful time it had been one too many and he'd fallen face forward onto a paving slap and nearly smashed his teeth) and turns to the waiters to signal his wish to pay up and go. As he turns the voices began to break over him, singular now, distinguishable.

"Famous Victory!" yelled one. "Borghese CC for ever!" shouted another. "Down with the CMCC!" the first one again. "Aubrey what a wrist!" "Constant practice!" "Totty's catch!" "Totty saved the day!" "Three cheers for Totty. Hip, Hip!" "Hooray!"

Now what was happening? The group seemed to get nearer. Much backslapping was going on. "Come on where's this party of yours, Henry?" "Dragged us all the way over to this godforsaken..." "Let's have a sharpener here." "No come on, there's whisky galore up at the Contessa's." "My god have you seen it? Isn't it precious?" "Catch!" yelled someone and an ashtray, deftly swiped from a table, went up into the air.

That's glass, thought Percy.

Up sailed the ashtray, up until it caught some of the evening light. The bar, the patrons, the cricketers, the waiters all freeze as it begins its descent towards exactly where he's sitting. Like a star it flickers as it falls. "Bloody...!" was all Percy heard before he saw a figure, a long-armed figure, fling itself from out of the group, hands cupped together.

The figure hit the paving sideways, neck strained upward to keep head from ground, arms stretched out, muscles and veins straining, hands miraculously grasping the ashtray. The figure rolled immediately onto its back, head still up, hands and ashtray over its chest as it, with a huge effort from the diaphragm, curled upward until forehead touched knees. All had been going so well, so fast, until forehead and ashtray connected with a sound like "tock" and the figure flopped backward landing, so very fortunately, on the plimsolled feet of one of the group.

"Fuck me," said a voice. There was a pause. "Catch!" they all yelled as one. "Bravo!" yelled the waiters. The air was full of the clattering sound of the wings of pigeons getting away from the scene and in the near distance a Toppolino coughed. Tableau.

One part red vermouth
Percy looked at the figure now prone on the ground, observing that the ashtray, smooth-cornered, appeared at first sight to have broken the man's nose. Blood ran down from the nostrils in a wide trickle. The long head with its grey-blond hair turned sideways, looking up from the ground. Were those eyes focused on him? Like the eye of Marsyas times two. It was hard to tell. Still no one moved. One second, two seconds. They seem, thought Percy, his thoughts occupying only a fraction of this fraction of time, like a Quattrocento painter's throng. Magenta. Mantegna. "For they have brought," came up like subtitles on a film "no fabulous symbol here but my heart's victim and its..." The blood reached the man's lips.

Suddenly all was action. Someone inside flicked a switch and the bar blazed with bright blue light. The scene exsanguinated leaving the wounded man looking like a pale corpse and the throng of English cricketers ghostly, grey and startled like chiaroscuro figures in a late Titian. "Ghiaccio!" boomed a voice from the doorway into the nether bar. "Prontissimo!". The English fell back a little as one of the waiters dashed over with cubes of ice bagged inside a clean white towel. The catcher pressed the towel to the apparently broken nose to the sound of "Ouch!" followed by "Grazie," (most properly pronounced). "Niente di rotto. Andra tutto bene," he said.

Still the English didn't move. Sunstruck, probably, thought Percy. Sun's fried their brains. The man, the catcher, sat on the ground only a matter of four or five feet away from him. The man looked at him. "Close shave," he said and then, shrugging off the hands offered to raise him to his feet extended that golden hand of his toward Percy. "Aiuto," he said. Percy put his own to the arms of his chair and levered himself upright. The drink made him sway, very slightly, as he stepped forward and, avoiding the hand extended to him, leant forward and grasped the figure under the pits of the arms, then, bracing, canted backward so as to pull him to his feet pushing up from a squat to a stand taking the figure with him. Inevitably they were close, very close. Percy being the shorter by a foot found his face in the man's clavicle, his forehead feeling the pulse in the throat. He smelt sweat, smelt the iron smell of blood, he felt the press of another body against his. The head, the grey and golden head, tilted oh so slightly toward the crown of his own and he heard, sotto voce, in his ear; "Knew you would."

A hand patted his back and the body was absent. The world returned to a chorus of "Are you alright old chap?" "Well held!" "Thank Christ or this chap here would have bought it." "Who threw the bloody thing?" "Totty you prat!" "David can you walk? Do you want to sit down?" David, heard Percy. David.

"No I'm alright," said the David. "Look here chaps you go on to the party without me."

Cries of "No!", "You sure?"

"No really I just need to sit down for a minute. Look I've dropped the bloody ice. Cameriere? Dell'altro ghiaccio per favore. Look I'll just sit down here for a bit."

"You must come and join us.'"

"Yes of course in just a couple of minutes."

"You know the way"

"How can you ask?"

"See you in a minute or two."

"Five, just five."

"Umberto will be there."

"Yes I know. Just five, really. On you go, you chaps."

"Get yourself a brandy."

"Looks like he needs one, too."

"I think I will. Cameriere, Cosa stava bevendo questo signore?"

"Negroni, signore."

"Portami due. No," turning to Percy, "I insist."

The English figures melt away down the Piazza, plimsolls squeaking on the paving. A late swallow cries and with dusty clackings the pigeons return to the Nettuno.

One part bitter Campari

The tall man sits down easing his bony frame into the creaky rattan chair opposite Percy. His shirt is unbuttoned almost to his waist revealing a virtually hairless, sunburnt chest, slightly sunken belly, ribs prominent. Down his thighs his trousers, striped elsewhere with dust and pale green, have carmine tracks where a cricket ball has rubbed against them. He crosses his long legs and Percy sees the bare tanned flesh of slim ankles between plimsolls and the cuff of his trousers. Someone has dropped a leather bag next to him, something like a briefcase and with its top rolled back Percy can see inside it a pair of studded duck cricketing shoes. Around the man's waist an MCC tie has been casually threaded through the belt loops and knotted at the front. Percy's eye tracks upward from his groin, along the placket of his shirt and up to his neck where a pulse beats below a prominent Adam's Apple. A day's stubble gives this face a vulpine look despite the deep tan, a face arranged around a prominent chin, a large nose and wide-set grey eyes. Tawny hair is receding from a high forehead and the skull is narrow and long. An aristocratic face, Reynoldsian. A cocksure smile hangs about the mouth and the eyes gaze at Percy full of benignity and, in Percy's view, condescension.

"What are you doing here?" says Percy, breaking the swallow-slashed silence that is descending with the Roman August dusk.

"I could ask you the same thing," says the man David.

Percy says, "I shouldn't be having another. It'll be my third and they're only meant for aperitivi. I might fall over."

"Says the man who was just nearly brained by an ashtray. You can thank me if you like."

"Thank you," Percy pauses, "David."

"Cin," says David raising his glass.

"Cin," says Percy doing the same.

"I suppose," says David, "I should say something like 'Gosh, it's been ages. How the devil are you?' You're looking well. A touch pasty perhaps."

"You look well despite the blood on your chin."

"Good lord am I dribbling?"

The David lifts to his chin the bag of melting ice and dabs it here and there causing the blood to thin and drip. Reaching out to the pavement he empties out the ice and brings back the wet towel that he wipes over his face before letting it fall to the table. A waiter comes over. "Altro ghiaccio?" he asks. "No grazie. Grazie per la tua gentilezza." The waiter smiles and takes the towel away. This is the first time Percy has seen him smile.

"Percy Langrigg," says David.

"Lord David Augustus Brythnoth Sopley Earl of Maldon," says Percy.

"Fancy you remembering all that."

"Brythnoth isn't the kind of name you forget."

The dark is falling faster and now only the top windows of the facade opposite are reflecting back the flaring orange sun; those on the piano nobile are lit with interior lamps.

"I imagine you won?" says Percy.

"Won?" says David. "Oh, you mean the cricket?" He gives a little laugh. "I expect you find it funny, don't you? Us playing cricket here."

"Not really," says Percy.

"Because you've some gobbet of knowledge to cough up that will tell me Shelley and Byron formed their own club here in eighteen-something with Keats as wickie."

There is a silence.

"Where do you play?" says Percy.

"Now from anyone else I know that would contain a double-entendre but from you little Percy, I take it as a question about fact. Our home pitch is in the Borghese Gardens the other lot use the Circus of Maxentius. We have nets every other Saturday afternoon in the Circus Maximus. Care to join us?"

"You know perfectly well that I don't take part in games."

"Yes of course. How is your eyesight?"

"I have a new optician, thank you, in London and he's..."

Quick as a flash David has reached out both hands, slid them down the side of Percy's face and gently lifted the arms of the spectacles off from behind his ears before sliding them over his own nose. 'Strewth," says David. "No wonder you never risked losing these. They're like bottle ends."

David takes off the spectacles and makes to hand them back to the other man but instead pauses. He moves his face closer to Percy's and looks at him intently. "You haven't changed much," he says.

"Appearances can be deceptive," says Percy.

"When did you start to talk in clichés? You must be living on your own. Yes indeed they can. But in your case, in your case Percy I'd say you're just the same inside that you ever were. The inside outsider shall I call you? Never joining in the other boys' games. Always something on your mind. What did Boldero used to say about you? Ah yes, the fish that always gets put back."

"David please don't talk down to me. You're not Government House anymore. You're not the Jockey Club. This isn't Hong Kong."

"Are you going to cry, little Perce? Have you missed me?"

"Of course not."

"'But are you happy?' Now who said that, you fellow Enameller;

"'And art thou happy? I exclaimed.'"

"'Alas, she cried, and fled.'"

This was the game again. Their game.

"Well played, little Percy. I've missed our game. If only someone could invent a field sport where quotations get hurled around instead of nasty hard, red leather balls you'd never miss a catch."

It was an item of renown in the old days that David could move as fast as a snake; first mesmerising his prey with a stare from his grey eyes before moving to the kill. He could spirit anything away before the Japs could see it like a night-club magician at the end of a table with a watch or a silver dollar. It was the smile, thought Percy. That ineffable, inbred superior smile that made them fall under his spell. Now, before he knew it, David had reached out and slipped the spectacles back over his ears, moving his face close, so close that his lips brushed Percy's cheek just long enough to be more than an accidental proximity. Just on Percy's ear lobe he says, "I've missed you."

The Gin

Percy next sees David leaning back in his chair, tilting the glass back to his lips to drain the last drops. As the rim of the glass bumps his nose he winces. "We really must meet up."

"Must we," says Percy.

"That's rather unsociable isn't it, Mr Langrigg? We're school chums, aren't we? Not to mention our three and a half years in jug together. Then The Rally in the Alley and our Adventure-upon-Thames? What was that? Three years ago? How was France by the way. Oh no need, Lyle told me the lot. Now here we are bumping into each other in Rome. Our long delayed reunion. Shouldn't we be celebrating?"

"Did you plan this? Did Lyle tell you I'd be here? I've spent the last three years not expecting you. 'I live in calm,' she said, 'and there am learning to be wise.'"

"Dead Love? Oh dear. Have you no feelings for your old schoolboy crush? Your old Stanley mucker? I'm not going to give you a hard time for running away from that cushy billet in France. I wasn't suggesting a week of nights on the Via Veneto, old chap, just a bit of a get-together."

"We've barely seen each other since camp. Just that extraordinary drama in London. I haven't heard from you for the best part of three years. Not a word."

"But I've had word of you."

"From Lyle."

"Yes of course Lyle."

"She never said."

"I was categoric that she shouldn't."

"Spies. Both of you."

"This means I've saved your hide twice. Maybe even three times. Come on Perce; what are you afraid of? That I'll make a pass at you?"

"I don't want to say."

"Do you think I'm condescending to you?"

"No, even though you seem to think that you're some kind of deus ex machina in my little life. It's simply that I don't want to go back. Not everyone does."

"Too painful?"

"Too potent."

"Ah my dear Percy you're in flight. Yes you are. I see it. You're running away, aren't you? Again. And you want to travel light, is that it? Yes you wouldn't be the only one. I've seen chaps leaving the Service, going Home and they can't cope with the office so they run away to Somerset and start a muddy little smallholding. Their poor wives. Never thought of getting married?"

"No. Of course not. Are you?"

David looks at Percy."I know what you think of me," he says. "I know you think I'm some swing-both-ways, upper-class tart-without-a-heart. My face is my fortune, Sir, she said."

He pulls out a pack of Nazionali, taps one out, offers to Percy who shakes his head, lights and draws. The smoke ascends in a thin blue stream.

"You were a spy weren't you back there? Are you a spy again now? You'd make a perfect one. No one can ever tell what you're thinking."

"How are you getting by?"

"Lyle must have told you."

"Your legacy from that aunt."

"That's enough, David. We just don't run on the same lines. I want to make my home here. I have no wish to be among your cloudy trophies hung. How long will you be staying?"

"I merely suggested we meet for a drink and a chat. This is just two old friends catching up after all. Wouldn't you like to know what I've been doing the past three years? Hmm? Or why I'm here? Perhaps I've been questing for you, little Sir Galahad?"

Percy froze. That old, old fear of intimacy gripped him by the vitals and calcified him. His voice caught in his throat: "Are you flirting with me, David?"

"Would you like me to?"

"David it's been years and we were only children. We barely knew what we were doing."

"But we knew what we wanted. And there was camp. You know they used to call us Mutt and Jeff."

"Everyone thought you were having it off with that Flora Matthews. Among others."

Percy is silent, hunched up, David thinks, like an owl on a branch.

"Listen, Percy, you know I looked for you after we got out but I couldn't do what I wanted or go where I wanted. You were my talisman, Perce, all those years. Way back at Yantai even. Wasn't I glad to see you in London? Weren't you just faintly happy too? When you picked me up from the pavement just now you did it just the way you stopped me falling into the shit pit when I couldn't even stand from dysentery. Do you remember?"

A silence hangs over the table. The waiters are silent. The great theatrical space is silent, too.

"We were in a prisoner of war camp, David. Perhaps we depended upon each other for a while. Perhaps I was your comfort boy. Perhaps you were my Lord Protector at school but now we're not in some Noel Coward play. You aren't Elyot and I'm not your Amanda. There's no moonlight behind me and I absolutely doubt that what's going on here is true to any dream you've been dreaming moreover..."

"Moreover. Such an underused word. Will you come for a picnic with me tomorrow?"

"A picnic?"

"A handbag?"

"David it's been lovely to meet you again. Thank you for not letting me be brained by a glass ashtray. I hope you're happy and I hope your life is wonderful. I don't want to go back. I don't want to reminisce about my life because it didn't used to belong to me but now it does. I don't want emotion or daring repartee. I don't want Society. I don't want to be propositioned or proposed to. By anyone. Or be that anyone's bit on the side. If I want for anything it's companionship and to that end I will probably take on one of the kittens from the Quatro Coronati's litter and call it Rosebud. Moreover. Moreover I don't want anything, anything, that dare not speak its name from the rooftops if need be. The worst sin against the spirit is silence."

"Cameriere il conto per favore. Vorrei pagare per tutte le bevande di questo gentiluomo"

"Si signore, subito."

"You know I won't be able to come back here again after all this?"

"Find somewhere else. Find somewhere where they don't call you a finocchio behind your back."

"I like it here."

David stands up.

"It's like a flea-bitten waterhole in a desert. Tomorrow is Sunday. I'll call for you. We can call in at an Alimentari, make up a picnic and go out to Ostia Antica. Have you been there?"

"Thank you, David, but no. Thank you."

"I'll pick you up at one."

"You don't know where I live."

"The Embassy does. Grazie. Tiene il resto."

"Grazie signore."

"Now you can come back here if you want. A domani, tesoro."

David turns on his heel, his plimsoll squeaking on the paving slabs, then heads off toward Via Santa Maria dell'Anima and into the night, a freshly lit Nazionali trailing its foul smelling smoke behind him.

Percy sits a moment.

A tittering from the waiters behind grows in volume as a chorus of frogs crescendos at sundown. He gets up and sways a little before heading off to the Moro whose waters ripple in the descending dark and lap at his feet like a beach on the Styx. At the sound of the waters he turns and begins to follow in the direction of David.

New York, The Four Seasons, March 1987

Tom
Coda alla Vaccinara

"Hi there Janey. Shaney. Sorry. Yeah no fine thank you, my journey was fine. Yeah, good to meet you too. Okay sure, no problem. Can I smoke? Great, yeah. No I'm okay, yeah, so far. I had the test oooooh last week? Getting the results day after tomorrow so the timing is good here. Good. Yeah, good days, bad days. Not that I've had any symptoms or anything just a bit tired that's all but you know pace of life in New York and all that kind of crap. Yeah, I'm a copywriter that's it. 'It's the white, white smile' and that kind of garbage. No actually I'm proud of what I do. You know I wrote the copy for a pack of oatmeal cereal that's been read by over twenty-five million people in a year. Charles Dickens eat your heart out. Yeah. Yeah perfectly comfortable thank you. Yeah, I'll have some of this water. Thanks.

[Drinks]

"So this is for your thesis. A doctoral thesis. About Percy and..."

"Comparing Percy to Julia Child and Elizabeth David. As someone who popularised European and Mediterranean cooking in the post-War period."

"To Elizabeth Child? You sure? I mean, look, his classes were pretty small you know. You know he'd have been flattered but he wasn't out to do more than share what he'd learnt about Roman food. He didn't care how many people turned up. He didn't want a crowd. He didn't advertise. No shouting from the rooftops. That just wasn't his style. He thought Elizabeth David was populist. That's what he told me once. Doesn't that say it all?"

"His book is back in print. The Times did a feature on it. He's garnering a reputation."

"Okay well you're the expert. But you know he was a very private person. He wouldn't want you to be digging up stuff about him about his life. Cooking okay but you know he said food saved him but he never said from what. Capisco?"

"This is an academic study Mr Russo. A proper academic study. Please believe me."

"So, I'm going to tell you and your Sony machine what I remember about Percy Langrigg and his Roman cookery school right? Okay? Okay.

"Just one thing: can you remind me how you tracked me down? I mean it's years since he died. And I was only with him a few months. Oh Lyle Destrooper. Yeah that figures. The spider in the web. So she had my parent's address, huh? God, I don't remember giving it to her. She must have extracted it under anaesthetic. And you spoke to my parents? Did they tell you I was sick? I mean may be sick? They just gave you my number. That figures. So what did you tell them? Oh yeah that's right you told them you were researching the college in Rome. So how did you know I'd been at the college in Rome no don't say it was all there in the Signora's Rolodex. Have you interviewed Lyle herself? You must. You're going to. Well Best of British as Percy used to say 'cos hell's gonna freeze over before that one tells you anything except what she wants you to know. Protective? She's got Percy's memory all saran-wrapped up. It'll look like you can see through but it'll only be what she wants you to see. Why? She became his High Priestess over the years, guardian of his Privacy. Erebus. Yeah maybe I did mean Cerberus. Though Erebus is just as apposite. I have a smattering of the classics as Percy would say. There's more to writing about oatmeal than you might suppose and the key is grammar. And what you do with it. Okay. Is your machine switched on. Let's go.

"I first met Percy Langrigg in Rome in '70 at his cookery school 'L'Antica Tavola Romana'. It can't have made him much dough but the word was that some relative had left him some kind of legacy at least enough for him to live on and give what were effectively lunch or dinner parties and get paid for the ingredients. And the vino. Classes were never more than of five or six and they weren't advertised, you just found out about them at some drinks party or other. And while everyone at home was trying to cook like the Four Seasons and failing at every step, I mean spun sugar cases for profiteroles and that kind of thing with Percy it was rustic. Basic, even. I mean you had to want to eat weird vegetables and every kind of organ. And you had to cook and eat it the way they had since before Unification. Over the years he'd made himself a kind of native of Rome even though he'd been born in China. It may have helped that he'd grown up in hotels, his mother – an American – she'd inherited a smallish chain that eventually sold out to the Hiltons in the '50s. Maybe he'd just been brought up on the leftovers. Actually you know I think he had. Fried rice figured a lot. He used to mix it up with peanuts and raisins and cook it in a fry-pan then he'd make hollows in the surface and crack eggs into them then cover the pan up and a few minutes later there it would be. Chow Fan he called it. And he told me once his favourite food was yesterday's rice for breakfast with hot milk and brown sugar. Tientsin Breakfast he called it. The winters there can be real cold. So he said.

"So, I went along to one of his classes just to check it out because Lyle told me it would be 'interesting.' And you know it was. There were a half dozen American crème de la crème Alpha Kappa Alpha ladies in pearls sitting on rickety chairs in that tiny kitchen stripping the leaves off artichokes or gutting chickens or whopping bits of veal till you could see through them it was kinda surreal. Something almost like they'd gone back in time to ancient Rome, and they'd laugh and chat and Percy used to say that cooking is a social activity and he was right. Anyway I was the only guy there and I got on real well with the ladies I was slim and I had long hair and a cute ass and they'd ask me to help them like 'Oh Tom could you be a dear and pass me the prosciutto crudo,' and that kind of thing so then he asked me if I'd like to come along regular and help him set up and pack up and clean up and he'd pay me and I said yes. He liked my ass, too, said it reminded him of someone's. I said Michelangelo's David and he said almost right. Then he asked me to go and live with him. So I did. Those few months.

"Moving on? Yeah, sure. Okay so Percy talked to me. I don't think he'd ever really talked to anyone before. He told me about the war and how they'd lived off a bowl of rice a day. He was chief rice-stirrer so he told me. He had a way with cooking rice. Fluffy and nutty every time! No that was. Never mind. The client loved it is all I can remember. We used to have at least one rice evening a week. He'd sit there in that favourite chair of his and hold the bowl – he had these lovely blue and white bowls with rice grains baked into them – hold the bowl up to his mouth and just shovel the rice in with his chopsticks. Never left a single grain in there. 'The number of grains left in the bowl will be the number of pockmarks on your wife's face,' he always said. Apparently it was some kind of old North Chinese saying. Charming, huh? What about husband I once said to him.

"And then, yes, you're right of course, he went back to England after the war and worked in some kind of ancient hotel in London. Something went on there, I'm not quite sure what. 'Unsavoury' he said to me but he wouldn't go into detail. He was a regular clam, that guy. Then I think Lyle got involved for the first time and got him a hotel job in France somewhere in the South or near the South. 'I bolted,' he said. 'I became a bolter.' Apparently being a bolter gave him some kind of notoriety he felt. Anyway it amused him to say it. Then something went wrong there, too, and once again he was schtummer than a picket post about it. Except once when he said, 'I fell foul of a cock.' Like, take it or leave it. [He laughs].

"So, enter Lyle Destrooper once again. She had a house in the same part of France as the hotel where Percy worked. Natch. So after the debacle francaise she steered Percy to Rome in oh, late '48? And he never left. So in '69 when I trolled up he must have been – oh, fifty-eight? Fifty-nine? The school had been going a few years by then and he was getting a bit of a reputation. Even among the Italians. Though it was almost all Americans came to the classes. He didn't last much longer than that, sad to say. He died in '75. Some kind of complication brought about by something that went back to the war while he was what he called a prisoner of the turnip-heads. Of course you know that. Not one of the most brutal camps and nothing like the railroad or being shipped off to Japan but still nearly four years of pretty extreme deprivation. Where we he was head rice-stirrer, yes. He once showed me his camp notebook and it was almost all recipes. Recipes for things like custard and other English nursery crap and then lists and lists and lists of all the restaurants in London they'd go back to after the war and what they'd eat there and what the specialities were and the name of the maître d' at the Café Royal and Simpsons and this place called Odennino's and the Savoy Grill.

"He didn't talk much about what he called his 'adventures' and no I didn't suck his dick (it would have been vice versa anyway of that I'm pretty sure) but I have something here I want to share with you, something he did pass on to me, something that was close to his heart

so like it or not you need to settle down and let me give you his recipe
for Coda alla Vaccinara. Here, I brought it with me. He used to type
out his recipes and I'd 'roneo' them. This one I kept. It's in Italian.
He used to give his Roneo sheets to his ladies in Italian. He could be
brutal that way. Here goes:

Cosa serve per 6 pezzi per coda

> 1 coda du bue
> 1 sedano intero
> 1 cipolla
> 1 spicchio d'aglio
> lardo/guanciale q.b.
> olio extra vergine q.b.
> 1 kg di pomodori a pezzi
> 2 bicchieri di vino bianco secco
> 4 chiodi di garofano
> pinoli q.b.
> uvetta q.b.
> cacao amaro in polvere q.b.
> sale
> pepe
> acqua calda q.b.

"What does 'q.b.' mean? Quanto Basta. As much as you need.

"I once asked him why he loved this dish so much. There are
plenty of other Roman dishes he cooked like those Jewish fried
artichokes, pigs' trotters and spiced-to-death pig's cock. He called
them pizzlei. His made up word. Oh and he was strict about it all, it
all had to be not only done just so but the right foods had to be eaten
on the right days so gnocchi on Thursdays, salt cod on Fridays and
tripe on Saturdays. At least I think he said Saturdays. Tripe. Oh god.
And he had a mania that nothing could be wasted. I guess that went
back to his years in the POW camp. He'd scrape every mixing bowl
till it bled, never leave an atom on his plate and he once told me that
when he'd first come here and found a place of his own he used to
reuse the coffee grounds two or three times before he chucked them
out. Honestly. I think the careful way the Romans cooked, the kind

of thrift they had, chimed in some way with his experiences of being hungry. Greens of potatoes he told me they were given to eat. Greens of potatoes and rice husks sometimes.

[Pause. A cigarette is lit and the sound of an ashtray being slid across a surface can be heard]

"But he had a good head for languages and he soon picked up some basic Italian to help him along after he first arrived like 'che the cazzo' – what do I do with this? Only without the 'cazzo'. So he'd just stand there at a market stall or in the macellaria and say, 'How do you cook this or that?' and they'd tell him. He said they all used to chip in with variations and argue like blazes. He said he didn't always understand specially if it was dialect so then he had to do trial and error. So he told me this story about passing the window of a butchers somewhere fairly no-go like the depths of Trastevere or the wilds of Testaccio and he saw what he said looked like a haggis in the window. You know haggis, right? Well I didn't of course so he had to explain to me about the sheep stomach filled up with oatmeal and chopped up sheep liver and heart and what he called lights meaning lungs then all mixed up with enough fat to cause heart failure. Then you boil it. Boil it. I mean. Gross. So there in the window he thought he saw a haggis so being Percy he had to go in and ask about it and it was 'testicolo di vitello', only being Italy where they eat their veal older it would have been the size of a haggis about two or three pounds."

"And what did he do with it?"

[Pause while cigarette is drawn]

"Oh yeah okay apparently he sliced it up, dipped the slices in beaten egg then stale breadcrumbs with salt and pepper and fried the slices. He said they were like cod roe to eat. I haven't eaten cod roe either. Apparently that's their eggs, right? Or is it their jizzum? Yeah okay back to the script.

[Rustling of paper and clearing of throat can be heard]

"'Come si fa.' That means how do you do it. How you do it. How it's done. Okay, so first you 'sciacquare la coda'. That means rinse it, then 'asciugarla' it; wipe it, and, 'tagliarla' it 'a pezzi abbastanza grande'. Now he puts in brackets, 'i rocchi' which he told me was Roman dialect and it means big chunks, more or less. You see even in the language Percy liked to be as authentically Roman as he could. You want me to carry on reading? You sure I mean I can just give you this piece of paper and you can make a photocopy of it or whatever and give it back to me later. No? Okay. Your call.

"He liked me you know. He liked his men thin which I was in those days and a bit tall. Maybe because he was short and had gotten a bit plump on the gelati and the dolci over the years. Maybe he just had a thing about endomorphs. He liked someone to look up to, so to speak and no I'm not making any innuendo or shit like that. I respected Percy. I really liked him. You could tell he'd been kind of wiry when he was younger. He always wore a moustache and had a good head of hair. I think he'd played rugby football, what he called rugger, somewhere unlikely like Shanghai or somewhere. He was really proud of being Scottish, too. He had a set of Scotch bagpipes and at New Year's he'd get his kilt on and some kind of green jacket and walk up and down the Celio playing these Scottish tunes, you know, 'Auld Lang Syne' and 'The Bonnie Bonnie Banks of Loch Lomond' and that kind of stuff. Apparently at the beginning he scared the shit out of the locals but in the end they kind of liked it. They kind of adopted him. They called him froccio and whatever the latest word is for faggot and Lo Scozzese of course. Whenever he went out to eat locally they'd always bring him a whiskee and never charge him. Or they'd put it in his coffee. Corretto con Whiskee they'd say. They couldn't understand why he loved Roman food so much and they were suspicious at first but eventually he told me they'd bring out their family recipes and give him the inside track on where to buy the best what. They respected him. He had pluck. In a way he was a bit like them. He had a heritage and he was a survivor and he had values, they could tell. Old-fashioned, that's what it was. He was old-fashioned. You know he used to call me that, too. 'You Americans can be so old-fashioned.' That was it.

"Is this stuff any good to you? Can you use it? Am I just rambling? Go on? Okay, good.

"You know on this subject of liking tall men you knew about the boyfriend, yeah? I didn't meet Percy till after all that but there was a picture he had; a photograph of a tall man with that kind of British aristo look. With a kind of smile like he never had to worry about anything. Ever. No I never asked about the photo or the guy. It was Lyle Destrooper told me to lay off the subject with him. Yeah people talked. Not the locals but the expats but not to me they knew I didn't like it. They knew we were friends I guess they thought I was his boy so they kept schtumm in front of me. Anyhow, with Percy when one chapter closed it stayed closed. Did I say he used to sew on his own buttons and do mending and that kind of thing? Yeah. Well he kept all his sewing things so neat in this Chinese lacquer box that had more boxes inside it. It was a fancy shape and all the boxes fit in the outline and with each other and it had two layers so there were maybe two dozen little boxes and each one had something different in it. Buttons or thread or needles or I don't know; sewing stuff. He liked to collect buttons would you believe. And you know that was Percy. Blue buttons went back with blue buttons and red thread went back with red thread and everything stayed in its compartment and when he'd done it got closed up and put away and that's how he was about life, you know. The right thing in the right place and you go there when you need it then down comes the lid blammo and the buttons just sit there in the dark.

"Yeah sure. 'In una pentola alta e grande rosolare i pezzi di coda in un trito di lardo o guanciale e olio extravergine di oliva. Quindi.' He loved that word and 'allora' and 'dunque' and those kind of words that mean 'then' where you draw breath. He used to say that if you were an Italian learning British English and someone taught you Umm and Errr and you said one or both when you needed time to think what you were going to say next everyone would assume you were a Brit. Okay so, 'quindi, una volta rossolata' the rocks, 'aggiungere la cipolla sminuzzata'. Sorry, can I stop again? You know that word really brings Percy back to me and those cookery classes. He loved the word: he said it could be Scotch. He used to give a demonstration on how to cut up onions and carrots really small and he used to say this is an important skill to learn so we're going to have five minutes on the fine art of sminuzzi-isation. He cracked me up. I loved it. Not all the gals got it of course. Yeah so sminuzziate the onion 'quindi' errr yes, quindi, sorry have to go back a bit, 'quindi aggiungere l'aglio intero, i chiodi di garofano, sale e pepe. Lasciar asciugare l'acqua fuoriscita dalla code e, una volta asciutta, sfumare con due bicchieri di vino bianco secco lasciando cuocere circa quindici minuti.'

"He talked to me a lot. Yeah he'd talk to Lyle too. They were real friends. Well I mean he was sociable of course but there was a lot he held back on. He wouldn't answer questions about himself in the classes. No way José. It was about the food, you know? Well with me I think it was just right place right time right colour of hair right skinny ass. At least that's what Lyle said. She said he had to talk to someone, eventually. Yeah, there was something between us. He was like. He was like not a father, not the faggot uncle always cracking jokes. Not the friend you first compare dicks with. He was. This will sound strange. He was more like a brother. Comrade-brother. Yep there were what twenty-five years between us maybe more but it was like time didn't care about that. He once said I was his family. Why me? I asked. Why not? he said. What was I? An American student making the most of a year or two in Rome, folks back in Boise, Idaho..."

"You said you were from Fresno, California."

"Yeah, shit capital of America, yes I am. Boise, Idaho is just a metaphor. It means inconsequential. Unless you live there of course. Some of my best friends are from Boise, Idaho. Look I mean I was kind of naive possibly even a bit pretty back in those days. Perhaps I flashed my ass without even realising it. Perhaps it was my man-musk. I don't know. Something about me attracted Percy and okay let's be honest cards on the table something about Percy attracted me. And no, I've never asked myself what but since you're sitting there in that chair like Sigmund Freud maybe you can tell me what I look for in men. Not with the eyes, you know. Not with the eyes. The eyes are too easily deceived. They make things up, you know, the eyes. They only see part of a picture and they make the rest up out of other pictures they've seen before. So they see someone doing something you like to see people doing and they what is it they extrapolate 'friend', 'friendly' and miss the other bit that says 'bastard', 'avoid'. No, you're better off with your nose. People can't dress up their smell like they can the rest of them. Sure they can put on perfume or cologne but there aren't as many perfumes as there are physical disguises so they're easier to filter out. There's something else there isn't there? Signals our bodies send to other bodies about us. There has to be. Like dogs sniff asses for bitches on heat. Okay this is getting gross let's just say that for reasons unknown there was something about Percy that made me really dig him. Let's say something in the air. Okay? And for the record since you're recording it wasn't physical. Never. But he talked to me, yeah he talked to me. Well, that's why you're here isn't it? Okay so where was I? You know, Percy had a rule no perfumes or colognes to be worn in class, no stinky modern deodorants. No hairspray. He told me one woman broke the rule and came in bathed in some kind of expensive perfume and when he told her to go and wash it off or leave she said, 'But it's Joy, Mr Langrigg.' He said, 'Joy is in the nose of the beholder, Mrs whatever-your-name-is, and my nose isn't happy, so please go away.'"

"When did you first meet Percy Langrigg?"

"Let me just light this – [sound of coughing] – gosh let's see. Well so it was '69 and I was seventeen My parents wanted me out of the country. They knew I liked the Roman poets and Roman history and Did the Romans First Discover America and that kind of weird shit so. Well, so. There it was."

"Why did they want you out of the country?"

"[Laughs] Percy would have said you were impertinent. I love that word don't you? It's accusing you of not sticking to the subject. To what's pertinent. That's pretty darn bad, huh? [Pause] Okay so this is nothing to do with the Percy story, right? So you're not going to put this in right? Okay I'll tell you because I told him. That's the only reason, okay? So there were two things. No, three. I think. Number one, California was buzzing with rumours about a new kind of draft. A lottery draft. Two, my mom and dad weren't happy the way things were going at the schools in the US. It didn't help that I was totally set on going to UC Berkeley. Like, totally. They'd gotten rattled by the Kent State thing. They didn't like my clothes, they didn't like my hair, they didn't like my politics. So they thought of making me go East to School but Woodstock kinda blew that one up, seemed I wouldn't be safe there either. I don't blame them. They just wanted me to want to stay in Fresno and grow nuts. Not go crazy. Grow nuts. That's what my dad did. He grew nuts, walnuts, almonds. Nuts. So they thought a couple years abroad might help me see the family business for the great enterprise that it was so they shelled out – geddit? shelled out? – for me to go to this new school in Rome. Those fifteen minutes are up and that wine will have reduced by now. Next step? Oh, okay. Yep. All right.

"Yeah so there was something else. Or someone else.

"So there was this foreman on my dad's farm. Enrique he was called. Is called. Whatever. Dad gave me to Enrique to teach me the finer points of nut farming. Enrique was a dude. Everyone liked him.

He made people laugh, he fired up the BBQ on Saturday nights in Summer and fourth of July, drank his beer ice cold, stepped out in botas picudas weekends and wore his jeans tight round the crotch. Dad really trusted him. He was a whiz at his job. We got on real well. And then one day he put his hand on my ass and the rest is history. So that lasted all that Summer of '69. My own personal Summer of Love getting humped by a short, hairy Mexican every opportunity. Oh yeah, woo, Mister Big Stuff. No, he never got my love as such but he sure liked what he did get. Me too. I guess I'd found my type. The life and soul kind of man. The quart in the pint pot. Then my dad found out, I don't know how. He couldn't sack Enrique or rather he wouldn't. How was I to know he'd been taking Enrique up the ass himself till I came along and made him go back to Mom? Poor guy, missing his favourite nut tree. No, he didn't even talk about it to me directly. He just said, 'Well, son, me and your mom have got together a real treat for you. Something we'll know you'll like.' He gave me my airline tickets to Rome and a copy of Catullus bound in leather like a school prize and in it he'd written, 'Mens pratrepidans avet vagari' and that was the first time I realised he might be gay, too. And he gave me a letter of introduction to Lyle Destrooper. Letter of introduction! So Henry James. I found out later that mom and Lyle were related and it all fell into place like the Destroopers were these Fresno County millionaires from way back in California terms like all of 100 years. Lyle used to say, 'You can take the girl out of Fresno but you can't take the Fresno out of the girl.' When you first met her you thought Boston Princess but you'd have been wrong. So that's how I came to be in Roma and when I was once having supper with Lyle at her place she said, 'You like the local food, don't you?' and I said, 'Yes,' and she said, 'Do you want to learn more about it before you go home?' and I said, 'Yeah sure,' and she gave me a card of Percy's and I went along one evening. I was the only guy and we just got on from the get-go and I kind of became his sous-chef prepping all the ingredients for him, doing the washing up then we'd sit at that scrubbed kitchen table of his and he'd have an Amaro and I'd have a grappa or two and sometimes I'd stay the night on his couch and one day he woke me up with a kiss on my forehead. That was the only kiss he ever gave me. People called us Mutt and Jeff and we did kind of go places together. I'm over six feet and in those days I had hair down to my shoulders and was thin like a waif and Percy was what five feet eight if that and with a moustache and this brindled hair. 'I'm a Border Terrier,' he used to say. I once overheard myself described as his amanuensis so I thought, fuck it, and I went and bought a notebook and a Parker 45 and asked him if I could make notes and he said 'Yes, old chap, you could help me write a recipe book.' But I had to leave before it got very far."

"Did you know he published such a book soon after?"

"Yeah. Lyle sent me a copy. '71 was that? He'd inscribed it to me but he didn't know my address where to send it."

"It has the recipe for coda all vaccinara."

"Yeah."

"And you left Rome after just a few months?"

"Yeah. Excuse me."

[Coughing]

"Sorry. Okay where were we? Yep. It was all going swimmingly as Percy used to say until my dad and mom came over on a visit, realised I wasn't doing any studying, decide d I was aiming to become a kitchen porter, saw me hanging around with a guy at least twice my age, cancelled my fees and took me home."

"How did you feel about that?"

"I was young. I didn't have feelings. I told him I'd be back and he smiled at me. I wrote him once or twice but then I pretty soon went to Vancouver to dodge the draft and got into a load of weird shit in this crappy house that was about to fall down. We used to call it Le Voh. That's Hovel backwards. Then Lyle wrote me – I don't know how she got the address – to tell me he'd died and sent a bankers' draft for money to go the funeral but I spent it on weed. That was the lowest point of my life."

"Did he ever talk about someone called David?"

"No, he didn't."

"But you knew about David."

Well sure, everyone did. Every foreigner. I mean he was some kind of English Lord and there was a big fuss over his death but that was like the Fifties or something and like you say 'before my time.' Okay?"

"Did he talk about other periods of his life?"

"Yeah. Some. Not many. I told you he let me into all that stuff with the war and being in China as a kid."

"And London? France? His early years in Rome?"

"I've told you about as much as he told me. Really. Not much. You'll have to ask Lyle for the rest. Versare nella pentola i pomodori a pezzi..."

"Did he dictate that recipe to you?"

"Yeah. I wrote it down at his antica tavola romana. With my Parker 45. In my notebook. In 1970. Then I typed it up on that Remington and we got it copied. On the Roneo. The Roman Roneo. Coprire con il coperchio e lasciar cuocere per un' ora. You know what I'm getting kinda choked here. I can just hear his voice. I don't think I want to read any more. No actually I just want to say out loud a few more lines. So being Percy he even described how it would have been eaten in the old days so: 'la goduria che si prova nel mangiare con le mani e senza farsi tanti problemi e impagabile.' Priceless, that's what he was, priceless. 'Tempo di preparazione: Che tempi abbiamo passato insieme.'"

"I'm sorry?"

"No I am. Just let that one go. I'm winding up here. 'Tempo di preparazione: tanto, ma vale la pena.' Ma vale la pena: It's worth the effort. Valeva la pena old chum. Okay, that's it, I'm done. I'm sorry I'm not feeling so great. No, it's okay. I'll be okay. Think I'll get a cab home. Okay well that's very generous of you. Thank you. I hope I've been able to help you with your thesis. In bocca di lupa as they say in Rome."

"Thank you, Mr Russo. Thank you for your time."

"Ciao. I can find my own way out. Arrriverderla. Look forward to reading the thesis. Yep. Goodbye. Goodbye."

Yantai Missionary School, China, July 1924

Jiaotzi

The warm wind blew off the China Sea pushing the stale air before it along the open-sided cloister and through the arches of the Yantai School. It rattled and flapped the chicks on the windows. It pushed and pulled the trees and bushes around the sports ground. It nosed through classrooms and dormitories, bathrooms and storerooms, busy and bothersome as though, thought Percy Langrigg, it wants us out of here. It has come to winnow us. The heat shimmered on the sea; you could barely make out the bluff four miles across the bay in whose waters rocked a little British warship.

The wind was febrile, disordered; a changing wind, a wind that meant no good. It didn't freshen, it didn't cool. It didn't invite you down to the beach. It didn't like the verandahs and courtyards packed with foreigners. It wanted them empty and the place to itself. It was an end of term wind, come to blow boys and men away, away to Japan, to Shanghai, Tientsin, Kuling, Peitaho. Percy turned into the wind, eyes half closed against its push, and it seemed to him as though he were looking into the eyes of a dragon whose scaly tail lashed the air. I'm not afraid of you, said Percy to the dragon; "I was born here. We should be friends." His hand reached up to the dragon's nose. "Lao pengyou," he said.

"Langrigg, go to the dayroom." Teachers were like the wind, they got everywhere. Percy gave a little bow. "Don't do that you're not a native. Now go. Go!" Percy turned away from the warm, anxious wind off the China Sea feeling a scaly snout in the small of his back giving him a gentle, a tender shove along the verandah and toward an open door. He went inside.

"Here's Chink!"

"These are his! These are his!"

In the middle of the room stood a group of four or five boy-men, the prefects whose job it was on the last day of every term to order the younger boys to search every nook and cranny of the school for stray possessions. Anything out of a locker, under a bed, in a changing room, in a bathroom, anything not packed away in a suitcase was picked up and dumped in a pile in a middle of this room called the Dayroom, the room in which they spent any time not occupied in eating, sleeping, in class, at games or at worship.

Every object, every piece of clothing in the pile was picked up by a prefect in turn who held it up to the assembled boys and yelled "Quis?" The ritual was simple; the owner simply claimed the object by yelling back "Ego!" One of the boys was holding up a pair of maroon swimming trunks made of worsted wool. They were Percy's and he loathed them. In the water they ballooned up and slowed your swimming, when sitting on the sand they became encrusted with its grains. As they dried, they itched. He'd tried over and over again to lose them but they came back to haunt him. Percy had come into the room just in time to be shoved to the front to be forced to claim them. He took them, turned around and saw the jeering faces. This was how it was at end of term. Friends dropped out of orbit as they felt the pull of different planets: Home, parents, siblings. Percy puts his trunks in his locker and sits at a table to await his bath-time. He knows that all this is simply going through the motions. His parents don't want him this vac. For him 'other plans' have been made.

Later, bathed and dressed in clean clothes Percy trooped with the others into the school chapel for the end-of-term service. Simple and resolutely low church the chapel had white walls, dark oak pews and a floor tiled checkerboard black and white. Each boy went to his allotted place. Brass chandeliers in the ceiling held electric light bulbs and there were shaded lamps to light the choir pews.

On the walls above their heads plaques commemorated the school's founders and benefactors the Protestant All-China Mission and its martyrs. Percy contemplated the list of the twenty adults and eight children of the Mission who had been murdered in the Boxer Rebellion twenty-five years before memorialised on a wooden board directly in his view. Other plaques told the names and lifespans of missionaries who had died almost as far away from here as London was from Cairo; places in Manchuria, Sinkiang, up the rivers and over the mountains. The plaques were if nothing else a testament to the vastness of China with Yantai perched like a pimple on its Eastern extremity. Among the memorials were painted verses from the Bible:

'The God of Jacob is our refuge. Psalm 46 1:7 'A very present help in trouble. Therefore we will not fear, the Lord of Hosts is with us. God is our refuge and strength'. As the organ strikes up a sprightly voluntary Headmaster, staff and visiting missionaries begin to file in. If the missionaries look exceptionally clean and well-groomed it's because for the first time in months they've taken off their native Chinese gear and clambered back into Western dress.

"We will sing..." Really there was no need to announce the hymn. By ritual it was sung at every end-of-term service; 'Lord dismiss us with thy blessing, Fill our hearts with joy and peace...' Summer Term of 1924 at Yantai School was all but over.

It is now the following early-evening and the air outside the school has all day been full of dust from the movement of cars and charabancs emptying the building of boys. As the dust begins to settle darkness has slowly descended and Percy Langrigg is standing at the dead centre of one of the school's two courtyards. The winnowing wind has eased and he hears the hiss and crackle of a gramophone record beginning to play. It's Ukelele Ike and it begins 'Goodbye for ever, goodbye for ever, I'm going away for a long, long time' before the refrain swings out: 'California here I come, right back where I started from where bowers of flowers bloom in the Spring...' From inside the Staff Room a voice joins Cliff Edwards' and another until a chorus of three or four sings, lapses and laughs its way through to the end of the song. "What next?" hears Percy, outside. "Come on Morrison, pick another one." Morrison is the Classics master who combines an impermeable in-class lugubriousness with a love of popular music, particularly American and he will play it and sing along to it all vacation long.

Since about a week before the end of term parcels of the latest records have been arriving from Tientsin or Shanghai; jazz, variety, crooners, musicals, ballads. Hiss, crackle, now it's the sound of the tik-tokking of muyus, a cymbal and then a solo clarinet being played to a Chinesey take on jazz, its F Major key lending a touch of the Orient to a ground of Limehouse Blues. Of course, it's The Shanghai Shuffle. "Listen out for Louis Armstrong," says a voice. "He's the tops." Percy edges a little closer to the window. It isn't late but he's tired and hungry and full of vague fears about the long eight weeks that stretch ahead of him until a new term begins and 'Lord accept us with thy blessing' rings out in the chapel.

A head with a cigarette in its mouth pops out of a window. "Crikey, Langrigg, is that you skulking about? Come on lad, come in here, nothing to be afraid of." Percy goes back to the verandah, turns into the block and knocks on the Staff Room door just in time to hear Fletcher Henderson and his band play its last note. As the door opens he takes in the rattan chairs, the book-shelves, the gramophone and its speaker horn, the pile of records in brown paper sleeves, the punkahs working away, the ashtrays and the glasses of beer. As he goes in one of the Chinese 'boys' brushes past him with a tray-full of empty glasses.

"Look here chaps, look at poor old Langrigg abandoned to our company this evening. He's not going home this vac. Where is it you're going, Langrigg? Somewhere up-country?"

"Yes sir, Mr Thomson," says Percy. "Kiukiang, sir."

"Kiukiang?" says another voice. "Shanghai and up-river?"

"Yes, sir," says Percy.

"Got someone up there, have you?"

"Yes, sir. My uncle, sir."

"Honorary uncle?"

"Yes, Sir. I just call him that sir. But he's wizard, sir. He always sends me a book for my birthday."

"Drop the sir old chap," says another voice, Mr Gent the games master. "It's the vac."

"Yes absolutely, the blessed vac," says Thomson. "Not a moment too soon."

"It'll be warm down there," says Fitch, the English master. "Got someone looking after you in Shanghai?"

"Of course he has," says Gent. "Parents are hotel magnates. Probably putting him up at the Cathay." A pause. "Is it the Cathay, Langrigg?"

"No, sir, it's the Atholl Palace, sir."

"Alright for some!" says Gent and everyone laughs.

"Ever been to Shanghai before?" says Thomson.

"Of course he jolly has, haven't you Langrigg? Movie palaces, The Sincere, Nanking Road, the racecourse, he's seen them all, haven't you lad?" Percy nods. In fact, he has seen them all but only through the windows of cars from the Bund to the French Concession and back again, once or twice, when he'd lodged briefly with one of his parents' contacts in the Rue Ratard. He's often heard people talking about Shanghai as though it were some kind of what Headmaster would call a 'Den of Iniquity' but what he recalls are quite normal things: the tennis parties, teas on the verandah, shopping at Sincere or Wing On for new socks and shirts. He prefers Tientsin.

"Yes," he says, "Thomson."

There's a pause followed by gales of laughter.

"One of us already!" hoots Davison, the maths master.

"Well said, old boy. Quick off the mark" says another voice and he's given a slap on the back.

"Coca Cola?" says one of the adult voices.

"Yes please," he says. The door gets flung open and a voice yells down the corridor "Boy!" and is answered by the sound of slippered feet running on terrazzo. A figure dressed in black trousers and a white jacket approaches, bows and when he looks up glances at Percy with the faintest of smiles. It's Ah Sup, his friend among the Chinese servants. "Fetchee Coca-Cola young master!" Smiling, Ah Sup rushes off on smooth-sliding feet.

"More music!" yells a voice. "Come on Morrison be a good chap!" Morrison goes to the gramophone, carefully lifts off the disc and puts it back into its brown paper sleeve before placing it gently down (shellac being brittle snaps easily) then picks up another envelope and slips out its shiny, jet-black record.

"Come on, old thing!" says Gent.

"Let him take it steady," says Thomson. "Get any dust on them, scratch them, it ruins them."

"We know that, thank you," says Gent.

"All right," says Morrison, "keep your hair on." With that he winds the handle, lowers the arm and the record begins to play: Fizz, crackle, pop, music. Jan Garber and his orchestra with the "Hinky Dinky Parlay Voo". Within seconds two of the younger men have leapt to their feet and begun to march around the room singing the words they'd heard their elder brothers, their older schoolmates sing back in England just a very few years before: "Three German officers crossed the line, parlez-vous? Three German officers crossed the line, parlez-vous? Three German officers crossed the line, shagged the girls and drank the wine! Inky-pinky parlez-vous?" The older men sit it out. Chairs are pushed aside and two of the men kick off into an energetic foxtrot that weaves precariously around furniture, potted palms and people. Silently Ah Sup comes back into the room with a Coca-Cola for Percy who's sitting quietly close to the door and away from the mayhem. As he offers the tray he whispers in the boy's ear; "You come jiaozi. One half hour." Percy nods and Ah Sup vanishes.

The record winds to its end and the singers and dancers collapse into chairs. Morrison goes back to the gramophone, takes off, puts away, puts on, winds up and the voice of Noel Coward streams into the room: "Parisian Pierrot, your spirit's at zero..." Up jumps Thomson, tall, dark and very slim, sliding a chair away from under the writing table, lifting it up and dropping it into the middle of the room. He sits, straddling the chair and lets his arms drop over the back of it creating a mime of exhaustion. Raising his head he tilts it to one side before making a shelf of the backs of his hands on which he rests his chin in a well-known aesthetic pose. Turning the corners of his mouth down completes his Pierrot. He mimes the light, drawly, tenor: "The world may flatter, but what does it matter, as long as the clock. Goes. Round." Leaping up he continues to mime, using his arms like the hands of a clock, raising them up then flopping down to let his fingertips touch the ground until. at the last verse, Thomson slides across the room to the hatstand, wraps a leg around it and, tilting himself backward, flings out an arm. Tableau.

Some of the audience roar "Encore!" Others mutter something that sounds like 'Bloody powder puff!' and one mutterer leaves the room. On goes the record again, one more time. Up from his seat leaps Gent the games master, his arms slim, strong and smooth and his hair razored at the sides but soft and floppy on top. He takes the dark, willowy Thomson in his arms and the two men begin to tango. "The Quai de l'Orsay the Rue de la Paix are under your sway..." The two men prance, pirouette, sway up and down the centre of the room, now close, now apart, now wrapped around each other, now at arm's length. "Divinely forlorn, with infinite scorn, from midnight till dawn," croons Coward, scratchily. The music ends. The two men make formal bows to each other and separate.

"Of course the Argie cowboys invented the dance 'cause there were no girls for a hundred miles," says a voice in the silence that follows.

"Bit like here then," says one wag and there are laughs from around the smoke-filled room.

Someone else, Fitch, sandy-haired and thin-lipped, leaps up and makes for the pile of records. "Something a little different, I think. Can't bear that pansy Coward. What else has he got?"

Silence and smoke rose up to the ceiling in a cloud before Thomson gets up from his rattan armchair and crosses to the upright piano almost imperceptibly brushing the shoulders of Gent as he passes by. At the piano he shuffles through a pile of sheet music until one catches his eye. Picking it up he sits down, places the sheets on the bracket, and, already jacketless, rolls back his cuffs from the wrist exposing long white Beardsley-like hands and fingers. These fingers play an arpeggio up, another one down before Thomson raises his elbows, leans in and begins to play the opening bars. Tilting back his head he kicks off in a bright tenor voice:

"'Someday he'll come along

The man I love

And he'll be big and strong

The man I love

And when he comes my way

I'll do my best to make him stay...'"

Fitch is noticeably glaring toward the figure of Thomson whose floppy hair is falling in his face as he sways to the music. He languidly tips his head backward to dislodge it. A man, not Gent, gets up from his chair and comes over to the piano to turn the page. It's Morrison, bulky bespectacled Morrison with his spotted bow ties and trousers held up about his round waist by striped suspenders and he joins in with a rich, surprising baritone at the line "Maybe I shall meet him Sunday..." Thomson looks up with surprise at Morrison. His face becomes surprisingly lovely around a frank, winsome smile. Relaxing, the two men carry on their duet until the melody wraps itself up on "I'm waiting for the man I love." The two men hold their gaze, notes fade, the smoky air is still but for the ticking of needle on record.

"I say, is this a tricky moment?" says a voice, a young-sounding voice from the doorway. Most eyes turn in that direction.

"Sopley?" says Morrison. "What on earth are you doing here?" A tall, dusty athletic-looking blond boy steps forward into the room a brown leather suitcase in hand.

"Tuchuns," says Sopley. "Tuchuns having a spat and one of their armies hogging the railway line all the way from Hsuchow to Pukow. They knew at Tsingtau so I thought I might as well just turn around and try and get a coaster tomorrow."

"What about the others?"

"Pretty much everyone else headed up to Tientsin."

"Damn shame the Hsuchow to Haimen line isn't open yet, you'd have got around them."

"Sticky wicket?"

"No Europeans involved if that's what you mean. But the word is the Tuchuns are headed down to Shanghai for some kind of big show."

"Langrigg, aren't you going to Shanghai?" This is Wedderburn, English master and deputy head. Eyes turn to where Percy has been sitting near the door waiting for the half hour to be up so that he can get out of this cloud of sickening smoke and disappear off to the kitchen for the promised jiaozi. Eyes that include those of Sopley whose body is surprisingly close, closer to a junior than a senior would normally stand.

"Yes, sir," he says. "But that's alright, sir. I can go up to Peking and down to Hankow then I can get a river steamer. Sir."

"Good lad," says Wedderburn, holding a match to the pipe in his mouth. "We'll wire the mission tomorrow."

"Sir?" says Percy, "Please may I go, sir? Cook said he'd make me some supper, sir."

"Yes of course, boy," says Wedderburn. "Should have said before. Off you go."

Percy gets up to find the doorway blocked by the figure of Sopley with his suitcase. Even though term is technically over deference is still called for when addressing the Head Boy.

"Excuse me, Sopley," says Percy, "Please may I get past, Sopley?"

The elder boy stands aside but only just. Percy has to wriggle past. Once out into the corridor Percy hears voices start up in the Common Room behind him.

"In you come, Sopley."

"Come and join the congregation."

"This is a fine how-de-do."

"That showed pluck!"

"Give the lad a beer. Boy!"

Percy is greeted in the kitchen by Ah Sup nodding his head and pointing him to the rough scrubbed table in the centre of the room. Young Chinese men in the black and white uniforms of house servants sit on benches on either side. Ah Sup tells them to shift up for the European boy. Some of the older men comply, smiling, nodding with favour toward the young white man who, of all the pupils in the school has been in China the longest, since birth, who understands the niceties of keeping face but who speaks a fat, fleshy Shanghainese. Some of the younger men look with disfavour on the foreigner but keep their opinions to themselves.

The table is covered in a fine dusting of flour and almost all the men are engaged in a chain of production. At the head of the table a putty-like pastry is being rolled out into thin sheets. These are slid along the table and circles are cut into the pastry with the rims of Chinese teacups that are then dipped in bowls of water before being used again. Leftover pastry is passed back to the head of the table to be amalgamated and re-rolled. The circles are moved down in turn to the centre of the table where there are two large bowls containing a mixture of minced pork, finely chopped cabbage, ginger, salt and pepper. Using spoons and their hands the men at the centre are dipping into the mixture and forming tiny meatballs that they drop into the middle of the pastry circles. The circles are turned and moved down again toward the end of the table where fingers reach out and make half-moon envelopes of the pastry, twisting the outer edges into a frill to seal the filling inside. The little pasties are slid down to the end of the table on a schuss of flour and into bamboo baskets. Percy, at the foot of the table, automatically picks up a filled basket and takes it to the stove. There boils and roils a huge pan of water into which the pasties are slid. Within minutes the pasties, like the embryos of small mammals, are bobbing around in the water and are then scooped up in a huge bamboo slotted instrument half way between a spoon and a shovel before being dropped into earthenware bowls lined with cloths.

Someone calls out. The production line has stopped. The table is wiped clear of flour and debris and within seconds bowls and chopsticks are dropped down in front of each diner. A minute or two later and large tureens of jiaozi have arrived on the table. Short men stand up, taller or longer-armed men merely raise their backsides off the bench and for a few seconds there is a frenzy of clicking and stabbing as each diner spears or traps the slippery jiaozi between chopstick points and flicks them into his own bowl. It is as though a flock of pelicans has landed on a shoal of fish. Percy is as skilled as any of them in making his catch and he too has his bowl held up to his lips, his right arm raised to shovel the hot, slippery pasties into his mouth with a flick of the sticks of bone. He slurps, all slurp. Bowls go down, someone burps then another.

"Wo chi baole!' says Percy and the laughter begins with Ah Sup who has been sitting next to him and who now slaps him on the back.

"Ni kan yige lian!" says Ah Sup, beaming.

The door opens and the tone quiets. There are some hostile looks toward the door. It is Sopley.

"Thought I'd find you here," he says. "Come on, we're all going for a bathe. You too. Morrison wants you there." Percy casts a regretful glance at Ah Sup before he slips off the end of the bench and turns to face the cooks and the company.

"Xiexie," he says. "Na tai ding hao."

"Hen hao!" they yell at him with smiles and laughter. He bows at the cook, shakes hands with Ah Sup and follows Sopley out of the room. "Forgot you were half Chink," says Sopley. "Don't know how you can eat that muck. Come on." They walk down the terrazzo corridor Sopley leading, Percy trailing behind.

There's already a good congregation of staff on the beach. Men only. The few Staff wives have already made the trip to Peitaho taking their own children with them. The moon is up casting a gold-yellow path of light onto the dark sea, utterly calm now that the wind has abated. Someone has lit a fire. Someone else has lugged the gramophone down here and set it up on a folding table. No one is drunk. This is absolutely frowned upon. But there's a sense of merriment, of delight that the holidays have begun. The sandy beach is all but the property of Yantai School. To the local people beaches are for landing fishing boats and they regard sea-swimming as yet another sign of Gwulo mental deficiency. Staff bungalows fill the ground between the school and the shore.

"The China Sea," says someone out loud.

"It's a long way to Tipperary," says a voice in the dark and the end of a cigar glows.

Percy has been back to the dormitory and struggled into the maroon worsted swimming trunks. His tender skin is already itching even before he and his plimsolled feet arrive at the beach. There are one or two paraffin lanterns and by their light he realises that of all the party he's the only one wearing any form of clothing. Accustomed to the light dustings of pubic hair and soft skins of his immediate contemporaries, the only bodies he's seen naked, he's completely taken aback and simultaneously transfixed by the variety of musculature, texture of skin, body hair and sizes of cocks and balls surrounding him. He knows from the talk that the staff often go swimming naked. It's just that none of them have ever seen it.

There are fine, long, hairless bodies on long legs with low-set balls and meaty cocks, thick-set bodies with huge bushes of hair and smaller cocks, muscular bodies, scrawny white bodies with caved-in chests and an ingrain of what could be chalk. There is dry body hair and wet body hair with water streaming down it in runnels. Some men glisten others fade like ghosts. Percy has brought a towel and he puts it on the ground a few yards away from the lights and the gramophone close to the border with the dark. Sopley is nowhere to be seen. Perhaps he's in the water. Percy hugs his knees and keeps quiet hoping he won't be noticed. His stomach is full from the jiaozi and how many times has his mother told him that if he doesn't wait for at least an hour after eating before swimming he'll drown?

A naked Mr Morrison, tubby-chested but scrawny-legged and small-balled, sets to winding the gramophone. The tune opens and it's the American Mr Armistead who steps into the middle of the circle miming something and with a strained look on his face. Yes, the mime is that he's holding a hat, a boater, and the side-set to the mouth with the fluttering of eyelashes is Al Jolson. The disc must be bran new. "'When the Summer wind starts blowing,'" he sings over Jolson, "'And the school is closing till the Fall, then my eyes went Eastward, knowing, that's the place I love best of all…'" From thereon he sticks true to the lyrics that Percy has heard him singing before now, his voice carrying through the Staff Room window. When he gets to the bit about the sun-kissed maid who said, "Don't be late," Percy thinks of the smiling, red-hatted figure on the boxes of Sun-Maid raisins his American mother occasionally sends him with jars of Radio Malt, "to build you up."

Percy has little hope that he will grow tall like his father accepting that he's fated to be small like his mother. He's already started to take on, though, some of his father's bristliness. His head-hair is wiry and little tufts of it have started to appear around his cock, around his nipples and in his armpits. And like his father he loves food and is chubby. "Puppy fat," says his mother confidently. "It'll go." But with incipient acne flaring on his face, with his wiry head-hair greasy and his body still egg-shaped Percy is deeply unhappy with appearance, with everything about his body except that he's shaving with his New Improved Gillette Safety Razor, a gift from his mother, followed by a stinging splash of Aqua Velva. Although he's always tried to find a time for his fortnightly shave when he can be private and alone it was only two days ago that Sopley had strolled into the bathroom during the act. The elder boy, whose golden skin was all but hairless, stood looking at Percy's face in the mirror with mock-admiration.

"My goodness," he'd said. "You Tarzan."

"You Paulovich," said Percy.

"Ouch," said Sopley. "So sharp and you'll cut yourself." With that Percy had nicked his cheek and a little stream of blood began to flow down among the soap. "Told you," said Sopley and disappeared.

Percy considers himself lucky that Sopley still can't be seen. The elder boy's slim body, his ready smile and general grace would have made Percy feel like one of the warty frogs that can be heard croaking in the distance away toward the village. Sopley hasn't ever been physically cruel to him unlike some of the elder boys. Towel-flicking, fagging duties, being baited with fantastic tales about his parents, called "half Chink" or "Yankee Doodle" went on and on. Only on the rugger pitch did he ever manage to shake off the jibes. There he became a "useful little fellow" for an hour a week during the Winter months.

Percy sat, quietly, thinking about tomorrow and the start of his journey to Kiukiang to stay for the Summer with James Kinghorn, the "Uncle Jack" he had met only once in '22 at the newly-opened Majestic Hotel in Shanghai where his parents were staying on what they called a "spying mission". Mother was gunning for the family hotel firm to buy into the booming Far-Eastern market. She and his father had spent a year or more on their "spying missions" in Peking, Tientsin, Shanghai and Hong Kong sizing up the assets of the Compagnie Internationale des Wagons Lits and the newly amalgamated Hong Kong and Shanghai Hotel Company, getting the low-down on their investors and keeping their ears to the ground. It was around this time that they'd come across Sopley Senior, the second son of an English Lord brought out to add some class to what Father called 'a bunch of sharks' trying to carve their own slice of the Shanghai cake. Father saw more opportunity in hotel-supply and was in discussion with a local firm to start making cutlery and metal tableware. "The Flatware King," mother used to call him or "The Toast Rack Tsar".

How they knew Jack Kinghorn wasn't entirely clear to Percy. Father had described him as "an old school chum" but the two seemed to come from entirely different eras; his father the well-dressed international businessman, and Jack, a frock-coated British Treaty-Port Customs Official, a position cynically regarded as both a sinecure and a dead end. Percy would have been delighted to have spent the vac. at the newly acquired Atholl Palace reading, exploring and hiding away. This year, however, talk had already been circulating about the possibility of troubles in Shanghai over the Summer and so it was decided to package him off to Uncle Jack up-country.

"You'll love it," his father had said. "Jack loves fishing and tennis and all that manly stuff. Do you good."

Back in the present laughter came in waves from the circle around the lanterns and the gramophone. The evening had turned into a wine-less Bacchanal. Feet flew in the sand, elbows shot out, knees twisted, cocks and balls swung as a line of men took on the Charleston to The Golden Gate Orchestra. The American tutor Armistead's accent and baritone were in demand to over-sing Eddie Cantor's "If You Knew Susie" followed by an a cappella version of "Yes, Sir, That's My Baby!" There was shoving in the row for the can-can line-up ("Used to be danced by men, you know," said the French master) that turned into a mock wrestling match.

Then out of the group came Morrison.

"Forgot you were here," he said. "Sopley told you to come down?"

"Yes Sir."

"Seen him?"

"No Sir, I think he's swimming, Sir."

"Must be bloody cold by now, then," said Morrison. "Are you

going to bathe? No? I think you've seen enough. Time we got you to bed. Follow me." Percy was glad to see that Morrison turned towards a pile of clothes and put on trousers, hooking the braces over his shoulders before putting on his plimsolls.

Tired and itching under the swimming-trunks he followed the man up the path. Even in the warm wind he was glad to have a towel around his shoulders. Morrison walked on ahead. As the Latin-master led on he whistled then broke into the chorus of, "Yes, We Have No Bananas" as he walked. Breaking off he turned around and said to Percy: "So, young master, you're off to Kiukiang for the vac, are you?"

"Yes, Sir," mumbled Percy as he tried to keep up.

"Speak up, boy."

"Yes, Sir," said Percy more loudly.

"Ever been there before?"

"No, Sir."

"Some of our fellows are heading up to Kiukiang. Is your uncle a missionary? Playing for one of the other teams? London Society?"

"No, sir, I don't think so, sir. He's in the customs, Sir, that's what Father told me."

"He's your father's brother? Your mother's brother?"

"No Sir, he isn't, Sir. I just call him uncle, Sir."

"Have you stayed with him before?"

"No, Sir, but he came to visit us in Shanghai, Sir. He and Father went to school together, Sir."

"Drop the sir, Langrigg, it's getting on my nerves. Is there a Mrs Jack?"

"No, Sir, I think they were killed in the Boxer, Sir. But he's got a big house, Father says, and he's hardly ever there but he's good at Latin Sir, and Father says he's going to give me some coaching in the vac."

"Won't you be worried being there on your own?"

"Oh no, Sir I mean Mr Morrison. Uncle Jack lives in a compound, sir, and I probably won't go out much."

There's a pause as they walk.

"Have you heard that Liddell's back?"

"Yes, Sir, isn't it ripping, Sir? He's my hero, Sir!"

"Even though he's London?"

"He's still one of us isn't he Sir? I mean he was born in Tientsin, Sir and I was too."

"Do you like Tientsin, Langrigg?"

"Oh yes Sir it's my favourite, Sir. It's not big like Shanghai but there are shops there and cafes, Sir, with English cakes and all the Hongs are there too, Sir and there's the Club it's ever so big and Father and Mother go there for balls."

"When did you last go home?"

"Well never, Sir. Father said we were going to go home in '16 Sir but we didn't because of the War and since then he and Mother have been too busy."

"You haven't ever been to England? Would you like to?"

"Father says he's going to send me to school there to do my matric."

"Do you want to go?"

"Yes of course I do, Sir. It's home, isn't it? Father showed me a house in Victoria Street in Tientsin that's all black and white and he says that's how houses in England look and there aren't any warlords in England are there, Sir and nobody throws bombs or spits at you do they, Sir?"

"Will you miss China?"

Percy is silent for a moment. "Yes, Sir, well you know they call me Chink, Sir."

"Will you come back after school?"

"Mother says I have to go to University Sir only she calls it school. She wants me to go to school near Boston, Sir. That's in America, Sir."

"Will you go into hotels, too?"

"I want to, Sir. Sir, but Mother doesn't want me to. She wants me to be a lawyer, Sir."

"They play lots of rugger in England."

"Yes, I know, Sir, and I'm looking forward to that."

"Not cricket?"

"I don't like cricket so much, Sir. Or perhaps I could join the army, Sir and come back and defend us from the Tuchuns, Sir and fight the warlords."

"You've been reading too much Henty, Langrigg. Life's not really like that. And the next war's going to be different, mark my words."

"There's going to be another war, Sir?"

"Not in the next eight weeks Langrigg. No need to worry."

The two had reached the school buildings. Lights still showed along the verandahs but the rest of the school was dark. Percy could tell from the click of mah-jong tiles that the Chinese servants had set up tables to play at while they waited for the teaching staff to get back. "Wait there," said Morrison and went off to find the tables and the players. Out of sight Percy could hear him telling them in pidgin they could pack up and go to bed. There was a squeaking of chairs and the sound of tables being folded up. Footsteps disappeared. Morrison came back and stood, looking at Percy. Percy shivered.

"You're tired. Better get you to bed, young man."

"Thank you, Sir," said Percy. There was a stillness. Neither moved.

"Won't you feel lonely in that dormitory all on your own?" Percy didn't respond. Lonely? Did that matter?

"Why don't I come up with you? Would that make you feel safe? You know, in case the Tuchuns are massing to attack."

"They won't, Mr Morrison. There's one of our gunboats in the bay I saw it earlier. They wouldn't, Sir."

"I think I'll come along with you anyway, Langrigg, just in case. Hmm?" Percy said nothing. "Langrigg you're shivering. We need to get you warm. Come on, this way." Morrison turned toward the stair that led up to one of the two dormitories.

"That's not my dorm," said Percy.

"Never mind," said Morrison, "This is where we're going. Come along." Percy held back but felt trapped, pinned down by the man's masculinity as if by a heavy weight. "Come along," he said again. They groped their way up the darkened stairs, Percy following as if drawn along by a magnet. Morrison's plimsolls slapped on the concrete risers. Up they went until Morrison pushed open the door and held it for Percy to enter.

"Excuse me, Sir," said Percy as he tried to get past, but the man was standing solidly in his way. He ducked to the left then to the right to try to get by but without success. Either way he found himself colliding with Morrison, his face ending up in flesh and body hair. A smell came from the master's armpits and another, sweeter smell seemed to seep up from the waistband of his trousers. These odours contrasted with those of floor polish, of boiled laundry, of thickly painted cast iron that were the familiar smells of a dorm. Finally, Morrison stepped back to let Percy into the room.

"Get ready for bed, Langrigg," he said.

"But I haven't brushed my teeth," said Percy. "And I don't have my pyjamas. Sir."

"Sit down on the bed," said Morrison and, kneeling down, started to take off the seated boy's plimsolls. Percy sat transfixed. And silent. Morrison leant forward and took off the towel from around Percy's shoulders. Percy shivered.

"We'll soon get you warm, boy," said the man. Still kneeling he leant forward again and grasped the waistband of Percy's swimming trunks. "Put your legs out straight," he said and pulled the swimming trunks down and over the boy's feet and reached behind to drop them on the floor.

"I expect you were a bit shocked," he said, "seeing all those naked men?" Percy said nothing. "Did you see mine?" Percy thought a lie would help and shook his head. "Would you like to? Here, let me show you. But listen," here he leant forward so that his lips brushed Percy's ear "This is our secret. You must never tell a living soul. Or you'll never get Home. Do you understand? They wouldn't let boys like you on the boat. Do you understand? Do you?" He withdrew his face slightly, cupped Percy's chin in his hand. Percy saw his teeth between his open lips. He nodded. "Let me hear you say yes," said Morrison.

"Yes," said Percy and the word felt so heavy that it seemed to plop out of his mouth like a brass ball that thudded onto the parquet and rolled off, making a thunder across the room.

Morrison stood up to slip off his braces first from the left shoulder and then the right. Sliding his hands down to his belly he undid the top button of his trousers and, jutting out his arse, pushed them over his buttocks and onto the floor. Straightening, kicking them aside he moved a step closer to the seated Percy. Now Percy understood the source of the sweetish smell. It came from the man's cock, thick now and jutting to within an inch of Percy's mouth. Morrison reached his hand around behind Percy's head and let it rest on the nape of his neck.

"Now be a good boy and open your mouth," he said. Percy parted his lips and then his teeth. His mouth, that had been dry, suddenly filled with saliva. The end of the man's cock, he noticed, had begun to dribble out a clear liquid. The hand behind his head brought his mouth closer and closer to that purple bell of flesh. Percy involuntarily closed his lips but the bell kept moving, pushing them apart until it grated over his teeth and came to rest on his tongue. "Aaaah," said the man and began to push Percy's head further forward until he could feel the thing on his tonsils. He started to gag.

"Sorry boy," said Morrison, withdrawing a little. "Suck," he said, "Suck hard. That's it." Percy sucked so his cheeks hurt and the piston of flesh went in and out, in and out. Percy spluttered. The rod withdrew.

"I can't, sir," he said.

"No such word," said Morrison and with a thrust of his arse pushed further into Percy's mouth than before. Percy felt as though he were choking but found himself exploring the alien flesh with his tongue, round and round, as though he were licking an ice-cream cone. "Ah!" said Morrison and Percy felt a rush of liquid over his tongue that cascaded down his throat. He had to swallow to keep breathing. The liquid was warm, first sweet then sour and rank. "Ah!" said Morrison again and another rush filled Percy's throat for him to swallow then a third then a fourth, but less. The man's legs started to shake and it seemed he was about to topple forward. The boy pushed his head into Morrison's bush, butting at him to move him away. Salty sweat from among the man's hairs ran into his nostrils and over his lip. "Want more? Eh? Good lad. You'll have to wait till later. I'll come back and we'll play a different game eh, Percy?"

"No you won't," said a voice at the doorway and the light came on. Morrison pulled himself out of Percy's embrace and turned sideways so that Percy was able to see the figure. At least, he saw the figure of a blond-haired youth.

"Rex," he said. "Rex's revolver crackled out."

Morrison was silent but the youth, Sopley, came forward into the room and spoke. The silence broke.

"Langrigg, are you alright?"

Percy couldn't speak and realised he had started to cry.

"Wrap yourself in your towel and come here. Now."

Percy levered himself off the bed, found the towel, wrapped it around his waist and crossed over to stand next to Sopley. He raised an arm and attempted to brush away the tears with the back of his hand. He didn't feel sad, he remembered later, or outraged or violated, he recalled just being full of a tide of emotion that welled up and overflowed. Like the feeling he sometimes got at the end of a movie when the hero turns up and saves the girl.

"Get dressed and get out," said Sopley to Morrison. As Morrison reached the door Sopley spoke, softly but with a force that seemed to blow over Percy's head like a typhoon. "He isn't going to be your bum-boy you crapulous pig. Get out before I box you to a jelly."

"Ang zang de jidujao zhu," said Percy.

Morrison, now an ashen colour, tucked his shrivelled rod back into his trousers and hitched them up, still unbuttoned, before turning and leaving the room.

Sopley turned to Percy. "Go and wash yourself," he said. "Wash yourself all over then brush your teeth and rinse your mouth out. I'll wait here for you."

When Percy got back Sopley was at the door holding a pair of pyjamas.

"Get into bed," said Sopley. "I expect you feel cold."

Percy shivered even in his pyjamas and under the sheets and bedspread.

"It's all right," said Sopley. "I'm just going to lie on the bed next to yours."

"Don't," said Percy.

"I won't leave, it's all right."

Percy felt the tears coming back to his eyes. "I'm sorry," he said, "for being soppy."

"You can't be as soppy as me little Langrigg. Sopley by name, soppy by nature."

"But you're the cricket captain," said Percy, "and you're the Head Boy. That isn't soppy."

"But there are things that make me cry, you know. Now you," he said, turning to face Percy so they looked at each other in the moonlight that streamed in through the windows, four feet apart, "Now you, you're a Scotch terrier. Look at you on the rugger pitch. I've seen the way you hold on to the ball."

"I'm not much good," said Percy. "It's my eyes. I can't see very well. Father says I shall have to wear spectacles. He says I'll be an owl and I won't be able to play games or do things proper men do."

Sopley reached into his trouser pocket and brought out a yellow tin of the latest cigarettes to come to China; State Express 555s. Choosing one he put it in his mouth, put back the tin, pulled out a box of matches and by the flare Percy saw his face intently focused on the cigarette's now glowing tip. He chucked the spent match on the floor and inhaled.

"But Sopley," said Percy, "That's not allowed. You'll be caned if they find out."

"This is the last day of term, I don't care."

They lay on their separate beds in silence.

Sopley got up and went to the window. The smoke from his cigarette flowed up until it met the light of the moon over the China Sea.

Percy gazed at the elder boy, blond and perfect like a vision of adolescent beauty so unlike his own chubby frame covered over with its spotty, chameleon skin. One, two minutes passed while the cigarette burned down and down and the trail of smoke thinned. 'Its little smoke in pallid moonshine died,' thought Percy as though for the first time truly feeling the line. His heart heaved into his mouth with a sensation he struggled to understand but which caused him physical pain like a bolus of unchewed rice in his throat. Sopley opened the window and threw the butt to the ground.

Then he turned around. "Did you enjoy it, Langrigg? Be honest. If you're honest now you can save yourself a lot of bother in the future."

"How do you know, Sopley? Has he done it to you?"

"Answer me, little Langrigg. Did you enjoy it?"

"I don't know."

"You mean maybe you did? Look, I'm going to tell you something." He closed the window. "What was wrong was that he took advantage of you, do you know what that means?"

"He's a master and I'm a boy."

"Yes, that's right. But when you get older you can do it if you like it. There's nothing wrong with it whatever anyone says. If you like it. But if you don't like it and you don't want to do it then you mustn't do it. Ever. That's all."

"So I can do it with Mr Morrison again if I like it?"

"Langrigg I really wouldn't. Just listen to me when I tell you that the worst thing about that Morrison is that he will tell you he loves you."

"Did he say that to you?"

"Yes and I believed him. Mater and Pater are a long way away and here it's all about God our Father but God isn't an actual parent who buys you things or takes you out on exeats or show He cares."

Percy was now sitting up in bed, his legs tucked under him.

"Did you love him back?"

"Yes, I suppose I did."

"Do you still love him?"

"Yes, I suppose I do but that can go to heck."

"Does he do it with lots of boys?"

"Only a few. He calls us his special ones. You know he gives us extra tuition and he says we're going to be great shining stars, luminaries he says, at the University or the House of Commons or the Bar or whatever and you feel he's even better than your father and then," he pauses, "then you find out that he's said exactly the same thing to I don't know - Farrar Junior. Has he offered extra lessons to you, yet?"

"No."

"Well, my advice is if he does, say no."

Percy lay back on the bed, his head out toward where Sopley lay. Sopley also lay back and turned toward Percy. Their faces were now no more than a couple of feet apart. Percy breathed in the aroma of State Express 555.

"What do you want to be, Sopley?"

"Oh, I don't know. Well yes actually I'd like to go to America, to California and I'd like to get into the movies."

"You mean and be like Douglas Fairbanks? You could do it!"

"No really I'd like to be what they call the other side of the camera. You know, the chaps who make the film."

"Like DW Griffiths."

"Griffith. But yes."

"I'll come and see all your films!"

"Thank you, Little Langrigg. I believe you would. Don't fall asleep, now."

"I wouldn't!"

"By the way, what did you say when I came into the dorm? It looked as though you said something."

Percy remembered and blushed in the dark. "I said," he said, "Rex's pistol crackled out."

"You are a strange one, little Langrigg. What was that all about?"

"Oh well it's nothing really although you know the way you came through the door?"

"Yes."

"It was like as if you were rescuing me from the bad person and I thought of the book I was reading and it has a picture just inside the front where it says 'Rex's revolver crackled out". Only his name's not really Rex it's Reginald. Reginald Bateman but everyone calls him Rex and in the picture Rex has shot one of the Boxers."

"Is this a Henty you're reading?"

"Yes, Sopley do you like Henty?"

"I used to."

"Well, this is the new one I've got and it's called With the Allies to Pekin and Rex is the hero. He saves the Legations. By himself." There's a silence in which they hear each other's breathing.

"What did you call Morrison in Chink?"

"Dirty Christian pig."

Sopley began to laugh and then they were both laughing and laughing and laughing. Percy laughed so much he half fell between the two beds. Sopley's arms came out to grab his shoulders and pull him up. They pulled him up so that their faces were level. Then they kissed. Percy opened his lips and teeth and tasted tobacco and beer. Just for a few seconds. Then Sopley pushed him back onto his bed and stood up in the space between. Leaning forward he lent over Percy and kissed his mouth once more. Then he stood up and went to lie down on his own bed, on his back.

"Do you like poems, Langrigg?"

"Yes, Sopley I do, very much."

"So, do I. You know they call it girly to like poems."

"Yes."

"But you still like them?"

"I do."

"Who do you like best?"

"I think I like Keats best of all."

"Why?"

"I think it's because he's so lavish."

"That's a good word."

"It's one of mama's favourites. Everything nice is always too lavish she says. So I like it."

"Do you know what it means?"

"Well it means too nice I suppose."

"It comes from the Latin, lavare, to wash. Can you see how it means what it means now?"

"Well maybe, Sopley. If it means to pour out water it could be saying just pour things out in a torrent and that could be being spendthrift, that's one of Papa's favourites, so it could mean being wasteful. Like washing something down the drain."

"That's good. So how is Keats wasteful?"

"Well, he spends a lot of words. Valuable words. He doesn't worry about it he just dishes them out. Like people at a casino. In Shanghai. If you see what I mean."

"I do. And that's why you like him?"

"Yes, it is."

"What's your favourite?"

"I like 'The Eve of St Agnes' best of all."

"Why?"

"Well, you see I love the opening when it's bitter chill and the owl, that's me you see, for all his feathers is a'cold and when you're reading it you can really actually feel cold too. And then later on when Madeline goes to bed and starts to take off her clothes you can feel your skin really going cold and she gets into bed and it's freezing and she's like one of those chain-mail knights lying down in their tombs all freezing cold too and then," he pauses.

"And then?" says Sopley.

"And then the man opens the cupboard and brings out all this beautiful food and it's all glowing and the stained-glass windows are glowing too and you go from cold to warm and you feel warm inside and if I was ever starving I think I'd think about Madeline's feast and I wouldn't feel hungry anymore even though it was only in my imagination. What poems do you like, Sopley?"

"I like Tennyson."

"Which ones? "

"'Now sleeps the crimson petal, now the white. The firefly wakens, waken thou with me.'"

"Oh yes Sopley I like that one too but it's hard to find; you have to look through all the rest of the poem first and it's quite long and it's quite boring, too."

The boys lie on their backs and look out at the window. A shooting star falls. "'Now slides the silent meteor on,'" says Sopley. "I like that line. Up there in space the meteor is barrelling along at thousands of miles an hour and is probably whooshing away and creating a right din and is huge and boiling hot and dangerous but down here you see it sliding gently. Ever so gently."

"Ever so ever so," says Percy.

"Ever so ever so ever so," says Sopley. "Ever so beautiful."

"My papa doesn't like me reading poems," says Percy. "Not the ones I like, anyway. He wants me to read Kipling and WE Henley and what he calls Manly Stuff. Like If and out of the night that covers me and books he calls 'improving'."

"Don't you want to be improved?"

"Not if it means having to read Kipling."

"Why not?"

"Because it's all about stupid men and beating and flaying and marching and rifles and war and armies."

"But it's still poetry."

"I suppose so. No wait, it isn't. It's verse. That's what it is. It's just rough. And hairy. Like Mr Morrison."

"Hairy poems?"

"Rough horrible hairy poems by rough horrible hairy men."

"That's quite funny, Langrigg."

"Thank you, Sopley."

Sopley turned and lay on his side to look at Percy, brushing back the lock of hair that had fallen across his eyes. "What's the difference between poetry and verse?"

"Just because something rhymes doesn't make it a poem."

"What does then?"

Percy turned to gaze on the smooth perfection of David Sopley.

"It has to make you feel something not just tell you something."

"Something that exists?"

"Everything exists in words."

"Tell me what poems you like. Not the hairy ones. The smooth ones. Tell me and I'll tell you if I've read them too."

"Do you really want to know?"

"Well yes or I wouldn't have asked you."

"It's just that you're senior and you're head boy and why would you want to know what an owl like me likes?"

"Owls are wise birds."

"Chinky owls?"

"Yes, owls that are Chinky, too."

"Maud."

"You like Maud? Fitch says it's melodramatic and silly."

"I don't care. I like it."

"Why?"

"You have to read it out loud I mean really read it like it's a theatre play and then it sort of starts to make sense."

"And?"

"You have to be the man in it. You have to really be him and go mad like he does. It's like you said, it's like a vision and you have to go in and share it, not just say it's silly."

"Do you remember any of it?"

"Yes."

"Well say it."

"Alright:

'All night has the casement jessamine stirr'd
To the dancers dancing in tune...
Till a silence fell with the waking bird,
And a hush with the setting moon.'

Jessamine means jasmine. You know you can dance to the words? It's like music."

"Show me."

Percy gets up from the bed and walks into the centre of the dorm. The pyjamas he's wearing are too big for him and he looks undersized and grey in the moonlight like a baggy children's toy. Sopley gets up too and stands opposite him. He bows to Percy. "May I have the honour?" he says.

Percy curtseys then holds out his hand. Sopley takes it and puts out his arm to encircle Percy's waist. Sopley leads off and they step out in a gentle, clumsy waltz.

"Say the words," says Sopley, "Sing the words." Percy sings and they dance until Percy trips over his pyjama trouser cuffs.

"Sorry, Sopley," he says.

"I see what you mean," says Sopley. "It's music." They bow to each other then go back to their beds.

"I know," says Sopley. 'let's start a game. I say a line from a poem and you..."

"Guess which poem."

"No. That wouldn't be fun. I say a line or I say a couplet and you say a couplet or I say a verse and you say a verse."

"Is it a competition?"

"No not at all. It isn't that kind of game."

"I don't understand."

"If I start with some Tennyson but you think Browning should be the next line then you do your Browning."

"As long as they fit together."

"Yes, as long as they fit together."

"But not if they don't."

"No. Then you carry on with the next bit of the same poem."

"I don't know where to start. Oh yes I know one that doesn't sound good at all unless you say it out loud. Fitch found me reading it and said it was doggerel. But I said it out loud and then he went quiet and walked off. It's Rossetti."

"Dante Gabriel or Christina?"

"Dante Gabriel. We can do Christina later. If you like." Sopley was silent. Percy began:

"'The wind flapp'd loose, the wind was still,

Shaken out dead from tree and hill:

I had walk'd on at the wind's will,–

I sat now, for the wind was still.'"

Sopley's voice emerged:

"'Between my knees my forehead was,–

My lips, drawn in, said not Alas!

My hair was over in the grass,

My naked ears heard the day pass.

My eyes, wide open, had the run

Of some ten weeds to fix upon;

Among those few, out of the sun,

The woodspurge flower'd, three cups in one.
From perfect grief there need not be
Wisdom or even memory:'"
Together they spoke the final couplet:
"'One thing then learnt remains to me,–
The woodspurge has a cup of three.'"
"That's one of my favourites too."
"Is England really full of green hills?"
"Yes, it is."
"You're very good at remembering."
"So are you."
"Have you read any Morris?"
"Gold Wings?"
"Oh yes!"
"'The Haystack in the Floods?'"
"'Make sure thy way lies backward to the Chatelet!'"
"'And he moaned as dogs do being half-dead.'"
"All the ones you like. We like. They're all quite bright, aren't they?"
"Bright?"
"I mean they have lots of colourful words."
"'Haystack' and 'Gold Wings', they're so..."
"Real."
"Yes, real like the movies but in colour."
"Or dreams."
"Yes dreams."
"Real but different."
"Real but brighter."
"I think they're better than real."
'So do I.'
"I'd like to live in a poem."
"So would I. Which one would you choose?"
"'Childe Roland to the Dark Tower Came.'"
"Gosh. I'd like to be in 'Ode to a Nightingale' and look through
the magic casement. Or 'Bright Star.'"
"Somewhere hard and beautiful and very bright and shining."
"Like cloisonné? My mama collects cloisonné. She has a beautiful
bowl it's all blue with scarlet and white fish swimming all around it.
And she has some birds and all their feathers are red and blue and

they have a gold line around them."

"Enamelled. Like enamel. What do you think? Enamelled feelings that will last for ever."

"Let's make a club. The Enamellers."

"In secret! A secret Club!"

"What do you think? We promise to love the bright and colourful poems with words that make things enamelled and everlasting. To love Morris and Keats and Tennyson and Rossetti DG and C and everyone like them."

"And know them all by heart."

"Yes, so wherever we are even if we never meet again we can think about our poems..."

"The enamelled ones."

"Or say them out loud and it'll be as though we're there."

"I hope we don't never meet again."

"Yes."

"And when we do see each other again whatever we look like or however old we are and fat and hairy like Morrison we can say a line and the other one says the other line and we know it's us."

"Yes. But it's a sacred pact and you have to keep it secret."

"Of course I will, Sopley. You're the best friend I've ever had."

"And me too."

"Thank you, Sopley."

"Don't thank me.'

"All right, Sopley. Sopley?"

"Yes?"

"I'm tired."

"I should think you are. Go to sleep."

"Will you be here when I wake up?"

"No I don't think so."

"Goodbye then Sopley."

"Goodbye Langrigg."

Sopley lying on his back on the bed began to sing, softly:

"What'll I do when you are far away and I am blue, what'll I do?"

The next morning Sopley was gone. Percy, prepared for his journey, went in search of Ah Sup and gave him the money he'd been saving. He shook Ah Sup's hand and headed for the Buick in the courtyard. Fitch would drive him to the station. Before he stepped into the car Morrison came up and stood with one foot on the running board.

"I'd like to take you for some special tuition next term, Langrigg. Latin. I think you have a great future ahead of you. University and then perhaps the Law. You'll need a good grasp of Latin. Aren't you going to say thank you?"

Percy rolled up the window. The hefty car drew away from Yantai School. Ah Sup was running beside and waving. Percy rolled the window down again and stuck his head out. "Lao pengyou!" he yelled and Ah Sup trotted on in his black satin slippers, smiling and waving till the car was out of his sight, his pigtail bobbing up and down behind him as he ran.

London, Bloomsbury, The Sherborne Hotel, August 1947

Poire Belle Hélène

"Open the door, Richard!"

That was everyone's catchphrase that Summer at the Sherborne Hotel, Bloomsbury. You couldn't stand by a door, outside a door, inside a door, with your hand on the doorknob or even walk toward a door without someone (provided the public weren't in earshot) carolling it out. But what to say? Life wasn't so rosy for the average Londoner. Singing was about all some of them had. The man who'd sung the line was standing just inside the office door, tray in hand loaded with coffee pots, cups and saucers.

"Be a sport, Mr Langrigg and open the door for us would yer? Only of me appendages I'm using the two that's allowed out on show if you'll pardon the expression."

Percy levered himself out of his chair, a wooden revolving chair, its veneer peeling and its leather upholstery frayed to the jute backing. As he walked toward the door he felt envy for the waiter, it was Frederick, for being able to get around the hotel in a simple uniform of black trousers and white regulation bum-freezer jacket while he himself had to be got up at all times on duty in full fig; polished shoes, pinstripe trousers, stiff collar, tie and morning coat. On a taller man this panoply could look elegant but Percy had suspicions that dressed like this and wearing his wire-rimmed spectacles he looked like Dr Crippen and had become morbidly sensitive to the sight of anyone drawing out of his way. He opened the door. "Thanks, Perce," said Frederick, "you're a gent." And he went away, clanking.

The Summer of 1947 was proving to be what the staff called A Scorcher although not all that warm by Hong Kong standards. Percy imagined The Heat as in 'oh, this Heat!' or 'I can't, it's The Heat!', as a tawny old lion, its dusty coat covered in sores and flies, padding around the city on its last legs, skeletal and sad, sounding off a cross between a roar and a cough when it could summon the energy, a sound that frightened no one. It looked as though it had walked here from India across all the pink on the map bearing bad news of the Empire and asking for safe retirement in Regent's Park Zoo. While a strand of public debate over the last two years had whiffled on about Imperial Commitment and holding on to the reins, both for and against, it appeared that the Empire had started to vote with its feet and was already leaving; first Burma and now, soon, very soon, India itself. Percy hadn't particularly liked India, British India, from what little he'd seen of it. Riddled with convention and snobbery it had been a far cry from the cosmopolitan worlds of Tentsin, Shanghai and Hong Kong. At least before the War. 'Before the War, Before the War,' said Percy to himself. There was then and here is now but what happened in between? "Inbetween" – what a gorgeous word. It sounded Dutch, they liked whistly diphthongs like tw and long eees. But he'd looked it up at one stage and of course the Dutch word was much more practical "tussenin" – "two things in" – whereas the Old English word was as hard to pin down as an elver in a misty Anglian fen. At one stage he'd have had the means to look it up. At one stage? Yes, at that quite long stage of being in Stanley Camp with not much to read other than the Bible and an Etymological Dictionary – the Oxford in its ten-volume 1928 edition – found in the looted school.

The Romance of Language, thought Percy as he tried to look through the streaked, brown film that covered the window into the alley outside, picturing The Romance as a quest, remembering the glorious tapestry by Burne-Jones where a knight, himself, Percy, Percival, Parsifal finds a way through thickets of obfuscation and trickery and sees a vision of the Vessel of Truth while outside the Grail Sanctuary, beyond the glow of the lamp that lights up asphodels and lilies of the field, hovers the deep, deep blue mist of un-meaning, of night. Now where had he seen it?

"Morning, Percy," said a voice, "Penny for 'em." That's more than they're worth, thought Percy, turning to see McAlise heading into the room and toward his desk.

"Morning McAlise," he said. "Coffee's gone. Shall I ring for more?"

"Not much of a tea drinker are you, Langrigg? Practically a Yank. Still, you're on the winning side as long as your coffee stays un-rationed and no mistake."

"And no mistake," thought Percy. How the English loved their little linguistic tics: "In point of fact. In actual fact. I'll have you know. I must say. I says it as shouldn't" – the phrases they used to add weight to their statements. The middle classes, he'd noticed, tended to use these phrases before, the lower classes after.

"As a matter of fact," he said to McAlise, "I'm not sure that Mrs Bell is in this morning. She said yesterday her youngest was down with whooping cough. I'd better go and see how the rota's bearing up."

"Absolutely," said McAlise, "Good show. Off you toddle. And have a word with Frederick if you would, en passant as they say, and see if he'll bring in my tea. And a biscuit." Ah, the biscuit, the tea biscuit. Talk about Holy Grails, biscuits were rarer than unicorns in the shops. And yet there were always plenty of them at the Sherborne. Funny, that.

Percy shoved his nose outside the door and into the corridor. Was it there? No, it wasn't, thank the Lord. The air was musty and close even at this time of day but the Odour was missing. And that meant no Mr Smetka. If Britain, home, was a wounded lion looking for a cage into which to crawl Mr Smetka was a black panther in its prime, padding about the corridors of The Sherborne; and where the lion was followed by the stench of decay from Mr Smetka's sleek pelt came the bracing aroma of Vetiver. Perhaps he bathed in it, thought Percy, so that it inhabits every pore. It was like an early warning system, the sort of thing we could all have done with in '41. Like Smetka's Succubus his Odour nosed into corridors before him and wafted behind like a fresh, woody green cloud of gas that told of his recent passage.

From the way in which he prowled about anyone would think Smetka was the owner of the Sherborne and not just its General Manager. Percy had often to remind himself that the owners were in fact the decrepit Beaumont family (known here as the Bewmonts) of whom the last survivor may or may not have been Miss Adelaide Beaumont ('Aduh-lah-eed Bowmon') who rumour had shut into a suite on the second floor like a Miss Havisham or worse; Mrs Rochester. Percy, whose parents had known the Beaumonts Out East knew full well what the actual circumstances were having met the lady in question a few months before when he'd come with letters of recommendation looking for a job. In her seventies, with a suite always kept for her here, yes on the second floor, she was wildly unmaterialistic in an upper-class English way, had no idea of the measure of her wealth and having founded what was to become the national antirrhinum collection at her home outside Winchester had no real interest in the running of her hotels either. Smetka knew all this and regularly disappeared to a small cottage in the country, close to the River Test and within a mile of the Beaumont pile which he would visit to update the old lady on the accounts or at least his version of them. It was the Beaumont connection alone that kept Percy, as well he knew, from being savaged, as most of his colleagues had been, by the panther's claws. And yet, thought Percy today as he did every day, the knowing could kill me still, and he felt as uneasy about sharing a secret with Smetka as if he'd been asked to hang on to a live grenade "for a tick."

Percy set off as quietly as he could down the long corridor, papered in anaglypta, brown as if stained by strong Indian tea and with a carpet that might have once been patterned brown on beige. At the end of the corridor was the staff room. He knocked on the door and entered.

"Well she said, I dunno she said, well I said if that's your attitude you can keep it I said. The cheek!"

Mrs Abbott, head char and head stirrer of the pot, aproned, scarf wrapped around the head and tied in a large knot at the front, beige lisle stockings well pulled up onto her suspender belt and her polished brown shoes. With her mud-coloured apron, brown hair, yellowish complexion and face wreathed in cigarette smoke she appeared today to Percy as she always did: the personification of Britain. Britannia, even, standing rather than seated as on the currency, mop and bucket instead of spear and shield, she represented to him that other country, the country he hadn't known that the chaps were fighting for, the country whose citizenship had cost him years of freedom, the country that was, he realised, two countries. Not so much yin and yang as yolk and white, Romans and Britons, Normans and Saxons, Nabobs and Nobodies, Kings, Queens and cleaners, Picts and Scots.

"Morning Mister Langrigg," came a chorus of about eight women's voices.

"Morning ladies," he replied. He liked them and the odour they generated of polish, smoke and Gumption. Gumption. "Mrs Bell not here?"

"No Mister Langrigg her nipper were took bad in the night. Had to send fer the doc."

Well that must mean it's serious, thought Percy, let's hope he doesn't hop straight from cradle to grave. If he could hang on another few months he could get doctoring for free.

"Well how shall we divvy up her duties this morning? Mrs Timmins and Mrs Catling could you kindly take her floor and share it between you when you've done yours? We're down on occupancy this week as you know so that shouldn't be too much of an imposition. And you can be excused staff quarters. I'll tell them to clean up after themselves."

"Dirty, stinking place that is," said Mrs Abbott, "I hates me turn going in there. All them socks and them stinking underpants and them sheets what they never change in a month of Sundays. Disgustink. As if I didn't have enough of that already what with 'Im and four boys one of them demobbed and nothing doing but lolling around on his bed all day. What you doing I says, cogitating? You could call it that Mum, he says, well I gives him the back of me 'and I'm telling yer and no mistake. Dirty little bugger."

"Thank you, ladies, best feet forward."

Percy lets the group out of the room ahead of him, giving his customary starchy little bow. Mrs Abbott does a courtesy and smiles at him before shuffling off with Dolly Dollis. "As in 'Ill," she tells people. "He's not a bad sort that Langrigg," he overhears Mrs Abbott saying as she turns the corner knowing she's still in earshot, "except he's one of Those yer know."

"They all are in 'ere ain't they?" says another voice. "You gotta have a nice long tongue to get a job permanent here you know."

"Or a nice long something," says another.

"Dream on, Dottie," says another.

"Back on the Bromide, you are," says Mrs Abbott and they all laugh before they take their various ways about the Sherborne Hotel. Percy stands at the door a moment. He knows that popular myth casts Bromine as an inhibitor of sexual urges, in men at least, and the same myth has it tipped into soldiers' tea with the sugar. But he also has read that Bromine was given to women in the Nazi camps to stop them menstruating. Camps, he thinks, when can we ever go back to tents, cooking pots, singalongs, straw and sparks fluttering up into night skies? Never. Not me. And if you don't want men to have urges, just don't feed them, he concludes, pat, before setting off to the Foyer to have a chat with the Concierge.

As he rounds a corner heading for the Foyer door he notices too late that the odour of the passageway has changed. Converging on him from the other direction, speeding along on well-soled patent shoes is Mr Smetka perfectly turned out as ever, hair brushed back over his temples like raven wings. Percy is reminded of a picture he had seen recently of the always immaculately attired and groomed Ataturk, but shorter, not much more than his own height. "Good morning Pearsay," he says in what Percy thinks of as his Ascot accent. "And how are We today?" Percy has a particular phobia about the use of the first person plural pronoun in place of the second person singular when addressing another party. Or, he thinks tangentially, possibly the second person plural if we were talking a more formal language like French. It's an affectation, he thinks, and not only that but he's using it to snare me, to trap me under the net that covers his shady little world, to draw me in to an "Us". Smetka always, as it's commonly said, "puts his back up" and he can almost feel hairs rising and stiffening along his spine. "Mr Smetka?" he says instead and gives the little bow. His Hirohito bow. His very bad habit. Mr Smetka gives a little bow back, stands up and smiles. "Uvijek tako formalno, dragi prijatelju," he says. "Such perfect manners. There is something of the Continental about you my dear Mister Langreeg. A hint of the Swiss, perhaps? But then of course they are the masters of our trade, are they not? To be Swiss trained is the apogee (he pronounced the word as though he were speaking French) of the hotelier (ditto). Perhaps the Major (pronounced my-or) Domo at the Atholl Palace of Shanghai was Swiss? Or at the Repulse?"

"I don't think so," says Percy not thinking about it at all.

"Ah well," replies Smetka, 'the war has washed our memories clean, has it not?" I hope it has yours, thinks Percy, but if it's true you were Ustase then not all the rivers, lakes, seas or oceans of the world will ever wash you clean, erase from the earth the memory of you from the few that managed to get past you or the memory of those who didn't. And you ran over the mountains through Austria to Switzerland did you, when the balloon went up? Clever Mr Smetka. He chooses not to reply.

"Would you care to take a cup of coffee with me in the Foyer Mr Langreeg? Now it is August and we are quiet we may get to know each other better. Should you like that? I should like that. Come," he says, opening for Percy the door into the lobby. Won't catch him singing Open the Door, Richard, thinks Percy. Not on your nelly. Percy walks through, uncomfortable to have Smetka behind him, thinking ridiculously of those knives attached to gloves invented by the Ustase to speed up the mass cutting of their victims' throats from behind.

Smetka struts into the Foyer as though he owns it. The Sherborne is not a large hotel and is Edwardian to a degree. Standing near the British Museum it escaped the Blitz and still offers the dowdy rooms and authentic English cuisine it has maintained over the past sixty years if not to the dignitaries of Empire, then their secretaries, governesses and all the human paraphernalia of the worldwide downward-sliding Raj. The Sherborne is the cadet sibling of the Beaumont, the perpetual spinster of the family of London hotels, tucked away behind Clarence House, never advertised, always full. How much longer can this survive? thinks Percy. That the vultures were circling before the war he had on good authority from his father and now that staging posts to Southampton or Tilbury, rooms heated to Calcutta temperatures and pink gins are less in demand how will these places go on? Which will go first? he thinks, old Adelaide or her hotels?

Smetka has seated himself at his favourite table, the eyrie from which he can view the revolving front door, the desk and the entrance to the restaurant. His hand dives into his white waistcoat pocket from which he produces like a magician exhibiting a multi-coloured handkerchief a box of Balkan Sobranie cigarettes.

"Do you like Turkish tobacco?" Smetka asks Percy. "I send to Fribourg and Treyer for these. Do you know it? At the Sign of the Rasp and Crown! So very British."

Percy takes a cigarette from the proffered case. Now, he thinks, now comes the lighter with the Ustase insignia. Got you, my lad, got you. Smetka picks up a book of matches from the table and hands it to Percy with a smile. This bastard can read my thoughts thinks Percy then lights and settles back a little into the worn cut moquette that gives off a graveyard smell. Smetka's movements on the other side of the table mirror his with a slight delay. Cigarette lit Smetka claps his hands. Oh dear, thinks Percy, so bloody Habsburg, European refinement with Slavic feudalism. It makes him wince.

"This is so much more. So much more civilised than standing in a dirty alley to what do you say, 'have a drag'?"

"I suppose so," says Percy, almost embarrassed by his answer; the answer of a social inferior. Suddenly he finds himself saying "What did you do in the War Mr Smetka?"

The panther's eyes stay open with not a flicker of an eyelid. "Ah, Frederick, we would like. What would we like Mr Langreeg? Caffe mit schlag? Do you know Kaffe mit Schlag? Or perhaps you would prefer a caffe mocha? These are popular in Vienna yes and in the cafes of Zagreb also. Let me recommend, Mr Langreeg, for you a caffe mit schlag und schnapps. This will see you right!" Pleased as punch with his little vernacular dropping, he turns his face toward Frederick. Has he blinked yet? wonders Percy. "Zwo davon," he says. Frederick, left forearm crooked into the small of his back, right arm extended holding a tray, right forearm draped with a white napkin inclines his head very briefly and stalks away, brilliantined hair reflecting the lights as he recedes toward the kitchen. "You are wondering perhaps what is a caffe mit schlagobers? It is a caffe au lait in the Viennese style with a hat of whipped cream. I have taught the sous how to whip the cream correctly. It has taken some time. Yes, it is indeed An Extravagance as dear Miss Aduh-lah-dee would say but when one is so far from home, an exile indeed, one must be allowed one small tasty memory nicht war?"

Percy makes a small smile.

"You asked me what I did in the war, Mr Langreeg? This is a question that some might have asked but not lived to hear the answer yes I may tell you." He stubs out his cigarette. "Ah this is ein witz Mr Langreeg, uno scherzo! Do not be afraid of Mr Smetka! Mr Smetka is a friend of the British for a long time." Here he waves his left hand back over his shoulder casting aspersions behind him. "Mr Smetka was a Partisan do you know? In Croatia yes and Serbia and Bosnia Herzegovina also and sometime Albania." Here he shudders. "Sheep grease. The fat of sheep Mr Langreeg. It is not possible to think of that benighted country without tasting the sheep grease again on one's tongue."

"Did you kill people?" asks Percy, emboldened by he knows not what.

The panther's pupils dilate. "Ah Mr Langreeg you are a man of the world are you not? You are a sophisticated man. This is not a subject for a Palm Court I think, Mr Langreeg? It is not," he pauses, "Foyer Material. Here we should talk the small talk, eh? We do not talk of killing it is not Chit Chat. It is not nice to discuss the shedding of blood in August in the Hotel Sherborne in public. I may have mistaken you Mr Langreeg. If Smetka had thought you wished to discuss the War in what I may refer to as Schoolboy Terms I would have suggested the alleyway after all. Alleyways are more a setting for the knife would you agree?"

"What did you do after the War Mr Smetka?"

"Ah this is the Safer Ground!" says Smetka. "We have passed through the minefield! Ah well Mr Langreeg I was for a time working at the Hotel Sacher in Wien where I met a very kind British man most impressed by my Command of English. He Engaged my Services On the Spot and I was most fortunate that he was able to bring me back with him to England on his Staff. Most sadly he died a short little while ago but not before, ah there you are Frederick, not before he had recommended my services to Miss Aduh-lah-dee. Is this what you wish to know Mr Langreeg? Does it make us Buddies?" Smetka smiles at Percy but makes merely a ducking nod toward Frederick who stoops to put the tray on the table. That done Frederick pulls himself up to his full height, towering above Mr Smetka. "Will that be all, Sir?" he says. Smetka nods. Frederick glides away silently, his back speaking volumes.

On the tray are two large cups, breakfast cups, piled with pale yellow cream whipped to a peak. The cups are not monogrammed to the hotel so they must, thinks Percy, be Smetka's own. Next to each cup is a port glass of clear liquid. Smetka picks up his glass, holds it up to Percy, then pours the contents through the cream before raising the glass to his lips and with a long tongue licking out any remaining drops. "Ah," he says. "The sljivovica. The plummy schnapps." He then picks up his coffee with the now-deflated peak and, lifting it to his lips drinks the coffee through the cream, silently. After each sip the tongue comes up and licks the upper lip.

A pause.

"I was fortunate enough to spend first before Wien one year, the year of 1946 almost all of it, in a training establishment in Luzern to perfect my skills as a manager of hotels. Here I learnt many things, many professional things including," he leans in toward Percy as if telling a secret, "the not discussing of the cutting of throats in the Foyers." He smiles. Percy doesn't recall that cutting of throats had been mentioned and a small chill creeps around his vitals.

"But you, Mr Langreeg, I think you did not have a Good War?"

"Not exactly," says Percy.

"It was written on your Curriculum Vitae, Mr Langrigg that you resided in Hong Kong and that you were taken prisoner by the Imperial Army of the Japanese?"

"Yes, that's right," says Percy. '

"And did you fight Mr Langreeg? Did you fight for your King and his country?" Smetka smiles.

Lord, thinks Percy, the same bloody question everywhere. He wanted to say No, I bloody didn't. I wasn't Army and I didn't volunteer for the HKVD. I helped keep the hotel open. I did my job, Mr Smetka, he wanted to say. I just did my bloody job for the seventeen days it took for us to lose. "I was in a reserved occupation," he says. "Senior management kept hold of a few of us when the others went to volunteer. They thought it would be good for morale – to have somewhere for the chaps to go and let off steam, you know. Somewhere to have a bath and a whisky."

"Ah the whisky, Mr Langreeg and the Hot Baths. The Blessings of Empire, yes indeed."

"But in the event the fighting came to us. There were some skirmishes up and down the beach. Some men were killed. Some we took into the hotel. It was pretty near the end. Burns victims mostly. The Japs were using flamethrowers on the pillboxes."

"Ah yes, the fight did not last long."

"Seventeen days. Look here, Smetka, what are you trying to say?"

"Please to keep your voice down Mr Langreeg here in the foyer."

"Sod the foyer, Smetka. Are you trying to say we were cowards in Hong Kong? That we didn't put up a fight?" Percy's colour was up, he was breathing through his nose in and out and he looked like a Border Terrier about to spring upon a rat. Just in time he recalled that this was no rat, it was a panther. Touch not the cat but a'glove.

He held back. Steady the Buffs. "It was a short campaign Mr Smetka but that doesn't mean that it wasn't fought with courage. We put up the best show we could. Whatever we were doing."

"And of course, Mr Langreeg there was not the option for you to take to the jungles and become Partisans, this is true. It would not have been possible for you to," he pauses, "blend in." Smetka finishes his coffee and says, "There was much looting I expect. Did you 'hang on' to your personal property?"

"No. I lost everything. I left the hotel with just what I stood up in, a sponge bag, the Bible and a pair of pyjamas."

"But I have seen the photo on your desk Mr Langrigg. You are smoking a pipe and there are two doggies. What became of your two black doggies Mr Langreeg?"

I think you must have been an interrogator, you nasty piece of work. "Katie and Kirsty," said Percy. "They were Scotties."

"And what... Oh of course Mr Langreeg, they became food for the Chinese. Let us hope their throats were cut with skill."

"You were saying, about subjects not fit for the foyer Mr Smetka?"

"I do so apologise."

"And is this a belated interview? Listen to me Smetka." Here Percy dropped his voice. "You know I've met Miss Beaumont; you know I was recommended to her and that she gave me my employment. Herself. I know how to do my job and I intend to do it well. I'm not here at your invitation or by your leave. You're the new General Manager and I know how to behave correctly toward a General Manager and that is how it will go on. I won't have this coffee, thank you, I have work to do. If you'll excuse me?" Percy stood up to go.

"This is Never Mind, Mr Langreeg," said the still-seated Smetka. "I do not take offence. Smetka is sorry to have opened such a wound. Of your time in the camp you can perhaps tell me when we talk again. Smetka is interested. If you will oblige him?"

"I don't want to talk about it Mr Smetka."

"Of course Mr Langreeg I will respect your wishes from now on. I merely thought we could," he paused, "find things in common." He smiled.

"I must get back to the office," said Percy.

"Grüss Gott," said Smetka and in the rolling Austrian rrr Percy thought he could hear the purring of a large and satisfied cat.

Percy set off for the men's loo off the foyer, technically out of bounds to staff other than cleaners, and he washed his hands thoroughly. He looked into the mirror and looking back at him was a roundish face, small mouth hidden under a well-tended moustache, high cheekbones and a lowish forehead under bristly hair that had turned grey before its time. You do look like some kind of Border Terrier he said to himself. His pulse was racing and he leant forward against the solid Victorian hand-basin to steady himself. It was as if he'd gone five rounds with Smetka. What was it about the man? How old would he be? How old am I? Thirty-six? He must be about the same age. Young to be a General Manager even of a stuffy old dump like the Sherborne. Wonder how he managed that? Must have impressed the old girl mightily. Probably came all over Habsburg and kissed her hand or what-not. Having a Continental running a hotel was all the rage. Swiss ideally but they were harder to come by. Swiss Efficiency, that was what they talked about. Hotels running like well-oiled machines.

No one liked Smetka, he was already a kind of bogey figure among the staff. They accorded him respect but probably one born of fear. His past, his origins were a source of discussion but Smetka was right that a cloud of forgetting, of un-knowing had settled over Europe and few, thankfully, discussed What They Did in the War. Was this progress or simply delayed shock? Percy suspected the latter. Books were beginning to come out and having been starved of information through the past five years there was a great appetite to read what had happened, what had really happened in the great theatres of the war; the desert, the North Atlantic, D-Day, Burma, The Railway. But not Hong Kong. Frankly no one cared, that much he knew. Somewhere very, very far away. A pimple on the arse of China. A coaling-station made good. Britain's most distant Imperial possession, indefensible, expendable, forgettable. Only three thousand dead in action. Only a few hundred executed, only a few score of wounded soldiers murdered and bodies butchered, no more than a dozen military nurses raped and killed, some Indians dead, some Canadians and then a mere ten thousand Chinese shot or tortured and then shot. Just a few hundred Europeans dead of disease or starvation in the following three and a half years. Nothing. Just a load of high-living, gin-drinking, money-making, rickshaw-riding, middle-class types who thought they could carry on partying safe from Hitler's bombs. A footnote to the history of the Second World War in the Pacific, attacked on the same day as Pearl Harbor, Malaya and the Philippines, but of so much less importance. And a defeat for the British. A speedy defeat. Given up to the Japs in a fortnight. Best not looked into, best not discussed. O tempora, o silentes.

Percy looks into the mirror and begins to shake. No longer a mirror it has become a movie-screen, Pathé News, Movietone News. Filming the Canadians coming ashore to defend Hong Kong. Every one of them looking like a lost lamb as they troop down the gangway. Now shots of them taking their first rickshaw ride. Now focus on the fresh-faced HK Volunteers elevating and sighting their howitzers. Try to look as though you know what you're doing. Put the instruction book away! Now look down at the harbour and wonder where the Royal Navy has gone. Let's go up to the Peak. Look into the distance. Can you see the five thousand Japanese soldiers coming over the hills? What's that you say? No, only five thousand. Fifty thousand? Tommy Rot! Talk like that can have you had up, you know. Lights twinkle in the harbour, bars are open, the Canadians and the British soldiers are splashing the cash in Wan Chai. Refugees in Kowloon? Perhaps a few. D'ye know my tip? If you run over one of those beggars reverse and finish the job. Don't stop and get out or you'll end up paying the funeral fees. Gin Drinkers' Line abandoned? Never. The Scots Guards are out there you know, they'll give 'em what for. Aeroplanes? Ours. Up from Singapore. Zeros? What the hell's a Zero? Churchill abandon us? Send a load of untrained boys from Winnipeg? Keep face, the Japs will come to terms. They don't want a war with the British Empire. Now rest easy; the Japanese can't see at night. Boats crossing the water from Lyemun in the dark? Don't be ridiculous, Nips get seasick. Yes, this is HQ. Brigadier simply doesn't believe you. Get back out there and look again. If they do try anything the show's going to be on the South coast. Our guns will blast them out of the water. Wong Nei Chong Gap lost? All the godowns on fire? What's that you say about St Stephen's College? Bit of a scrap was there? Executions? Don't be ridiculous; the Nips have signed the Geneva Convention. Stop now, don't film anymore. All the wives, all the men, the VADs down from Bowen Road, the bankers, the soldiers, the sailors, the volunteers all lining Connaught Road and bowing to the Japanese flag. Merry Christmas 1941.

And that was just the beginning. Percy lights a cigarette, a Du Maurier, and continues to look at himself in the mirror. A million scenes go by on its silver screen. Percy shuts his eyes but he can't stop shaking. The cigarette waggles up and down in his mouth. His knees start to wobble. Adrenaline, that's what they said, it's a chemical. It makes movies in your brain you can't destroy; you can't burn, you can't bury in a vault. Just something, some little trivial thing, a cast of the light, a half-heard sound can turn the projector on. You're strapped into your seat, forced to look at the screen. All for your own good, you know. It's so that if the same things start to happen again you'll know what to do. It'll all become clear, so clear. It's in our nature. Fight or flight. Fights, flights, camera, action!

In his stressed imagination he hears the voice of Mrs Abbott: "Remember that film, the one with Percy Langrigg where he puts his hands in the air and marches off to Stanley? Proper little John Mills he was! Stiff upper lip, I should say! Like in Goodbye Mr Chips who else was in it? Of course, Lesley Howard. No, Leslie Howard was killed. Who was it? It's on the tip of my tongue. Come on Vera who was it? I know! Robert Donat. It was that one where he plays a hotel manager what spots an escaped war criminal on the staff. You know, black market gangs all undercover. This war criminal thinks he 'as it all stitched up on account of his other war cronies are stockpiling black market bourbon biscuits and selling them to people what's addicted to them. Or is it eating bourbon biscuits stops yer getting newmonia so they're like gold dust can't get them for love ner money? Can't remember. Anyway this one's a right nasty villain but Percy Langrigg spots what they're up to but he don't call the police, oh no not him; he has to do it 'is way. Only his mate, what's 'is name, he works out there's something queer going on and he calls the police, only by this time Percy's on the 'otel roof and he corners this foreigner who's only got a knife stuck to his glove for cutting throats chop chop and he slashes away at Percy but then the coppers come along so he looks round, then Percy socks him one and he falls over the edge and hits the tarmac like a pot of strawberry jam. I know, a bit like Waterloo Bridge. No, you don't forget a film like that do yer? 'Ere you know what? Me and Jim went to see Waterloo Bridge again at the Pally and funny thing was when he socks him this woman gets up from her seat and starts yelling 'It 'im. It 'im!' really loud and the man with her nice looking he was, grabs 'er and shoves 'er back into 'er seat. Well I never, I says to Jim, whatever next? Looks a bit loopy that one. Then when we come out after the end there she is with the man; really tanned skin he 'ad and Jim says she's a ringer for Rosalind Russell and I says, give over she's got goo-goo eyes, there's something not quite right there I says looks like she's seen something what's made her go funny in the 'ed. Black Magic? Oooh I don't mind if I do!"

Percy puts out his cigarette in the hand basin, washes it away, takes off his spectacles and laves his face with cold water then washes it again, lathering it with soap from the egg-shaped cake on the revolving dispenser that sticks out from the tiles on a sconce above the basin. The soap has a pleasant scent of sandalwood. It's a good soap, well made. He dries his face on the towel, puts his spectacles back on and looks up. The mirror meekly reflects him back. The shaking has stopped and he walks out. Behind him a tap drips and a cistern fills with a long sigh.

It's time to go to the kitchen to discuss the day's menus. After the latest reductions in the meat ration followed by, to a general clamour of rage, the potato ration, the menu is a shadow of its former self.

"Here's Mr Langrigg," says Tommy, one of the sous chefs, "come to cheer us up with his Marshall Plan for noshin'. Tournedos Rossini on yer mind Mr. Langrigg? They ain't 'alf on mine."

"Morning Tommy," says Percy, "Where's Mr Lopez?"

"Loopy? In the store cupboard, Mr. Langrigg. Won't be half a mo."

Percy looks around the kitchen where young men in off-white uniforms are peeling and chopping vegetables while the porters are scraping the orts off the breakfast plates, spooning out whatever's left in the butter and marmalade dishes to be reborn fresh tomorrow, tipping coffee grounds down the sink and noisily washing up. They must all be what age, eighteen? No one wants to employ de-mobbed men.

The boys talk as they wash dishes:

"Saw that Margaret Lockwood at the pitchers last night."

"*Wicked Lady*?"

"She's old enough to be my Mum. Bet yer there was more wicked going on in the back row."

"Why's it always them old birds in the flicks?"

"That Mae West come inter Southampton."

"She looks like my gran."

"Your gran got lils like Mae West?"

"Them's her arse cheeks."

"You should go and see *The Lone Wolf in London.*"

"I seen the others, what's this one like?"

"Got a new wolf. Gerard More."

"What not Warren Williams? I liked Warren Williams."

"Got his picture up on yer wall, powder puff?"

"'Ere who are you callin'?"

"Knock it off, lads, Loopy's comin' back."

And indeed, the tall, slender figure of the Sherborne's Head Chef is at that moment walking back into the kitchen. The washing up becomes more vigorous. A faint air of lugubriousness hangs about Mr Lopez, a sadness suffuses his thin, beard-shadowed cheeks and dark eyes.

"Mornin' Mr Langreeg," he says. "You 'ere about the menus? I got today's. Fancy a nail?"

Percy has ceased being surprised at Lopez' command of idiom. He has, after all, worked at many London hotels, had a spell in the Merchant Navy and until last year and the death of Mr August and the closing of his restaurant had cheffed at Odennino's. The two men, the tall and the short, head off to the area at the front of the hotel below the railings and out of sight of guests. Lopez spreads a piece of paper out on top of a rubbish bin: the Carte du Jour.

"I still looks at the Repertoire, Mr Langreeg. But it like another lifetime."

Percy takes two Du Maurier out of the box and hands one to Lopez. Both men put the nails in their mouths. Percy lights a match and holds it up to Lopez. Lopez leans forward and takes Percy's wrist between both his hands, guarding the little flame from an unlikely gust of air on this stifling August day. His cigarette alight he leans back and breathes out, smoke billowing through his nostrils. Percy lights his own.

"So, what have we got today? Potage DuBarry. Have we got the butter?"

"Leftover from breakfast."

"No toast crumbs in it this time?"

"I say croutons."

"Eggs?"

"Mr Smetka, he says don't worry."

"Hmm. Navarin d'Agneau. Mutton stew."

"Clever Mr Langreeg."

"Mashed potato. Potato powder? Carrots Vichy. Do we have any Vichy water?"

"Château la Pompe," says Lopez.

"Dessert: Foule de Groseilles Normande. Have you made that one up Mr Lopez? It's just gooseberry fool isn't it?"

"Just, Monsieur Langreeg? Just? With fresh cream what come from Miss Bowmon's own farm!"

"Sorry, Lopez. And the six and six menu?"

"Now you talking. With the stew: boiled onions."

"Good Lord, Lopez. How on earth did you get onions?"

"I got mate at the market."

"And for dessert? Poires Belle Helene? Are we expecting royalty?"

"You not hear, Mr Langreeg? We got Jean Simmons table three and Barbara Stanwyck table eight."

"Very funny, Lopez. Yes, the menu sounds good to me."

"You should not laugh Mr Langreeg. We got the Sunday Pictorial Film Garden Party, we got the British Film Festival, Daily Express Film Ball, we got it all goin' on. All the stars in London."

"I'm not much of a movie man, Lopez," says Percy.

"You not go out? No more bombs. Anyone can go out. Kiss a girl in the dark, eh, no one see. Maybe get second base, eh?" Lopez smiles and a gold tooth flashes. He goes on, "Kiss who you like in the dark, eh, no one sees. Blackout was good times. Everyone randy, eh, Mr Langreeg. Boys and girls go out to play, eh? You got another gasper? Smetka he gone up the Bowmon' he not here."

Percy digs down again for the flat cardboard case in his pocket. They go through the lighting up ritual again but this time Lopex holds his wrists for a second or two longer.

"What you like going to, Mr Langreeg? You go to the Music Hall? Max Miller Cheeky Chappie. Miss Gracie Fields, Georgie Formby?"

"A bit blue for my taste."

"Ah you missing something, Mr Langrigg."

"Come on Lopez, you're Spanish. Half of it must go right above your head."

"Oh no, I understand perfect. If I don't understand I ask my chums."

"What chums?"

"Ah you are interested, Mr Langreeg? You want to meet my chums?"

"Theatre, Lopez. I go to the theatre."

"Bless the Bride!" Lopez begins to sing with in a surprisingly rich tenor: "'This is my lovely day!'"

"Plays without songs, Lopez."

"Not so much fun, Mr Langreeg."

"I like them."

"You go see a play with chums?"

"No."

"You go on your own? No songs, no chums?"

"That's right."

"You go to a play this week? What you seein'?"

"Not this week, Lopez. End of the month. I'm going to see the new JB Priestley. *The Linden Tree*."

"Ah Mr Langreeg you no have much fun. You come out with Lopez and his chums end of shift. The chums of Lopez they know places you can drink all night."

"Thanks, but I'm on earlies here most days."

"Hey Mr Langreeg, you not mind me sayin' you not havin' much fun. War's over, you got to live a little. You come out with Lopez and his chums we have a good time. You no be a fuddy-duddy."

"A what?"

"A fuddy-duddy Mr Langreeg? You not know American? Fuddy-duddy, khaki-whacky, active duty. Lopez knows. You make sure you no flip your wig Mr Langreeg!' Lopez laughs a pleasant, tenor laugh, throws his cigarette butt down on the area floor and makes to go back inside. "Hey, Langreeg, you know 'ow we make a Poire Belle Hélène? No? Come, I show you."

Percy follows Lopez into the kitchen where he's given a white apron. He puts it on and Lopez ties it from behind, his hand accidentally brushing Percy's buttock. Lopez moves off, his stride purposeful and full of authority. This is Lopez in his element, thinks Percy. Lopez signals to him with a flap of the hand, not turning round. Percy follows. "Walter!" Lopez shouts, "That ice cream ready?" "Yes chef!" yells a voice. There is always much yelling in the kitchen, that much Percy knows. It isn't that the place itself is so noisy it's that each man or boy working there is so intent upon their work that only a shout can break the barrier into each exclusive world.

Lopez picks up a bowl and spoon and strides back out into the area and across it, Percy trotting after, to open a black-painted door. He reaches to the left and switches on the electric light. That the Sherborne was one of the last hotels in London to install electricity is notorious. The floor here is made of brick and in front of them a cellar stretches half way under the street. It's like a crypt. It's cool and it smells fresh. Lopez hands Percy the bowl and spoon. "Sosten," he says. Half-crouching Lopez works his way inside to an ancient, duck-egg blue painted cabinet and opens the door. It's the icebox. He takes out a lidded tin pail and opening the lid gestures to Percy to bring the bowl and spoon. Percy holds them forward, Lopez takes both and from the bucket carves out a scoop of pale, churned and frozen custard. Ice cream. He hands the bowl and spoon back to Percy. "You no touch that with your 'ands direct. 'Old it in your apron." Lopez closes the bucket, shuts the cupboard and re-emerges. "Chop, chop," he says. Percy struggles to keep up as Lopez walks back to the door and turns off the light leaving Percy momentarily in darkness. This is precious stuff, this ice-cream. Other hotels have banks of refrigerators and even freezers imported from America. Not so the Sherborne where ice-cream is still made the way it has been for many years in a metal pail that fits inside a wooden bucket. The gap between the two is packed with a mixture of ice and salt. Inside the lid is a rudimentary whisk connected to a crank and handle on the outside. Pail in, lid on, someone, one of the kitchen boys, turns the handle for half an hour until the custard is set and cold. This custard has been made in a double boiler where a eggs and sugar are slowly thickened then cooled until whipped cream and seeds scraped from rather ancient vanilla pods are folded in. The mixture is cooled in turn before being tipped into the pail for its transformation into ice- cream.

Back in the kitchen Lopez is already melting chocolate broken into squares in a double boiler over simmering water. "Chocolate," says Percy.

"No shortage 'ere," says Lopez. "Nor sugar neither. You wanna know where it come from ask Smetka."

While the chocolate melts Lopez has called for and been handed a hotel-silver footed cup. With two spoons that have just come out of a bowl of warm water he makes two rugby-ball shapes of ice cream. Immediately he takes the cloth cover off an enamel bowl that's already standing by at the dessert station and using a slotted spoon has scooped out a naked, shaven, glistening pear still with its stalk attached. The pear drips and oozes syrup down its flanks back into the bowl. Holding the pear by its stalk Lopez puts it carefully down next to the ice-cream in the bowl so that it lolls seductively. "This dessert like a naked woman in bed," says Lopez and he grins at Percy. The chocolate by now has melted and picking up another spoon Lopez dips it into the bowl of water that's standing nearby. He slowly pours hot water from a kettle, just a little, into the chocolate and stirs the mixture once or twice with a wooden spirtle. Lifting the top pan of the boiler by the handle he pours the contents, with one movement of the wrist, all over the reclining pear on its soft, yielding mattress. The chocolate runs unctuously down the pear and onto the ice-cream. Percy can see that as it coats the pear it slides and shines. Where it meets the cold ice-cream, it slows and lightens in colour as it chills and hardens. "You better eat this time." Lopez' hands hold out the bowl and a spoon. The poaching juices of the pear are mingling with the melting ice-cream. "You don't say no to summat like that Mr Langreeg. That a work of art. You take it from me." Still holding the bowl, Lopez sinks the spoon into the glorious, sweet, Helen-celebrating confection and taking a scoop holds it to Percy's mouth. Percy leans forward toward it. His mouth opens and Lopez gently slides in the spoon. It was the fruit and he ate of it.

Percy reaches up to take the spoon from Lopez' hand and finishes the job himself. "Jolly good," he says to the beaming Lopez. "Haven't eaten one of those in years." The tip of the empty spoon that he holds shakes slightly like the needle on a seismograph delicately tracing a shape that shadows a shuddering movement, a shock of pleasure.

"Three soup, one eggs mimosa!" yells a voice. Service is under way.

Two minutes later Percy is back on duty at the entrance to the restaurant having been called to stand in for the maître d'hôtel. Percy's looking forward to his getting back so that he can sit down for a few moments. Since the war, since the diet of Mars bars and tinned pilchards came to an end, Percy still has moments of exhaustion particularly during the winter. His doctor has told him to get out and see more sunshine but work in hotels is the only labour he knows. It's a shame that the Sherborne must be the dingiest, most Edwardian, most net-curtained, velvet-draped and airless in London, but with so many men without work he knows he's lucky to be employed at all. Thank God for strings you can pull. Probably not where the parents would have expected me to end up and who would have thought Adelaide Beaumont would have carried a torch for the old man? But what a stroke of luck.

"Good morning, Sir William, Lady Gibbins. Yes, what a warm day. We've put you by the window... Not the window? The sunlight. Of course. Jacques will you show Sir William and Lady Gibbins to table twelve? Potage du Barry, Lady Gibbins, but for the six and six menu chef has added croutons. Yes, proper ones, Lady Gibbins. With actual bread."

Here the head waiter arrives to take charge of the diners.

"Bon appétit," says Percy. What are they doing over here, he thinks? There's bugger all in Bloomsbury. How do people sniff us out? Gamages? A bit populist. Lincoln's Inn Fields? More likely. St Pancras? King's Cross? Perhaps it's the Beaumont effect. Why not the Russell? Or the Imperial? Maybe they don't like big spaces anymore. We're certainly discreet here at the Sherborne, perhaps that's it. But that wouldn't account for the Gibbins.

"Mrs Perdue, good afternoon. Ah, Maples of course Mrs Perdue. Indeed, if it was good enough for the late King. Jacques will show you to your table. Poire Belle Hélène on the six and six, Mrs Perdue. Yes indeed a red letter day."

Percy looks around the dining room. Perhaps I do the old place down. And he remembers the Grand Atholl in Shanghai, the Repulse in Hong Kong and realises that he has more in common with Lopez than he realises. It's the American that's missing. What I call stuffiness the British think of as tradition and heaven knows we're traditional here. These are the sort of people who probably don't want rationing to end. It's too much like their nursery and boarding school food. Cosmopolitan it isn't. How he'd loved that American brashness leavening Hong Kong. His cherry-coloured drop-head Pontiac, his friend Carmichael who had the radio show sponsored by Jell-O.

"Jello, jello, jello," he'd begin each broadcast. Then he and the gang nabbing a launch to go out to the American warships in harbour to bargain with the captain to allow his black musicians ashore to play jazz at the Shek-O Club. And later; the bomb. The American bomb. The divine wind of liberation. American battleships in the bay. We'd seen the machine gun emplacements going up on the flat rooves. We knew what they'd do if the Americans invaded. Percy put a hand to his head. Not now.

"You alright Mr Langrigg?" It was Frederick. "Nothing like a 'ot day for bringing back the memories is it Mr Langrigg? 'Ere let me get you a glass of water." Frederick trotted off and came back with a glass that Percy downed in one. "Yer can't rush it Mr Langrigg. Funny how it's the 'ot days that gets yer. Come back when you least expect 'em, ain't it? Don't expect ghosts on a scorcher does yer?" Percy handed back the glass and Frederick trotted off.

Percy went back to his station for another hour until the maître d'hôtel came back on shift. With money so tight most of the management were doubling up. Other than Smetka.

"Poire Belle Hélène!" giggled a customer. "My goodness that takes me back! How on earth do you do it?"

How on earth do we do it thought Percy.

"Navarin d'Agneau?" said another, more hostile. "Nothing wrong with mutton. If you mean mutton, say mutton."

"Mutton," said Percy under his breath.

"What's that you say? Speak up!"

"I said it could be hogget, Colonel Dashbury."

"Bloody sheep-farmer now are you Langrigg? Hogget! Dashed good. Hogget!" and he wove his way to his table steering with his cane.

Percy looked around the room and imagined the Technicolor food in Hong Kong restaurants right up until the end of '41. The emerald and dark green lobsters in tanks at Aberdeen, amber smoked ducks, gleaming vermilion char sui, bright green bak choy, saffron orange sweet-sour sauce, all the table of Southern China laid out before us Europeans. Not for ever by still waters he said to himself.

"Chef is rather old-school, yes, Mrs Patterson. Yes, he trained in France. Yes indeed there could be a New Look in food. After rationing of course, Mrs Patterson. Yes, we must all do our bit." And then to himself: "Bet you'll take the six and six you snobby old lump. Bon appétit!" out loud. "No, we don't seem to have a similar expression in English. Funny, that."

Diners wove in and diners wove out, mostly older people up from the country and girls of a certain age shopping the summer sales. No film stars that he could see whatever Lopez had said. Lopez, now there was a cove. He was always talking about his chums dotted all over Town; one a waiter at the Café de Paris, another a sous at the Maison Française. Apparently another one had opened a restaurant in Greek Street and called it Trattoria something-or-other. All of them Spanish. Not an Italian in the place. Couldn't he get a job there? And there was an MTF if ever there was one. Decidedly NSIT. Those long arms, thought Percy, simian, all over you.

"Thank you, Mrs Freer, Mrs Delahoy. Thank you, yes, chef made it himself. Ah the milk and eggs come from Lady Beaumont's estate in Hampshire. I believe it is allowed Mrs Freer. Did you enjoy it? No, she doesn't grow cocoa plants. That was our ration for some time I'm afraid. Yes quite, if you've got it. The pears are an early variety I believe. Yes, Beaumont House. The potager, yes, Mrs Delahoy. Kitchen garden Mrs Freer. Thank you, ladies. May I book you in for next week? Thank you." Clearly old Adelaide must be on some faddish diet that denied her, or her staff come to that, milk or eggs or anything very much judging by the quantity of produce that flowed from Hampshire to the Sherborne. Managed by Mr Smetka. Didn't he say he had a house down there somewhere? On the Test? Well, if it had fishing rights it must have cost a pretty penny. Don't see Smetka as your Izaak Walton type somehow. Wonder what his hand is in all of this. Wafting around drenched in all the perfumes of Arabia won't wash Mr Smetka clean. "Ah. Pierre, you're back. Almost over. Just the Timmins party on table nine. Frederick's trying to move them into the drawing room. Frederick can hover for England, look at him. Well, à bientôt, Pierre. Thank you, strictly schoolboy French I'm afraid."

What was next? Percy suddenly felt hungry but equally not inclined to go back to the office for a sandwich and coffee at his desk with McAlise and his war record that he kept winding up and playing over and over again. It was hard going with McAlise to keep off the subject off the Far East and the mass surrenders. The bastard had it in for anyone who'd "thrown in the towel." Let him go a round or two with the Imperial Japanese Army with one or both hands effectively tied behind his back, and he might think differently. These "heroes"; so bloody self-righteous. But Percy had no more defence against McAlise and his ilk than poor Hong Kong had had three thousand to fifty thousand. Maybe four thousand if you counted the HKVD. We paid for our pleasures, he wanted to say. In fact, we all, all of us who stayed, paid the price of Empire. You lot back here took out a hell of a lot more than you put in and when the time came you left us to fend for ourselves with some Scots, Rajputters and that boatload of lads from Winnipeg to defend us. But you took the money when times were good; the money for your pension funds, your shipping companies, your banks, your traders and tea barons, your merchants and your stock market johnnies. And the taxes you took from the Chinese Hong Kongers? Were your four thousand to defend them, too? Some people were saying that ten thousand Chinese in the territory had been killed by the Nips. Nothing to Nanking of course but on that basis a Chinese life was worth, let's see, thirty percent of a European one. Sounds high when you think of how we acted in Shanghai in the emergencies. Put barbed wire around the bits that belonged to us and let the Nips slaughter the local Chinese pretty much willy-nilly. McAlise wasn't concerned about justice so no point in bringing any of that into it. McAlise had simply found a dial on Percy he could turn up and down, off and on as he chose. The dial marked guilt. The guilt of having given in. And what would he have wanted? thought Percy, vaguely heading toward the kitchen. That we should have set the place on fire and leapt into the flames, women and children first? Leave that to the Lycians at Xanthos. Perhaps Hong Kong simply wasn't sacred enough to us. Not our citadel after all. To those born there, home, but to most of us not Home. In it but not of it. Too complicated for McAlise, too subtle and orientally philosophical for one who divided the world into those who'd fought in D-Day and those who hadn't. We are so steeped in blood, thought Percy, as he found himself at the kitchen door. He opened it and went in.

"Mr Langrigg! How the devil are you?" This was Tubbs, one of the sous.

"Afternoon Mr Langrigg," chorused the other staff.

Percy felt oddly at home in the kitchen, in its hierarchy and rituals, its camaraderie and cheerfulness. Simpler somehow than the backbiting, status-obsessed world of front of house and even worse, management.

"Afternoon all," he said. "All of you drinking plenty of water today?"

"Yes Mr Langrigg," came back a ragged chorus.

Frederick bustled in through the flapping doors to the restaurant. "Bugger me blind," he said. "Thought I'd never get them Timminses to shift. Who went an' put Bostik on their ruddy chairs?" He swept past Percy. "Loopy's saved some dinner for you Mr Langrigg," he said in a stage whisper as he went by.

Percy began to make his way to the Head Chef's office, knocked on the door and entered. Lopez was sitting tilted back in his chair reading a copy of H&E that he made no pretence to hide, simply chucking it down on his desk open on a double page spread showing two naked couples playing doubles at tennis. The women's' breasts could be seen above the net that obscured their bushes. The men were seen from the back, but no attempt had been made to brush out the sac that flopped into the perineum of one of the men, the one bending down. The other, poised on his toes to serve, all the muscles of his calves and buttocks tensed, showed a furred cleft to the camera.

"I can come back later, Lopez," said Percy.

"Nah, Mr Langreeg. You sit down. Look I saved you some dinner." And here he slapped a plate and a spoon down onto the magazine spread making a mat of it. "Mostly meat, hardly no carrots."

"Thank you, Lopez," said Percy. Lopez had placed the plate in such a way that Percy had to draw his chair close to that of the chef.

"Carroty George, Clara Carrot, Dr Carrot, Potato Pete ain't it Mr Langreeg? Still, they ain't thought of all the things you can do with a carrot have they Mr Langreeg?" Lopez smiled wolfishly.

"Probably not," said Percy. "Although in the Middle East they grate them up, mix them with sugar and spices and shape them into balls." Lopez stared at him. "Probably wouldn't work at the Sherborne, too foreign," continued Percy, trying to develop enthusiasm for the congealing mutton stew.

"Who does work at the Sherborne, eh, Mr Langreeg? Not that Smetka. He don't work. That Smetka only work for himself. You listen to Lopez."

"I don't really take much notice, sorry," said Percy.

"Ah that because you friend of family get you job."

"Not really," said Percy. "And who says that anyway?"

"If you took notice you'd find out, my friend. Smetka knows, Mack Alice knows, Lopez knows you work in fancy hotel in Hong Kong, Mummy and Daddy own hotels in America. You got shares in Miss Adelaide."

"Yes, they're all gone and no," said Percy.

"So Lopez is right, you a spy."

"I don't think I can eat this, Lopez, I'm sorry."

"You a spy or you not a spy?"

"Rather on the not side. I work here because I need to. My parents are dead, their investments went bad and Miss Beaumont gave me a job on a letter of recommendation. Smoke?"

"I don't mind if I do," said Lopez. "Always smoke Du Maurier? Natty chappy. Me I smoke Craven 'A'. You like a Craven 'A'?"

"No thanks, Lopez, bit rough for me."

"Will he, won't he?" thought Percy as he once again extended his lighter to Lopez. Yes. He felt the warm enfolding of hands around his wrist, the slight rasp of body hair against the smooth of his palm, a pulse. This must be the first time in how long? A year, longer since he'd felt human contact that was anything more than an accidental brushing-by?

Lopez looked at him. "So Langreeg, you gonna come out with Lopez and his chums tonight? What time? Ten? I meet you here foyer. Okay you stay there I get you dessert. Lopez saved some for you." The chef went out of the room.

"Hells bells," said Percy to himself. "And buckets of blood. Why on earth did I agree to that? Easily led, that's what your mother used to say. And how right she was."

In his mind Percy envisaged that Burne-Jones tapestry, the one he loved, the one of the Grail. But now the glorious aureole of light was diminishing by degrees as the dark surrounding night of fleshly desire swallowed it up. Away flew the angels with a clash as of cymbals, the asphodels and lilies went out like candles, the golden chalice turned to lead on its frost-white cloth and a cold wind began to blow. Childe Roland to the Dark Tower Came. Parsifal has been judged unworthy of the Quest and now is just a man on horseback amongst the ignorant armies, left to fend for himself.

A noise came from the windowsill and Percy looked out through the smears to see two pigeons mating, the wingtips of the male beating against the glass making patterns in the greasy dust. He toppled and flew away, followed by the female, their flight making dry clackings in the torpid air. A feather spiralled downward to the alley floor. Danger, he thought. Or freedom? The sedge is withered from the lake. Are you a monk? Two years you've lived like one. Palely loitering. The narrow bed, the open window summer and winter, a handful of possessions; the bottle of sherry for Sunday, the one, squat, dark amber Peking Jesuit glass to drink it from, the picture postcard of Diana and Actaeon from the National Gallery, its browns and russets and the gaping wound; fresh blood and dried. Anything else? Yes, the snap of you and the girls on your desk that you'd sent home to your aunt. And beside the bed your Bible, the one with the red and black Japanese stamp of approval stuck to the inside cover. And when the gates of passion are opened what then? Will you gorge and make yourself sick as many of us did, unable to cope with the richness of ordinary food? If you stop starving yourself your libido will come back and when it rises up again after all those years where will it point? Do you want to know? Don't you want to know? There's no one left to nag you to get married, continue the line. Their line. My line? A line of beauty? Now slides the silent meteor on. Probity. Wholeness. A soft mask of snow upon the moors. Thine immortal soul. Percy imagined his soul as a draught of cool, clear English water scooped up from a chalk spring among green-tipped hills, the stony font surrounded by celandines coming into flower in March. And take the April winds with beauty. Scooped up in a pewter cup and set on a bare table. Christ at Emmaeus. The fire in the glass. The stretching arms. Lopez' long arms and hairy-backed hands? I struck the board and cried, No More! I will abroad. O fons Bandusiae! Splendidior vitro. We have put rancours in the vessel of our peace. He comes to set the captives free. Let me hide myself in Thee. Those lovers long ago are fled. A waste of spirit? O brave new world that has such creatures in it.

Stuff it. The game wasn't so much fun when you played it by yourself; you needed someone else's stock of quotations to stop you from getting stale. And what was this all about anyway? A load of kapok wrapped around the thing itself; the question. Would he do it with Lopez? Could he do it with Lopez? It was a long time since he'd last had sex with a man. Who was it? Oh yes, that Taff sapper in the Repulse. That had left him winded. And afterwards they'd stood at the window together, naked, and someone, an officer he thought, had seen them from below and looked up in amazement. Or was it jealousy on his face? And Sopley, once or twice, in the pines overlooking the college running track. David Sopley had seemed to keep his motor running the entire time. How had he managed that? Must have been in overdrive to start with. I wasn't the only one he took up to the pines, he thought to himself. Possibly the only man but there had been women, he knew. Not for him except the once before the War with that English woman at the Repulse who'd practically raped him. She'd cottoned on pretty quick but kept going with him anyway. Did he want to do it in her backside, she'd asked? Was he bull or cow? He hadn't understood at first but then the penny had dropped. "Who's the bull then?" she'd kept saying. "Keep going, think of him," was what she'd told him. "Think of him, Keep going." It had been three years now without sight or sound of him. Not long when you compared it to their time in camp but it felt an age, now, with all the deflation of peace, the dullness of Home, the listlessness that so many men suffered, trapped still between two opposite realities. He could do with David now. He really could. But if not David, would Loopy Lopez do? Let's see what happens. Let's just see.

At nine-thirty Percy went back into the kitchen and into the Head Chef's office to retrieve the box of cigarettes he'd left there. He turned on the light. The magazine had been folded up and the Du Mauriers sat next to it on what looked like a tradesman's receipt. To it was paper-clipped a note in Smetka's handwriting. It read, "Tell them do this again." Bacon, mutton, steaks, joints of pork. "Abernethy Scotch Butchers of Smithfield," written across the top. Each total had been crossed out and another figure written next to it. Percy judged that each new figure was fifteen percent greater than the original. He moved the receipt and found another underneath it. Same butcher, more or less similar order but this time the figures were as Smetka's corrections.

Percy sat down in chef's chair. Dirty double-crosser, he thought. And Lopez, too? But Lopez loathes Smetka and that seems genuine. Lopez doesn't have a fancy bolthole in the country. As far as he knows he and his chums, or some of them, share a flat at the top of

Frith Street by the nurses' home. Lopez doesn't stink of fancy eau-de-cologne. In fact, he rather stinks. So, can they possibly be in on this together, this cheating of Miss Beaumont? And even if they are, why leave this out so obviously on show? Any of the staff could have spotted it. Unless it's meant for me to find? Had Lopez seen that he'd left his cigarettes then positioned the receipt and note in such a way that, knowing he'd come back in, would see them? That Smetka's skimming would then be exposed? Listen to yourself, 'positioned', 'exposed', too much Margery Allingham. All the same; fishy. Percy picked up the box of cigarettes and left. Then he turned. Picking up the receipt with Smetka's note attached he pocketed it and headed for the door.

At ten o'clock Percy was standing in the Sherborne's foyer wearing his going-out clothes; beige trousers, a cream aertex shirt and a light checked jacket. At the bottom of his suitcase he'd found the pair of co-respondent shoes he'd bought when he'd first come to London. His wiry hair was brilliantined and his moustache neatly trimmed.

"Nice rig," said Frederick rushing by. "I'd say yes."

Percy smiled faintly.

Frederick went on, singing, "'While I'm away... purrrrleeeze remember me...'"

Lopez appeared, grinning. "That little tick annoying you? Hey, Percy, you look natty. No so fuddy-duddy. Come on, lez go."

Out they went onto the street. The air, thick with fumes and dust, was still a treat to Percy who on the instant realised he hadn't left the hotel for days. "Where are we going?" he said to the long-striding figure of Lopez dressed for the occasion in fawn trousers and a white shirt whose collar-tips had been carefully positioned outside the lapels of his light, Continental jacket. His feet however were clad in plimsolls and Percy noticed that he wore no socks. The straw Panama on his head was tipped raffishly back.

"Keep up, Perce," was all he said.

On they went. Bless us all, thought Percy; the long and the short. Along Great Russell Street they walked, turning left into Museum Street and past the Museum Tavern.

"Fancy a sharpener?" said Lopez.

"No thanks," said Percy.

"Suit yourself."

Down Museum Street and across to Shaftesbury Avenue, Monmouth Street under the huge plane trees, past the French Church and into Seven Dials following St Martin's Lane as it broadened into a wide crossroads then narrowing as it swept like a river down to Trafalgar Square.

"Here we are," said Lopez.

Percy squinted into a blaze of light and a riot of noise. So this was it. The Salisbury. Tiny, crowded and airless it was still the queen of London gin palaces. Lopez turned into the side alley, Cecil Court, opened the door into a miniscule lobby, opened the next door and shoved Percy forward into the heaving, shouting, laughing, sweating mass of people inside. Percy felt Lopez' lips brush the lobe of his ear as he leant forward and said, "Welcome to the Stores."

Percy felt winded by the crush and the bright light, so bright it hurt his eyes. Lights, faces, glasses, brass beer pump handles and soldiers' badges, teeth and beer froth, glowing cigarette ends, sleek pomaded hair, white shirts, gold jewellery, paste earrings, sparkling tonic water found their luminescence returned by mirrors, by glass screens etched with fantastic curlicue designs and bevelled to reflect more light back into the room. Bronze nymphs held out light bulbs wrapped in glass flowers whose radiance burst onto the polished wood of the bar and bar surrounds increasing still further the general brilliance. And hand in hand with the light, the noise. Ridete quidquid est in domus cacchinorum, thought Percy just as Lopez' hand came to rest on his shoulder. "What you say?" he yelled and then "Here my chums! What you wanna drink, Perce? Hey this is my mate Perce I tole you about." Percy realised Lopez had already gone to the bar as he found himself pushed into a group of five or six men, each one smiling, holding out his hand as best he could, hampered by the crush. He could hear "Pleased to meet yer," "Any friend of Trini's," 'Shubbin," "Tom," "Jerry," "Encantado," coming fast from a set of mostly moustachioed lips.

"I, errr," started Percy, "I haven't ever been here before."

"Your first time?"

"First time for everyone!"

Laughter.

"You work with Trini?"

"Hey, estupido, this Trini's boss."

"No, no, I'm not."

The air was so thick that Percy struggled to speak and he found that his larynx hurt as though he were shouting across a parade ground in what came out as a whisper.

"Eh, Percy, we call you Percy no Mister Something?"

"Just Percy," said Percy.

"What kind of name Percy?" said one.

"Inglés," said another.

"No, no actually," said Percy. "It's German I think. You know, Percival, knights of the round table and all that."

No, they didn't know that. Someone blew smoke straight across his nose and his eyes started to stream. Lopez returned and shoved a warm gin and tonic in a wine glass into his hand. He drank. Completing the sensory assault came Lopez' hand resting in a proprietorial way on his right buttock. Percy looked around anxiously but in this press the caress could not be seen. Lopez started to address the band of chums across Percy's head in fast Castilian Spanish. Percy shifted his buttock from Lopez' palm and started to look around.

Every available square foot of space on the squelching carpet was now occupied as was every bar stool, every inch of velour bench and every recess in this bar and the other that he could see mirrored toward him. In the crowd were soldiers in uniform, men in demob suits, men who looked like Admiralty or Civil Service. Older men in pinstripes and ties, younger men in sports jackets and open-neck shirts. One or two women in black taffeta with heavy makeup and gaudy rings over thick fingers. One or two girls with triumphant scraps of millinery pinned fast to their hair, lips red and cheeks blushed. Two girls in WAAC uniform were squeezed tight into a corner. There seemed to be no designated area for the women or at least if there were, it was being ignored. Younger men laughed uproariously at the jokes of older men, heads thrown back showing pink tongues and throats. Eyes darted everywhere, never still. Looks went out across from one side of the bar to another, looks whose warmth seemed to set the room on fire. People pushed and swayed, hands cupped, and fingers explored. Faces came together to exchange whispers and stayed just a heartbeat too long. Smoke filled the air and hovered up at the yellow-stained ceiling in a cloud. Down below, vetiver, sandalwood, Mennen, Old Spice, Dunhill, Vol de Nuit, Ma Griffe. A young man to his left sweated Shalimar.

Lopez' friends were talking to each other mostly in Spanish. Lopez leaned in in a gesture that implied that he, Percy, was spoken for. Someone began to sing, "Here we play in a different way, Not like you but a bit more gay," and the house erupted in laughter.

"He's got the Mayfair touch alright!" someone yelled out.

"I've gawn and lost me Lambeth Pal."

"Look behind yer!"

Sweat rolled down faces, matches flared, little quarrels broke out. Percy did what he very rarely did and looked at himself in a mirror. The mirror had a small crack in it and a cobweb floated across the glass. A face reflected in the mirror smiled at him. To hell with it, thought Percy, let me look down at Camelot just once in my life. The face smiled back.

"Who you lookin' at?" said Lopez. "That one there he's no a good man."

Percy looked away. One by one the chums peeled off to the bar and came back cradling more drinks that slopped and rolled in the glasses as though they were all at sea. Four or five times Percy headed off toward the bar only to be held back by a restraining hand.

"This my treat," said Lopez.

The noise if anything was getting louder, the room hotter, the lights brighter. None of this seemed to disconcert Lopez, the chums or anyone else in the room. This is Pandemonium, thought Percy. But these aren't demons. Not like the bars of Shanghai and Hong Kong where men were knifed by other men, where the rooms were divided into two cohorts only, cheongsams or trousers. Where women danced and men wilted. Where bottles were hurled up to ceilings and came down as sharp crystal rain. Where whistles blew and shorts-wearing police charged in waving batons. The chums were speaking to him off and on or looking at Lopez first and then at him, then addressing Lopez. Lopez stood smirking. Percy needed a pee.

The crowd slowed Percy's progress but after a couple of minutes he found himself down some rickety stairs in tiny, the rank-smelling lavatory that was thick with cigarette smoke and the odour of raw kidney. Eventually he reached the porcelain wall and the gutter running with yellow liquid and cigarette butts. Unbuttoning, Percy looked straight ahead at the word "Doulton". There are things to be said for a boarding-school education he thought as he ran through the etiquette of pissing at urinals; no looking, never stand in the middle, more than three shakes is a wank. Nevertheless, he could feel the eyes of his neighbour upon him, a man who seemed to be taking his time about it.

The man breached every rule of bog behaviour by speaking to him: "First time at The Stores is it?"

The man was looking down at Percy's cock while gently stroking his own. Fixing Percy in the eye he jerked his head toward one of the cubicles. And then again. Looking sideways Percy saw the man's member growing as it was stroked. Realising that he was in the same, compromising position, cock out and hardening, he blushed.

"S'alright mate," said his neighbour. "Come with me and we'll sort you out."

Percy blushed again thinking of Lopez back in the bar, Lopez his work-chum and host this evening. Lopez who had already staked his claim. This was too easy. Talk about low-hanging fruit it was everywhere he looked, ready and inviting. Is this how everyone carried on, in places like this? Going with whoever? How long would it take? Three or four minutes? Would he be missed? Was that the point? Yes, he could probably get away with it, say there had been a long queue or make up some kind of story but then of what would Lopez suspect him, having been away so long? That he'd had some kind of sex with a stranger in a lavatory cubicle? He'd be right, wouldn't he and what would that do to their nascent understanding? What would Lopez do if he were here? Percy suspected that Lopez was sufficiently sure of himself not to need his attractiveness confirmed or his availability tested standing up in a men's urinal. Not to mention the risk of a police raid bursting in on them. Cock still in hand Percy looked around at the other man and said, "Thanks mate but I'm on a promise." Then he shook, buttoned, and headed back into the bar.

Lopez looked down at him with a fuzzy but confident smile. "No one tried pick you up in there?" he asked.

"Probably," said Percy.

Lopez' smile grew broader and his hand went around Percy's shoulders drawing his head toward him. "You mine," he said.

A gin and tonic warmer than the last was shoved into Percy's hand by one of the chums. There were cheers and clinking of glasses all round. Was he on the point of becoming Mrs Lopez? He thought of all the times he'd been asked why he wasn't married. No point in running through the obvious answers but the simple fact was that he hadn't ever wanted to own anyone in the way that laws of church and state gave a woman to be the property of a man. Of course things had changed in this liberal century but to have another being dependent upon him even metaphorically was more than he could contemplate. What did that mean in reverse? That he should give up his freedoms in return for what? Protection, financial security? He didn't need either of those things from anyone else, never mind a hotel chef. No, that was sheer snobbery. From what he'd come to know of Lopez he genuinely liked him but to enter a relationship with him? Everyone around him was laughing at something that Lopez had said. Monogamy? Perhaps he should have gone with that man and found out what it was that he wanted to do. Percy still had no idea what would please him most in sex with a man. He had the impression that Lopez must think that he, Percy, was more sexually experienced than he was. Yes, he would like another drink, please. Lopez slipped his hand down inside the waistband of Percy's trousers at the back and with his long fingers felt for the cleft. The man who had accosted him out in the loo came back into the room and looked at him. Percy looked back. A cat may look at a king. Turning his head now toward the mirror he saw that Lopez' eyes had tracked his own and were narrowed in the classic frown of control. The pressure of Lopez' fingers on his cleft increased and began to caress his ring. You either learn the rules of this world or you go back to your own and stay there, Percy realised. Pick up your part or leave the stage. An ingenu role is not going to suit you. Lopez slid his hand out of Percy's trousers and then raised his middle finger to his mouth and began to suck it. For the first time that evening Percy began to laugh and thought he wouldn't ever stop.

A bell rang. "Time ladies, please!"

The hubbub was barely dented but the chums began to look at each other and at Lopez as if waiting for the signal to leave. Lopez downed the remains of a pint of that warm British beer that Percy found nauseating. "'Nother round?"

"No thanks, boss," "'S'alright," "Nosotros vamos," "Disfruta tu noche." This last comment earnt the speaker a clip around the ear from Lopez' big hand that came whirling out of nowhere like a Macau pelota player's. "Doan you be cheeky," he said. The band of chums all smiled again and each one shook Percy's hand, nodded and said something along the lines of, "Pleased to meet you," followed by a look at Lopez to make sure they'd said the right thing. Lopez looked happy. The chums smiled yet again and began to shuffle out between the crowd.

"What you wan' do now?" said Lopez, slightly swaying.

"I should be getting back," said Percy. "I've got an early tomorrow."

"We can go night club," said Lopez. "I know great club not far."

"I think we should leave, anyway. I need some fresh air."

Lopez looked at him keenly. "Okay Perce, okay." Pause. "Tell you what you come home with Lopez for a nightcap."

"Oh, I..."

"Oh, you what? You no gonna be no cocktease eh Perce? No need be shy. Lopez knows," and here he tapped his long nose with a long finger, "Lopez knows what you like."

Well, thought Percy, if one of us does that would be a start. The start to my education. Lopez was standing directly in front of him, their bodies not quite touching although every now and then a departing drinker would push one or the other of them forward and closer.

"Just get on with it, you daft dago," said one of the bar staff picking up empty glasses from tables. It was a girl. She looked at Percy. "Aven't seen you in here before." And then to Lopez: "He the new one you've been on about? Little cutie, ain't he?" With her free hand she grasped Percy by the chin and bringing her face close to his said softly "You be nice to him, mate," she said. "He may be just a bleedin' dago but you could be doin' a lot worse I can tell yer. And that means you," she'd lifted her head up and was talking over Percy's shoulder to a man he couldn't see but whose erection he could feel brushing up against his backside. "Sling yer 'ook," she said. "Spencer Tracey's taken." Turning back to Percy she said with a starlet moue: "Our very own Liz and Phil."

"He's Spanish," said the man behind him.

"And you're a proper arsehole," said the girl. "Now 'oppit."

Lopez grabbed Percy by the arm and spun him round so that they were facing the side door onto Cecil Court. Spaces had appeared on the velour banquettes. A man in a trilby glanced up at Percy. It was the man from the urinal who smiled a smile that turned Percy's insides to water. The man spoke with no sound: "I'm going to fuck you," he said.

Percy felt the beginning of a smile on his own lips but controlled it just in time to hide it from Lopez.

"What you wan', mate?" he said to Trilby Man.

"Your boyfriend's arse," said Trilby.

"'Ere," said Lopez, trying to push Percy aside, fist raised, to get to Trilby. Luckily, at least by Percy's lights, Lopez already had a foot into the lobby while he, Percy, was still inside and blocking Lopez' room to manoeuvre.

"No," said Percy. "Ignore him."

"What you say to him? You say anything to him?" Lopez was getting angry, making threatening gestures around Percy's shoulders.

"No," said Percy, "I haven't said anything to him. The only thing that's talking is the beer. Come on, let's go," and he began to push Lopez into the lobby.

"Fancy a threesome I'm your man." said a voice that might have been Trilby's. Percy carried on pushing Lopez and a moment later they were out in the wide alley.

'You say anything to him? Cos he English, eh? A dago not good enough for you?"

Percy had the common sense not to set too much store by what Lopez was saying. And while not entirely drunk himself the alcohol in his blood had been oxygenated and sent straight to his brain in a couple of gulps of fresh air. He pushed the yielding Lopez back against the bit of wall between two doorways and held onto him by his lapels just in case he should slide to the ground. With Lopez slightly recumbent their faces were almost level. Percy looked at Lopez. I do like you, he thought. You're kind and you're funny and you're a good cook and you may be good at other things I'm about to find out about.

A whistle shrilled at the end of the alley where it met St Martin's Lane. "Come along!" yelled a voice. "Ain't you got no homes to go to? No mate, I'll be tucked up in bed with the missus, thanks anyway. You too, dearie, mind how you go. Yes night, Blossom. Night Mrs Miniver, Move along, last bus'll be along any minute. No mate, you can 'ave 'er."

Laughter. A voice sang out: "You can 'ave 'er I doan wann 'er, she's too fat for me!"

"There's no call to be rude," said a deep Welsh voice.

Percy glanced over to see that the one the copper had just called Mrs Miniver had landed a punch that had knocked her insulter to the ground. The copper didn't seem unduly concerned. "Come on, Ted," he said. "You two kiss and make up and get on home the pair o' yer. Now." He extended his hand to a recumbent man in evening dress and helped him to his feet. The man smiled, took Mrs Miniver's arm and the two turned into St Martin's Lane. Percy heard them singing as they headed down to Trafalgar Square; "No you can't trust a special like an old-time copper when you can't find your way," "Can't find your way," "Can't find your way," "Home!"

Lopez seemed to come to. "Gracias a dios e B Squad," he said, grinning. "Or they'd have been straight down the nick. You gonna kiss me or what?"

"Not here," said Percy. "It's a bit public."

"A beet publeeek," said Lopez. "You ain't half a posh bird, Perce. Okey dokey, let's go home." Levering himself forward he started to stride off toward Charing Cross Road past the entrance to Sheeky's, past bookshops with their Georgian bow windows and under the old gas lanterns. He turned right and Percy followed him under the lit canopy of Wyndham's and past the mouth of Leicester Square station belching its hot breath into the night air in windy gusts. At the intersection with Shaftesbury Avenue, he crossed over, narrowly missed by a taxi that hooted at him indignantly. Standing outside the Cambridge he waited for Percy, hands in pockets, smiling. As soon as Percy was across the road he turned and marched on again North up Charing Cross Road. Percy struggled after him, weaving through groups of drinkers heading out of Old Compton Street. Up ahead he saw that straw trilby speeding along until it got to the lit vitrines of Foyles. The lights shone and glittered on Lopez' dark hair and thin moustache. He was gazing through the glass but not really looking, Percy could tell. When he caught up he could see for himself a display of titles among which the new Ngaio Marsh caught his eye – *Final Curtain*. Looking closer he saw a spread of new crime novels, new cosies: *Swan Song*, the new Gervaise Fen, *Crowded House*, by Agatha Christie, and a new title by the mysterious Lorna Nicholl Morgan:

Another Little Christmas Murder. He liked her stuff; he'd come back and get it on his day off.

Lopez saw him scanning the display. "You a book worm, eh?" he said. "You always reading, reading, reading time off. Bet your 'ead like a book all full of words. You always think before you say, eh Perce? You gotta have the right word, eh? You a brain like a biblioteca, eh?"

"I'll take that as a compliment," said Percy. "Yes, I like reading."

"You gonna teach Lopez some posh English words, eh, Perce? Lopez he gonna do things and he gonna teach you Spanish words. Te voy a follar. I teach you what that means."

Lopez leaned forward toward him but Percy ducked away. This was too public, too bright. He walked briskly around the corner into Manette Street where Foyle's had its non-fiction displays. He was enjoying this, this chase. He felt wanted and it was delicious. A whole window was devoted to the books of war experiences with at their centre *The Diary of a Young Girl*. Surrounding her was a show of titles that could have burst out of the window shattering the vitrine with the force of their horror: *Survival in Auschwitz, This Way for the Gas, Five Chimneys, Every Man Dies Alone, Eclipse of Reason*. Incongruously the next display was of the latest children's books: *Mrs Piggle-Wiggle, The Saggy, Baggy Elephant, The Valley of Adventure, Do You Know Pippy Longstocking?* And then, one along, recent translations into English from other languages: Jean Cocteau's *The Difficulty of Being, The Plague, Dr Faustus, Querelle of Brest*. Moving along and very much aware that Lopez was standing to attention just a few inches away Percy stopped at the last window where, on its own and brightly lit stood a copy of *The City of Tomorrow* by a Le Corbusier. Percy stood and looked, trying to imagine what that city would be like and how it would survive a war.

Lopez came very close. Percy could smell Pino Silvestre mixed with beer and cigarettes. "You clever man," said Lopez. "You read books." Now he could feel the brush of Lopez' moustache against the back of his neck. "Lopez, he cooks. You learn how to cook Spanish. Lopez teach you."

Percy turned toward him. Lopez' straw trilby was pushed to the back of his head. Although his face was in shadow Percy could feel the man's eyes intent upon him.

"You like that?"

"Yes," said Percy with a flash of intuition that yes, indeed, he would. He would very much like to learn how to do that. "You come with Lopez to Spain. We open 'otel. With ristoran. People will come." Well why not? thought Percy. I expect they will. The traffic on the street had died down. There still wasn't much money around. People with debts and families went home early to Acton, Romford, Haringey, Penge. Lopez took his hand and drew him along Manette Street past one or two houses and a tiny Byzantine-style church half hidden behind fig trees. Here Manette Street became a tunnel under buildings that fronted Greek Street. In the tunnel were a couple of doorways, dark retreats between the sodium-yellow half-night of the two streets. Lopez guided Percy into one of the doorways. He felt no fear despite knowing that what they were about to do. To give each other even the slightest physical signs of affection in public, could, if a copper were to walk in from Greek Street during the moments to come would see them arrested, imprisoned on remand, tried for indecency and sent to gaol. Their careers would be ruined and they would carry the stigma for the rest of their lives.

"No importa," said Lopez, quietly, sweetly, as though he had read Percy's thoughts. Tall, thin, Lopez. Quick-to-anger, droll, bristly Lopez. Head Chef Lopez from somewhere in Spain, Percy didn't even know where. Lopez the Fascist or Lopez the Republican. Had he lost family, friends? Who had he loved before he came to England? A man, a girl? A wife? Lopez with his flashy clothes and terrible taste in shoes. Lopez who somehow managed to make a five-shilling menu taste like what you'd get at the Savoy. Of course. that was why they came to the Sherborne. They were there for the food. Lopez' food. Give us this day. Percy opened his mouth to take communion from Lopez' tongue. It ran over his lips, then his teeth. Their moustaches bristled against each other. Then the tips of their tongues touched like an electric shock. Lopez leaned onto him so that Percy staggered against the weight of his body and leant back further against the door. The doorknob caught him in the small of his back and it hurt. The pressure of Lopez' mouth on his increased and Percy put his hands around Lopez' waist. A car went by in Greek Street and footsteps sounded on the pavement. Percy closed his eyes. He leant back so that he could speak. Kiss me goodnight, Sergeant Major he said and he was sure that Lopez smiled.

Lopez' head was jerked backward, and he stumbled away from Percy into the roadway of the tunnel. He staggered and a hand came from behind him, knocked off his hat and tightly grabbing his hair pushed him to his knees. There were other eyes looking at Percy. Eyes from a face that he knew. Smetka. Smetka, dressed in greatcoat and hat was holding a knife, blade flat, to Lopez' throat. Poor Lopez. From Latin lover to sacrificial animal in five seconds.

"The pieces of paper, Langreeg. Give me the pieces of paper."

Percy couldn't speak. The knife made a tiny nick in Lopez' neck and a little trickle of blood drained toward his shirt-collar.

"You have them with you?"

Percy shook his head.

"You tell me where they are."

Why is he asking me questions? Does he think I have a choice?

"I could ask you nice Langreeg but nice is for English. I like you Langreeg but I not like this one. Where are the papers?"

Papers? Papers? Shit, the receipts. The receipts he'd picked up. They were in his morning-coat pocket, weren't they? Were they? What had he done with them? He noticed Lopez' right hand come up palm raised to make contact with the right wrist of Smetka, the wrist with the hand holding the blade. Lopez moved fast springing up like a jack-in-the-box to push Smetka's hand and the knife away. As his knees left the ground Smetka twisted Lopez' head to the left, away from Percy, toward Charing Cross Road and the lit windows of books and for the smallest part of a second Percy thought Lopez' throat was cut. Instead Smetka had pushed the Spaniard to the ground where he lay, sprawled, flat on his face, his straw trilby rolling off down Manette Street.

Smetka turned toward Percy, breathing hard. "I cut many throats in war. Many. I good at my job. Bring papers to me tomorrow morning. We have nice caffe mocha, eh? Just like in Cafe Sacher, Philharmonikerstrasse Fier, Innere Stadt, Wien."

"I don't believe you were ever in the Café Sacher, Philharmonike-whatever or even in Vienna."

"If you know that, Langreeg, if you know anything about story of Smetka you bring papers. No papers no Lopez. Wish your boyfriend goodnight." Smetka turned and walked away down Manette Street past the vision of Le Corbusier then under the eyes of Pippi Longstocking and Anne Frank.

Percy unfroze and looked over toward the figure of Lopez prone on the dusty street, one arm out, one crooked to shield his face as he went down. His legs were bent at the knees. How dirty his plimsolls were; there was a ring of dust around his ankles that were brown-skinned and striated with black hairs. Lopez' calves were fine and muscular, his thighs long and tapering and his buttocks, visibly detailed by the line of his underwear, were oval and flat. His waist was narrow and his shoulders wide. Lopez like this stirred his desire. Lopez flexed his hands and turned his palms down, bent his elbows and pushed himself on to his knees. He breathed there once, twice, then pushed himself to a kneel, then paused. Percy went over to him and put a hand under his armpit to help raise him to his feet.

"Non me toques."

Percy stepped back. Lopez uncrooked one leg and setting a foot flat on the ground pushed himself up to standing. He paused again, looking at his hands that he then rubbed together to remove the dust and gravel of the roadway. He didn't look at Percy.

Percy made his mouth move and his voice box sound: "Lopez," he said, "Are you alright?"

Lopez' hand went to his throat where it smeared the already-drying trickle of blood. What's he going to say? thought Percy. "A close shave"? and he wanted to laugh, giggle with shock.

Lopez turned toward him, a look of utter seriousness on his face and Percy swallowed his smile. "How he know where you are?" he said.

"I don't know," was the best Percy could say although he knew he meant I don't want to know. I don't want to think that Smetka had overheard us planning to go out, that had been following them like a malevolent shadow. He would know where Lopez lived from the hotel records but that he'd worked out that the two of us would head there at the end of the evening? Was it that obvious? Who else knew they were an item? Frederick? Mrs Abbott? McAlise was too stupid, surely? Who knew Lopez' regular haunts? This was like the world of a cosy but Percy felt cold, very cold and began to shiver in the warm, muggy air. The lamp in the dust lies shattered, he thought. Lopez is wounded inside. He looked at him. There was a trace of kindness on his mouth but his eyes were blank.

"En otro momeno tal vez," he said and turned away.

"Your hat," said Percy. Lopez took two, three steps and stooping picked the hat up. He looked once at Percy before walking into the dark tunnel. Percy saw him re-emerge into the light and turn right up to Soho Square.

"'So this was the parting that they had,'" said a voice behind him. A familiar voice. What now this evening? thought Percy as he turned around. There in the yellow light was a tall figure, a tall figure with blond hair and a narrow, Reynoldsy face. The face was smiling.

"Boyfriend dumped you? Never mind eh, little one, let's go and drown your sorrows." David Sopley.

"David. What in heaven's name are you doing here?"

"Hello David," said David, "how lovely to see you. You're looking well. What are you up to these days? Muggy old weather, eh? Shouldn't be surprised if they hoist the signal tomorrow."

"David," said Percy.

"Thought it was the third man coming back, did you?"

"What third man?"

"The one that ko'd your boyfriend."

"You saw him? How long were you there?"

"Oh, not long, just a couple of minutes. Long enough to see that he looked a nasty piece of work. What on earth kind of company are you keeping little Perce? Not a black market runner are you?" David laughed. "Are you?"

"'No, David but I think he's something to do with it."

"Who? The dago or the weasel?"

"The weasel."

"And the dago? Is he a waiter round here somewhere? Nice looking if you go for the Ramon Novarro type. Can't say it's quite my taste. Cigarette?" David pulled out a scuffed and mottled flat tin that still had traces of yellow on it and the number 5.

"You've still got it?"

"Never without."

Percy took a cigarette. David took one, pocketed the tin and lit up for them both. As the match flared Percy could see that David's eyes were intent upon him. Then they disappeared in a cloud of smoke.

"And the weasel?"

"I'm not sure I should tell you anything."

"What? Mystery and suspense? You always said you'd write a cosy one day."

"This is real."

"Do you want to tell your Uncle David?" said David and laughed while the tip of his cigarette waggled up and down.

"Come along gentlemen, please. Loitering in dark alleys can be classed as suspicious."

"Good evening officer," said David to the bobby who'd materialised beside them. "This is a friend I haven't seen since the war. We've just bumped into each other. Isn't that extraordinary?"

"Happens a lot I should think," said the policeman. "To the lucky ones. Now if you don't mind taking my advice and moving on, I'd be obliged to you and no mistake."

"Aren't you going to say 'ain't you got no homes to go to?'"

There was a silence.

"An' here was me thinking we were getting on rather well. Move along now or I'll book you for loitering and if that don't shift yer I'll have you for indecency in a public place, now be good chaps and scarper."

"Indecency?"

"You'd be amazed what goes on in the dark round here. I blame the blackout. Now don't waste me time and just clear off like good gentlemen. Please. Sir."

David gave his sweetest, most aristocratic smile and said, "Of course, officer. Good night. Come along Douglas," and he grasped Percy by the elbow and steered him out of Manette Street and into Greek Street. Percy looked right up to Soho Square.

"Still hankering after your waiter? He's probably up there in the shrubbery. Want to take a look?"

"Don't be ridiculous. Douglas?"

"Well, you do have something of the Bader about you in the face at least. I mean if he wore spectacles."

"He isn't a waiter."

"Oh my dear how fascinating. What then is he? Do you have to pay him? I must say I'm glad to see you choose the tall good-looking ones. Makes me feel as though I'm in with a chance."

"David you're insufferable."

"And you're a stuffed shirt. Now come along with me."

"I want to go home."

"Don't fret, child, we'll be back in time for tea."

"Where are we going."

"To see a friend of mine."

"Where?"

"Just down there."

"I don't want to end up in a night club."

"I doubt one would let you in. You have the look of Vice Squad about you."

"It's late."

"It's morning in Hong Kong."

"We've been back nearly three years now. At least I have. Stop walking." David stopped. "David, I have a job. I start at six. I go to bed early. I have something important to do tomorrow and I mustn't get drunk."

"Aren't you already?"

"Possibly."

"Oh, I see. You were out with Ramon. Where? Crown and Two Chairmen? Can't have been the Admiral Duncan or I'd have seen you."

"I don't know either of those two places."

"Percy, don't play green."

"The Salisbury."

David gaped. "The Stores!' Bloody hell!" he laughed. "Camp as a row of tents. Did he take you there?"

"Yes. Look. David, this isn't the kind of conversation I want to have in the street and anyway…" he paused.

"Anyway what? Look Percy you're acting rather agitato if you don't mind my saying so. I would have thought you'd have been pleased to see me. What's going on? Did I interrupt a threesome? Were you being fought over? Good gracious please say yes."

"It isn't funny."

"So there was something going on? Something to do with the weasel?"

Percy was silent.

"Are you in some kind of trouble? Look I'm sorry if your date went south but if you're in trouble, spill the beans. Shared and halved."

"I don't want to share."

"Churl."

"Look David this is serious so…"

"Oh, it's serious is it? There, you've admitted it. Does that feel better?"

Percy was silent.

"Look here, little Perce, you seem completely out of your depth. Dear duffers don't drown so come along my knight at arms and tell me what ails you."

"Not out here."

"Very well then. Back to my original proposal. Follow me." And he strode off down Greek Street.

Percy, trying to keep up, noticed that they'd passed a Trattoria and he wondered if that was the one Lopez had been talking about. The fast walking and the shock of what had happened became mixed up with warm gin and tonic and Percy suddenly stopped and was violently sick over the railings into an area.

"Dirty bastard!" yelled a man's voice.

"Wass going on?" screamed a woman.

"Another load of spew," shouted the man. "Come back 'ere you dirty bastard! I'll give you something to make yer sick!"

David had stopped, turned around and grabbed Percy by the arm. Percy was hauled off down past the last of the old Georgian houses, along a modern brick facade and shoved inside a green door just before they heard footsteps on stone stairs and a metal gate clank to.

"Evening George," said David. "We aren't here."

"Best get off out of sight then Milord," said the doorman.

Inside there was dim wartime lighting that showed a long concrete-floored corridor walls painted dark yellowy-green and with noticeboards along either side of its first few feet. "Move," said David and gave Percy a shove along the corridor. Percy stumbled then slipped along the glossy concrete. Half self-propelled, half propelled from behind he seemed to be flying into the bowels of the earth. They rounded a corner and Percy lurched for a wooden railing that helped him go sideways down a short flight of steps. A push to the right shoulder sent him leftward around a corner. The wall in front of him turned into a door that opened and he was propelled through.

Inside was bright, too bright for him. He blinked and swayed before finding himself dumped into a broken armchair covered in cracked leather. The room swayed round and round. Percy leant forward and was violently sick a second time.

"Charming," said a woman's voice. "Too bloody charming. I say, David, won't you introduce me to your incontinent friend?"

"Save that," said David. "Where do you keep buckets and cloths?"

"The sluice. Turn left, three doors down." "Wait with him. He's just had a nasty shock." David left the room.

"You alright? You look like you just seen a murder. David take you out drinking did he? He's a devil that one. What's your name duckie? Oh second thoughts don't try and speak you might. Oh well, he'll soon be back. Don't worry about that. Happens to the best of us. Me I only got to look at a glass of champers and the old insides is doing the can-can. Sorry."

David came back into the room with a bucket of water, a cloth and a mop. He began firstly to sponge down Percy's trouser cuffs then wiped the vomit from the arms of the chair and the tatty rug and lastly mopped around the concrete floor. That done he disappeared back to the sluice. All the while Percy stared straight ahead, eyes blank, mind blank. David came back.

"Looks like what he needs is a cup of sweet tea."

"Coffee."

"No ducks you just listen to me. What that man needs is a cup of tea with sugar. You wait here while I fetch it." She left the room.

David laid the palm of his hand flat on Percy's forehead. "Clammy," he said and standing up brought a blanket from the corner of the room and laid it over Percy who in the meantime had curled up in the armchair teeth chattering.

"David why were you there?"

"Saw you go by the end of Moor Street with the dishy waiter. I was just curious. So I followed you and watched you looking in the windows at Foyles. The chap didn't seem your type but I didn't want to interrupt. You seemed like an item. Then you went into Manette Street and I just assumed you were heading for somewhere dark for a bit of how's your father. Didn't seem to be the Percy I knew so I thought I'd stay and see. Shortish chap in a greatcoat went by me. Next thing I knew the waiter was flat out on the pavement and that weasel with the mad eyes came back past me at a rate."

"Head chef. Not waiter. Head chef."

"Head chef. So where does the weasel come into it?"

"Here you are dears. Nice, sweet tea freshly made proper. Pot to kettle never kettle to pot as my old gran used to say. Shall I be mother?" The woman put the tray down on a make-up table and poured tea and milk into a green opal-ware cup with saucer, added four teaspoons of sugar, stirred it in a dainty way and handed cup and saucer to Percy with a smile. "Just call me Nippy," she said. Trying to grasp the saucer Percy's hand shook so uncontrollably the cup rattled and tea showered over the armchair and his trousers. David stepped in and took the cup away. He pulled a tatty chair up next to Percy and held the cup out toward his lips. Percy leant forward and drank.

"Seems to be doing the trick," said the girl. "Here. Your friend looks like he's walked out of the Café de Paris straight after the bomb dropped. It's shock he's got. Where was you drinking?"

"Dutch House," said David.

"Not your sort of place, Lord Marmaduke."

"We talked about it in camp."

"Boy scouts?"

"No, Far East."

"Oh yeah come to think of it someone told me you'd been banged up by the Chinks."

"Nips."

"Same difference. So you and him was room-mates?"

"No. We were just in the same camp."

"See something nasty in the old Dutch woodshed, did he? Run into a Nip with his sword out doing the hari kari?"

"Something like that."

David proffered the teacup again to Percy.

"Come on ducks, drink up," said the girl. "Made that with the last of the Assam from before the war. Nothing but the best for Lord Snooty and his Pals." Percy smiled at her. "Aw look he's sweet when he smiles. Looks like a little Scotch doggie. What's them Scotch doggies called? More tea, vicar?"

Percy handed her back the cup and she filled it again, handing it back to him. His hand had steadied. Turning to her make-up table she picked up a pack of Du Maurier, took one and handed the box around. David and Percy both declined. Lighting her cigarette, she leaned backward to take her first drag, crossing her knees as she sat on a rickety stool. Tilting her head back further she exhaled a perfect smoke ring while holding the cigarette at arm's length in the style of Clara Bow. Percy noticed for the first time that she was dressed in coffee-coloured negligee in what looked like silk and on her feet were crimson kitten-heeled slippers finished in ivory swan's down. She noticed Percy looking at her.

"Listen up, duckies," she said. "I'm not so sure about this drunk story. Wait, David. You've had a shock, my man, no point in hiding it. I've seen more than my share of shocked people in the Blitz and during the doodles to know what I'm talking about. Here, did I tell you the one about my Aunt Nance? Going to Woolworths she were down New Cross one fine morning on account of some saucepans had just come in and she's just got to the door of the bank opposite when the manager comes charging up behind her grabs her by the waist opens the door shoves her inside and chucks himself on top of her. Well, my luck's in thinks Aunt Nance and no mistake. Here we go, nice semi-detached in Purley and no shortage of knitting wool. Finally someone's noticed me attributes. Anyway, suddenly there's this almighty crash and that was Woolworths copping it from a Vee Two. Then you know what happened. Well, I don't suppose you do not being here an' all. No David, you can wait." She took another drag of her cigarette and adopted a different pose, arm extended, bracelets tinkling. "So what you gentlemen have been doing I dreads to think. Only I don't wanna know. Mum's the word. What's your name ducks?" David leaned forward as if to intervene. "Hold your 'orses Lord Marmaduke. He can tell me hisself."

"Percy," said Percy. "Percy Langrigg."

"I knew a percy once. Come to think of it I've known a few percies in my time. Sorry ducks! It's a nice name. Me Grandad was called Percy so there. My name's Laetitia West on account of me titties and how I made it up here out of the East End. Since we're friends I can tell you me real name's Flo Waters. From Silvertown. Can you believe it? Couple called Waters they call their daughter bleeding Florence. I'd have killed them if that Goering hadn't have got there first. So now we're all cosy. Anyhow," and here her voice changed completely into a rich, brown, velvety purr that somehow went all of a piece with her Titian-coloured hair, 'should a girl be heading for a night club or bed? What do you think, my fine fellows?"

"That's her stage voice," said David. "She can do deb as well."

"That's right I can bless my jodhpurs and mounts," said Flo in an uncannily accurate upper-class accent. "Pig he calls me," she said in her best Docklands. "On account of the play. Pygmalion."

"I guessed," said Percy.

"He walks, he talks!" cried Flo. "Of course Lord David here will have told you how he's in the films? Rosegarden Pictures out at Denham. They done some crackers. David's going to get me in there aren't you Davey-Wavey?" Pouting at him Flo waggled her eyelashes and put her hand up to them. "Fuckin' hell are they still in? 'Oppit chaps I gotta take me slap off and get home. David, darling," picking up the deb, "Be a sport and give me a tinkle about ten thirty tomorrow. Now," back to Silvertown, "You two what the cat brought in, drag yourselves off before you gets thrown aht. Goodbye," the deb voice, "Percy." She extended her hand as if for him to kiss but looking at him again withdrew it. "We simply must do dinner and a show. Here David," Silvertown, "Touch Teddy for a couple of comps and you can bring him here. Would you like that, Percy?"

"Here?" said Percy.

"Here, Scottie dog, Here. Centre of the universe. The Prince Edward Theatre, The Dancing Years starring Laetitia West. You only just got off the boat? Now 'oppit both of you." Ushering them out of the room she put out her cheek for David to kiss, made a coy courtesy to Percy saying "Night, night Scottie," winked and shut the door behind them.

"Come on," said David. "Let's get you home."

"Not a cab in sight," said David as they got to Old Compton Street.

"I'd rather walk," said Percy.

"Spill the beans," said David.

And so as they walked to Charing Cross Road, crossed over, turned left then right into Phoenix Street, Stacey Street past bomb craters alive with purple loosestrife glowing in the street lighs and into New Compton Street Percy told David much of what had happened to him since he got home. By the time they got to St Giles Percy had arrived at the Sherborne Hotel and the immediate problem of the receipts and Smetka's threat.

"You think they're the evidence that he's diddling old Miss Beaumont?"

"I'm sure of it. And it won't be just chops and steaks. I've no doubt that he's doing the same thing across the board. Drink, repairs, staff, even the heating and lighting I shouldn't wonder. You know he has some bijou cottage on the Test down between Southampton and Winchester?"

"Isn't that near where the old bird lives?"

"How do you know? But yes."

"You told me."

"No, I didn't."

"And you're trying to say that he couldn't possibly afford that on his salary and, no, let me finish, and that he feels he has to be near to the old bird when he's not on duty to keep an eye on her and ward off suitors."

"Something like that."

"So he's a crook."

"More than a crook."

"How much more?"

"He told me some sort of story about having been a partisan in Yugoslavia."

"Why this is Illyria, lady."

David stopped to light two cigarettes and handed one to Percy. "So he's a commie. That doesn't make him a crook. Necessarily."

"I think it's a cover story."

"Well hello Eric Ambler."

"You can mock; you haven't met him."

"Only very briefly."

"He told me that a year or so after the war he went to Vienna and got a job at the Hotel Sacher."

"That should be easy to check."

"You're right I should give them a call."

"And put your hand in the hornets' nest? I'd be jolly careful. It could get back to him."

"Perhaps you're right. Just keep going on. Very top of Shaftesbury Avenue."

"You don't believe him? Why not just let sleeping Yugos lie?"

"Because of what he said next."

"Yes."

"He said that a British man, I took him to mean Army, took some kind of fancy to him and added him to his entourage and got him into England."

"Would have to know all the right people."

"Exactly. And he also said that immediately after the war, before Vienna, he'd spent some time at a hotel management school in Lucerne."

"Well, why not?"

"Because let's say he was Ustase..."

"Crikey that's going some, my lad."

"But just say that he was. Say that he got out through Austria over the mountains and managed to get to Switzerland."

"Money?"

"Friends along the way."

"Changes his name, new passport, past behind him, enrols at a nice establishment, grows wheels and turns into the perfect Swiss waiter. Well I suppose it could be done. Then someone clocks him so he does a bunk and heads to Vienna."

"Friends along the way."

"The place is crawling with them you know."

"Friends?"

"Nazis, Ustase, Italian Fascists all doing the washing up and carrying luggage. You may well have a few here."

"My point exactly: Smetka."

"Or whatever his name is."

"Or whatever his name is. And whoever got him over here will be a Friends sympathiser."

"And what about your boyfriend? How did he get here?"

"That doesn't come into it. We cross over here."

"Spanish, is he?"

"Yes."

"Red or black?"

"It isn't the sort of thing you ask point blank. And anyway, I doubt he'll speak to me again."

"Too much Latin pride?"

"But I know he loathes Smetka and I think it's more than just a clash of personalities."

"What if he isn't Spanish?"

"Eh? Museum Street."

"What if he's Yugo. What if he's the actual partisan and what if he's recognised Smetka or whoever he is?"

"Then he'd have killed him by now, wouldn't he?"

"This isn't quite the Wild West, Percy. Whitehall one two one two and all that. There's a good chance he'd get caught even if your Ambler-esque fantasy were to turn out to be true."

Percy, walking along, seemed barely to notice.

"What makes you think he's Ustase? That's a hell of an accusation."

"I asked him what he did in the War. I think he made it clear that he'd been in those awful camps where they killed thousands and thousands by cutting their throats en masse. And you should have seen what he did to Lopez. Had him on the ground in seconds."

"Saw that."

"But you didn't see the knife. Or how he used it. And he more or less threatened to turn it on me. Turn right."

"Knife?"

"Yes, he had a knife out and was about to cut Lopez' throat."

"That would have ticked him off. I can see that. You think that Lopez is here because he's on Smetka's trail. He isn't a cook?"

"Yes, he is. He's a very good cook."

"With a phoney Spanish brogue."

"He has Spanish chums."

"Why not if he's been posing as Spanish for years."

"How did he learn the language?"

"Perhaps he did fight in Spain. People went there from all over the place."

"We're nearly there. Perhaps he was in Vienna too "

"Lopez?"

"Yes, Lopez."

"Or Sigismund or whatever he's actually called."

"He's certainly learnt to cook from somewhere pretty high falutin."

"Percy, stop."

Percy stopped.

"Look here, little Perce, this is all very interesting and imaginative and a darned sight more dashing then I'd have expected from you but look here, take this from me, Europe is full of exes of all kinds of hideous organisations. And if for a moment your story should turn out to be true then leave it to the professionals. If Smetka's ex-Ustase someone in Whitehall will know about it, you can be sure. He may also be a crook, most of them were or are, but my advice is to not just keep your nose out of it but keep your cock out of it, too."

"But even if I don't think he's got a shady past he seems to have a shady present and don't I owe it to Miss Beaumont to go to the police?"

"But you don't think you'd get that far."

Percy shivered. "Perhaps not. Or I wouldn't put it past him to at least threaten to hurt Lopez to stop me from doing anything."

"And you think he would hurt Lopez?"

"Based on this evening's show, yes I do. And you."

Both men went quiet.

"Percy what are you doing here?"

"I'm standing in Great Russell Street talking to you."

"I mean, really. Never mind what you seem to have got yourself mixed up in like a silly ass. What are you going to do with the rest of your life? To be honest, wee Perce, it seems to your Uncle David that you've got out of one camp with poor service, awful food and no mod cons into another camp with mediocre service, mediocre food but more of it and still no mod cons. And all this not to mention that our what shall we say shared proclivities their own kind of prison do make. Even if you and Lopez are headed for the happy ever after then for goodness sake how and where? Let's face it Perce, what on earth kind of future have you got?"

"Lopez wants to open a hotel in Spain. He wants me to go with him."

"Perce there's a fascist government in Spain. What do you think they do to homos there? Let them run hotels together? Face facts, Perce, there isn't a yellow brick road. There's only the Wicked Witch of the West waiting to get her claws into the likes of you and me."

"What do I do? We're here."

"Go in there now, pack a bag, go to bed with the door locked, get up tomorrow, give the receipts to Smetka with your notice and get a train to Maidenhead."

"Maidenhead? And what about Lopez?"

"You'll be taking him out of danger. At least the danger you've created for him by taking those receipts. If he wants to go back and take a pop at Smetka that's his lookout."

"And Miss Beaumont?"

"She's old, she doesn't have children, she's happy. Isn't she? Perhaps Smetka is just what she needs."

"She just has to pay through the nose for the privilege."

"It'll all come out in the wash, Perce, mark my words."

"Maidenhead?"

"See you at the steps by the bridge, South side, at one o'clock. Look out for a flashy little boat called the Way Foong."

"Dear Duffers don't drown?"

"Something like that. Good night, Perce. Hasta la vista." David turned around.

Percy felt for his night key and headed to the staff entrance, quietly. He could hear David whistling as his steps receded down Russell Street, "'The golden evening brightens in the West...'"

Joyous Gard, Cookham, August 1947

Caesars and Cocktails

It was a quarter to one by the red brick, stone-trimmed clock on Maidenhead's main thoroughfare. Percy, dressed today in white trousers, white shirt, canvas shoes and a striped jacket with boater on his head, suitcase in hand was heading North away from the railway station and toward the river. Never in his life had he been to Maidenhead before. Ahead of him was the Eighteenth-Century bridge that had replaced the ancient ferry and on the other side the Skindles Hotel reputed to be a dirty-weekend resort of Londoners. In fact, yes there was something of the air of Brighton about the place, thought Percy. Something jolly, something naughty, something a bit blowsy. Today was a Friday but this time tomorrow, if the weather were to stay fine, the Thames would be full of little boats and launches heading upstream to the cool, willowy eyots down below Cliveden, to the meadows of Cookham and all converging at some stage on the organised chaos of Boulters Lock. Percy had seen the painting in the National Gallery in which men in boaters (he tapped his head) and women in frothy hats and furbelowed skirts jollified together in their boats and skiffs. He imagined shrieks, singing, ribald laughter, the pop of corks, barking of little dogs, wailing of children, splashes as young men dived into the river, the creaking open of wicker hampers, even an organ grinder supplying a tune. All the sounds of an Edwardian Summer where light receded for just a few, warm moments illuminated only by the red glowing tips of cigars before the sun rose again and blackbirds made trails over dewy lawns. The English paradise? Strange, really, he thought, as he walked along, when you considered that only a few miles upriver at "the village in Heaven," Cookham, the same Edwardians, of the local variety, had been portrayed as so energetically, so muscularly rising out of their graves and seeing God, Jesus, in their very, rather grey, flesh. Was this stretch of river England's Jordan? With Cliveden as its Camelot? What a shame, thought Percy, that we've left the river behind us and more or less forgotten about it except on Bank Holidays. Perhaps we de-natured it, he thought, dirtied it, over-used it, abused then abandoned it. Or was it just that this England, this Home of myth and desire was simply exhausted, bankrupt, hungry and grey. The sedge really had withered from the lake, he thought and he hoped that further upstream the willow-lands of Morris and of Ratty and Moley had been spared.

Behind him lay London and an empty staff bedroom at the Sherborne. Lopez hadn't been at work that morning; the 'flu apparently. Percy had left a note for him in his office couched in the most general terms since it was sure to have been opened and read by now by who knew who. It said that he, Percy, had been experiencing periods of anxiety brought on by his captivity – this much was true – and that having been offered the chance of a talking-cure, an offer rarely made, had accepted and joined immediately. He wished Lopez well in his career. No hopes of meeting again, no conventional phrases to finish. Yours, Percy. I wish I had been, he thought. I really do. Smetka was also out that day and Percy left on his desk the two receipts in an envelope. To Miss Beamumont he would write a letter in the next couple of days when he'd had time to think about what to say. The upper classes could sniff out a platitude at twenty paces so whatever he wrote must at least in some sense be true. Putting on his civvies he had walked out at six in the morning and set off for Paddington.

Down at the wharf below the bridge Percy looked around for a launch called Way Foung. The river flashed and sparkled, ducks quacked, wooden hulls knocked against pontoons, bollards, piles and other wooden hulls with hollow clocking noises. Motors coughed and raced sending blue smoke out across the water and the smell of unburnt petrol hung on the air, the weedy, mulchy, rivery air. Across the water half-hidden by willows stood the Edwardian confection that was the Skindles with its long-glazed frontage behind which, Percy imagined, were pink-shaded lamps and polished spirit stoves for the making of crepes Suzette at diners' tables. He put his suitcase down. It was peaceful. Then the sound of a boat's klaxon broke out, rudely. One or two people looked out to see where the noise had come from. It isn't really done, you know. The prow of a launch shot out from behind a tethered line of boats for hire, the full length of the hull came into view and made a tight, sweeping curve in toward the bank to come to rest up against the side, rocking wildly. The Way Foong.

"Chuck in your suitcase." said David, "and hop in after. Come on."

"Stop ordering him around, David," said a rich, brown, purring voice from near the stern. Laetitia.

Percy held out his suitcase and David, steadying himself in the still-rocking boat by holding on with one hand to the white bakelite steering wheel, reached out and took it. Percy put one foot on the gunwale and, unsteadily, followed with the other. At that moment a larger cruiser that had just passed sent back its wake and the launch began to bob about. Percy flew forward. Laetitia shrieked. David left the steering wheel and, bracing himself, caught Percy under the armpits so that the two stood, rocking and clasped together.

"Go on, give him a kiss," said Laetitia. "You know you want to."

David and Percy unclasped. The nose of the boat nudged into a bollard and the motor went put-put letting off a little fart of blue smoke. Percy looked around. The boat was beautiful. The prow was long, sleek and its polished planks honey-coloured with narrow lines of white wood between each strip, gleamed. The windshield was steeply raked back, divided by and fixed in with bands of shining chrome. The well of the boat was fitted out with duck boards made of a rich, dark wood. The sides were wood panelled behind wide cushions of dark red leather piped in white. Behind the wide back cushion, on which reclined Laetitia, was a short white mast from which hung an ensign. From there the back of the boat shelved down toward the water in a long, long, graceful slope made from the same gorgeous wood as the prow. The boat was perfection, a natural denizen of the river, made for taking pleasure in the cool water as would the white, long body of a swimmer, a Hero. For goodness sake, thought Percy, why can you never get this right? Hero or Leander? Which one was the boy?

Laetitia patted the seat next to her and said, "Come on Perce. Let's be 'avin you."

"Go on," said David, "Go and be Rudi."

"Yes," said Laetitia, "I'll be Grete and you can be my little Rudi and I'll sing you all the way home."

"Your luck's in," said David.

Percy headed, unsteadily, for the back of the boat. David had been toggling the motor and feathering the steering to keep the launch up against the bollards while this had been going on but now he'd turned the wheel gently and put the propellor into reverse to glide backward and away from the side leaving more and more space between the prow and it. Now, standing upright and glancing behind, he gunned the motor and flicked the wheel to send the boat roaring backward and curving out into the river. From behind them there came a shout; "Oi!". The Way Foong stopped, its prow plunged downward. David grabbed the wheel, flicked the shift, gunned the motor and sent them careering forward. "Lout!" came the voice again. Predictably Percy lurched and came crashing down next to Laetitia but not before seeing a small boat rocking uncontrollably behind them, its master white-faced and shaking his fist at the cloud of exhaust that burst out of Way Foong's arse.

"That wasn't very nice, David, I must say," said Laetitia who turned around to wave an apology that must have looked like an insult, the rocking man now shouting even more loudly than before.

"Bloody rich bastards!"

"Poor little man." said Laetitia. "Never mind. Turned out nice again, ain't it?"

Once out into the channel David reined in the motor to send them chug-chugging upstream toward Boulters Lock.

"Where are we actually going?" he said to Laetitia.

"Trust David not to tell you. It's this house. Belongs to a friend of his what's away on business for a while. If you catch my drift." Percy looked blank. "In jug," said Laetitia, "banged up. Nicked."

"A criminal?"

"Not half. King of the Swindlers. Dunno how he managed to keep the house but Rosegarden Films, you remember I told you? - they rent it for their stars and whatever "cos it's only half an hour in the car from Denham."

"Is it nice?"

"Nice?" Laetitia roared with laughter. "It's the 'ouse of me dreams, honest."

"Where is it?

"About an hour up river."

"Does it have a name?"

"Yes, bloody stupid and all. Joyous Gard. Now what the fuck does that mean? I ask you."

Joyous Gard, the home that Lancelot prepared for Guinevere. Just a short drive from Rosegarden Studios and Maidenhead railway station. It must be true what Morris had complained of before retreating to Kelmscott; that the Thames had become cockneyfied and ruined. "Never mind," said Percy to himself. "'Spect it'll turn out nice."

The Way Foong put-putted onward, David not leaving his position as steersman up front. Sometimes he stood, sometimes sat down on the forward bench. The front of the boat, David's domain, was fitted out as though it were some great American land-barge with chrome-surrounded dials, chrome levers and chrome fittings all set into more gorgeous wood. The wheel was a huge affair, white-rimmed and chrome-spoked. At the back end Percy and Laetitia were sprawled on the cushions. Percy felt uncomfortable sitting there next to the beautiful Laetitia dressed today in the very latest New Look dress made from white material printed in a chintz. On her head she wore a hat like an upturned saucer made of coral-coloured straw. Her sandals too, and her toenails and her lips were all the colour of coral. Her sunglasses were of tortoiseshell. The brocade curtain is drawn back, behold the Princess of Wei.

"Penny for 'em."

"I was just thinking of a Chinese poem. David might remember it. David," he called, "the poem, the one about the Princess of Wei."

"She was a hooker. Calling her princess was a joke"

"'Ere, were you calling me a tart?"

"No. Well if I did I didn't realise. I'm sorry."

Laetitia laughed "Don't care if you are. Don't take everything so serious, Perce. "'Ere, David, don't he take everything so serious our Perce?"

"Always did," said David.

Laetitia curled her legs up on the seat, grasped Percy's upper arm and pulled herself into him until her chin was resting on his shoulder. They were getting close to Boulters Lock, slowing down and drawing into the bank. People were looking down at them. Laetitia glanced up and waved. She looks like a film-star, thought Percy. And I must look like some awful casting-couch producer who's buying her favours. Up on the bank the women looked dowdy with their dark brown or bottle-green suits, cream or grey blouses, felt hats and stout brown shoes. Some were wearing scarves around their heads either tied beneath the chin or up on top of their heads like charladies. Something white fell into the boat and landed on Laetitia's bare arm. They both looked at it. It was a small piece of stale bread.

"Oops!" said a voice up above them, "Sorry, thought you was a duck."

This set off a wave of giggles among five or six younger women in clothes that were less drab but definitely not New Look.

"You a film star?" called out one of them.

"Can I 'ave your autograph?" said another.

"Who you got with yer? Yer dad?"

Ahead of them the lock gate began to swing open. David began to nose the Way Foong inside. It felt to Percy as though they were headed into a trap. The crowd of girls seemed to have scented blood and began to head toward the lock side arm in arm. Steadily, slowly the boat began to rise as the girls to assemble. For a second it looked as if David were about to clamber out of the boat and confront them.

"Hello ladies," said Laetitia, standing up, perfectly poised, in perfect command. "Now me ma always used to say that what goes around comes around so," the water lapped and Way Foong uttered a poot but all else was quiet. "So I says you wanna watch what you chuck at who in this life if you gets my drift. You with the pink 'ead scarf what's yer name?"

"Pearl."

"Well, Pearl, I forgives yer for chucking the bread but you wanna watch it next time, alright?"

Pearl looked down stony-faced and pugnacious.

"And don't wear pink it don't suit yer complexion. What colour's yer eyes? No they're not. Try cerise. You're the bold type. What you giggling abaht? The little mousey one; you? Well you should get her pink scarf off her and try it yourself. You need a bit of prettying up."

The girls stood in their little group, spellbound.

"You, Pearl, get yourself a wider belt and pull it tight round yer waist. All of you, get some colour. Got any clothes dye? This year it's cerise, emerald and turquoise. Got that? And florals. Like this,' She stretched out her skirt to reveal the pattern and also the yards of fabric that had gone into it. The girls gasped.

"This was me Grandma's curtains," she said. The girls were goggle-eyed but when Laetitia laughed they all laughed with her. "'Ere," she said to the one called Pearl, "you need some accessories, know what I mean? Cop this." And here she took from off her arm a band of big, coloured beads, balls almost and chucked them up the few remaining feet to the side of the lock. The girl caught the bracelet and put it over her forearm.

"Thank you miss," she said. "Oh thank you."

"'S all right," said Flo. "If you're up the West End I'm on at the Prince Edward. Come to the stage door and ask for Flo I'll get yer some comps. That goes for all of yer only," – she waggled her finger at them in Lucille Ball style – "only if yer don't like it don't yer dare chuck no bread. Got that?"

"Yes miss, thank you miss," they all chorused and led by Pearl, braceleted wrist and forearm high in the air, they turned and went laughing away.

Laetitia sat down. Percy looked at her profile. David turned round. "Want to take over the wheel?"

"No thanks mate," said Laettia "Me an' Perce is talking make-up. You just keep yer eye on the road."

The Way Foong nosed out of the lock. Laetitia leant back and waved up at Cliveden above them in the trees. "Cooo-eee!" she called, "Wotcher Nance!"

David laughed. "Flo, you're a card."

"Queen of diamonds that's me. Once I get a part. 'Ere, David."

"No shop till later. At the party."

"Oooooh yes!" Laetitia clapped her gloved hands together, "Party!"

"There's a party tonight?" said Percy. "I don't have party clothes."

"You sound just like a girl, you do. Them trousers is alright. We'll find you a shirt that's a bit more party and there you are. They're mostly Americans and they don't dress up anyhow. Ever seen a Waian shirt?"

"Hawaiian."

"Ta Prof. A Waian shirt. David's got a couple from when he were Stateside. You can have one of them. Blend right in, you will."

Laetitia put her arm back around his shoulders and they cruised slowly on past the maze of islands and weirs below Cookham, past the village, under its swan-crowded bridge and out again onto a smooth, broad stretch of Thames like a lake.

Soon David began to throttle back the motor and steered the boat toward a line of willows. Into the branches they went so that they were in a marquee of bright green, shimmering light. David deftly cut the motor, stood on the gunwale, lifted a painter, leapt ashore and bobbed the Way Foong gently along the wooden embankment. Laetitia had already run up and down the side of the boat chucking over the side the three or four bollards that had been neatly stowed in readiness. Hooking her bag over her shoulder she held out a hand to David who stood aside to let her step lightly ashore, her coral pumps touching the fine yellow gravel. David made the Way Foong fast. "Chuck your suitcase up," he said to Percy. Percy handed it to him then clambered ashore pushing back with one foot so that a gap opened up between boat and verge into which, for a minute, he thought he would fall.

Laetitia was going on ahead. With her hands outstretched she parted the willow branches and through the gap Percy caught his first sight of Joyous Gard. The house was an Edwardian confection of red brick; a crazy variety of white-painted windows, roofs, bays, verandahs and even a turret all brought together into a completeness by sheer exuberance and the confidence of cash. It stood on a red-brick platform about six feet high that would, Percy assumed, keep it safe in times of flood. Its many windows reflected bright sunlight, its tiles sparkled and the brickwork seemed to throw back warmth like the fur of a large, ginger cat asleep in the sunshine. Between the river and the house stretched a long sward of green lawn, perfectly mown and at its centre a large circular flower bed stuffed with begonias yellow, cream, scarlet and lavender. In the centre of the bed stood a stone urn of some size and magnificence filled with trailing geraniums in blood red and orange. It could have been modelled on a hat worn by Lillie Langtry or the girl on the arm of the Prince of Wales at Longchamps, Vincennes, Fontainebleau. Laetitia reached down and took off her shoes and dashing up to the circular flowerbed began to run around it skipping and posing in the style of Isadora Duncan.

"Come on Tits," said David, "let's go and find a drink. You can show Perce his quarters."

"Aye aye," said Laetitia, "All ship shape and Bristol fashion." Here she hoiked up her breasts and squashed them together before laughing and running ahead toward the steps that led up to the front door of the house.

"Well, here you are, Perce," said David. "Consider yourself rescued."

"'Summer cometh to an end, Undern cometh after noon.'"

"What's that? Can't play the game if you don't speak up."

"Morris," said Percy.

"'Gold Wings?' Thought so, you gloomy little bastard. Cheer up and come on in."

Up the steps he went behind Laetitia and into a wide foyer off which to the left was a small, gold-wallpapered smoking room with a view out toward the front gate. The carpets were thick and plain vermilion. Rooms went off to the right, stairs to the left.

"Come on, ducks," said Laetitia and led him upward. They passed a landing, wide with tall windows and huge chairs. A landing as big as a room. Percy could imagine a conversation between Edwardian visitors meeting: "Good morning. We seem to be early for breakfast. Shall you sit with me a minute and we may have a moment's idle chat?"

The next floor was gloomy by comparison and seemed to be all bedrooms with a wing heading off to the left. They went on up to a floor of small bedrooms and with a low ceiling. Servants' quarters?

"No more servants," said Laetitia. "At least there are, sort of, but they live over the garage at the back." She showed him into a small room with a small bed and a small window.

"Thank you," he said. "Perfect."

"You're up here on account of you're family and all the big knobs are in the big rooms. I'll go and get some lunch organised. You must be starvin'. I am!" And she went away.

Percy dropped his suitcase and went to the window to look out. Far more garden extended out from the back of the house than down to the river but here instead of lawn there were outdoor rooms: a row of horse-chestnut trees bounding the property, then inside a miniature orchard, then a concrete pond heavily overgrown with bulrushes with a lead fountain at its centre. The pond and its surrounding path were hedged in with berberis. A miniature sunken rose garden hedged in box, a trellis walkway covered in tiny white stars of jasmine, a croquet lawn to the other side of the plot below a line of Lombardy poplars mixed with aspens trembling in the breeze. Beyond that it looked as though there was a kitchen garden, possibly one or two more enclosed outdoor rooms and then, beyond, the tiled roof and boarded gables of the former stables. Cockneyfied it may be, thought Percy but it's enchanting. Multum in parva. Midways of a walled garden in the happy poplar land. At least some of Gold Wings was happy. A gong sounded from downstairs.

"Lunch!" yelled Laetitia.

Percy quickly washed his hands and his face and went downstairs.

"We're just slummin' it in the kitchen," said Laetitia, "staff is 'avin its rest on account of they've got to get on with the party stuff in a minute. We just got time to nosh and scarper."

David wandered in through a back door and sat down at the big kitchen table. In the kitchen all was American; a huge refrigerator opened by treading on a pedal, an American range stove, electric beaters and blenders, at least two sinks including one with a Tweeny.

"That thing's vicious," said Laetitia as she fed it with eggshells. "Dunno how many teaspoons and wedding rings it's eaten. 'Ere you are, egg sandwiches. Now don't say yer Auntie Flo don't look after yer."

"Why don't we take them outside?" said David and so they wandered, plates in hand, back down to the riverside and took their places on a bench beside the water and under the marquee of the willows. Within a few seconds a flock of ducks came quacking up.

"In a minute," said Laetitia. "Lucky you lot, I've saved the crusts."

Sure enough, as soon as they'd eaten she began throwing crusts of bread into the water in among the birds. Bread fell onto backs, into the water, occasionally straight into beaked mouths. There was a scramble, splashing and loud quacking. "Come on, Whitey," said Laetitia, "Mummy's saved one for you special," and she lobbed a large piece of bread straight at the white duck hanging back from the press. "Go on littley," she said. The other ducks descended on the small white one but not before it had managed to ingest most of the bread.

"He's your friend," said Percy.

"Always go for the underdog, me. Bit like you, Perce."

"He hasn't always been," said David. "He's just having a bad patch, aren't you, Perce? We'll soon get you fixed up with something. Can't keep a good man down and all that."

Laetitia opened a flask of coffee, sweet and milky, and they shared the cup around them.

"'There were five swans that ne'er did eat the water weeds for ladies came each day,'" said Percy.

David said, "'And young knights did the same and gave them cakes and bread for meat.'"

"'Ere," said Laetitia, "you two talking in secret code? You Russian spies or something? I knew there was something funny about you two."

"Yes, there is," said David, "but it isn't that and," holding up his hand palm towards her, "it isn't that either."

"Wass goin' on then? Share."

Percy cleared his throat and began; "It all started when we were at school, in China."

"You was at school in China? Eton not good enough for yer?"

"Our parents were working out there." said David, "and they didn't want to send us Home.

"Though they might as well have done," said Percy. "So we both ended up at a school on the coast run by missionaries."

"You're vicars in disguise," said Laetitia, "come to show me the error of me ways and save me from a fate worse than death."

"Too late," said David.

"You watch it, mate. So, Percy, you and him were school chums in some kind of monastery where you had to lash each other every day,"

"Twice," said Percy.

"Three times," said David.

"Go on with yer," said Laetitia. "Was you two bum-chums then? They say it shows you're a proper toff." "

No," said David. "We weren't".

"It didn't really happen," said Percy, "there was no privacy for a start. Even the loos had no doors on them."

"You couldn't even crap in private? What kind of place was that?"

"A place where you had to keep your hands on view at all times," said David.

"Even in bed," said Percy. "So you made up a secret code so you could say naughty things to each other? Is that it?"

"Sometimes we had to stay there in the holidays," said Percy.

"You poor little waif!" said Laetitia. "Come 'ere while I gives you a big kiss. You too, David. Oh it breaks me 'eart to think of you two little chaps being abandoned months on end."

"There was a library."

"Very Victorian, most of it."

"Tennyson, Macaulay, Dickens, Trollope."

"Arnold, Morris, Rossetti, Keats."

"Browning, both Brownings, George Eliot, Collins."

"And there was some newer stuff too, be fair. They had some of the Yellow Book poets. Even Wilde had survived somehow, the poems at least."

"Yeats, Allingham, lots of Irish."

"Yes, Yeats and Kipling of course."

"And some of the Great War poets, too."

"Quite a liberal library."

"Yes, surprisingly."

"And the Latin poets. Hours and hours of prep on those."

"And we started this game: one of us would say a bit of a poem.

"And the other would have to come up with the rest of the line or the verse."

"We each had different favourites. So we covered quite a lot of ground between us."

"Well aren't you just the Tweedle Dee and Tweedle Dum of the Remove? You sure you're not brothers separated at birth or something?"

"Do we look like it?" said David.

"What about the masters? Them missionaries? Weren't they around?"

"Some of them were," said Percy, "one or two but mostly it was just the Chinese staff."

"Any of them masters 'ave their wicked way with you? Go on. Must 'ave 'appened."

There was a silence and a motorboat purred by.

"Not really," said David. "You're very prurient, you know."

"Doctor can make you a cream for that. I can tell you my Mum if she'd found any vicar or teacher with his hand down any of my brothers' trousers she'd have killed him on the spot. An' your Mums and Dads they just left you there. Shocking, that is."

"It wasn't like that."

"Much."

"We had some good times."

"Record-playing evenings in the staff room."

"They had a wind-up they called a Phonogram."

"And one of the masters got all the latest American records from Shanghai."

"Dance music? I love to dance! 'Ere, we can have music later. They've only got a radiogram. He got the lot. Nothing this year mind since he went inside. They got Bing, they got Frank, Perry, Nat King Cole, they got Dinah Shore, they got Doris Day they got the Andrews Sisters." She got up, hitched up her skirt and sashayed along the path as she flicked the fabric to left and to right, kicking and stepping, "'If you go down Trinidad they will make you very glad.' Oooh can't remember the verse. 'Rum and Coca-Cola, everything get much better. Both mother and daughter working for the Yankee dollar.'"

Percy was silent.

David leant across and said "You haven't heard her sing before. Isn't she fabulous?"

Percy sat still, watching the girl singing and stepping under the tent of the trees, the fabric of her dress scattering roses right and left.

One hand she raised above her head. With the other she flicked the fabric as she danced. "La la la, la la lah, lah," she sang, "Working for the Yankee dollar!" She stopped. "'Ere what you two looking at. You look like lovebirds on a perch. It's only me, Flo. Come on you two lunch is over. I'm going for a nap. Coming, David?"

She held out her hand and took his. "See yer at six for a snifter," she said and waved as she and David stepped out over the grass.

The water rocked and shimmered sending flashes over the boat and into the willow-tent. Percy sat down and looked over the Cockney Thames at Cookham's meadows. Not a single line of anything came into his head.

He took a wander around the gardens, skirting the house to its right. The wide border at the front of the house was thick with more begonias, astilbes and huge mauve daisies. Around the side was an Italianate pool, marble-bordered, rectangular with lunette recesses at either end. Cypresses were planted at its corners and they made the waters black and mournful. To his left he could see figures coming in and out of the back door, the staff and hired staff starting to make preparations for the party. As quietly as he could he passed them by keeping to the line of the jasmine-covered trellis he'd seen from up above. The little orchard was on his right; miniature apple trees hung with fruit. Thereby the apple hangs and the wasp caught by the fangs. The three of them; Miles, Giles and Isabeau. Why Gold Wings? Why had it been in his head since they arrived? Was disaster just around the corner? Someone, a man, running along the jasmine alley cannoned into him just as he stepped back onto the path pushing him back into one of the uprights. Losing his balance he slid down onto the ground and ended up in a patch of hellebore.

"Oh god I'm sorry," said the man. "It's just I'm late for work. I'm sorry Mister. "'Ere, let's get you up again." The man held out a hand. Percy grabbed it and hauled himself upright. "Sorry mister, I just didn't see you was coming out. I'm sorry."

Percy said, "That's alright."

"Thanks guv," said the man, a youngish man, thirty perhaps. "You all right?"

"Yes, thank you," said Percy.

"You one of us?" said the man. "You on the staff for tonight? Shit, no, you're a guest ain't yer? Oh god I'm sorry. Do you wanna sit down or something? Shit you're all covered in green stuff." The man turned Percy round and began with the flat of his hand to brush Percy's back trying to remove the stains of lichen and sap. Percy could feel a graze or a bruise on his shoulder-blade. "Shirt's ruined," said the man. "'s'all green. 's ruined. I'm so sorry guv."

"It's all right," said Percy, "There'll be plenty more shirts in the house. Not to worry."

"Thanks guv," said the man who was of a bit less than average height, with brown curly hair shaved up at the sides to sit on top of his head in a mop. He had a pleasant face.

"Cigarette?" said Percy.

"Guv I shouldn't, I'm late."

"Have a couple for later," said Percy, taking a dented box of du Maurier out of his pocket.

"Don't mind if I do. Thanks guv." He pocketed the fags and set off down the alleyway. After a few paces he turned around, stopped and blew Percy a kiss.

Up the jasmine alley, around the vegetable plot, down into the sunken Jekyll-style rose garden went Percy. The air was full of light. The sun warmed the old grey stone of the rose garden made vivid by the surrounding hedge of box and lit the remaining roses like Chinese lanterns. There was a bench, there, a stone bench, mossed and lichened. Percy sat down and lit himself a cigarette. What a day it had been already. This time yesterday he'd been finishing his shift as maître d' at the Sherbrone. Or perhaps like a baby eating Poire Belle Hélène from a spoon. Preparing himself to take the huge step of going out with Lopez. Lopez. Best not to think. David was right to have rescued him. He'd needed rescue. Where on earth did he think his life was going? To Spain? Ridiculous. And yet. And yet what was keeping him in England? Not family, not property. What resources he had were as mobile as had been his parents' lives. America then? But as what? He'd met his mother's family once? Twice? They were as austere as she had been and probably dead, too. They'd sent him formal condolences after it was certain their sister and her husband's lives had been lost in the Coral Sea heading toward Manilla. No ties there, then. He had some cash. Not a lot. Some. He dragged on his cigarette, thick and pungent in the hot summer air. "And it was not a time in which we think about the dead." Who was that? Not Allingham. Not Blunt. Stephen Phillips, that was it. The Apparition. Not the one by John Donne. Percy tapped the ash from off his cigarette into a rose bush crowned with a huge, pink flower. The last of the year? "And close beside me a great rose had just begun to die." What had young Tommy said just yesterday? Or was it Frederick? About death in Summer being different. Harder to bear, somehow. The hot sun, the old stone, the lack of shadows, the scent. Phillips had been onto something there. To be gripped by Schadenfreude but without the schaden. That was frightening, other-worldly. Percy leant over and did his best to bury the cigarette butt in the flakes of dried manure surrounding the rose. His eyes hurt. He wished he'd brought his hat. Up he got and wandered into the line of horse chestnut trees, conker-pods already showing. It wasn't exactly a Walk. Just one line of trees and then a fence. But Percy meandered happily between the trunks, in the shade, looking down at where the roots broke the ground, where the grass retreated and where the ants ran hither and thither in the thin and dusty soil. Seeing an opening in the hedge he went through and found himself by the bulrushed round pond. In the centre a concrete putto held a scallop shell that gurgled water that dropped into the green pond beneath. A slight breeze blew up. Across the moat the fresh West wind in very little ripples went. Golden Wings will be here soon. He walked round the pond once, widdershins then turned around and walked the other way. A spell against Disaster. What was this strange, fluttering feeling? Too little time asleep last night, too many cigarettes. That was it. Time to get a grip. Does David have a plan for me? Why can't I plan for myself? What do I actually want to do with my life? And company? A companion? A woman who would understand? Or a man to set me on fire? I cannot stay here all alone or meet their happy faces here, and wretchedly I have no fear. A little while and I am gone. I'll have to go tomorrow. I'll go to the solicitors in London and see what I'm worth. Then I'll go to Spain. Phone Lopez. That kiss in Manette Street. Manette. A man and woman in one. That's me

The smell of something cookin.g caught his nostrils. Walking hesitantly through the gap in the berberis he headed into the shadow of the house and found himself outside the kitchen door. The door was protected from the north by a glazed porch in which dead pheasants hung from hooks. One had already dropped to the floor leaving its head still in the noose of string. A maggot crawled out of the carcass. The pungent smell of rotting guts got in the way of the cooking smell. I should stay out, thought Percy. I'm a guest, I'm not in charge, I have no right just to wander in. He went up the steps and through the doorway.

Inside, a team of about five or six men were preparing, cooking and washing up. He saw the curly-haired man, or at least the back of him. He was wearing an apron and scrubbing pans in the sink. He caught the smell of something rich, buttery and sweet. Sure enough two beautiful pastries with fluted edges sat cooling sweetly on the side. He remembered these from before the War. Where? Paris with his parents in when? '30? He'd joined them briefly when they were in talks with the Compagnie Internationale des Wagons Lits, hoping to get in on the act in Shanghai. At least they'd got him his ticket back via the Trans-Siberian if nothing else. They'd taken him to a restaurant? Where? Clos des Lilas? And there he'd seen and tasted it; Gateau Pithivier; that confection of pastry, almonds and apricots. Gorgeous. A young man brushed by him carrying a wooden bucket with a handle inserted in the top. Percy felt a rush of nostalgia through his heart. Only yesterday Lopez had scooped ice cream for him out of just such a bucket. The young man sat down on the step and started to churn.

A voice spoke to him; "You the replacement? Look at that shirt. What happened, someone roll you in the long grass? Get to the storeroom get yourself a clean shirt, tee shirt will do and get your apron on. You're with me. Terry!"

The man with the curly hair turned round, wiped his hands on his apron and came up to him. "So you is one of us after all? Took yer for a toff. That was a mean trick." He smiled. "You alright? Come with me."

Terry led him out of the kitchen down a corridor and through a cream-painted door into a room that functioned as sluice and linen-cupboard. "Better give me that shirt," he said. "You can have a wash in the mop-sink. Won't hurt. Blimey looks like that might."

Percy had taken off his shirt and was standing with his back to Terry. Terry's fingers went up to his shoulder-blades and pressed on the place where he'd fallen onto the trellis post.

"Just stop there a minute," said Terry. Running a clean cloth under the tap he gently sponged the place where the skin was broken. "There you are," he said, using the other end of the cloth, still dry, to pat the water away. "Now all you need is someone to kiss it better. Aprons there, tee shirt there, laundry bag there. See yer back inside." He walked out of the room.

Percy put on the tee shirt and donned his apron. This was strange. He felt ready, complete, or at least, somehow and for the first time in years, a work in progress.

A voice shouted from the kitchen "Get yerself in 'ere now!"

For the next three hours Percy skivvied as he'd never skivvied before. This was to be a running buffet for the guests and because most of them would be American, David had hired two American cooks for the evening from USAF Croughton, one for the side-dishes and one short-order, to work with the brought-in Head Chef whose training was French and who was sticking to his classic menu, including the Pithiviers, come what may. Percy was assigned to the Americans and to the cook in charge of salads and sauces. Here he would be handling ingredients he hadn't seen since Hong Kong pre-war, and all supplied, probably, by a sideways-looking PX. Percy scrubbed and cooked potatoes before boiling and skinning them hot, scorching his fingers, before he chopped them into regular cubes. Into a suspiciously white-looking mayonnaise from an enormous jar labelled Hellman's he mixed bright yellow French's mustard before chopping pickles from another vast jar and blending them into the mix followed by a dose of paprika. The cook had given him the kitchen's copy of *The Joy of Cooking* that he had open and laid flat on the counter ahead of him. Opening a giant tin of frankfurter sausages and draining them he chopped them up and mixed them in with the potatoes adding a pinch of salt. Into the fridge covered with a plate they went to be amalgamated with the mayonnaise dressing later when the potatoes had cooled. Next? He shredded cabbage and onion as fine as he could, cut carrots into the thinnest of batons, drenched them in the juice of lemons and mixed in yet more of the inexhaustible supply of white mayonnaise before adding celery salt and yet more paprika He chopped the crusts from slices of thick, white American bread, cut them into cubes before frying them in Mazola oil until they were crisp and brown.

"They's for the Caesar's," said Jimmy the cook. "We don't put no anchovies in our Caesar, no sir. We're pure Cardinis. See I'm from San Diego, my friend. Only Woostershire sauce."

"Thank you," said Percy.

Next to the fry-pan for the croutons was a small vat into which the cook tipped bottle after bottle of ketchup, bottle after bottle of Coca-Cola, powdered onion, powdered garlic, lemon juice, black pepper and streams of the "Woostershire sauce".

"This here's my Mom's barbecue sauce," he said. "Stanley's outside getting the barbecue ready. You ever seen a proper barbecue? Man, you're in for a treat. This one's gonna hum and ding together."

Percy played the same instruments to a different tune for his next creation, Thousand Island Dressing. Going back to the store-cupboard for yet more white mayonnaise he bumped into Terry.

"How yer doin'" mate? Like fuckin' Christmas round 'ere innit? Could feed me entire street on this lot for a week. Fancy a snout?"

"Have we got time?"

"Workers of the world unite," said Terry and winked. "Got your fancy cigs on yer?" Percy nodded. "Right, follow me."

With Jimmy the cook engaged and intent on preparing his sauce Terry disappeared out of the back door in the blink of an eye. Percy followed, narrowly avoiding slipping in rotted pheasant. Terry darted off to the enclosed pond garden and sat down on the stone bench. Percy trotted up and took from his pocket the box of Du Maurier, offered one to Terry and took one for himself. Terry produced a box of matches and Percy lent down toward the flame. As he glanced up he saw that Terry was looking at him. Their looks met, their eyes about a foot apart. Percy stood up, said thank you.

"Better siddown," said Terry, "or they'll see yer." Percy sat. "How you get in on this caper?" said Terry. "I ain't seen you on this gang before. You one of the Pinewood bunch?"

"Pinewood?"

"Yeah the Pinewood catering crew. You're not Korda are you?"

"No," said Percy. "Gainsborough."

"What's it like over there?" said Terry. "My mate Reg says the pay's lousy but with it being so hard for a demob to get a job you gotta take what yer can he says. No mistake, I says."

"What did you do in the war?"

"That yer best chat-up line?" said Terry. "No, honestly, I was catering corps, Life Guards. Palestine I saw; Egypt, Italy. I loved Italy."

"Yes?"

"The food, mate, the food. It wer like 'eaven if you was brought up on pies and sugar sandwiches like I was. Mind you the fighting were terrible. Thought the Jerries'd never let go, like Italy was theirs forever."

"What did you cook out there?"

"Well it were different weren't it? We had our own stuff comin' in and tons of stuff from the Yanks like what we got 'ere this evening but more Spam. And the locals were starvin' so we couldn't get much from them but it was the fruit, mate, the fruit. Everywhere you went was like the Garden at settin' up time. Peaches, the size of 'em. Apricots like 'oney they were. Huge great plums. Watermelons, 'adn't ever seen one of them before. Bunches of grapes and figs, blimey those figs. Me and me mate ate 'alf a ton of 'em one evening and next day we couldn't stand and we couldn't sit down neither; 'ad to keep running to the khazi. And the wine. Lots of wine got liberated I can tell yer. And your brandy and this stuff they called grappa. You can keep that grappa gives you a 'ead like a statcher. 'Ere, me rattlin' on; what did you do in the war then? What's your name?"

"Percy."

"Fancy. Me dad's called Percy. So, Perce, what you do in the war then and that is me best chat up line I don't waste on just anybody."

"I think we should be getting back in."

"I think you're right but tell you what you're going to tell me more later "cos it's always the quiet ones. Mrs Perce know you'll likely be out all night?"

"There isn't..." said Percy.

Terry winked and led the way back in.

"Had your fag, faggots?" said Jimmy.

Percy blushed. Terry glanced over from the washing-up station and winked. Percy washed his hands and went back to work mixing in a large bowl yet more so-called mayonnaise, tomato ketchup, yet more paprika, lemon juice, orange juice from a bottle, an unheard of luxury, woostershire sauce, Tabasco and cream. He beat it in bowl, vigorously.

"Use your forearm muscles," said Jimmy. "Shoulder muscles tire out."

Percy smiled and went back to his mixing.

"Next up," said Jimmy, "I wan' yer to make a cream-cheese frosting for the Angelfood. Look it up."

"Yes," said Percy. "Yes, chef."

Jimmy froze solid and Percy saw him gape toward the doorway. Almost everything in the room went quiet. There was just the sound of heels clicking on linoleum.

"Hello, boys," said a rich, velvet voice, "how's it all going? Percy?" A laugh. "What on earth are you doing here? Playing cookie? Come on, it's six o'clock and I've been looking for you everywhere. Come on, David wants you."

Terry looked at him. Percy finally lifted his head up from the cookbook and turned around. There she was, Laetitia West in her finest incarnation, dressed in full New Look, pink and purple like an exotic flower, a bougainvillea, or a double-hued fuchsia. She smelt wonderful. Joy? Yes, probably. She might as well have been naked and robed simply in the 10,000 jasmine flowers and 26,000 roses it took to make one bottle of Jean Patou's creation. The scent vanquished even the odours of cloying mayonnaise and bubbling barbecue sauce. Jimmy was pop-eyed. Everyone was silent.

"Thank you, boys," she said. "You're doing such a marvellous job. Listen, why don't you take a break? If you look in the other fridge you'll find some cold beers. Buds? Is that what you say? See you later!" And like the sun she smiled on all alike. "Come on Percy," she said. "David's waiting." And she turned around and left the room.

"What a broad," said Jimmy and looked at Percy. "You know her?" Percy nodded. "She in the movies?"

"Soon."

"What's she to you?"

"My aunt," said Percy.

Terry sniggered.

"You," said Jimmy to Terry, "get over here and take over the frosting. You," he turned to Percy, "one more thing before you skip off to Auntie. Clear up that mess on the back stoop. Now." Percy hesitated. "I said now, you limey faggot or you leave here minus your dick. Comprende? You make a fool of Jimmy Jericho pretending you're in his brigade and you pay for it. Now get shovelling pheasant stew."

"Thank you," said Percy, "Did I do okay?"

Jimmy looked fit to explode then with a visible muscular effort calmed down. "Okay faggot, you did okay, whoever you are you could make a kitchen porter. But not on my team. Now get lost."

Percy went off to the sluice and got a dustpan, mop and filled the pail with water and Clorox. Going out of the back door he slid the decayed pheasant corpse from the floor into the dustpan and took it round to the bin where he tipped it in. Back in the porch he grabbed one carcass after another, the flesh disintegrating and in some cases just sliding off the skeleton like a glove from a hand. If he pressed at all then guts, yellow, magenta and brown slid down to the floor preceded by a gobbet of white maggots. Feathers, feet and pulp were pretty much all that was left of the birds. Each pile he scooped into the dustpan before taking its contents to the bin. Then he used his mop to wipe clean the floor. He was just about to leave when, looking round, he saw six pairs of hooded eyes, six beaks on six heads hanging from nooses of string like the chorus from an absurd and cruel children's rhyme. He unlooped each and disposed of them, too. As he got back to the sluice-room he heard someone come in behind him. Terry.

"So what are you mate, toff or not?"

"I'm not a toff," said Percy. "I've worked in kitchens before."

"But not Gainsborough."

"No."

"So who are you then? Where you work? I dunno why I bother to ask, tell you the truth. You spun me a line, mate, that's what you did."

"Look don't raise your voice. We'll have Popeye in here."

"You've gone and rubbed his whiffle up the wrong way and no mistake. You bugger off with the Belle of the Ball and old Cinders here's gonna cop it in your place. I could swing fer you, mate, right now I could."

"I'm sorry," said Percy. "It's hard to explain."

"Tell yer what," said Terry, "I'm gonna give you the chance to do just that. Ten o'clock, do you hear me? You meet me on that bench where we had a gasper at ten o'clock and you tell me all about it. "

"But why?"

Terry stepped close enough for their bodies to touch. "'Cos I wanna know what you did in the war, mate," he said then turned and went out.

Percy went up the corridor into the other world. He looked around for Laetitia. Scent and cigarette smoke floated down from the landing above. He turned and walked up. As he got there Laetitia was sitting on the wide, cushioned window seat. She patted the cherry-coloured fabric. "Do sit down," she said in her stage voice. Percy hesitated. "I said, siddown," said Flo. Percy sat.

"Where's David?"

"Denham."

"I thought you said?"

"Listen Perce I got a message for yer. From the man hisself. He says in case he don't get a chance this evening you're to make yerself known is what he says to Gaston le Frog."

"Who?"

"Oh I can't remember. Some French geezer with a French name. He says there won't be any other Frogs at the party so you'll be able to spot him easy."

"And then?"

"Then you talks to him."

"About what?"

"About the rest of your life mate."

Percy was silent, trying to work this out.

"Poor little Perce. All confused. Look I'm not supposed to tell yer but David's only gone and fixed yer up with a job. In France."

"France?"

"Yes Perce. French man with French name offer you job in France. That's the plan."

"So this man has a hotel?"

"You cotton on quick, don't yer. Honest, Perce, you're like one of them Nazi interrogators you're gonna draw this out of me slow like. All I know is this man gotta hotel, tres posh one, somewhere in France and he wants a new manager, one what speaks pukkah English on account of he's expecting the English back and the Yanks. Oh sorry, Perce, I don't mean to be mean to yer only if you wanna know the truth I don't want yer to go. We've only known each other a day but I likes yer Perce. I really do. 'Ere, we got a few minutes. Tell me a few things."

"What things?" "Well I know you've known David ages and ages. Are you in love with him?" Percy was silent. "Tough question? Ciggie help?"

Laetitia reached out and picked up a silver box from a low rosewood Oriental table. The open humidor revealed a wooden lining and two trays packed with filter-tipped cigarettes. Laetitia offered the box to Percy and then took one herself. Putting the box back on the table she then lifted a heavy, oval silver table lighter in the shape of a classical urn and flicked on the flame. She held it to Percy's cigarette. "Come on mate," she said. "This thing weighs a ton." They both drew and looked at each other.

Laetitia saw a man a little below medium height, hair prematurely grey, with an open face and wearing gold-framed spectacles. He was wearing cotton trousers, a food-stained tee shirt and canvas shoes. Good-looking? No. Nice, yes. Something from inside.

Percy saw a beautiful woman, perfectly dressed, hair in a chignon above a long but perfectly proportioned face, perfectly made up. He gazed.

"Tell me about *The Dancing Years*," he said.

"No good changing the subject, Perce. That's me job. I like it. I'm good at it. I wanna get into films, into musicals, there's a load of 'em comin' up and I gotta fair chance with a bit of 'elp from David. End of story. Now back to you my little chickadee. Are you in love with him?"

"I don't know."

"Whaddya mean you don't know? Being in love's one of them things you know about when it happens like a bomb goin' off. So kaboom or not kaboom: that is the question."

"It isn't like that."

"But you like men don't you. 'Ere, Perce," putting out her cigarette in a huge glass ashtray she then placed her hand over his. "There's no one around. They're all in the kitchen or 'avin a zizz. You needs a bit of sorting out, you do. You're like one of them waifs and strays me Mum were always on about. Bit lost, ain't yer Perce." She patted the back of his hand and then sat up straight. "Talk to Flo. You might not get another chance."

Percy put his own cigarette out. "I don't want to get married," he said.

"I ain't asked yer," said Laetitia. "But if you were worth a million I might."

"My Mother and Father wanted me to. They were always going on about it."

"But they shoved you years on end into a boarding school with a whole load of randy missionaries and no doors on the bogs and they thought you'd come out normal?"

"It wasn't really like that. The school in England was worse."

"Was David there too, at the school in England?"

"No, he was at Eton. I'm a Dellingpoleian."

"I'm sure you are, Perce, but what's that when it's at home?"

"Dellingpool School. It's in Dorset. I was there from sixteen till eighteen."

"Sounds like you really loved it."

Percy smiled. "Are you sure there's no Gipsy in you?"

"You mean like read your mind and see your fate? Well as it 'appens I 'ave got a bit of second sight."

"So can you read my palm?"

"It ain't like that, Perce, it ain't a performance. Take your specs off." Percy obeyed. "My, Percy, what lovely eyes you've got. Close them up." Laetitia brushed her hand all over Percy's face softly and gently and leaning forward enveloped him in Joy. She took her hand away and leant back. Percy opened his eyes and put back on his spectacles. They looked at each other, eyebeams entwined. "Well I'm sorry to tell yer Perce," she paused, "yer gonna have a long and 'appy life but yer happiness don't start yet. Whatever's messed yer up it's not going to vamoose just like that. 'Nother couple of years."

"Am I going to find love?"

"When you know what it is, you will."

"Can you look at your own life?"

I've tried but I can't see nothing. Now," she said, "Percy. If I said to you we got an hour or two till the guests arrive let's go up to that room of yours and have a shag what would you say?"

"Well," said Perce. "Thank you."

Laetitia began to laugh; great peals of merriment resounded through Joyous Gard. Finally she stopped. "I ain't laughin' at yer Perce honest I'm not. Well maybe I am. Listen, Perce, I'm no Betty Grable but I know that most men would have either tried to 'ave their way with me already by now with us being alone up here.. As it 'appens I ain't that kind of girl. I do what I gotta do but no more. But I ain't ever been with any man who said thank you!" Here she began to laugh again until her mascara began to run at the corners of her eyes. "Now look what you made me do! I'm gonna have ter do me slap all over again!"

"I'm sorry," said Percy. "Don't be," said Laetitia, "I ain't had a laugh like that in years."

"I just want to," he hesitated, "I just want to treat you with respect."

"Is that what you calls it Perce?" said Laetitia, the backs of her hands dabbing at the corners of her eyes to dam the flood of tears and mascara. "'Ere, give me half a minute." Gradually she dabbed her eyes dry, took a deep breath in and sat bolt upright. "Thing is Perce respect is nice like a bunch of flowers but it ain't much good in the bedroom, know what I mean? 'Ere, are you a virgin?"

Percy blushed a deep red. "No," he said.

"I mean with a woman not with a man."

"No," said Percy, "Neither."

"So, didn't yer like it with a woman? Did you finish off?"

"I don't know. And yes."

"So it's all working down there? Well that's something? So what didn't yer like?"

"I," said Percy, "it didn't feel right."

"Well it is," said Laetitia, "They don't call it doin' what comes naturally for nothing."

"It wasn't doing it," said Percy. "It was doing it to a woman."

"So yer just don't go in for clits and flaps and minge and all that kind of stuff. Puts yer off does it?"

"It isn't that," said Percy. "It just didn't feel," he paused, looked out of the window, looked back, "Equal." "

"What if she'd gone off her rocker and shouted give me more Perce give me more? What if she'd gone round on top would that 'ave made it equal?"

Percy began to sweat a little. "No I don't think so. Maybe at the time, not afterwards."

"I broke her heart, pet, after the ball?"

"Something like that. I just don't think. I just don't want."

"Love?"

"No, no I do want love. I just don't want."

"Children?"

"Well, I wouldn't send them away to school."

"You're no Tin Man, Perce, I know you gotta 'eart. Trouble is I think it's too soft. I think you thinks you gotta be responsible for women, gotta take care of 'em, always be 'olding doors open for 'em. I think your ideal woman's Queen Victoria. You know what Perce? I blame your parents, honest I do. Well," she held up a hand to fend off a protest, "If it wasn't them it was someone else what done it to yer. Put yer off women for life."

"I don't think so," said Perce. "I had my first crush on a boy when I was, oh, eight or nine. I think I've always known."

Laetitia was silent. "What about David, then. He does it with women."

"I'm sure he does. I don't think there's just one kind of queer."

"You're saying David's queer?"

"Well."

"It's all right ducks, I know he swings both ways and I know it's complicated. One day in the future we'll just be able to be who we are but everyone's different, I know that. 'Ere, talk about Nazi interrogators!" They both fell silent. "He loves yer, you know. Not like that well maybe it is like that sure you'll find out one day but he loves yer. He does."

"Will you and he ever?"

"Fuck? Only we already done that as I'm sure you've worked out. You ain't as green as you're cabbage-looking."

"No, I meant get married."

"If he asked me."

"I think he loves you."

"Well, isn't this a fine fol-de-rol. You can have Monday to Thursday and I get Friday and the weekends?"

"I'm going, though, going to France."

"He ain't trying to get you out of the way or nothing. He thinks it's best for you. You'll see him again, you mark my words."

"With you as Lady Maldon?"

"It has a certain ring to it, don't it. The ring of utter bollocks. Nah, why would I want to marry 'im? I'm just using him for me career ain't I. I'm a man-eater, me. I chews them up and spits them out."

"You're no Tin Woman."

"Oh I did 'ave a 'eart, Perce only I had it surgically removed along with me tonsils. Come on then, we better get goin' since he's left us in charge. Enjoy your skivvying did yer?"

"As a matter of fact, yes."

"In that case can you be maître d' tonight?"

Percy stared, taken aback.

Laetitia said "I ain't just trying to make use of yer and you are my friend. It's just that it's gonna be boring for you listenin' to all these hot shots bangin' on about themselves and me and David just smilin' and makin' up to them. It ain't pretty. Some of 'em like blokes and you'll get a pass or two but I know you, you're a professional, you'll deal with them alright. An' it might get a bit rowdy and we gotta have someone in charge so it don't all go tits up. Will you do it for me Percy. For us?"

"Yes," said Percy.

"God love yer," said Laetitia who leant over, hugged him and kissed him on the forehead. "You're a pal." She went up two steps and turned back. "Oh, by the way," she said, "he told me to tell you dear duffer don't drown. Toodle-ooh!" She went upstairs and out of sight.

Laetitia ran upstairs to her bedroom. Percy followed more slowly on the way to his. He took off his shoes and lay down on the bed. Light filtered into the room through the golden leaves of the horse-chestnut tree outside. Why, he asked himself, why did I talk to Laetitia about myself? Talking about oneself just isn't on. Nothing's clear. It's all just a great mess. Some things feel true one day and a whole pack of lies another day. He felt in his pockets for the pack of Du Maurier. Terry? Terry did he say his name was? Look how I'm getting to know my way around this maze.

For almost six years I didn't even think about sex despite the Mars bars and the pilchards to oil the mechanisms after we got out. Why now?

There may have been opportunities back at the Sherborne. There was that man on the boat back Home. Williams? He was very friendly. Perhaps he wanted more. Gave me his address, perhaps I should have gone and looked him up. No, sorry, I just didn't feel like it. And then comes this Great Awakening. In just two days I've found a boyfriend, gone out to a queer pub, kissed a man in a dark alley, lost the boyfriend and then bumped straight into. Into David. What is David to you? Percy tapped a cigarette out of the box, got up, went over to the window to light and smoke it. He's your family, isn't he? Father, mother, brother and sister. All mixed up. Like me. All mixed up as they say in the movies. He blew smoke out between the bars. The gold bar of Heaven. She wept; I heard her tears. Always made me think of a barmaid having a bad day. You could be a teacher. Go to the University, you could get in, read English Literature then go and teach. Where? Some dusty provincial private school with ghastly, superior boys like Dellingpool. And your fellow teachers, all of them wounded in places you can't see. Wounded in the mind. Fighting the Battle of the Blackboard, perfecting the forehead-shot with tiny pieces of chalk. And holidays. Where would I go? I'd have to stay on. That would be circular. Could I be trusted not to take advantage of the boys? Even the older ones? Yes, I think so. I think a certain incident will have made sure of that. Even if I wanted to I just don't think I could. I don't think I could help perpetuate that. That sort of thing. That sort of thing. That sort of chap. The queer sort. A school would probably only take me if I were married. Could be a perpetual engagement of course. But the poor girl. Or maybe not so poor. Perhaps Laetitia was right, perhaps it might suit her. There must be as many kinds of girl as there are kinds of men. But who am I? Let's take a look at myself. The Tin Man. The perpetual openerof-doors. After you. But never crossing the threshold. The Knight Errant. Sir Percival. Now put your armour on, wrestle and fight and pray. Tread all the pow'rs of darkness down and win the well-fought day. There's a thought. Go and be a missionary. You'd be a natural. Childe Roland. The dark tower doesn't exist. He was sick in the head from riding about in armour all day long in the hot sun and baking his brains. It's all rather sexual isn't it, the two low hills and the squat tower. Was Browning queer? Oh Percy, you dunce. It was women, women's appurtenances he was afraid of. It was the thought of getting his lance ready for it that was really troubling him, riding off into that mounded gully, that horror of self-obliteration, that death-in-life that Shakespeare and his chums were always on about. And you have the same problem, don't you? Afraid to sully your shining armour and your flaming greaves. Afraid that having sex with a woman will disqualify you from attaining the grail. Disqualified, Langrigg. Go back to the changing rooms and await your punishment. One of them had tried, hadn't they? He'd forgotten about that. What was that boy's name, waiting for me, naked in the showers. And when I wouldn't do it he'd threatened to get me expelled. Said he'd say I'd tried it on with him. Maybe I should have just done it. He'd been really lovely down there. Wonder what Lopez was like. Down there. Wonder what Terry's like? Come on Percy, the expense of spirit and all that. Even if it were legal. I know what David's like. That practically did it for me on the intimacy front. When you've seen them covered in shit, wiped them down, wrapped them back up in their loincloths. When you've a shower-block full of walking skeletons. That made our things look bigger, you know. When the rest was so thin.

The rapes. And the bayonetting. Right at the beginning. Death by penis or death by bayonet, care to make a choice? Scabbard. Vagina. Just putting my bayonet away. It happened right there, you know. St Stephen's. Violence. That's what I think. Sex is violence. Yet they say she asked for it. Did she really? Let's play bayonet and sheath. I know men do it the same I saw it at school, not Yantai, Dollingpole. I saw the games master and that boy, Griffiths? doing it in the gym office when they thought the place was empty.

To nouns that cannot be declined the neuter gender is assigned. Examples fas and nefas give and the verb-noun infinitive. Est summum nefas fallere. Deceit is gross impiety. Vix vivunt mutandi luandi. They eke out a miserable existence by taking in one another"'s washing. Neuter.

The cigarette had long burnt down to the stub. Percy put it in the ashtray and went back to lean on the windowsill and looked out onto the garden of rooms. Gold Wings. Oh Lord, is it me? I thought it was Laetitia. Midways of a walled garden. Percy the Passionate. So you want to be a girl? No I don't. So what do you want to be? Something in between? Do I have a choice any more than what was her name? Jehane. Outside the wall is red. And the love-crazed knight kisses the long, wet grass. So here we are. The Dark Tower and Ladies' Gard all rolled into one. Tall Jehane du Castel Beau. You're Percy and you're what they call medium height. And I have hope. He could not come, but I can go to him. Go to whom? Go to the devil.

Think for yourself. I can't. I can only think in other people's lines. Runes, it's like casting runes. Auspices and Haruspices. What's my line? Who knows? No one knows. Clotho and Lachesis. You don't find out until it's cut. Once the vision that delighted. No answer in the cold grey dawn. Cold. Don't be a cold Cape Cod Clam. Even educated fleas do it. What did Lord Sheere say to you last night? Not much but he was very ardent. He will propose marriage. He seemed last night to wish for something a little less binding. When may I love somebody, please? Don't be silly. Emotion is so very untidy. No matter what price is paid, what stars may fade. Crickle, crackle, Frances Greer. Yvonne Printemps. Printemps. My heart in hiding. The foul rag and bone shop. AND the fire that breaks from thee then. Come on Percy, be a dragonfly and draw flame. We all go up like candles in the end. As the sparks fly upward. And when a lovely flame dies. The worst you can expect is a bit of smoke in the eye. Time for a wash. Time to let yourself love. No more rusting flowerpots. America is here or nowhere. Forth in Thy name O Lord I go. Percy stripped off his tee shirt and headed to the bathroom.

It was now nine o'clock and the party was, as the Americans say, getting started. David was there looking superbly elegant in a Savile Row suit as understated as the Hawaiian shirts around the room were not. True to her word Laetitia had got Percy into one of these, loud and brash. Percy found he rather liked it. "Gives you a bit of colour," she'd said. Percy was spending some time behind the bar dishing out the less complicated drinks. For the cocktails David had got a couple of professionals down from London. The rest of his time was spent watching the rooms making sure that glasses were full, that ashtrays were emptied, that tables were cleared, that the food was kept topped up. In came the food in wave after wave and Percy saw his own concoctions among them. He'd enjoyed that time in the kitchen. David had just wanted a cocktail party. It was Laetitia who'd persuaded him that offering up food would extend business hours. Guests came in, went out to the barbecue around the side of the house, walked up and down the long lawn to the riverside. A vocalist sang mostly Sinatra numbers at a piano in the hall. David had wanted a swing band but had again been overruled by Laetitia not only because the house was simply too small but also because, she said, "that stuff is over." Car after car rolled up into the little drive, let out their precious cargoes and went off to park or come back later. "The neighbours are going to be onto us," said David. Many of the guests were American and Percy even heard the words "swell party." It was swell. David had managed to fill the rooms with a heady mix of producers, scriptwriters, talent-scouts, one or two directors and even a couple of American B-listers. Rosegarden Studios had brought out practically all its team, its starlets and some home-grown big names. David had arranged a photographer to record the event for tomorrow's newspapers and the monthly magazines. At stake was a Rosegarden/American co-production of a musical. Talk had it that the studio planned to film The Dancing Years and the chatter in the rooms was talking it up.

The noise levels went up and up, laughter became louder, more square feet of carpet were ruined by smouldering cigarette butts and smoke got in everyone's eyes. Beautiful girls leaned on the arms of big men with cigars. One or two beautiful men held court. Out by the barbecue stood a heavy-set man wearing a loud shirt and a white Stetson hat. In the gilded lobby by the front door a party-within-a-party had started for the younger local talent. Laetitia steered people round the room straight up to other people, talked for a few minutes to each and then left them to hunt for more power to connect to even greater power to brighten the room still further. She was gorgeous. Her Titian-red hair jarred so slightly with the colour of her dress that it made her even more watchable. David's tall figure stayed in a small group of people most of the evening.

"Hello," said an American man's voice.

A West Coast voice? Percy couldn't be sure.

"My name's Perry Portree. With whom am I speaking?"

"Langrigg," said Percy, "Percy Langrigg."

"Oh my goodness, so British to put your second name first! You know, Niven David, Coward Noel, Shakespeare William oh but did they have your public schools back in that time? Isn't that where they teach you to put your tribe before your itty-bitty self. You know, Atahualpa Bernard, Khan Ghengis? Do you have a cigarette? I seem to have run out."

Percy pulled out the almost-empty pack of du Maurier and offered one to the American. Why didn't he help himself from any one of the silver boxes of them dotted around the rooms?"

"You gotta light?"

Percy took out a box of matches, struck and held out the flame. The American pulled Percy's wrist in toward his face, close, in a Lopez moment of intimacy.

"So which side are you?" said Perry, "bride or groom?

"They're gonna make a swell couple don't you think?"

"Who?" said Percy.

"Oh my, I like a gruff little bear. Why Miss Laetitia Rosegarden actress and Mr Levy La Brea Wolff studios of course. The English Rose and the cinematic Semitics. Have you heard the one about the studio where they had to stop saying Cut because..." he trailed off and touched Percy lightly on the sleeve. "I think something is about to get lost in translation, don't you? Listen, why don't you show me around the grounds. Is there a deer park? I've always imagined a kind of drive-in with antlers where they censor the death of Bambi's mother. Plus it's getting kinda stuffy in here and I'm personally not a Sinatra fan. Too cocky for my taste. Why don't we take a little walk? What do you guys say? Constitutional. Constitooshonal. Let's go and constitute something, whaddya say?" Portree took Percy's arm and marched him through the hall toward the open front door past "It Had to be You" and the English in the lobby, the girls hanging on to the every word of a well-known, ruggedly handsome American actor.

"What you looking at?" said Perry. "Oh him. They won't get far with him I'm gonna tell you. That one ain't for the birds."

They went out into the flower-scented night, weaving through the cars on the red-tarmacked drive to reach the path that followed the East side of the garden down to the boat house.

"Why this is nice," said Perry. "So, tell me something about yourself I haven't already guessed. You're on the staff but you're actually, isn't that British; "actually", you're really in a menage a trois with the divine Miss West boy can she work a room and the sexy English Lord. He's the brains, she's the bait and you're the, what are you, what's the word? Retainer. You're the retainer. Oh my that sounds like I'm saying you're anally retentive or something. That's just what my analyst said; Perry you're all compacted, you gotta let it all come out. Oh I can do grosser than that, believe me. So how did I work this out? It's the way you three look at each other like you're British Secret Service and you're infiltrating us. Tell you what, you can be infiltrator and I can be infiltratee. Would that work for you? Got another cigarette?"

Perry had abruptly left the path through a gap in the laurel hedge and stepped into the gardener's area, an enclosure that contained a greenhouse, incinerator, tool-shed and a pen of lawn mulchings. It was dark except where the river reflected the moon and the party lights along the walkway. Percy reached for the box of cigarettes. There were two left. He offered one to Perry and was about to take the last one for himself when Perry reached out and grabbed it.

"Oh no," said Perry. "We'll share this one. Put that one back in the holster. We'll need it for after."

Percy leant forward with a lit match and Perry, leaning in, shot out his other hand and grabbed Percy's crotch, hard. Leaving his hand there he took a drag of the cigarette then brought his mouth to Percy's. Percy opened his lips and felt Perry's move onto them. Perry breathed out and the smoke went into Percy's mouth and nostrils. They broke apart, both breathing smoke. "There," said Perry, "we're sharing. That's cute. So tell me about yourself. You worked for them long? I admire them, they're verrrry professional. Gonna go a long way. If the price is right. The scouts have spotted Deborah Kerr and Stewart Grainger but it'd be a pip to have an English Lord instead."

"But he isn't an actor."

"Okay you win, same difference. Golden couple." Perry's hand was massaging Percy's penis, stiffening it. "That's better," said Perry, "we got you flying the flag."

Handing the cigarette back to Percy he slid his hands around Percy's waistband looking for the buttons. Skilfully he popped the top one open then followed downward opening the rest until he could pull Percy's trousers knee-ward. Squatting down he began to coax Percy's penis out of hiding and into his mouth, licking around the bell end. Percy gasped. Perry began to rock back and forward on the balls of his feet, taking Percy's cock into his mouth right down to base then out, then in. Percy went to put his hand around the back of Perry's head but Perry brushed it away. Then he went back to work. Percy exploded into the back of Perry's mouth once, twice. His knees began to wobble.

Perry came to standing. "Mmmm," he said, "want some Benny?" Percy was pulling up his trousers and fiddling with the buttons.

"Benny?"

"Benzedrine, speed, benny. Have you dancing till dawn." Perry pulled an elegant little case from his pocket. "Go on. You know you want to."

Percy took the pill and swallowed it.

"What you doing after the party? Don't tell me you're all going into the closet to compare notes. Come back with me to the hotel. I can show you the rest of my portfolio. No? Silent Sam? Never mind honey, see you in Hollywood. Hasta la vista, baby." He came close to Percy, put his hands around Percy's neck and planted on him a strong, deep kiss that all but sucked the air out of Percy's lungs. Then he turned and walked away.

No sound but the rhythmic slapping of the water against the boarding of the boat-house berth. Was that what they call intimacy, thought Percy. Or an encounter? He turned and set off back up the path. The lawn now damp with dew changed from blue to yellow as he walked from night to light. The Frenchman, he thought. I haven't found the bloody Frenchman. As he stepped back into the party he found himself face to face with Terry. "'Ere where you been mate? They had to bring me in 'ere 'cos you went AWOL."

"It was five minutes."

"Quarter of a bleedin' hour more like. It's quarter to ten. 'Ope you ain't forgotten."

"I haven't," said Percy. "Have you seen a Frenchman?"

"I dunno. What's a Frenchman look like?"

"Someone speaking French."

"Oh you mean Maurice Chevalier? He's over there."

Percy headed off toward a group standing in the bay of the dining room's great window and drew up next to the man Terry had pointed out. "Excuse me," he said, "I'm Percy Langrigg."

The man, a little shorter even than Percy, turned toward him. His head was bald at the crown but the hair on either side had been carefully combed over and brilliantined into place. Above a small mouth, tightly clipped moustache, and long nose shone dark eyes full of humour.

"Eh bien?"

"David, Lord David suggested I come and talk to you. About employment."

"Ah mais oui," answered the man turning back to his companions with a smile and a flap of the hand, "Desolé," he said to them "I must talk shop for a moment, please excuse me," and he made a little bow before putting his arm around Percy's shoulders and drawing him away out of the room. "So you are Percy Lanreeg," he said. "Where can we talk? Houp, quelle foule. Au dehors. We go outside."

Unhitching his arm from Percy's shoulders he led down the front steps and then right, around the back of the house, into the darkened garden. They came to the pond garden. The Frenchman sat down on the stone bench.

"A swell party," he said to Percy who sat next to him. "Why I am here I do not know. Perhaps Milor wanted to bring a touch of Paris to his party, hein? The Americans they are falling in love with Paris again. Soon the studios will follow. When Paris has been made safe for les cinéphiles Américains. Quand la tache nazie a été nettoyée. Vouz fumez?" The man brought out an elegant silver case filled with oval cigarettes. "Turques," he said, "les meilleures." Percy took, the Frenchman lit. "Ah je m'excuse. My name is Dinant, Gilbert Dinant. It is a pleasure to meet you." He took Percy's hand and shook it. "David tells me your family has also been in the business of hotels, this is true?"

"Yes, my mother inherited some hotels in America. They lost it all in the war."

"Et l'enterprise Américain a été vendu? Dommage. Vos parents, mort dans la guerre?"

"Yes."

"Dommage, quel bordel stupide, la guerre. Et maintenant, l'existentialisme. Chacun pour soi, c'est la nouvelle vérité. But we are not at Les Deux Magots. We are here to discuss your employment. David tells me you are an excellent directeur. You work in Shanghai, Hong Kong?"

"Yes I worked at my family's hotel, the Atholl Palace from '30 to '37. I went to Hong Kong in the Emergency, got a job at the Repulse and stayed there."

"Un bel hotel par tous les comptes. And now you work for Miss Beaumont? At the Beaumont?"

"No, at the Sherborne."

"Ah, le cadet. This is an old-fashioned place I think? Un peu démodé?"

"Yes, very."

"And you must work? You are a rich man I think from the sale of l'enterprise familiale. For you this work is a game, ce n'est q'un jeu." He took a puff from the cigarette, blew the smoke to one side and looked Percy directly in the eye.

"My mother had borrowed a great deal of money from banks in Boston. To finance her drive into China. The sale paid the debts off. No more. I work because I need to."

"And how do you like this England? Froid et humide? You want to go back to Hong Kong perhaps?"

"Perhaps I should. They say if you fall off a bicycle you should get straight back onto it. Otherwise..."

"Sinon vous en aurez peur."

"That's right."

"Mais ce n'était pas un accident de velo. C'était une guerre mondiale"

"That's right."

But you do not like London? Mais je ne vous en veux pas. C'est une ville de cauchemar. Les Britanniques sont en faillite. Il n'y a pas beaucoup d'espoir, pas de plaisir."

"The old girl will come back."

"Esperons. And David he told you I have a hotel."

"Yes."

"It is strange that un hotelier is at a party for le monde du cinema?"

You do not ask why? This is good. We will get along. Très professionel. On va bien s'entendre."

"Where is the hotel?" "

"You know the Midi?"

"The South of France."

"Yes, almost, presque le Midi. On l'appelle Midi moins le quart. Vous connaissez le pays du Dordogne."

"The Hundred Years War."

Gilbert looked at him. "Quelle drole de réponse but yes, it was the place. Now it is très touristique. It will be très touristique. Les meilleurs touristes. Les Anglais riches. Les Américains. My hotel is outside Sarlat. Sarlat-la-Canéda. Hotel Mirabelle. Je l'appelle Menton-sur-Dordogne. It is bijou, exquis, most elegant. Its restaurant is the finest in the Dordogne. L'Epergene d'Or. But it is something lacking, mon hotel. I have stayed at Savoy, Clareege, it is familiar, it is like the homes of the Milors Anglais, the country houses. I want my hotel to be like the English country house. Faut qu'il fonctionne comme une machine exquise."

"Don't you want a Swiss?"

"I want the friend of an English Milor."

"You want David to bring his friends there."

"But of course. The milors, their maîtresses, the film stars."

"But you can't compete with the Riviera."

"I do not compete. I excel. My hotel is for les touristes culturels. It is not big. It is not Georges Cinq or La Negresco. You will see."

"Did you offer me the job?"

"Bien sur Monsieur Langreeg. Now. One must travel by car from Paris. I see you at my office in Paris in, alors, two days. We drive together into ce pays inconnu. In Paris you stay at this hotel. I have written down on my card. A l'envers. You will see." Gilbert, M. Dinant, handed Percy his card. "In Paris we find you clothes. You bring nothing. Jettez cette chemise danse le bac s'il vous plaît." He stood. "A bientôt, Percé."

Percy stood and merely nodded. He could find nothing to say. Gilbert walked off back to the party. This was the dream come true. Or was he just a rat leaving a sinking ship? He felt wild, wired-up, he wanted to run, to shout, to tell someone the news. It was the benny, surely. He started to run on the spot, faster and faster, knees almost up to his chest, arms pumping up and down.

"'Ere, wass goin' on?" It was ten. It was Terry. Percy stopped his running abruptly. "You gettin' ready for the Olympics? You still got a year, mate. Don't bust a gut yet. You two getting' on well was yer? Bit of slap and tickle was it? I'm gonna slap you my son for walking out and leavin' Terry to take over. You been a naughty boy."

It must be the drug. Percy felt as though he was caught up in a revolving door. Scenes shooting by like anonymous stations seen from a speeding express. What else did this night have to offer? Had he stepped out of Athens into the magic forest? Lord what fools these mortals be. Terry was moving off out of the pond garden toward a gap in the hedge and into the horse-chestnut walk. Percy pushed past him and set off toward the top of the wall furthest away from the house.

"'Ang on mate," said Terry. "Something got the wind up yer?"

It had. Percy, his hearing must be extra-sensitised, had heard a woman's voice. A woman approaching the little round pond. A woman with a man. Laetitia and a man. Not David. He hurried off up the line of trees like a ghost seeking familiar darkness. The sound of the voice faded.

Terry came up. "Well mate," he said.

They mustn't speak. Percy reached his hand around the back of Terry's head, his thin curly hair, to the nape of his neck and pulled his mouth forward and his face so close that his spectacles were squashed into him and the metal frames embedded themselves into his cheeks. He pushed Terry's face away, reached up and took the spectacles off then shoved them haphazardly into his pocket. Then he grabbed Terry's head again and pressed their mouths together. Terry started to mumble and pulled away a little.

"Blimey Sergeant Major," he said, "you can kiss me goodnight any old time"

"No!" yelled a voice just ten yards away. "I said no!"

The first Laetitia, the second Flo.

Percy turned to ice. Terry stared at him, the fear of discovery in his eyes. They looked at each other for one second with full understanding before Terry disappeared back down the line of trees toward the house. Percy turned and ran toward the sound. Rushing through the gap in the hedge he saw Laetitia being bent over the stone bench her head held down and the berberis thorns catching in her chignon, teasing it apart. Her beautiful dress was pushed up toward her back and moonlight caught on white flesh between the top of her stockings and her knickers in the moonlight. Her arms were flailing but the hand that held her down had pound upon pound of bone, flesh and fat behind it. Suddenly David was there drawn by a psychic tremor from the garden or just coming to check up on Laetitia, have a chat with the American. Who knew? David stood stock still for an instant. The man let go his hold on Laetitia's neck. Laetitia kicked out a heel fast and strong and the man staggered back. The man tottered, the three stood stock still until Laetitia turned round on the bench and coming to a stand gave the aggressor a shove in the stomach. Like a child's toy he began to rock forward, backward, forward, backward, arms going round like the sails of a windmill as he tried to maintain his balance. Percy stepped forward into the garden room.

The big man gave a kind of squeal of surprise and tipped over backward. There was a splash. The water rushed up in waves to the lip of the pond and over it. Rush, retreat. Rush, retreat. Diminuendo. Silence.

"Shit," said David. The American had disappeared under the water. "Get in," said David and Percy jumped into the water fumbling along until he found the man's head.

"I can't," said Percy trying to lift the heavy head above the water. David moved around to the other side of the pond and half walked upon half waded through the bulrushes until he was on the opposite side of the body. They looked at each other. David nodded and they both reached down under the man's head and began to lift. The water was what? Two feet deep? They brought the man up to sitting.

"Hold him there," said David. "We need help." Clambering up to the edge of the pond he struggled for a short moment in the thick mud around the bulrushes before he managed to heave himself out and onto all fours. Standing, he began to stagger then run down the walkway and toward the house.

Laetitia was back sitting on the bench, head between knees, retching.

Percy went over and shook her shoulder. "Get up," he said. "I'm sorry, get up."

Laetitia looked up at him. Their eyes met. She stood, swayed a little. "Shit," she said. "Shit." She turned round to look at the stone bench behind her. "Not much of a casting couch. Is it Perce?" And she began to sob.

"Go to the garage," said Percy. "Wait there." Laetitia began to cry. "Now, please, now," said Percy.

Laetitia turned and ran into the dark, leftward toward the garage.

The sequence of events that followed he was to hear from David later. It seemed that no one had heard the noise or the splash and that no one could say with certainty that if David hadn't been with them that he wasn't with someone else at the time. Gilbert claimed to have been talking shop to David in the patch of darkness between the kitchen porch and the tulip tree ascending the house wall. Some butts of the cigarettes that only he smoked were on the ground. The music was loud here. Loud enough to conceal sounds that were already wrapped in thick summer foliage. Terry was nowhere to be found. He'd disappeared. The other staff were annoyed he'd "done a runner" but said nothing about him to the Police. Terry was a good lad. He'd probably got a date somewhere. Little bugger.

A couple of men out for a stroll in the dark saw the American in the pond with Percy cradling his head to keep it out of the water. One of them, white-faced, ran back into the house and killed the party like Banquo's ghost by calling for help. A couple of other people arrived and got into the pond to drag the man toward the edge. Percy stayed at the head-end to stop it slipping into the water. The man wasn't conscious.

"Grab his feet," said someone at the edge of the pond as the body came closer.

People grabbed at the man's feet and pulled. One of his shoes came off and he started to slide back.

David reappeared. "Heave," he said.

The body began to move up the lip of the pond and his feet came up over the edge.

"There isn't room," said David, "move him round to the gap."

The pulling men began to circle over toward the gap in the hedge. The man's feet and legs went round like the hands of a clock. "Pull," said someone. With a final effort the rescue party managed to beach the man on the concrete surround before standing back and looking at the prize flounder they'd landed. "Who is it?" asked someone. "Taruccio," said another. There was a collective drawing-in of breath. "My god," said someone else.

"He isn't breathing," said Percy.

"I know the Heimlich Manoeuvre," said one of the attendants, "roll him on his side. Lift him up so I can get my arms round him."

Kneeling, the speaker wrapped his arms around the huge waist and pushed his fists into his abdomen while he hugged the body in toward him. He was strong. The victim was lucky. "Uh!" went the rescuer as he hugged and pushed with all his might, "Uh!" and again "Uh." On the third uh the half-drowned man coughed a little and with the fourth he coughed more loudly. On the fifth vomit and froth came from his mouth and once expelled he took a huge croaking in-breath. He was alive.

Then a flash popped blinding them all.

"What the fuck?" said David.

The hired photographer: Pop, pop, pop. The whole scene was captured in chiaroscuro. Pop, pop, pop.

"Enough," said David to the photographer. "Show some respect."

"Is he dead?" said a voice.

"Someone go and get a blanket," said David. "Wrap him up. Get him warm. I'll go and call an ambulance."

"Dear God," said someone. "Dear god." "Is he okay?" "He has kids." "How many?" "That's a good question."

"Get back, please," said David to more people arriving. Luckily the narrowness of the path and the trellis that covered it constricted the flow. No one had thought to come around by the line of trees. "There's been an accident." said David, loudly. "Someone's had a fall. It's alright now. Go back inside please. Go back inside."

The line of people up the path and under the trellis was being pushed forward.

"Don't push!" "Hey!" "For fuck's sake!" "Wassgoinon?"

David lifted the camera from the photographer by its leather strap.

"Hey," he said, "that's a Leica!"

David barged into the walkway pointing the camera at the line of people and popped the flash. Flash, flash, flash. Hands went up over faces and people began to turn away. Flash, flash, flash. They started to retreat.

"That's not my good side," yelled one.

"Better not print that," said another.

The crowd started to move back toward the house.

"Ouch!" "Quit shovin'" "Pray this don't make the LA Times." Hollywood Enquirer." "Hold the front page." "Let's get outta here."

Gradually the line moved backward and turned around. David suddenly stumbled and fell. He let go the camera and flash. The apparatus hit the ground and the back of the camera flew open.

"No!" yelled a voice, "You fucking exposed it! You fucking ruined it!"

David stood up, bent down and retrieved the bulky camera and the crushed and dented tinware of the flash. Getting up slowly from the ground he handed it back to the photographer.

"Look what you..." he said.

"Just needed to get them away," said David, "I'm sorry. Add it to the bill."

Percy had already clambered out of the pond glad not to be noticed or needed. His first thought once out was for Laetitia. She mustn't be connected with this or it could surely ruin her career. Sploshing and dripping he'd made for the walkway and headed toward the garage. He reached it and felt his way around to the front and the car-doors. As he got there he saw a succession of flashes from the garden behind him like a pattern of incendiary bombs and with them loud voices, many of them. Reaching the garage doors he heaved at the end one that slid smoothly toward its neighbour. Percy squeezed through the gap and pulled the door shut before crouching down on the floor, panting. All about him was the smell of petrol and warm metal from the bodywork of cars and motor-mowers. Where was Laetitia? There was a movement at the back of the garage and Percy crawled toward it. Laetitia was slumped in a huddle against some gunnysacks. He could just about make out her figure. As he got close she held out her arms and threw them around him.

"Tin knight," she said, "I loves yer." She was in shock.

"We want you out of here, don't we?" he said. "Come on, we have to go. Which car did you come down in? The Alvis?" Laetitia nodded. "Where are the keys?"

"I dunno," said Laetitia. "Oh god are we stuck here? They'll find us. They'll get me."

"No one knows what happened. Only David and me. No one else saw."

"But when they see I've gone they'll think there's funny business."

"David will fix that. I know he will. He'll paint us out. Look he'll tell them you and he had a flaming row and you stormed off. I bet you. Something like that."

The sound of an ambulance bell broke like an enemy assault outside the garage before the vehicle made the sharp turn down toward Joyous Gard.

"We could take the boat," said Laetitia.

"And get past the house?" said Percy.

"Does he keep a spare key?"

"There's one for the driver somewhere."

Looking around Percy saw the flash of metal in the moonlight from a rack on the side-wall close to where the stairs went up to the staff quarters. Staff? All at the party. He moved toward it. Headlights shot down the road outside and glared through the glazed upper quarter of the garage doors raking across the back and side walls. Percy ducked down, catching his cheek on the wing mirror of the nearest car. The force knocked off his glasses and in the darkness he went down on his knees tap-tapping the dusty concrete till he found them. Putting them back on he was about to stand when another set of lights blazed in like the beam of a lighthouse. Again he ducked, carefully. When the car had gone by he stood up and reaching for the key-rack lifted key after key until he found one with the word Alvis etched into it.

He showed the keys to Laetitia.

"Can you drive?" she said.

"After a fashion."

"Want me to drive?"

"Might look strange a woman driving at this time of night. And you've been drinking."

"Sicked it all up," said Laetitia.

Percy opened the driver's door, got into the seat and fired up the engine. They were drowned in noise, smoke and stench. Laetitia ran forward and shoved the end door that folded neatly into the next and into the next until there was room to get the car out. Percy put the car into first and lurched it forward onto the roadway. Laetitia was sliding the doors closed. Then she hurried round to the front passenger side and was getting in when Percy said "In the back. Lie down.". Percy crashed the gears into second, the mechanism protesting loudly.

The car lurched but didn't stall. Percy put his foot down hoping that the Alvis would be synchronised between second and third. It was. With a roar the car headed for the tarmacked road. Left or right? Left or right? Percy swung the car to the left and put his foot down. With the engine screaming he raced a quarter of a mile to where a signpost indicated a minor road on the right. He swung the car about and pointed its great long nose down the lane. Shit. Best not to wake people up. They'd notice a car going down this little road at this time of night and might tell the police. Dropping his speed Percy let the car glide forward as quietly as he could and switched off the headlights. There was moonlight and with that and the side lights he could just about keep out of the verges. Stopping the car he turned round and stage-whispered to Laetitia to get out of the back and come and sit next to him. After a quarter of a mile at a triangle of grass he turned left barely missing a cattle trough. A huge owl flew straight at their windscreen. Percy could see its yellow eyes and heard its talons rake the tonneau above his head. The car went forward with soft putt-puttings and the sound of tyres on gravel. Percy turned right, tapped the accelerator and moved smoothly from second to third. They were under way. The road was quiet and they sped through villages and then up the steep hill to the main road to London. Here there was some traffic, just a few cars and lorries heading toward the London markets. Eastward they went down the old Oxford Road by Beaconsfield, The Bull Hotel at Gerrards Cross facing the pale blue moonlit space of grass on the other side of the road. Denham. It would be Denham. Then Uxbridge. Through the town they went then out the other side and onto the broad, modern Western Avenue that had only just recently become the main drag into town. Down to Shepherd's Bush through mile after mile of peeling stuccoed houses. From Hammersmith Percy headed into Town then down to the river past Earls Court until they picked up the Embankment. There on their left was the bulk of Dolphin Square. Laetitia grabbed at his arm and told him to slow down. Percy slowed and pulled gently in under the arch. Rolling down the window she smiled at the gate porter. Somehow she'd managed to repair her make-up as they drove.

"Miss West," said the porter, "late one for you."

"No show tomorrow, Freddy," said Laetitia West. "A girl's got to have fun, Ramon," she said and tapped Percy on the shoulder, "drive on." The window was rolled up. "Park over there," said Laetitia, "on a bit, left a bit. There, that one."

Percy brought the car to a halt and switched it off.

"Come on," said Laetitia, "I need to get indoors."

Percy followed her to a doorway. Laetitia strode toward the concierge at his desk.

"Hello sweetie," she said. "How's Bill. Operation a success? Oh good! Listen sweetie I seem to have left my key somewhere. Would you be a darling and let me have the spare? Thank you, sweetie. Kiss, kiss, night-night. Love to Bill!"

Laetitia headed toward a set of stairs, opened the doors letting Percy follow her. She ran upstairs, two flights, four flights. They went down a long corridor until Laetitia stopped outside a door and wielded the key. The door opened and they went in. Laetitia flicked a switch and led Percy from a tiny hall into a small living room. She kicked off her shoes. "Whisky," she said and headed toward a trolley of bottles and glasses. She stopped, turned around, came back and lifted Percy's glasses off his face before taking his head into both her hands and drawing their heads together kissed him long and kissed him passionately. Then she replaced his spectacles and let him go.

"Me Tin Knight," she said. "On 'is flamin" steed. Thank yer Perce. Me friend of two whole days. I don't half owe yer one."

She poured two whiskies.

It'll happen soon, thought Percy. Laetitia sat on the sofa and reached out for a box of cigarettes. As she put one into her mouth her hand began to tremble violently. Throwing the cigarette down onto the floor she collapsed sideways onto the sofa and began to cry wretchedly and howlingly. Percy went over to her and kneeling down held her gently to his chest to smother her cries.

Her next words came out in a whisper; "I killed him, Perce. I'm a murderer ain't I?"

Percy got up off his knees and squeezed onto the tiny sofa next to her, holding her to his chest and talking into her beautiful, fine hair that got into his mouth and onto his tongue. "No, but he certainly deserved it. He was assaulting you. It was an accident. You haven't killed anyone."

Tears flowed onto the front of his tee shirt that had not long ago dried up. "Killed me career, though, ain't I? He told me. He told me he was going to get me a part in one of his films. Lead role. Oh god I'm so stupid. I'd have let him if he hadn't jumped on me."

"He tried to rape you."

"He did didn't he? Oh god I ain't worth jack shit to no one. I'm just a piece of meat ain't I? Only I had to go and throw meself to the bleedin' lion stupid fuckin' cow that I am." She jerked herself free of Percy and began to slap herself on the head, the shoulders, the face.

Percy managed to grab hold of her wrists and stop her though she struggled. "Shhh," he said but thought, "Let her talk".

"He said he wanted to talk business. You know who he was? Only Tony Taruccio. Most of the producers here are queer. I just didn't think. He's never gonna give me no job now I mean is he?"

"No one saw. No one knows except David and I. He's not likely to make anything of it is he? He's not going to say Laetitia West shoved him into a pond or people are going to ask why. He knows that, I bet you he knows that. He's going to say he was tight, had a turn, there was no one around. David'll fix it. We're all in this together."

"I don't wanna be in anything together. I wanna be me. I wanna be a star. I don't wanna have a secret like that in me. I'd rather get cancer!" She began to cry, loudly, painfully.

The phone rang. Laetitia, to Percy's amazement, stopped crying and slowly, majestically even, got up, walked over to the instrument and lifted the receiver. A man's voice broke into the room, distant, crackling.

"Yes," said Laetitia. There was a pause. "No, no I won't. Yes alright I will. No. No I'm okay. Yes 'ere 'e is. It's for you Perce. David."

She handed him the receiver. David was short and to the point. The police had come and gone; they weren't interested. Taruccio had told them it was an accident, there was no one else involved, he'd blacked out for a second. But the press were another matter. They wanted a scandal with a home-grown star and Laetitia West fit the bill perfectly. She must never have been near the pond. She and David had had an argument and she'd taken his car and left for London before the incident. If a journalist bribed the doorkeeper at Dolphin Square then Percy was just a Joe, another man. Laetitia wouldn't ever mention his name. But he must go. He was to disappear, vanish. Had he money? There was a hundred pounds in the safe in the flat. Laetitia would give it to him. In the morning he must go straight to

Victoria and take the boat-train to Calais then onward to Paris to meet Gilbert. Then to Sarlat and to the Mirabelle.

"Passport?"

"At the Sherborne."

"Go now while it's quiet. Take a cab. Get your things then go to the station. Just clear out. It would be best for all of us. How's Flo?"

"Fine, I think."

"Tell her I won't see her for a few days. Tell her I'm sorry that bastard spoiled the party for her. Glad she made it back to Town alright. I need to stay here. It's going to be a close run thing that this doesn't scupper the studio. I've got work to do. Bonne voyage and, Percy,"

"Yes,"

"Thank you."

The line clicked and went dead.

"You off then?" said Flo.

"Yes," said Percy.

"Some sunny day," said Flo, handing him an envelope of cash. "Hope yer meet someone nice. Someone what deserves yer."

"Thanks," said Percy and turned for the door into the future. His future. He went through and Laetitia closed it behind him.

Quercy, Les Rossignols, September 1948

Foie de veau, pommes purées

There was in the mornings a hint of autumn in the air that the bright day would later sweep beneath its colourful carpet so that one could see that summer was ending. The swallows still wheeled all around the hotel, the town and the rocky crags above it. There were still the long shadows at lunchtime, the delicious transition between the hot day and the cool of the hotel foyer where unplastered stone walls gave off the fertile scent of cellars. Cats still lazed, dogs still hid under shrubs in yards and the denizens of Sarlat-la-Canéda still waited until after eight in the evening to take their stroll through the Place and down by the river.

It was September and the year had made its mind up to change. For three weeks now the farmers of Quercy, Quercy Bas, Quercy Blanc, Perigord and the Agenais had been harvesting their Ente plums from the trees and taking them back to their farms to pick them over before spreading them onto meshed trays to be stored in the sécheries, the wooden drying houses on stilts that sat among and beside the orchards. The earliest-picked plums had already begun their transition from vermilion to black. Driving wasps to a frenzy amber bead of sweetness had burst out on the skins of the fruits like a golden sweat before they were to pucker into leathery ridges, become brown and contract around their fibrous flesh and the skeletal stone within. Reines Claudes hung pendulous and gross from branches and figs had begun to fall to the ground and burst making dark, sticky messes on streets and garden paths. Kee kee called the swallows looping and gliding in the air like a swarm around the great rose-coloured cathedral of Toulouse but their talk too had changed as the heat slid back to Africa on a tide that would soon take them with it.

But not yet. Only by getting up early in the morning did one sense the cooling of the earth and feel the increasing weight of the dew. And not until the evenings on the terrace of the restaurant did shawls go from the backs of chairs to the backs of diners as the soft dusk fell in a mound of rose, sand and mauve. Feeble streetlights began to make pools again on stones, cobbles and tarmac and somewhere in each rocky causse the autumn crocus had risen up out of the dry land. Pigs and dogs snuffled for truffles in woodland of oak and scrub. On the farms the carcasses of sangliers had begun their transformation into dark bacon and charcuteries. The talk in the villages has switched from what kind of Summer it had been to what kind of Winter it might be. Winter among these limestone hills can be viciously cold. But in the meantime golden Armagnac is to be drunk from tiny glasses, the year's harvest of walnuts and honey has already begun to appear in pastry tarts and many ducks and geese that waddled contentedly around the basses cours of Aquitaine are now dead, dismembered and preserved in their own luscious fat.

Poor, rich Quercy. A land of rocky outcrops and level plains between the Dordogne and the Garonne dotted with tiny villages and castles. Its chief glory, the bastide towns, perched on hills for defence against the French, the English, the French, the English, the French. A whole century passed in which the two cousin-nations battled each other for supremacy. This was the land of Froissart, of William Morris's early romances in prose and verse and on every day off Percy was on their trail, looking for shudders or shadows, ripples in times that might give physical substance to Morris's cinematic episodes, scenes that had flashed across his imagination with enamelled, pre-Raphaelite vividness.

And so, close to Montaigu one day he found himself driving in Gilbert's huge white Lagonda after a storm along a metalled road slightly elevated above the surrounding fields of stubble, sunflowers and burst, over-ripe melons. The intense rain had created pools and ponds alongside the road giving it the feel of a causeway across a marsh. He slowed the car and coasted to a halt at an unmarked crossroads. The little lakes bubbled as the water sank back into the ground through the cracks in the sun-baked earth. Pools reflected the greying magenta sky and showed subaqueous strips of emerald like rice paddies. Percy wound down the window and gazed out. As the sun began to set bright colours heightened and sharpened the landscape until every detail was as distinct as a Pre-Raphaelite pastoral. There was a haystack soaked and dark. The pile of hay where Jehane the Brown had lain in her sleep for an hour. There she stood and was saying "I will not." Percy got out of the car and went to join Robert's soaked and terrified band of knights. Over there Godmar had cut Robert's throat and the darker stain spread across the ground was where his soldiers had kicked his head to pieces. A signpost had appeared at the crossroad and it pointed Jehane to Paris, the Chatelet, turbid brown waters and her miserable end.

With the vision came a trembling in his chest. His hands shook. He was overcome by a sensation of intense joy. Was this what Morris experienced? The visions that gave him the material for those electrically real vignettes: Silent Dawn, The Prisoner. Scenes from a country that Morris hadn't even visited, only known because of Froissart. And yet he was there. He had known it. Was it the recollection of The Haystack in the Floods that had triggered all this for Percy? The scene in the poem first read alone, then emotionally recreated, internalised, reproduced, projected, once even acted out with David, and now lived? And the soaking clothes on his skin, the smell of wet leather, the sobs from the man on his right, the breathing of the horses. How? Percy clutched at his heart. He opened his mouth and his soul went out and he could see it condense on the cool air above the little pond.

What had knocked at his vestibular cortex, the door into his mind? Percy stood, swaying a little. A hoopooe stood on the brown earth. His hands stopped shaking and from a nearby village the angelus began to ring. Tolling me back from thee to my sole self. Percy's heart rate slowed. Gone was the vision. The dead man, the murderer, the weeping woman. He had sweated and the sweat was cold. He was standing on a narrow road between fields in Quercy. There was a round stain in the stubble a few yards away. He felt a chill and saw the sky cloud over like an October sky and with it came the smell of fires and dead leaves, the promise of frost, the muddy ways, the great coat of grey wool over Quercy and he heard and saw above him the huge wheel of time and seasons turning, churning, creaking over his head.

The sun came back out. It was hot in the car. The leather of the seats was warm and it dried the sweat on his back. Exchanging his normal spectacles for the dark glasses he'd put in the glove box Percy launched the huge car out onto the road and headed toward Montaigu where he would turn right onto the long stretch that would take him to Domme then up to Sarlat. An hour's journey? This car ate miles as it whooshed along. Percy hadn't ever driven a machine this powerful before and it took all his strength and concentration to steer it. Gilbert had been unfailingly kind and generous to him in the year that he'd been at the Mirabelle. The affair at Joyous Gard had not been mentioned. If Gilbert were in touch with David, and Percy was sure that he would have been, nothing had been said. The hotel, his duties, the restaurant, the celebrated Epergne d'Or, its kitchens, the cafés of Sarlat had become Percy's world.

Percy spent as much time in the restaurant kitchen as he dared. By getting up extra-early to help with the morning tasks he gradually made a little, invisible place for himself among the brigade. It helped that the head chef, Bricqout, was a genial soul. At first he'd taken Percy's interest as English eccentricity. For himself, he had a genuine like of Les Tommys that counterbalanced his hatred of Les Boches. Les Rosbifs versus Les Têtes de Caboche. Food larded his language and his thinking just as bacon fat was threaded through the skin of a roasting guineafowl. He had first seen Percy standing beside the kitchen door not long after his arrival as the brigade, les gars, worked on that day's lunch, always a more rustic and humble meal than dinner. That day, Percy remembered, calves' livers were being sliced thinly, all suggestion of gristle and tissue removed before being soaked in milk. Onions sliced as fine as paper were stewing in butter in a copper pan. Another lad was forcing boiled potatoes through a sieve to be puréed later, after the addition of butter and seasoning, into an unctuous cloud of starch that was as close to English mashed potato as gravy-powder was to a sauce brune. Another lad was making and rolling out pastry to form into tart cases for the local speciality the tartes aux noix, a sort of apotheosized treacle tart made with the celebrated local walnuts. Bricqout had smiled and waved him in, showing him a place to stand where he would be out of the way.

That day, his day off, Percy booked himself into the restaurant for lunch and as he ate these refinements on simple, local produce he first understood the difference between cuisine and cooking. He felt at home at last in a place where tradition and skill focused on just two or three ingredients could produce a feast. Not since China had he enjoyed such a transformation of bits of flesh and pieces of vegetable and he thought of those jiao-tzi, those flour and water envelopes of minced pork, cabbage and ginger and how delicious they were and how superbly simple. What a shame it had been that Lopez, a natural cook, had been made to churn out standard British Restaurant stuff back at the Blandford. Even with rationing, even without the delicacies of Smetka's black market larder Lopez could have produced something remarkable. What was it that Lopez had offered to make for him one day? A paella. What fun that would have been. Percy imagined a family party for which Lopez had cooked and at which he had greeted, seated, looked after grandparents, children, aunts, cousins, nephews, nieces. My god, thought Percy, we would have been a couple! Two people sharing a home, a bed, hopes, ambitions, news, sickness, health, holidays, chores, fears, bad times and good times. Two men. It could not have been. It could never be. He was violently glad that his almost-affair with Lopez had been swiftly and simply castrated. How could it have ever come to anything? But, oh Lopez, he thought, another time, another world. Please come and find me again.

On his next day off it was the same dish. Percy went into the kitchen for a couple of hours keeping out of the way, observing. He watched techniques; how that knife was used, when and where. How that was filleted, that sliced, that chopped. How long until the butter foamed, at what point a custard came together, at what moment to check a seasoning. How many times the pastry was turned for a pâte feuilletée, when the cold butter was added and how much or how little flour was used for dredging. How a chicken was eviscerated and then boned, how a trout was prepared, how quenelles were made of pike-flesh. A turbot had arrived from the North and he watched it being cleaned and cut into tranches to be served with a reduction of veal bones and herbs that had been cooking for twelve hours. The whole fish must be consumed in one evening so it must be beyond delicious. He gradually learnt when to skim a stock, how to make a sauce mayonnaise, hollandaise, béarnaise. Above everything Percy came to love the making of sauces, the fineness of adjustments, the timing of additions, the speed of beating, the patience required to wait, to wait for the moment when butter, lemon and egg yolk emulsified, when a roux blanc was ready, how a simple bechamel could be transformed into something extraordinary, how to peel, seed and concasse tomatoes, how to create a deeply flavoured reduction over hours and hours of patient attention.

The Mirabelle was as good as any hotel in Paris; *The Red Guide* noted it, for service and for cuisine. The English and the Americans came and kept on coming until winter descended on the Dordogne. Then the stone-built hotel was just about kept warm with fires burning in the downstairs rooms and in any guestrooms that were used. Winter here was exceptionally cold with heavy, heavy frosts and falls of snow. Now the preserving skills of the Quercynois came to the fore when it was time to eat. Kitchen guests and staff ate goose and duck, roasts and salamis of wild boar, pastry tarts of prunes or walnuts, game of all kinds, truffled chicken and guinea fowl, cassoulets of goose, duck or salted pork. It seemed as though almost every part of every animal was cooked and eaten from the breast of a duck to its gizzards, fried. Their rendered fat was used again and if it were goose fat then there were the local Pommes Sarladaises, the potatoes sautéed until crisp on the outside and almost melting within. There were sausages, hams and of course foie gras. Percy had seen the process and found that it took him back to China and the cruelty of its livestock markets. But he ate the unctuous liver all the same. During this season he was allowed more often into the kitchen on his days off. Bricqout would set him going with a glass of home-distilled liqueur, walnut or pear, at whatever time he arrived. When kitchen staff were held back at home with coughs and colds or because there had been a heavy fall of snow Percy was given more complicated tasks and, gradually, gained competence at his beloved sauces but also at pastry-making. He'd succeeded at a pâte brisée followed by the usual pâte sablée for the prune or walnut tarts. He loved working flour with butter and sugar with his fingers, loved understanding when enough was enough, when to rest and when to move. Picking up a circle of pastry to release it over a buttered tart-ring, letting the cool, fleshy disc fall just so, tapping it lightly into the metal, trimming the edges with a sharp knife and setting the orts aside for fleurons. All this gave him intense pleasure.

And the staff were beginning to accept him: they made jokes about English cuisine. "Show us what you'd do with these Monsieur," they'd say or "Make us something a l'Anglaise." In other words, boiled till flaccid. He'd have liked to have made them jiaozi but he couldn't expect to find ginger-root. Not having ever made a steak-and-kidney pudding or a pork pie he couldn't demonstrate the points at which the two cuisines, the country English and the country French touched;

the traditional dishes where the ingredients that most people could lay their hands on were transformed through careful preparation and slow cooking. They mocked him for his fastidiousness, his near inability to ever throw everything away. They called him the ménagère prudente. Percy hadn't mentioned his imprisonment during the war although he was certain that they all knew about it. At first he thought they were mocking his horror at wasting anything edible but gradually he realised that after five years under German occupation, the food shortages of these last three years, they were actually declaring him one of them.

Outside these very few hours a week in the kitchen Percy was either running the hotel or sleeping. These routines were enough for him. More than enough. His bedroom in the greniers was small and white and cold with a dormer window and an iron bedframe. Here Percy had pinned a couple of coloured postcards to the wall, from the National Gallery in London, Caravaggio's Christ at Emmaus and Titian's Diana and Actaeon. He'd brought his few books with him; Morris's early verse, his Keats and his Tennyson and Bleak House to be read, rested and read again. Occasionally he thought of his other books, his school prizes and the ones he'd collected in Hong Kong. After liberation and before leaving he'd been back to the Repulse Bay and to his room there but it was bare of anything.

For long summer days on his day off Gilbert had given him use of that white Lagonda 4.5 litre V12 Rapide drophead coupe that had spent from 1940 until 1945 hidden in a barn. Sometimes he'd drive distances to Bordeaux, Toulouse, to Poitiers. Now in the summer he was using it to take him to small towns like Lauzerte from where, on the bicycle stowed in the back he could take his time to discover their localities, their satellite villages, their beauty-spots more slowly. Even the bicycle had a war story to tell; used by at least three British SOE parachuted in to aid the Resistance. None had survived until 1945.

Today had been tiring and now Percy was enjoying the comfort of the car. This stretch of the road was long and straight and bordered by poplar trees. The stroboscopic effect of light, shade, light, shade along the road confused him and without realising it he'd veered the right-hand drive car over to the left-hand side of the road and had begun to nod off to sleep. Absolutely in the nick of time he heard the klaxon of the oncoming car. Fighting the weight of the Lagonda he managed to only just move out of its way without losing control. Nothing else was on the road. Heart racing and skin sweating Percy slowed the car to a halt and looked behind him. He couldn't see the other car but could easily make out swerving lines of black on the road's surface where he'd missed it. He switched off the engine, leant back and with gratitude listened to the slight rustling of the poplar leaves, the only sound around. After half a minute he restarted and pulled out heading toward Domme at a very reasonable 65 kilometres an hour. Suddenly he caught sight in his rear mirror of what looked like an enormous insect with shining eyes rushing up behind him. It was the other car. It must have turned back to follow him. Closer it came kicking up behind it a cloud of dust and exhaust. The lit headlamps were low and set like bug-eyes either side of a fierce mouth shaped like an heraldic shield. It was black and yellow like a hornet. Its klaxon sounded again and again as it came up closer and closer.

As he slowed the other car pulled past and screeched to a halt in front of him. It was a Delahaye 35 1938 Competition with bulbous-fronted streamlined wheel arches. The dust settled behind it. Whoever was driving was in no hurry to get out. Its motor was switched off and the door swung open. Percy looked up to see an elegant shoe and a leg dressed in a silk stocking come to the ground. Above it a white headscarf turned in the same direction as the foot. A gloved hand grasped the doorframe where the window was wound down and as the door opened fully the figure of a woman dressed in a dark blue New Look skirt, boat-neck white silk blouse, string of opulent pearls about the neck and eyes shaded in dark glasses came toward him. Percy prepared to get out of the car to meet his accuser but he wasn't fast enough.

She was already next to him.

"You're not Gilbert," said a privileged American voice. "What are you doing in his car? You nearly killed us both back there. Get out and show yourself. At once." She stepped back to allow Percy to open the door and get out of the car himself. He closed it behind him and they faced each other.

The woman was tall and thin and very, very neat. She folded her arms and looked at him. "Well?"

"I'm sorry," he said. "I was confused by the flashing. The trees that is. I must have got into a state. I'm sorry."

"What's your name?"

"Percy Langrigg."

"You must be Gilbert's new manager from England."

"Not that new."

"Don't quibble. Do you know who I am?"

Percy vaguely did and opened his mouth to speak but the woman went on. "I'm Lyle Destrooper. I'm a friend of Gilbert's. And I shall tell him not to let you get behind the wheel of that monster again. I am frankly most put out to nearly have been killed and I consider you a menace to other drivers."

She put up her hand to take off her dark glasses. Her eyes narrowed as, Percy supposed, she sought some other shade to cast over him. But she paused and lifted the end of one arm of the frames to the corner of her mouth in a practised, elegant way. A different light came into her eyes. What was she thinking?

"You're the close friend of David Maldon?"

Percy was speechless. There was silence.

"Answer me please."

"Yes," said Percy, "yes I am."

"And you helped him out over that dreadful rape. I see. And you've been closeted here with Gilbert till the heat cools down." She paused. "Well done you. It could have killed that poor girl's career." Percy paused, heart in mouth.

"But it didn't?" he said.

"Not unless you consider taking screen tests in Hollywood the utter nadir of contemporary existence. And some might. I do."

Lyle Destrooper began to chew at the arm of her sunglasses. Then she stopped. "Bad habit," she said, "like playing with toys too big for one. Now Mr Langrigg when we meet again please do not approach me at a speed greater than one mile an hour, if that. And if Gilbert is fool enough to allow you to drive that monster of a car again then kindly do not kill with it. It would not be good for his reputation. Do you understand me?" Percy nodded. "Well Mr Langrigg; Percy," said Lyle Destrooper extending toward him a gloved hand that bore about the wrist an elegant bracelet made of links of yellow and red gold, "a la prochaine," and she turned away to walk to her car. Just as she was about to climb in and sit down she turned, dark glasses now back over her eyes and said: "Please to tell Gilbert that if he's down next weekend I shall be having a party at Les Rossignols. He is invited." She paused. "And so are you. Goodbye, close friend of David Maldon."

She sat down at the wheel, gunned the motor, executed a handbrake turn and sped off south leaving Percy covered in dust and fine gravel. The poplars waved like a long line of feathers on an alarmed hen before settling down once more. Percy began a slow drive home.

The next morning Gilbert knocked at the door of the manager's office. "Bonjour," he said, "ça va?"

Percy rose to greet him "Thank you," he said. "How was your journey down last night."

"Ah" said Gilbert, "it was slow in the Traction Avant. In the Lagonda, well," he shrugged. "But the Lagonda lives here, non? It would not be happy in Paris. The Lagonda is well?" Percy thought he saw the shadow of a smile around Gilbert's mouth. Had his little, trimmed moustache quivered slightly?

Gilbert went on; "You have heard of Castel Beau I imagine? And you have heard of its chatelaine?" Percy had. In fact he'd seen her on that pre-War visit to Paris when she was at the height of her fame; the black girl from New York who'd electrified the Revues and Folies of the capital with her singing and dancing. He nodded.

"Quel cul," said Gilbert and gave a tiny smile. "Le tout Paris l'a vue n'est ce pas? Eh bien. Mademoiselle Alouette is to give a grande fête at Castel Beau the weekend following this. She wishes it to be "catered," that is to say, approvisionné, and she wishes for the famous brigade and the exceptional staff here from La Mirabelle to delight her guests and to look after them. How do you think of this?"

"We're quiet next weekend Monsieur. One would hate to close the restaurant but..."

"Shall we weigh up the consequences? Here we disappoint perhaps a douzaine of people. There we make show of our wonderful kitchen and our wonderful service to one hundred, two hundred. It is la publicité, la reclame."

"And surely there aren't enough rooms at Castel Beau to lodge all the guests so..."

"Exactement. You are agreed?"

"Oui, bien sûr."

"And you will have some extra assistance of which I shall tell you more later. Please to look at these instructions from the Secretaire at Castel Beau and we shall meet later to discuss them. A bientôt." Gilbert stood up and turned to go out of the room, then turned back. "Ah mon Percy I almost forgot. The assistance I have arranged for you is formidable. Most formidable. It is someone above all who knows how a party for foreigners should be run and how it should be fed and how it should be staffed. It is a person for whom I have the most respect in all matters of the etiquette of the beau monde. It is an American lady. It is a lady who is a friend of a friend of ours. I believe you have met this lady, even. In fact Gilbert is delighted that you have made such an impression on this lady that she insists you are to accompany me to a reception at her house this evening."

Percy blanched. Gilbert smiled.

"She is a lady very fond of cars," said Gilbert. "Her husband made them. She has made an offer for the Lagonda but Gilbert said non. I tell her it is too britannique she will not understand its ways. A tout à l'heure, mon brave."

Gilbert left the room.

Percy spent most of his life these days walking around the hotel, constantly on the move, rarely staying still but now he sat back in the chair behind the desk and had a talk with himself. That lady, that American lady with a taste for fast cars could only be this Lyle Destrooper. Had David ever mentioned her? He thought he might have done. What had he said? What had he said? The connection, was it Shanghai? She was banking or was it railroads. Or was it shipping and department stores or cars and dairies? Now it came back to him, how the subject had come up among the general talk about America and Americans when it was clear that they were getting the upper hand in the Pacific. People in camp telling their stories of Americans. Yes, that was it. Someone had been talking about tootsie rolls and Hershey bars and a country without class. Someone had said that in America class was all about money and how it had its own royalty and someone who read a lot had cited Henry James and his heiresses and that's when David had said I met a true blue heiress once at the Cathay in Shanghai she was an Ice Queen and that must have been her. Lyle Destrooper. But she wasn't called that. Lyle what? Ferrand, that was it. Ferrand the car manufacturer out setting up concessions in China. Bit of a show-off by all accounts and addicted to danger; loved racing his cars in competitions. David must have seen her since the war or known her better than he let on in camp if she'd called him friend. No; they must have met at some London parties after the war that would be it; or she'd stayed at Maldon Hall on a huntin' shootin' fishin' weekend. Friend meant something different to the rich. More social equal than loyal supporter. He hadn't seen David since he got the title, not before Manette Street. His father had died and then his uncle or was it the other way around? Must have been the father who died first or the spoils would have been gambled away. David hadn't been particularly posh at school, hadn't played the aristocratic connections card. So what had it been about David? He settled back in his chair.

Looks. Charm. An easy manner. A certain smile. This is a song coming on, thought Percy. These foolish things. That old black magic. Icy fingers on my spine. Percy shivered. What had David done after Yantai? A couple of years at school in England. Eton was it? They hadn't kept in touch. And then what? He'd always said that he'd wanted to get into the business of films. But he'd come back to Shanghai in '38 to rescue his father from some shady cartel or doomed business proposition and pitched up at the Atholl Palace. My darling. Then the war. And now a title and a country estate in England. And Lyle Destrooper as a friend. I'm not sure I can think about him. He began to read the paper in front of him superbly titled Le Bal chez Castel Beau.

L'Alouette's secretary had a fine command of grammar and wrote the most beautiful French ringing with hauteur. An event that would in all probability be Rabelaisian was Racinian in its conception. And all at the command of a girl, a woman who, it was said, had been plumée by half the French cabinet and half the Russian aristocrats in Paris. In the end she had supposedly become tired of all her lovers and bored at the prospect of a worthless Russian title had decided, to the sound of a thousand Parisian jaws hitting the floor, to move herself South to the Dordogne to the exquisite manor house perched on a bluff above the river that was called Castel Beau where she would be chatelaine surrounded by her acres and her many dogs. And it had worked. It was miraculous and Castel Beau really was nothing less than magical. Here the hoofer from Hoboken who'd mistakenly joined the wrong troupe and ended up on the boat to Le Havre instead of the one to Panama had come to rest. And rest she deserved. Her sheer energy, her warbling voice, her extraordinary sliding dances, arms aloft, had won her the soubriquet "L'Alouette" and following Isadora Duncan's death here in France in '27 L'Alouette had taken on her mantle and worn it right through the rest of the Twenties to the end of the Thirties. Tiring of performing just, but just enough, before the public tired of her she'd apotheosed herself into the deity of the Dordogne. The locals loved her while visiting Parisian wags painted her as a latter-day Alcina who had with a conjuring trick turned a rocky desert into an enchanted garden, said that her dogs were all her boyfriends transformed by a black spell and that one day her magic would fail and everyone at Castel Beau and all its gardens would revert to their original states. But for the moment little Hetty Hill from Hoboken had done rather splendidly well. Percy read on. The kitchen was required to make a supper to be served at ten o'clock and a breakfast to be served at midnight. This didn't sound very French. Perhaps Mme Destrooper was behind it. Percy scanned through the paper and went off to find Bricqout.

Later in the day at about six o'clock Gilbert reappeared in Percy's office to remind him of the party tonight at Les Rossignols. He was coming of course? Of course replied Percy and yes he would be ready at 19 heures, naturellement. Up in the greniers in his room Percy sat on the edge of his bed. Parties had never been his bag. He didn't care for small-talk or for showing-off or loud laughter and declarations of common-cause or friendship that would be forgotten once the alcohol had worn off. From the other side of a bar or carrying trays of drinks around a room he'd seen so many people he liked become cruel, greedy, two-dimensional. People he'd thought were interesting flaunted their shallowness. He'd seen too many flirtings and chasings and even consummations between people who'd left wives, husbands, fiancés, lovers, partners back in the party to fend for themselves. And the thing was that all this dishonesty was in fact completely honest. People showed who they really were at parties. He had rarely liked what he had seen. Perhaps there would be a library at Les Rossignols where he could hide. Hunting around his wardrobe he found nothing that would be good enough for chez Mme Ferrand. Perhaps he should volunteer to join the staff? Having a purpose among the purposelessness would suit him better. There was a knock at the door and Gerard came in carrying a suit and a small valise, from M Dinant he said, putting them down on the bed. The suit was splendid and made of a pale mustardy-green cashmere weave as light as silk. The shirt was cream with an integral collar and with it was a silk tie of cerise interwoven with silver. In the valise with shirt and tie he found a pair of co-respondent shoes, tan and cream coloured and even a pair of lisle socks in beige. Percy spread the clothes out on the bed and felt a mix of rebellion and excitement. He didn't want to be dressed by his employer. On the other hand it would help him to blend in. He could wear it like a disguise. By looking like them he could pass for one of them. It was camouflage. French camouflage. He washed, shaved, splashed on a little Floris Special 127 that had been left behind by a guest and put his costume on.

"Tiens, c'est vous!" said Sandrine as he came down to reception to wait for Gilbert.

"Ah, bon," said his employer coming into the room with a cashmere coat around his shoulders. "You have no coat? Les soirs sont frais. Thierry? Allez à ma chambre apportez ici mon manteau gris. Merci. It is lucky we are similar construction."

"Build."

"C'est ça. Allons-y. Bonne soirée tout le monde."

"Bonne soirée!" called the lobby staff in return as Thierry came back with a coat that he thrust at Percy with an "Amusez-vous bien!"

The Lagonda waited outside and in it a driver, Marcel.

"Bon soir Marcel," said Gilbert. "Aux Rossignols."

The car rolled out of the drive.

They wound on in the direction of Montaigu getting deeper and deeper into Quercy. The light was limpid and the evening was still away from the roar and fuss of the car. Roads became narrower and signposts non-existent. Percy doubted he would ever find his way here again. Woods of oak and chestnut sprang up and on they went into the heart of them like adventurers in a magic forest, a Broceliande. Clearly Lyle Destrooper was the kind of woman who liked her privacy. No one would ever just happen to be passing. Eventually they came into a clearing of mown meadows and the road became a driveway not to a grand 0 or even a grand manoir. This had the look of an ancient Quercynois farmhouse that had reproduced itself asexually over the centuries. It was long, the length of three large farmhouses, and low with a red roof and overhanging eaves. The entrance side gave nothing away. A doorway and shuttered windows. Swallows wheeled and cried to each other, sounds of love on the wing. But the gravelled driveway and near field were full of cars and not, Percy noticed, great Lagondas or Delahayes. These were mostly Citroens, Ferrands and Renaults, the cars of professionals and wealthier farmers with one or two larger beasts among them perhaps from Cahors, Toulouse, Bordeaux. The entrance door was flanked by old stone troughs full of lavender. Percy breathed in. Truly this was what the French called La France Profonde. They went inside.

"Good lord!" said a woman's voice, "You know I haven't seen her since Benenden. Hasn't she got fat? Obviously not much rationed in their part of Sussex!"

"I know!" said another woman's voice, "and really puce isn't her colour. Someone should tell her."

"Bagsy not me!" replied the first speaker, "she was a demon with a hockey stick. Broke poor Buffy's nose."

"Have you seen Buffy recently?"

"Oh yes she's just moved in to Lauzerte with Baffy. Gorgeous townhouse up on the old walls. They're having the whole place completely re-done."

"Who's doing it?"

"Raymond."

"No! The little man from Le Mans?"

"Yes, that's him. Snake hips. He'll have it looking like a château by Christmas."

"What are you doing for Christmas this year?"

"Well George would just like to stay put of course but it gets so ruddy cold around here and we've had an invitation from Tubby and Dodo to go down to their place just outside Tangier."

"Isn't Tangier a bit you know."

"I do know. They lost Monty Mulligrew last year. Went on some kind of bar-crawl and ended up on a rubbish dump buggered to death apparently. But the villa's lovely and the garden's simply heavenly and one's heard talk that the Dockers may be pitching up."

"No! What a scream! On the Shemara?"

"Absolutely. Dear young newlyweds."

"Oh Bunny you are a bitch!"

"Isn't it delicious? Look that must be Tootsie Callaghan. Doesn't she look awful? Let's go over and fawn a little."

"Oh yes, do let's!"

The two women drifted away across the tiled hall. Gilbert had disappeared and Percy wandered out on his own through a large doorway that gave out onto the gardens. And what gardens. The house that looked as though it had grown in a straight line was in fact gently curved along the edge of a plateau. Below it the ground sloped down to a valley in a natural amphitheatre. Terraces ran down to, at the focal point, a swimming pool with an arched changing house at one end below which water cascaded down through a stone lion's head.

Junipers stood up in raised limestone beds of lavender, cardoon, echinops, Jerusalem sage, fennel and catmint. On saucers of sedum sat flocks of butterflies. Late roses flowered and walkways were roofed in honeysuckle and passionflower. Bright blue-purple Morning Glory grew up the walls of the house and mingled with Virginia Creeper just turning russet.

"Why my dear Mr Langrigg," said a voice, so near that it startled him. He turned and looked up into the grey solemn eyes of Lyle Destrooper. "Thank you so much for coming to my party. Clever of you to disguise yourself as a Frenchman. I'm sorry," she said putting her hand on his arm. "That was forward. I simply meant that local Society is almost exclusively English and for some reason I don't think that's quite you. That didn't sound right either. May we start again? Percy," she said, "it's lovely to have you here. Any friend of Gilbert's is a friend of mine. And we really should get to know one another better. But I have to go so please run along and mingle. Oh dear. I think you're not a natural mingler. Neither am I. If it all becomes too much for you there's scotch and soda in the library. Back to the world of Angela Brazil. What a lark what a plunge." Hoiking her dramatic black and white sheath dress to above her ankles she set off toward a group of men and women like a magpie falling down upon a covey of wood pigeon.

"Lyle!" screeched the women in English Home Counties accents, "Simply wonderful party." They mobbed her and she disappeared.

Percy wandered off around the garden. Colours began to deepen. The gravel in the walks was still warm and the flowers and leaves, perfectly still, seemed to be drinking up the late year's heat. Bats flew and screeched and in the woods one owl began to hoot its hunting cry followed by another and another. White flowers showed like giant moths and giant moths where they settled looked like white flowers. Anything purple or blue glowed with a deep intensity like Lawrence's gentians the dark-flaming torches of Dis. Percy sat down on a bench in the pool house, looked out at the purple water, took out a cigarette and prepared to light it.

"Mais vous ne buvez pas," a male voice came from inside. "Ce n'est pas fait."

"I don't seem to have a glass," said Percy.

There was a chinking. "Ça va. J'ai un verre de recharge."

Next came the sound of fizzing liquid being poured into first one glass and then another. One of the glasses was lifted and handed through the near dark to Percy.

"Toujours le meilleur champagne chez Ferrand. 1945. Une excellente année à tous égards. Salut." The stranger lifted his glass toward Percy's and they clinked rims.

"Cheers," said Percy.

"Alors, vous êtes Anglais?" said the voice. "Je m'excuse; je pensais que vous étiez Français."

"I'm sorry," said Percy.

"There is no reason to be sorry. You don't look English."

"I'll take that as a compliment. You don't like English people?"

"I am married to one," said the speaker. "But en masse, non. Here in Quercy we are being colonised."

"Better than the Germans, perhaps."

"Oui bien sûr. Je faisais juste une blague. Tu es très serieux. It is small talk. This is what we do at parties, hein? But you break the rules. You talk big of things in the past. Things we forget."

Percy took a sip of champagne. "Very nice," he said.

The man started to laugh and Percy caught a flash from even, white teeth. "Very nice! Toujours ce sang froid. Alors ton sang c'est froid?" He reached out and grasped Percy's hand and held it tight, thumb on his wrist. Eyes looked into his eyes. "Ça va – je suis médecin." He let Percy's hand go. "You have much passion in your veins. But you must give out your passion or it will turn dark et deviendra cancereux. Tu comprends?"

"Would you like a cigarette?" said Percy.

"Merci."

Percy reopened his silver cigarette case, a gift from Gilbert, and handed it over to the man who took one and put it to his lips. Percy did the same and then struck a match. In the flare he saw, turned down toward the flame, a face with matinée idol good looks, tanned skin, hair black and with a slight widow's peak brilliantined back from the forehead. The head was long, narrow. The eyes lifted. They were brown and glimmered like topaz. The man breathed in, the cigarette tip glowed. Then he sat up.

"Désolé," he said "I have not introduced myself. I am Lambert Loiret. And you?"

"Percy," said Percy. "Percy Langrigg."

"Enchanté," said Loiret. "We have touched hands, we have exchanged names. C'est ça. Les formalités ont été respectées."

They sat and smoked, glasses beside them on the stone bench. "Moi j'adore la crépuscule," said Loiret. "C'est une heure magique. Entre les temps. You recall Proust? Combray. L'homme qui dort tient en cercle autour de lui le fil des heures, des mondes, des années. But for me this comes before sleep. Quand nous somnolons. L'entr'acte entre la vie et la mort."

"Now it's you talking big."

"You are right. I am French."

The sound of a rising chorus of frogs came from terrace and valley. "Soon," said Loiret, "Les Rossignols."

"Your wife is English, you said."

"Oui. You have not met her? Lady Daphne." He pronounced it La Dee Daphnay and Percy was momentarily confused. "Lady Daphne," said Loiret again with a meticulous English pronunciation.

"No," said Percy, "I haven't."

"I must introduce you," said Loiret.

"Thank you," said Percy. "Won't she be missing you?"

Loiret made a kind of grimace that Percy took to mean no.

"She has many friends," he said. "Her family, you know, important in England. Many people want to know her. Many English people."

Loiret pinched the butt of his cigarette and threw it onto the gravel. "You have friends here? You come with someone? Ta femme peut-être?"

"No," said Percy and the word seemed to be weighty with a significance that escaped him. "No. I came with friends."

"Drink," said Loiret. They drank.

The pool bubbled and slapped its sides. A bat flew low down over the water.

"And you're a doctor," said Percy.

"Oui," said Loiret. "Je suis un simple médecin de campagne. The Bovary of the Bastides. Do you have a doctor?"

"I don't know." said Percy. "I imagine I must. We must. I mean there must be one for the hotel."

"The hotel?"

"Ah yes I'm sorry. I work at La Mirabelle. In Sarlat."

"You are married in England?"

"No."

"Fiancée?"

"No."

"Girlfriend?"

"No."

"No?"

"There was someone," said Percy trying to put the brakes on the revelations, "in England."

"Ah," said Loiret. "In England."

"Yes," said Percy.

In the silence that followed a tide of chatter, braying laughter, small shrieks of amusement and dull men's voices, raised, demanding attention, flooded downward from the terrace to their hideaway.

"Do you swim?"

"Well yes," said Percy, "a bit."

"You cannot swim a bit," said Loiret. "You might drown a bit." Would you care to swim?"

"What, now?"

"Yes, now before we are too drunk."

"But I don't have any. I don't have un maillot de bain."

"Moi non plus," said Loiret as he bent down to unlace his shoes.

Now Loiret has taken off his shoes, his socks, his jacket, his tie, his shirt and grasping the waistband of his trousers pulls them down to his ankles. His cock is stiff. Percy takes a step back and takes off his jacket. Sitting down to take off his shoes he feels Loiret's naked thigh brushing against his mouth. It's rough, hairy. Shoes and socks off, Percy stands up. His hands go to his waistband, undo the top button, more buttons and he pushes his trousers down. Bending down to pull the cuffs over his feet his forehead meets the end of Loiret's cock. He looks at it. It's beaded with a sweetish, saltyish, jellyish liquid he tastes when he licks it. Instinct? I do it because I want to. I want to do this, thought Percy. It's me. It's me. It's me. And this man smells divine.

Loiret stepped back. His legs were long and his waist slim. He walked toward the pool like a kind of gazelle and into the water made a perfect dive that scarcely broke the surface. Percy, naked, without his glasses now that he'd finally taken them off, fumbled around toward a rail and clambered in down some steps. The water was cold and he shivered before he felt the sensuousness of the water around his balls, his cock, around his buttocks and on the small of his back. Loiret surfaced next to him his head sleek like an otter. The water came up to their shoulders. Loiret grasped the back of Percy's head and pulled it toward his before planting his lips on Percy's mouth. Percy opened and felt the taste of pool-water flooding in. Loiret let go and took an elegant stroke backward. Percy grasped the stone edge and gasped.

"Pool Party!" screeched an English voice.

"I've brought my things!" yelled another.

There was a click and lights came on everywhere; around the pool, under the water, everything was lit.

"Oh good lord," said a voice, "someone's in there already."

Suddenly the air was full of moths swarming in such numbers that they created a kind of miasma above the pool scorching themselves on the lights and falling dead like grey snow on the surface of the water.

"They've got no clothes on!"

"Who is it?"

The voices were closer, close.

"Oh good lord, it's that Loiret. This is a dream come true."

"Who's with him?"

"Little chap, no idea."

"Two naked men? Funny business, I'd say."

"D'you mean..."

"Bonsoir mesdames," said Loiret standing in the shallow end, naked, hands on hips and facing them. "Voudriez-vous me rejoindre?"

"Oh my god he's gorgeous."

"Oh look at that."

With his hands on his hips, water streaming down the hairs on his chest making them track downward to his groin, his bush wet and shining and his bell-end purple Loiret looked literally divine, smiling and laughing as a good Celtic river-god should.

"Turn off those lights," said a commanding English voice. A woman's voice. "Now."

The lights went out. Spectators on the pool level, on the terrace above, the terrace above that and at the balustrade that fronted the area outside the house were plunged back into darkness and for one second, two seconds, three seconds the chatter ceased. Heels clicked down the steps. The silence held. Heels clicked nearer on the stone surround of the pool.

"Get out of there" said the same woman's voice. "Get out and put this over you. You're making an exhibition of yourself. Get out."

Percy, stock still, heard Loiret start to walk toward the shallow-end steps. The water rushed past his thighs and swished and swashed. Climbing out of the pool he walked up to the woman and stood still.

"Alors, cherie" he said. "C'est toi."

The woman was offering him her shawl. He didn't take it. Instead, squatting down he offered a hand to Percy. Percy grasped it and putting his other hand on the stone lip jumped up and half-clambered and was half-pulled out of the water. The stone hurt his knees. He knelt on the edge, water flowing off him, water that pooled around an exquisite pair of high-heeled party slippers. The hand was still holding his and now it pulled him toward his feet. He stood, naked and streaming water in front of the woman – she was someone out of a a Gainsborough or a Reynolds, slim to thin-ness, pale-faced, her hair, as far as he could see, short and waved in a pre-War style. Her nose, long and sharp spoke aristocratic breeding back to the Plantagenets. She could have been Eleanor of Aquitaine or an Eighteenth-Century countess. All that was required was a brace of wolfhounds.

"May I present," said Loiret, "Lady Daphne Loiret. Ma chère, Monsieur Percy Langrigg."

"Get dressed," said Lady Daphne. "We're leaving." She turned and walked off into the dark.

The noise of the party started up again louder than ever.

Now it was late, very late. Percy was still hiding in the pool house where he'd waited until he was dry and then resumed his clothes. He'd heard Gilbert's voice from up above asking for him until it stopped. Gradually the party sounds faded away. There was the night, he had his cigarettes. As he lit one, he heard the sound of shoes coming down the steps and onto the stone flags around the pool. A flashlight raked over the water. He shrank back against the wall.

"Are you there?" said a voice. "Don't worry. It's Lyle. Per amica silentia lunae."

The tall figure in the black and white magpie sheath dress came out of the dark preceded by a small pool of flickering light. Lyle sat down next to him. "Curse these dresses. They hobble you like a horse. May I have a cigarette?"

Percy offered her his open case.

"Not many left," said Lyle. "Will you be a dear and nip up to the house? It's all open. You'll find cigarettes in the armoire in the hallway. Oh and a bottle of champagne from the fridge. And a couple of glasses. Thank you, Percy. Oh, take this," and she handed him the flashlight. "There are some cushions and blankets around here somewhere. I'll find them. You must be frozen."

Stiff from being cold and wet and from sitting on the stone bench for, what? an hour and a half? Percy's legs barely worked and his knees wouldn't bend. He made his way slowly up the steps.

A few minutes later, back in the pool house he sat down on cushions and found one at his back.

"Champagne?" Lyle opened the bottle and began to pour.

Percy had the glasses at a tilt. Lyle poured a little into each at first and then when the bubbles had subsided slightly added the rest up to an inch from the brim. Somewhere she'd found a lantern and must have used his matches to light the candle that flickered and fluttered light into the pool-house. Percy noticed for the first time that back and side walls were covered in murals in which gazelles and panthers eyed each uneasily other over the tops of asphodels. Lyle handed him a glass.

"Cin cin," said Percy, gamely.

"No my dear," said Lyle, "not like that. You say cin and I say cin. Remember you don't get a double cin."

"Cin," said Percy.

"Cin," said Lyle. They waved their glasses at each other and drank a little.

"Cigarette?" said Lyle.

Percy took out two cigarettes. "Light for me," said Lyle. Percy lit both and handed one over to the tall, ghostly woman next to him, her black hair stiffly marcelled and gleaming when any light caught it. She was pale, tall and pale and her narrow head emerged on an enviably swan-like neck from a kind of cowl that fell back from the neckline of her dress. They smoked in silence.

"What on earth prompted you to swim naked in the literal middle of a party. You must have been neglected as a child. Or are you just easily led. Were you drunk?"

"No, not at all. I don't particularly like drink."

"Bad associations, eh?"

Percy was silent.

"Drunk on sex?"

Percy moved as if to demur but Lyle's wrist and that two-tone gold bracelet were on his knee, steadying him.

"Not a word," she said and putting her glass down beside her took a puff at her cigarette. "In fact don't explain at all. Anything." She took her hand off his knee. "There's no need, really. I've spoken to Gilbert and told him you were both drunk and having a dare. Like frat boys. He's not best pleased that his senior manager's pubes have been on display in front of Le Tout Quercy but as I've explained to him," she took another drag, "the local English rarely go out to eat anyplace good so they won't likely see you again clothes on or clothes off."

Percy breathed out. "Thank you," he said.

"Niente," said Lyle. "The Davidsbündler must stick together, isn't that right?"

The night was quiet.

"Did he proposition you or was it the other way around?"

"I wouldn't...," said Percy.

"You wouldn't aim that high?" said Lyle. "He is a bit Apollo-like isn't he? We wouldn't want you as our Marsyas. All that blood. On the other hand you had an experience that almost all the women at the party and some of the men would give their eye teeth for. Expect more jealousy than ridicule. Or jealousy disguised as ridicule. Did you?"

"No," said Percy. "We didn't."

"You should feel flattered that he chose you."

"Chose me for what?"

"To have his coming-out scene with." Another pause. "We've all suspected for some time that he was homosexual. Or bi-sexual. Gilbert and I believe that she married him out of sheer sexual jealousy. We think those two slinky leopards have the same spots. Now he's shown his wild side let's see if she steps out of her cage. If she does then head for the hills."

"Who is she?"

"Lady Daphne? Well," it came out in a drawl, "how best to describe her? Ghastly, isn't that what you English say? A Ghastly Gorgon. People call me the Ice Queen but at least I have a heart even if I keep it frozen. She has no... now what's the right word? Empathy. I have a friend back in Boston who treats rich women with no hearts. He calls them sociopaths. Apparently it's because they weren't ever kissed or hugged by their parents. But she's hors du genre by all accounts. The thing in the woodshed is more like to have been scared by her than vice versa. I rattle on. Do you get the picture? Well stay out of her way if you ever want to serve lunch in this town again. I mean it. Forget the wren in her nest, this one's a Queen Cobra."

Percy brought out another cigarette for himself and one for Lyle. "Keep the mosquitoes away," he said and lit again for them both.

"Have you heard from David?"

"Have you?"

"No."

"But you hoped to?"

"Yes."

"Do you get the English papers?"

"The Times once a week but I haven't been looking."

"Just in case."

"I suppose so."

"Well would you care to hear from the Lyle Telegraph?"

Percy nodded. "Yes please," he said.

"The lovely Laetitia is now in Hollywood auditioning for the latest Rogers and Hammerstein."

"Are they still together?"

"Who? Rogers and Hammerstein?"

"David and Laetitia."

"Were they together?"

"It looked like it."

"It was meant to. They're both actors," said Lyle, "call it a relationship of convenience. The prince and the showgirl. She was David's property. He groomed her up for the studio to sell on to the highest bidder. It was about their careers, Percy. What shall we say? Thespian realpolitik?"

Percy was silent.

"You thought they were lovers?" Lyle took a drag and blew out smoke. "Don't beat yourself up over it. So did most people. You have to admit they were good. They deserve an Oscar."

"What about David?" "

"Hmm. The little incident didn't do him any favours, I'm afraid. Most people guessed that Laetitia had been involved somehow. Only the police bought the drunken accident story. But sadly the party pigeons smelt cat and they all flew off toot sweet. David had to sell his share in Rosegarden to cover the cost of the party and have a war-chest in case of lawsuits. Then his erstwhile chums sold out to Rank just before Rosegarden hit the buffers, so those boys done good."

"And David?"

"Well, we had lunch a couple of weeks ago and he's cashing in the family silver so he can be 'mobile' as he calls it. Says he's had enough of movies for entertainment. Wants to get into the nitty-gritty. So possibly Paris. There's talk of a new wave of filmmaking about to hatch. And of course before the war, film was art there. Did you know Renoir's son directed a picture? Very poetic. You should like it."

"Me?"

"Yes. You're fond of poetry, aren't you? You know a lot of lines."

"Did David say that?"

"Possibly. In fact I'm expecting Tennyson. You know, standing at the gate alone. The black bat has almost flown. That's night. Not me."

"That's not what I was thinking."

"David says you're a fiend for quotations. He says you ate libraries on your school vacations."

"It was a game we had. A sort of poetry Pelmanism. So, David?"

"Ah yes of course, back to our moutons. Or mouton. It could be

Paris. He has to sell the country seat first. Apparently he's rejected all he learnt about film at Denham and wants to apprentice himself to a Continental master and start again. He told me how he'd gotten into films before the war. Do you know?"

"He told me he'd talked his way into a studio near London, somewhere that's since gone bust. That must have been in '33. Then he worked with Korda I think. On the production side. Then, it must have been '37 or '38, one of his school-chums suggested he talk to someone in the Army about filming the next war. They knew it was coming. That's how he ended up in Hong Kong in '41. That last summer. That and having been to school in China. Government House accredited him just in time before the Japs walked in or he'd have been shot as a spy. Or worse. His crew were all given uniforms. Some of them survived. He went back to where he'd buried all his equipment, but it'd been looted."

"You know he never told me that?"

"He'd always loved the movies, did he tell you?"

"Oh yes he told me about all the picture houses in Tientsin and Shanghai. Did you go there together for fumbles in the dark?"

"You're prurient."

"Yes I am. And you had a prof at school; what did you call them? Masters? No need for prurience there - the imputation is plain, one who took his special charges to the pictures in the vac?"

"Yes, we did."

"Was that the one that raped him."

"Raped him?"

"He didn't tell you?" "

"No. Well possibly. In a roundabout way."

"He said he once stopped you from being raped by the same man."

"Did he? Yes, he did. It's true."

"But

we don't talk about it."

"No."

"Natch."

Percy slapped his neck where a mosquito had landed on it.

"Natty togs," said Lyle.

"Thank you. Not my style, really. Gilbert bought them all for me. Told me it was camouflage just as you said."

"Then you should have kept it on."

"I didn't set out to attract anyone."

"No, I'm sure you never do. But that doesn't stop you from being attractive. There's no clothes can get in the way. No armour either. There is none. Tell me; where is fancy bred?"

"I think it's in the nose. I think there's something we give off, some kind of charge or odour that get's picked up by the people it's destined for. I think we underestimate our noses. I think we're more like dogs than we believe."

"So, you and Apollo just sniffed each other out?"

"That's a bit near the knuckle but yes, I suppose I do mean that."

"Extrasensory perception. Ee Ess Pee. It's the sixth sense apparently. A professor at North Carolina was doing some work on it, late Thirties. He and his wife did tests but it all got pretty much trashed of course."

"And it's all there in the ether?"

"I think it could be something more physical. You know, teeny tiny itty bitty little pieces of things carried around on the air. Like things that make up scents. Little globules of chemical compounds all floating around."

"Like perfumes."

"Yes, like perfumes. And who knows but we may all have scents of our own that we just try to disguise with something bought. Cheap or expensive. Now this could be our game, my dear. You and David have words. Perhaps we could play at perfume Pelmanism? What was she wearing? The La Dee?"

"Vol de Nuit."

"And him?"

"Neroli of some kind. Something French. I don't know." Percy paused. "But surely it's not just the smell or vibrations or monads or whatever we give off. That can only be half the story. Surely it's about the receiving equipment. How we're wired. What the signals tell us. That has to be already contained in us somehow."

"We're somehow predisposed to react to certain aromas?"

"It could be."

"There's no such thing as free will? We're literally led by our noses. Gosh this is like a High School debate."

"I'd say the messages can be strong, powerful, overwhelming but we don't have to listen to them."

"But you answered Loiret's siren smell."

"Yes I did and I was undone."

"Stop feeling sorry for yourself. You're very serious. You're like a serious sort of David Niven. With eyeglasses."

Lyle reached across and lifted his glasses off his face. "Let's look at your gorgeous eyes. David says you have extraordinary eyes. Lovat. Green or blue. Green and blue. What are you this evening? In-between. My favourite shade."

Percy peered across at her. "David said?"

"Yes, David said. Don't you know how much he loves you?"

"Loves me?"

"Yes, loves you. Maybe not in the Neroli kind of way but he told me he fell in love with you when you were boys. He calls you his Little China Friend and I thought he was talking about some porcelain doll."

"I idolised him, that's true. But I never thought he felt the same."

"You're right, he doesn't. He doesn't idolise you. He cherishes you. You mean something very important to him."

"Like Peter Pan and Tinkerbell?"

"You're vile. I'm trying to be serious."

"Please give me my glasses back."

Lyle handed them over.

"Thank you."

"You look different without them. Younger."

"I'm not all that old."

"You act it. You have to let go sometime. You can't spend all your life buttoned into your liberty bodice."

"This from the person who keeps her heart in the freezer and thinks she's a bat."

"We must give you champagne more often. I sense a loosening."

"Well I love David, in my way. But I can't see myself chucking off all my clothes and jumping into a swimming pool with him."

"More's the pity."

"It can't happen. You know it isn't allowed to happen and even if it were I don't think David can…"

"You don't think David can what? Swim?"

"Live with anyone."

"You mean like married?"

"Yes, like married."

"Because he's promiscuous? Because he goes with men and women?"

"No because he doesn't really go with anyone. Not in his heart. There's no other half he's looking for. He's on his own. Inside."

"My Boston friend would love this. You mean he has no empathy with other people?"

"Oh yes he understands other people. He understands their desires. He just doesn't share them."

"And this goes back to childhood I suppose?"

"You didn't have a childhood like ours."

"Maybe I did. Maybe I had a childhood just like yours. Let's face it. We're a bunch of Edwardian rich children kept in nurseries, seen but not heard, goodnight papa, goodnight mama, god bless papa, god bless mama, off to boarding school or shut away with a governess. No wonder we never grew any wings. We're permanently chrysalistalised."

"That's a good word."

"It's a wonderful word and I just made it up and it's mine and you can't have it."

"I don't want it."

"Yes you do."

"No I don't."

"Listen. Hear that? Sssh."

From the wood below came the song of a nightingale. Then another. Then another till the woods were full of music.

"Not communicating through their noses," said Lyle.

"I grant you that," said Percy, "Fancy could be bred in the ear."

"Deceiving elf," said Lyle Destrooper.

Percy began to laugh and Lyle, tilting her head back, began to laugh with him. They laughed and laughed until they had to clutch each other to stop themselves falling forward, until Lyle drew back her hands and began to wipe away smudged mascara from under her eyes. "Oh Lord if anyone should see us now. I bet I look like some kind of bat-woman for sure."

"I think you look..."

"Percy, let's just keep this at the cerebral level."

She paused and they looked at each other calmly.

"Come on now my friend Troubadour. Let's have another one of your ditties. Such a lovely word, a ditty. And Percy,"

"Yes?"

"I can cope with a little melodrama. It eases my weltschmerz."

"Are you sure? Most of the poetry we know is a bit..."

"Melodramatic?" "

"Yes."

"Well my dear you simply have a passionate soul. Passionate and frustrated. Aren't they the springs of the melodrama?"

Percy started quietly:

"'My dead Love came to me, and said:
God gives me one hour's rest,
To spend upon the earth with thee:
How shall we spend it best?

Why as of old, I said, and so
We quarrelled as of old.
But when I turned to make my peace,
That one short hour was told.

...

She touched me not, but smiling spoke,
And softly as before.
They gave me drink from some slow stream;
I love thee now no more.

The other night she hurried in,
Her face was wild with fear:
Old friend, she said, I am pursued,
May I take refuge here?'"

"My Lord, Percy. You remembered all that?"

"I learnt all that."

"At school?"

"No in camp."

"Oh dear."

"We had a sort of English Literature class. We didn't have any books so it came in useful I'd learnt all this stuff by heart. I often got bits wrong and still do. Usually Browning. Sometimes David would come along and we'd recite things together but he didn't come often."

"In case people got the right idea."

"Precisely."

Suddenly Lyle was singing in her best Gertrude Lawrence, "'Someday I'll find you, moonlight behind you...' Oh Percy how priceless. Here we are, Elyot and Amanda in the strictly chaste version approved by the English Lord High Censor for watching by frogs, bats and owls. Will you do the honours with the champagne, please, my dear. Ah. Thank you. Where were we?"

Percy handed her her glass and took his up again. They chinked the rims, raised the glasses up and said together "The Edwardians." They drank.

"And to absent Edwardians," said Lyle.

"To David," said Percy.

"Come on," said Lyle. "I'm getting the chills and you must be frozen. Let's get back to the house."

They got up and walked, Percy stiffly, around the gleaming pool past echinops, cardoons, stachys, convolvulus and sage all the grey-silver leaves that looked as though they were covered in frost. The lavenders' purple was mercurochrome, the last reds had turned the colour of dried blood, bright greens were black and the whites of cistus and oleander shone blue. The scent was warm and woody like garrigue with a cool undertow of decay. As they walked moths cannoned into them, big, solid creatures that buzzed and vibrated on strong wings. The hooting of owls came nearer as the voice of the nightingales faded. On the terrace up by the house all was stillness under the great face of the moon.

"Time to move on," said Lyle as they reached the double-door into the drawing room.

"Where?" said Percy.

"Oh South, I think. Just a couple of weeks at Cap Ferrat and then it'll be time to make plans for Winter."

Lyle's hand went straight to a switch beside the door and the drawing room, long and floored with dark oak, huge dark oak beams above, was lit in one corner by a shaded lamp.

"I'm hungry," said Lyle. "Feeding the wolves gives you an appetite. Come on, let's scout the kitchen." Setting off, hem of her dress swooshing along wooden then tiled floors, she led the way along the house until they reached it. Lyle lit it up. "Well, Sir Percival," she said. "Breakfast?"

Percy turned round to see Lyle leaning forward as she simultaneously kicked off her shoes and reached forward for a frying-pan. She busied herself looking for ingredients then stopped.

"Hey why am I doing this? Gilbert tells me you're learning how to cook. He says you may even be good. So, chef, apporte-moi un petit dejeuner a l'Américaine."

Percy first found an apron to shield his suit of camouflage before finding eggs, a glass of chives, a baked ham from the refrigerator and the remains of a baguette. But first he boiled water and made coffee.

"Attaboy," said Lyle.

About twenty minutes later they were sitting at the kitchen table in front of the old range now superseded by the American electric cooker Lyle had had installed and were eating omelette with chives, slices of ham and toasted baguette.

"This is good," said Lyle, "a good omelette. They say that making the perfect omelette is the first step to mastering the art of French cooking. How are you getting on? Gilbert tells me you spend half your life in the kitchen."

"Beginning to cover the basics," said Percy. "But French cooking is so much more than that. Proper French bourgeois cooking at any rate. It takes years of practice to do it properly."

"Do you think you want to do that? Do it properly I mean?"

"I'm not sure about the Northern style of cooking," said Percy, "I mean the Parisian, Alsace, even Lyons. I like the style around here. People have told me about the cooking further South, the herbs, daubes, cooking with oranges, something called bouillabaisse, cooking over embers. That's something I'd like to try. Cooking without cream. Or cabbage."

"When I head South," said Lyle, "would you like to come with me? You could work in the villa kitchen and learn about how they do it in Provence. Who knows but you might work your way up to being my personal chef." She looked at Percy. Percy looked at the remains of the toast. "You're interested, aren't you?"

"Well yes," said Percy, "I am. Thank you. It's just that..."

"Just that what?"

"I owe so much to Gilbert for giving me a job and letting me get in the way in the kitchen. But thank you. I'm very flattered."

"Good," said Lyle, "It's bedtime. Past bedtime. The black bat has to fly. I think I'm going to put you in the study. Sounds a bit backhanded but it's full of books. Don't stay up all night reading."

"I don't think I can."

"In its own way that was some enchanted evening"

An owl hooted from outside. Oh lord, said Percy to himself, lord and giver of life we look for the resurrection of the dead. And the life to come. "Amen" he said out loud. And the owl hooted, closer.

Castel Beau, Dordogne, September 1948

Pommes Sarladaises

Gilbert and Percy stepped out of the Lagonda onto the white-gravelled turning circle at the main entrance to Castel Beau. Percy slammed the door behind him.

"Silence!" said a uniformed figure that had appeared at his right elbow. "Mademoiselle dort."

"Je m'excuse," Percy whispered.

"Désolé Percy; I should have warned you. L'Alouette dort au nid entre dix-sept et dix-neuf heures," said Gilbert.

"Can we go in?"

"Oh yes. Her nest is at the back of the house. It is a long way from the kitchens. Alors, let us go down."

"Not so fast, Gilbert!" A tall woman swept in to grasp his elbow. "Percy's coming with me." said Lyle Destrooper. "I need to show him the ropes."

Gilbert smiled, bowed and backed away almost bumping into the same figure that had shushed them a minute earlier now carrying their suits in hessian bags out of the car. The man, thin and dark, gave Percy a little look before sweeping on, Gilbert in his wake.

"A bientôt, Gilbert," said Lyle, softly, with a smile and wave. "So, my dear, I hereby enrol you in the service of Castel Beau," she whispered as they moved away from the glaring white drive, "where we all have our part to play." She smiled. "Even American aristocracy gets roped in to help. Vive la Révolution. I just have to remember to keep my head."

"Is she that domineering?"

"Hetty? Oh, you must never call her that by the way. That's strictly for familiars. Mademoiselle L'Alouette exerts a spell over people. She can make anyone do her bidding. Few can resist her command."

"She's just a dancer, surely. And a singer."

"Hocus Pocus, abracadabra, riddlemeree. You are now under the spell and you will never say anything quite as disrespectful again."

"Never," said Percy, looking around him. "If this is magic give me more."

From the shade of a tulip-tree that created a tunnel over the tradesmen's walk they'd emerged onto a terrace that looked full over the river and down toward Sarlat. Balustraded terraces stepped down to a belvedere over the vista each terrace divided into geometric parterres of box and gravel. Fastigiate cypresses or yews pinned down the corners and the centres sported urns full of calla lilies bordered by begonias.

"Wait till you see the other side," said Lyle and so they walked on around the house passing under striped awning after striped awning keeping the sun out of rooms furnished in an Empire style. "Walk on the sides of your feet," whispered Lyle. "Old Shawnee trick. Keeps the noise down," and she pointed upward indicating the Swallow's nest. They crept around to the side of the house that bordered the turning-circle, the main gates and the road down to Sarlat. Percy hadn't really taken all this in as they drove through the gates. Now he gawped. The garden stretched for hundreds of yards either side of a stone-bordered canal along which were stationed at precise intervals more fastigiate cypress, yew or juniper. Trees, pleached limes, ran down either side of this natural plateau. At the far end the lines of trees gathered into a grove of some hundred more set into a lawn with an exact symmetry so they appeared as the pillars of some ancient basilica or the Great Mosque of Cordoba. In the middle of the grove Percy could make out a statue on a plinth.

"Diana," said Lyle, following his gaze. The canal itself was cruciform and at the centre of the cross was a stone island reached by a Venetian bridge. Stone tritons stood at intervals in the greenish water with their conchs ready to blow. Percy assumed they hid the marvellous jets d'eau he'd heard about. Either side of the canal marched a pair of long box hedges broken at regular intervals by outdoor rooms enclosing stone-bordered beds of foliage and flowering plants; lavender, artemisia, rue, echinacea, hyssop, santolina.

Hedges and rooms marched on. Between each room stood the statue of a mythological figure; Marsyas, Pan, Syrinx, Apollo, Orpheus, Siren; the singers and makers of music. Percy wished he'd brought a hat. The glare from the white gravel was intense. Lyle seemed as cool as ever. They crackled down along the walk until they came to the grove. The trees, trunks completely straight and bare, stood in a carpet of moss and flowers where they formed a kind of guard around the statue; watching, careful. Percy noticed that several trees wore a collar made of brass.

Lyle, close by, said "Dogs. When one of her dogs dies they get a tree named after them."

And there was Diana, white and chaste, guarded by the memory of her hounds; Rex, Tonton, Craquotte, Prince and so many more.

Percy, standing on the border of the grove felt like a trespasser.

"You can go in," said Lyle," "it's allowed."

"I'm not sure that I want to," said Percy, "it looks ready to repel any men visitors."

"Yep," said Lyle, "that's the idea."

A breeze came up and began to rustle through the tops of the trees giving them a voice.

"Like Dodona," said Percy.

"More like Delphi I think," said Lyle. "The oracle had a grove didn't it? Come on, I'll look after you."

Taking his hand she led him among the trees that were planted not, as he'd first thought, in exactly matching rows but offset so that one couldn't walk straight ahead, only on diagonals. Tiny flowering plants among them, thyme and chamomile, scented their footsteps. Moving between the trunks was oddly tricky. Together they wound their way round tree after tree until they came to the statue itself.

"Is this Diana?" said Percy. "It looks more like Mithras to me but without the hat."

The huntress in dazzling white was crouching, quiver over her shoulder, in the act of raising the head of the prone stag to slit its throat, just about to make the fatal incision. As he looked closer he saw that the stag's face was human. Looking up at its killer with fully human eyes it silently implored the goddess for mercy. The sculptor had caught Actaeon in the process of transformation. As Percy looked closer still he could see that the stag's hind legs were in the mouths of the pack of hounds. He shivered.

"People only tend to come and visit once," said Lyle. "It creeps them out, that look in his eyes. Let's go."

Percy half-turned to go and looked up into the face of the murdering goddess. It was tender and full of love. "Yes," he said.

Slowly they made their way back to the front of the grove and here they caught the full vista of the garden. "Did she start it?" asked Percy.

"She did," said Lyle, "but don't forget she bought Castel Beau nearly twenty years ago when she was raking it in. Like us all it's had time to mature."

Percy felt the pressure of Lyle's arm through his, attempting to pull him away, to move on, but he was as heavy as lead.

"Don't tell me her magic's worked," said Lyle. "You're not turning into a statue, are you?"

Percy put his hand over hers in a gesture to make her stay. She stood.

The breeze had died and now in the near absence of shadows, the shimmer of heat from the white gravel thickened and stilled. Like a metamorphosed host the pointed trees, hedges, urns, plants, statues stood imprisoned, held by a spell as cruel as the goddess of the grove, not magic but sorcery, in a wicked beauty.

Lyle gently squeezed Percy's arm. "Are you okay?" she said.

Percy felt his knees give way and he staggered. Lyle's arm alone prevented him from falling. He dipped, seemed almost about to fall but with a great effort pulled himself upright.

Lyle was speaking to him. "Oh my dear," she said. "Sunstroke? Come along let's get to that bench. It's in some shade. Can you manage?" Like a nurse she led Percy gently along to a bench under a pleached lime. They sat down. "You need water," she said. "We'll go back to the house."

"In a minute," said Percy. "Just a minute. I'll be fine."

"If it isn't sunstroke you look as though you've seen a ghost. Are you sure you're alright?"

"Yes," said Percy.

"You don't look too good to me but okay let's just sit here. Deep breaths."

"Thank you," said Percy.

"Of course," said Lyle, "no problem. Do you want to talk about it? Whatever you saw?"

"Saw?" said Percy.

"You have the look of an Old Testament prophet who's just seen the veil ripped back. Have you a message from the other side?"

"Is it that bad?" said Percy.

"You tell me honey," said Lyle. "But something's made your hair stand on end." Moistening her palm with her tongue she began like a mother cat to smooth Percy's hair back into its normal wave. "Can't have you going back in there looking like the Wreck of the Hesperus." She stopped and there was a silence. "Are you," she said. "Are you?"

"Alright in the head?" said Percy. "Yes I think so. There are times, not often, hardly ever. I get these feelings of joy or sadness. Sometimes both together. I don't know what prompts them. Just a sight or a sound or... They just seem to take me over. But not for long. For seconds. I haven't..."

"You haven't spoken to anyone about them."

"No."

"Listen. There are doctors back in the States beginning to talk about it. How we react to catastrophe. You know, like war of losing someone. These feelings. What sets them off maybe years later. What can be done about it. My dear you're not alone in this. Far from it."

"Don't dwell, my mother used to say," said Percy. "Let's not dwell."

"Okay," said Lyle. "Whatever bucks you up. How about I give you the inside track on L'Alouette? That's pretty diverting."

"Go on," said Percy, "please."

So Lyle charted the singer's journey from Gospel chorister back in Hoboken to the toast of Gay Paree. How her act had developed from risqué songs to the ethereal warblings and dances that had earned her her soubriquet. How she'd stunned Le Tout Paris with her barely veiled nakedness, how she'd slid her feet across the floors of stages and ballrooms and leapt, twirled, flown through the air like a bird only coming to rest to sing her signature song, "L'oiseau Libre." In the early days she'd usually end up on the lap of the wealthiest man in the room as if by chance, but as time went by her tastes and her wants became more refined. Yes, there had been other black American singers either resident in Paris or who'd included Europe on their tours. They'd been solo acts, fronted bands, danced like crazy and lived like mad but Little Old Hetty as she called herself to her inner circle of friends had simply outclassed them all. Seeing how fashions changed and not counting on professional longevity, though she'd done better than most, L'Alouette had bought the tumbledown

Castel Beau, installed American plumbing, planted a garden "like Versailles" and eventually retired here with her many dogs, then when the war came, kept her head down. Lately she seemed to have recovered her gaiety and it was possible, just possible that tonight she might sing again. There were rumours that a jazz band was on its way from Paris, a band with hot names from America.

"No men in her life?" asked Percy.

"Yes," said Lyle, "but they've all had their balls chopped off. The dogs. She has a major domo, but the talk is he's a eunuch or he's only got one cojone. She just loves it here. She doesn't want any man coming along and spoiling it."

"Tirra lirra by the river…"

"Sang Sir Lancelot. Yes, I know. But she's happy weaving her cushion-covers. She's seen Camelot and wasn't impressed so she rebuilt it right here. Are you okay to move on? We should be getting to work."

"Yes of course."

They stood and looked away from the garden at the château in its gothic-romanesque beauty, shining white and pure.

"Know what she calls it?" said Lyle. Percy, starting to move, shrugged and shook his head. "Her Honky Château."

Laughing, arm in arm, they walked back up to the driveway and headed back into the cool underworld of service.

Percy spent the next three hours doing the rounds of the party rooms checking, checking and checking again. Glasses, crockery, napery. Wine, cocktail ingredients, seltzers, waters. Of the major-domo there was nothing to be seen. It was said that he was upstairs, resting. Percy gathered his team to run one last time through how things were expected to work. They were all good people, well-trained and sharp. He felt confident. Now it was time for him to change into his tails. Even the major-domo had appeared to take his station by the entrance to the ballroom ready to announce the names of the guests as they arrived. "Here we go," said Percy to himself, "over the top."

Within an hour Castel Beau was pulsing with life; party-life and serving-life. The lovely, now-still evening encouraged people to mill on the terraces or walk through the gardens. Stationed in the ballroom helping to serve Champagne, Percy heard the names being announced; a rollcall of local aristocracy, Bordeaux wine barons,

Parisians, some locals, some English, a few Americans and of course Lyle this evening dressed in an emerald-green cocktail frock that flowed down her skinny figure and pooled over her neat black Mary-Jane dancing shoes. She wore no jewellery other than her two-tone gold bracelet. Her hair was as close to her head and tightly marcelled as ever. Now she was next to him. "Feeling okay?"

"Thank you," said Percy.

She touched his arm lightly. "Quel shindig," she said and moved on into the crowd.

A band with a girl singer had been trotting out some recent French dance numbers: Yves Montand's "C'est Magique", "Si tu viens danser dans mon village", safe enough stuff. A couple of Doris Day covers too; "Love Somebody" and for English-speakers "It's Magique", some Frank Sinatra hits; "Night and Day", "These Foolish Things", "People Will Say We're in Love", "Everybody Loves Somebody". She had a lovely voice; people had started to dance. Percy and his team withdrew to the doorways and worked the sides of the room. Then with a ripple of notes followed by applause the music stilled, as singer and band left the room shaking hands and dispensing smiles as they went. Percy had organised for them to have supper and drinks in one of the side-rooms. Standing in a doorway he noticed that Lyle had come up to his side. She had a smile of triumph on her face.

"No one's seen the host," he said.

"She'll pitch up in her own good time," said Lyle.

At that moment he felt an arm brush against him as a couple came through the door. Looking straight ahead was Loiret with Lady Daphne at his side. An ivory silk dress emphasised her pallor. She looked like a ghost. Glancing at Lyle and nodding she pulled her husband onward.

Lyle lent in toward Percy's ear. "Remember. Stay away. From both."

Percy tightened his lips and nodded.

Across the room a new band had started to file in, all men, about fifteen of them followed by a small, handsome, almost-bald, long-nosed man in a lounge suit, white shirt and tie. He was smiling broadly as he followed the musicians over to the dais.

"Mais non!" said a voice next to Percy.

"C'est impossible!" said another.

"C'est un tour de magie."

"Il y'a de la sorcellerie au travail."

"Mais non, c'est lui-même!"

The French guests had started to crowd toward the dais cheering, wolf-whistling and shouting; "Ray! Ray!"

The short handsome man turned toward them, held up a hand for silence then turned back to the band, raised his other hand and began to whistle a tune. The band began to whistle along with him. A guitarist, a good-looking man with a neat moustache, struck a chord. Some of the whistlers stopped, raised their trumpets, while the rest took up their own instruments and together, smiling broadly, they kicked off into "Siffler en Travaillant". The crowd shouted with delight and couples raced onto the floor and began to dance.

Percy turned to Lyle. "Disney-tunes?" he said.

"That man composed it," said Lyle. "It was French before it was Hollywood."

"Who is he?" said Percy. "

"My dear," said Lyle barely able to speak, "that's Ray Ventura. Lui-même."

"Did you get him here?" said Percy.

"Well as a matter of fact," said Lyle but her sentence was cut short as Gilbert, appearing from nowhere, grabbed her arm and practically pulled her onto the dance floor. The song so entwined in the feelings of all the French here tonight, a song of resistance, cheerfulness, the promise of better times returning, electrified the room. At the end everyone applauded but with a raising of the leader's hand the band were already off into "Tiens, Tiens, Tiens," and the room again heaved with movement. The band played and the band sang, bobbing up and sitting down. The music was light-hearted, loveable, danceable. On they went with "Maria de Bahia" and then "Le Nez de Cleopatre". "Oh non," shouted some of the dancers in time with the tune. "Oh non, c'est pas là!" they chorused. Ray Ventura turned around to encourage them. The band went silent on cue. "Oh non!" yelled the floor again: "C'est pas là!".

No one noticed a medium-height woman dressed in florid purple enter the room from the terrace. Just a few pairs of eyes picked out black skin in this entirely white assembly. No one, or almost no one as the band launched into "Shabada Swing" saw their hostess arrive unannounced except Percy who, looking across, involuntarily caught her eye. It was Alcina alright. L'Alouette was here. She winked at him.

The band paused to empty trumpets, take a glass of beer, retune guitar strings. Almost imperceptibly the woman in purple had made her way in front of the band to stand next to Ray Ventura who turned around to the audience and with downward motions of the palms of his hands managed to hush most of them.

"Alors, mesdames, messieurs," he said. "Cela me fait grand plaisir de vous présenter notre hôtesse," – he paused – "Mademoiselle L'Alouette!"

The lady in purple took a bow then straightened up. The room was quiet. "Well thank y'all for coming," she said. "And thank you too Mister Ray Ventura and Django and all your band." There were claps, cheers and shouts of acclamation from the audience. "And I'd like to thank my great friend Mrs Lyle Destrooper for doing all the arrangements here for tonight, thank my own wonderful staff and the staff of La Mirabelle for keepin' all our glasses filled and feeding us so fine." There was light applause. "Now some of you may know that my dancin' days are done."

"Dommage!" cried a voice. More applause followed.

"But I still got my voice."

"Brava!"

"Maybe that's from calling a whole pack of dogs to heel a hundred times a day." Laughter. "The Lord giveth and the Lord taketh away. He took my hips and I wish Him joy of them."

Pockets of laughter among the English-speakers.

"But as He seen fit so far to leave me my voice, I'm gonna use it ladies and gennermen to sing the praise of my adopted country. Ladies and gennermen, guests and helpers I urge you to join with me now to sing a certain song, a song that I never tire of singing."

Ray Ventura stepped down from the dais and with extended arm offered his place to L'Alouette who with stately steps and a rustling of silk ascended.

Looking around the room, extending her arms out to her sides she began. "Allons enfants de la Patrie, le jour de gloire est arrivé!" As her rich contralto rolled around the room all voices followed it. Many guests sang with tears streaming down their faces. Others held hands as they sang. Many, the grievers after the lost, perhaps, sang looking at the parquet floor. Lyle was back at Percy's side singing lustily. They both sang. Lyle's gloved hand gripped his. The anthem rolled on full of grandeur and bloodthirstiness.

Percy wondered if anyone ever actually listened to the words of any anthem. He hoped not. The band had stood up and as "the singing ended the trumpets" broke into a final peal of sound. "The silver snarling trumpets," thought Percy. Are they chiding us for having survived? I can't help it, he thought. I can't help not not having been killed. I should have tried harder.

Lyle squeezed his hand again and looked at him. "Here," she said, "Now. No backsliding. Promise?" Percy nodded and Lyle melted away into the crowd.

Now Ray Ventura was on the dais. Raising his hands for hush he spoke up: "Nous allons jouer pour vous un numero d'un film qui sort tres bientôt. Ce film s'appelle *Nous Irons à Paris*. Voici: A la mi-Août." The band stayed in their seats. L'Alouette began to sing solo, a cappella, just sounds, rich and strange, riffing on a samba beat, clicking her fingers. "Ba, ba-ba, ba-bahhh." The band smiled at each other, smiles broader and broader as she climbed up and down the vocal scale. When she jazzed it up she turned to the bandsmen who shouted encouragement and delight. Up the notes went, down, round and round twisting sideways, uncatchable. L'Alouette spread out her arms and began to twist and turn with the music. Suddenly she stopped and out of her mouth came a word that sounded to Percy like miaow. "Miaooh!" she sang and the band was on its feet. Off they went with the melody and L'Alouette was singing, turning round and round, samba-ing on the dais, hands in air, elbows crooked, swinging from side to side, shoving out her arse, flicking her pelvis forward. A group of people began to form a conga line hopping kicking their legs out to the lines of the chorus: "A la mi-aout c'est tell'ment plus romantique, A la mi-août y'a d'la joie pour les marous. A la mi-août on se sent plus dynamique, A la mi-août on s'amuse comme des fous." And they were. The party was flying with L'Alouette. Ray Ventura had joined her on the dais to take some of the words. The band popped up and down to chorus. The tune itself wasn't particularly strong, not that novel even but here, energised, infectious, it felt like an anthem to pleasure. When it finished the crowd roared and cheered. L'Alouette smiled and took a breath, hands together at her chest as if in prayer.

She began to speak but couldn't be made out against the hubbub.

"Taisez-vous!" yelled a few voices. "Mademoiselle veut parler. Taisez-vous!" The noise sank to a whisper.

She spoke. "Mesdames et Messieurs cela me fait grand plaisir de vous presenter un de mes amis, un camarade de ma couleur, un grand musicien, un trompettiste qui prend le monde d'assaut. Avec l'orchestre il vous donnera le nouvel hit qui fait fureur aux États-Unis. Mesdames et Messieurs, je vous donne Monsieur Louis Satchelmouth Armstrong!"

She gestured toward the same double door she'd appeared through. The curtain quivered and in came a man with the broadest smile Percy had ever seen. Waving and bowing he stepped up toward the dais where the band began to applaud him. Up stood the sax players and opened the number, dah, dah-dah, dah-dah, taking it slow. Up stood the band trumpeter and joined in with Armstrong. On they went, swinging. On came the tenor sax taking the lead, accompanied by the piano at walking pace. Gradually the rhythm picked up and the trumpets began to squeal. Armstrong's trumpet hit a note like a cat on heat, the piano broke into a jazz rhythm and all hell broke loose. The trumpet went wild. Two young people were out on the floor twisting and shimmying, the man behind the girl had his arms around her waist as they thrust their hips forward and back in a frank representation of sex. Several of the guests looked scandalised but L'Alouette was there on the dais urging them on. "Slither like a snake, wiggle like a dog, that's how you do, you do the Hucklebuck". More couples, those dressed in the newer, freer clothes came out and joined in. As the music got hotter and hotter one girl lay down on the dancefloor while her partner stood over her and gyrated his hips. L'Alouette clapped her hands above her head. The trumpet got wilder and wilder. More and more of the older people left the room including Lady Daphne, face pale and set, Loiret at her side. "Animal music," Percy heard her say. As they passed Percy felt Loiret's hands stroke his thigh deftly and invisibly. Armstrong's trumpet hit the high note and the song closed. People cheered. The music began again, trumpets squealing it out. L'Alouette was there: "Yeah my baby knows, Matilda Brown told ole King Tut Say if you can't pay me five just keep your big mouth shut Shoutin…" And they shouted "Hey! Ba-Ba-Re-Bop! Hey! Ba-ba-re-bop!"

Loiret came back into the room, grabbed Percy's hand, dragged him onto the dance floor and began to jive. Percy was horror-struck. "Bouge ton cul!" shouted Loiret over the noise. Percy bouged.

None of those around him seemed to care that he should be dancing with a man so, trying his best to pick up the rhythm and the movements, Percy danced. "Elle est ailleurs!" shouted Loiret "Danse!"

Freedom. This was freedom. Hidden in the centre of the mass of couples they were in the safest place in the house. Loiret smiled, he jived, he sweated. Percy for the first time felt the joy, the wonder of dancing with someone who wanted you physically. To be where the moves on the floor, fast, fully clothed, distanced stood for slow, naked, skin-to-skin action. Loiret danced like a man possessed. Only someone as naive as Percy wouldn't have realised that he'd been taking cocaine somewhere out of sight. He grabbed Percy, pulled him close, pushed him away, had his arm around his waist, his hand in his up higher, down lower. His fingers took every opportunity to brush across Percy's clothes. He'd taken off his bow tie and from undone collar black hair sprouted. He was light, he was lithe like a fox. Percy stumbled, tried to follow but Loiret was the perfect leader keeping control, adapting his moves to his, staying on the beat even when Percy let it go. And his eyes. Those eyes knew their way. They led and Percy followed. Girls on the dance floor flashed glances at Loiret with his film-star looks but otherwise none of the dancers seemed to notice or care about two men dancing with such passion. Loiret pulled Percy toward him, close, and Percy felt the hard flesh of the man's erection up against his thigh. This was extraordinary, paradise. "Why me?" said the voice in Percy's head, "Stay away. Stay away." He couldn't any more than a moth could steer around a flame. The danger only heightened the pleasure to bursting point. They leapt, swirled, jumped up and landed back on their dancing feet. In the midst of it all Percy felt his cock dribble something down his thigh. If Loiret had chosen to enter him there on the middle of the floor Percy would have been completely and utterly ready to receive all of Loiret, to give and to receive pleasure of which he'd only dreamed. To be a couple with someone at last. The number finished. Loiret with a smile on his lips came closer, put his arm around Percy's shoulders, drew them together as if into a kiss.

"Excuse me," said an English voice, a woman's voice. "I think the next dance is mine."

"Tiens," said Loiret. "Blanche Neige."

Percy stood, appalled, feeling as though he were actually as naked as just a moment ago he had wished he could be. Loiret let go of him and they both stood there like two Adams with mouths full of sweet, red apple facing the gaze of the exterminating angel.

"We take a break!" said Ray Ventura somewhere a hundred or more miles away. People started to clap and cheer, a trumpeter let off a screech of sound, the drummer drummed a set and gradually the music broke up followed by footsteps, laughter and loud chatter. In the vortex between Percy, Loiret and Lady Daphne there was utter silence, a disorienting, sick-making silence as though they were utterly still inside a tornado moving at hundreds of miles an hour destroying everything in its path.

"My husband is a wonderful dancer, isn't he? Now if you'll excuse us, Mr...? Mr Langrigg, thank you. Now if you'll excuse us Mister Longbrigg, I'm afraid we must be leaving. Isn't that right Laurent?" She turned to Percy. "Thank you for keeping my husband out of mischief. For an awful moment I thought I'd lost him to one of these little French girls. He's not picky. Are you Laurent? And I'm afraid he rather prefers the less interesting ones. Don't you, mon cher? It really doesn't matter what they look like. I've always said to myself one day I shall find him dancing with an ape. Mister Longbridge. Allons-y, Laurent. Il faut retrouver mon manteau. Do be careful Mister Shortwood. Many people catch a chill after leaving a dance floor. Isn't that right Laurent? Suis-moi, chéri. Au talon." Like an ivory statue she seemed to be turned rather than to turn herself. Her feet, invisible under her dress, propelled her across to the door. She disappeared without looking back.

"Merci," said Loiret and bowed to Percy, "Un jour je te baiserai." Turning, he followed his wife out of the room.

Supper was to served. Percy spent the next hour working with the staff bringing up dishes from the kitchen, carrying piles of crockery, folding napery, lightning spirit lamps under entree dishes. It was fast, it was familiar, it was the bliss of work. Gilbert came in and out, so did the major-domo, Bricqout and finally Lyle.

"Les jeux sont faits," she said to Percy giving him a cold, sad eye.

Picking up a stuffed quail's egg she wandered back out of the room. The guests began to troop in filling plates with paper-thin slices of Bayonne ham, beignets, brochets, gougères, tartelettes d'homard, ouefs a la mimosa, salade à la Russe, melba toasts with pâté de foie gras, carpaccio de boeuf, du Saint-Jacque, du thon, soufflés de fromage, du crabe, aspic jellies striated with vegetables, with ham, stuffed tomatoes, stuffed olives. For the Americans and the rock-and-rollers there were hot dogs, coleslaw, pommes a l'alumette all politely disregarded by the French. A plate-carrying diaspora headed around the public rooms and out onto the terraces looking for places to sit and chat. Later there would be ice-cream and for late stayers a breakfast at about two but for the next hour Percy and his joint team sped silently about the house and the terraces recovering crockery and cutlery, picking up empty glasses and exchanging full ashtrays for clean. The stairs down to the kitchen were constantly busy with up-traffic and down-traffic. In the basements a gang of washer-uppers recruited for the evening began to scrape off orts, wash and dry. The talk was mostly about the extraordinary appearance of Ray Ventura. Who next, said one wag, Yves Montand? Jacques Tati said another. Frank Sinatra said a third. Waiters who'd been in the ballroom during L'Alouette's set were retailing in scandalised voices how the ethereal swallow had changed her tune and was growling out jazz. Others related names of famous guests; the politicians, the aristocrats even one or two film stars. A radio was turned on and here downstairs had its music too.

The memory of the dance was making Percy's flesh smart and his conscience sting. To a nunnery, he thought. I'll go on retreat, I'll do penance only don't let Gilbert sack me. He prayed to Saint Lyle for assistance, patron of queer men who meant no harm. If only David were here. David would have just laughed, smiled Lyle on-side, broken down Gilbert's objections with his good humour. And what about Loiret? Ah, he thought, Loiret naked in bed, his long legs sprawled in sleep, his cock dozing on his thigh its tip oozing sweetness as he dreamed. And her? Snow White or Wicked Witch? He was suddenly afraid of her anger, her revenge. But surely nothing public? She wouldn't want her husband's proclivities talked about, made common knowledge. He would lose his practice and she would lose face. But they were rich. They could live where they wanted. Loiret would simply have to go into exile in Surrey or some cold English country house with only the stable-boy or the hunt-master for fun and games. Percy shivered. Lyle was standing next to him.

"You promised," she said with a hurt look. "Come with me."

Together they walked out of the basement by the servants' door and stood under the archway of the tulip tree smoking.

"I never expected that," said Percy. "I didn't go looking for him. I think I was just drunk with the music."

"And he was up to the eyeballs on coke. Shit." She flicked ash angrily onto the ground. "I don't blame you for losing your head that way. He's a sex-bomb just waiting to go off. Is that a hand-grenade he keeps down his pants? Lucky he didn't explode there and then." She sighed. "I know you didn't go looking for him. But I'm worried she'll come looking for you." She paused to take a drag of her cigarette. "Let's walk."

They went slowly, gravely, arm in arm around to the main entrance, to the sweeping stone steps flying upward in a double cascade to the grand doors open to the night with flambeaux either side. The air was still and cool the night full of stars. They looked upward and saw the great river of the Milky Way spangling and sparkling with such sublime ferocity it took their breaths away. Owls hooted from among the lime trees. From the horse chestnut trees either side of the gate leaves fell, conkers plopped to the ground. A fox screamed and a bat sped close enough to Lyle's head to make her duck and exclaim. Dogs began to bark.

"How many does she have?" asked Percy.

"Are you changing the subject? Well, why not. Don't dwell; isn't that right? I think twenty-three or twenty-four. Every one a mutt."

"She doesn't breed them?"

"Oh no. She hoovers them up when she sees them. Any stray by any roadside all the way to Nice and back."

"Where are the kennels? I haven't seen them."

"Cunningly hidden away in some old wine cellars under one of the terraces. They get the darndest view, the sweet creatures."

"You're being sarcastic."

"Actually, I love dogs. Just not packs of them. Did you ever have a dog?"

"Two." Their soles and heels crunched on the gravel marking their slow walk.

"And…?"

"I had to leave them when we went into camp."

"Didn't your servant or boy or whatever take care of them?"

"I'm sure he did. In his own fashion."

"Oh. I see. I'm sorry. Will you ever have a dog again?"

"I don't think so."

"Get a job here and you could have two dozen. I'm sure you and the major-domo would get on fine."

"I'm not thinking of leaving the hotel."

"What are you thinking of?"

Percy stopped, his arm through Lyle's braking her to a halt. "I don't know. I think I'd like to learn more about cooking but…"

"But what?"

"But what would I do with it?"

"You mean with what you'd learnt? You could open a restaurant. Or that offer's still there: be my private chef. Think of the parties we could give, the meals we could serve. I'd buy a house in… where would you like me to buy a house? London? Oh no, okay. Paris?"

"Not the States?"

"No, I don't think I'm gonna be going back. It isn't home. Just a source of funds. Does that sound callous?"

"Realistic."

"Thank you. So where would it be realistic for me to pitch my tent? I know. A Greek Island. Or the coast of Turkey. We could appear from the sea like deities. Or refugees. Or both. Gods on the run. Oh so Homeric. Can't you just see it? A great rambling Ottoman house? Or a blinding white modernist villa. Do you know I went house-hunting with Nancy Spain on Skiathos?"

"You know her?"

"We met at the Gateways in, oh, '39."

"That's a lesbian club."

"Why yes. It is. What? Prudery? While you boys haven't been daring to speak its name us girls have been keeping mum."

"Very droll."

"Thank you. We rented a house. Up there on a rock above the wine-dark sea. You know, one day we swam from Kanapitsa to Skiathos town. Later on we went snorkelling off the house and do you know there's the most enormous crater underneath you. It's an abyss. We swam over the top of an abyss. It just makes my skin crawl to think of it."

"Did she have her own cook?"

"Just a local. The food's not so complicated there."

"What did you eat?"

"That summer? A lot of country salad with that cheese they like. The spongey one. Heaps of fish. Almost always fish."

"How do they cook it?"

"Bake it in vine leaves, grill it, make skewers with it and cook it over charcoals. They paint it with bunches of herbs dipped in olive oil. While it's cooking. They chuck the herbs on the coals. Smells divine."

"Was that it?"

"No, we had meat. Not much. Skewers of pork bathed in oil and vinegar and herbs. Oh, and pies! Those pies they make with the flakiest thinnest pastry. Pies with that cheese, pies with spinachy stuff. Same pastry they use for those - baklava. Out of this world. But really very simple. Every morning the smell of eggs frying in olive oil. Heaven."

"The best meal you had there?"

"It wasn't really a meal at all. Jonny took two whole carloads of us into the town one evening and we just sat in this courtyard, and we drank little glasses of that ouzo, the aniseed thing, without water. Tiny glasses. Ouzaki they said. And we had pieces of octopus grilled on the charcoals. That was it. That aniseed. I love anything aniseed. And that chewy, salty meat all charred and smoky. I thought I'd died and gone to paradise. One night we didn't eat at all. We just drove and drove through olive groves and came to a taverna behind a great wall of shingle and danced Greek dances and drank wine made by Germans and there was just us and the owners. Then we walked over the hill of shingle and there was a beach like a scimitar. You know it shone in the moonlight like cold steel. And we swam and the water was very still and very deep. Then we drove back through the olives. The beach was called Wild Celery. It was just us women. The Maenads."

"Were you mad and terrifying?"

"No just drunk and horny."

"Bacchantes, then. A bit less ferocious."

"Unless you're King Peleus."

"He asked for it."

"So that was Greece. Very tactile. You kind of absorb it through the skin. I should like to go back there one day."

"To your villa."

"Well I might go to Lykia of course. It's such an undiscovered country. Full of huge, ruined towns and monuments and temples. Apparently Freya's planning a visit there. She says it's the most magical place full of huge, tall pine trees and doors in the hills into the land of the dead."

"Does she see herself as Persephone?"

"Well her mother's dead and I can't see Stewart following her into Hades. He's one of your tribe by the way. Everyone knew that except poor Freya."

"They might be getting along splendidly."

"There's no reason why not. I just don't think they are. Oh and I didn't tell you. That Summer on Skiathos. Noel came to stay."

"Noel Coward?"

"He and Nancy were great pals. He adored her. She had a piano and he used to sing his songs to us all in the evenings as the sun was going down and the air was just like a bath with pine essence in it."

"You had a ball."

"Yes sir we did. Did you hear music just now?"

They had walked along to the flights of steps underneath which were a pair of glazed doors leading into a room for footmen and coachmen. The doors were closed but through the glazing came the sound of a trumpet as self-confident and joyful as a young man setting out on a date. Then came the note of a woman's voice trilling up and down to a tune they thought they recognised. They crept up to the doors. Lyle put her beaky nose just a little too close and was spotted by L'Alouette. She waved at Lyle who opened the door a fraction.

"Come on in honey and bring your boyfriend. Me and Louis here just having a little fun. Come on in, come in."

The room was like a cave of golden stone under a cupola from which hung a simple brass chandelier. Around the wall were benches broken by a fireplace and its surround. "We just snuck down here for some reminiscing. Ain't that so?"

"Yes Ma'am," said Louis Armstrong.

"And Louis brought his trumpet. Hey Louis, let's see what we can put on for these folks. They're my friends. Hey! Negresco back this February. Suzy Delair," said L'Alouette, "Negresco Nuit."

"That song. First time I heard it," said Louis Armstrong, "Henry Betti."

"Andre Hornez. 'Cept it was Jerry Seelen wrote it up in English."

"I'd like to record it one day."

"I'm sure you will. But hey we keeping these good folks waiting. Hetty's ready, You ready, ol' Satchelmouth?"

"Yes I am."

"Take it away."

Hettie began: "Elle est vraiment toute la joie du monde Ma vie commence dès que je la vois. Et je fais Oh! Et je fais Ah!" Bah, bah, bah went the trumpet up and down the melody. Hetty swayed, Lyle swayed like a calla lily in the wind. Percy stayed still. Hetty waved at her friend to get him to stop. He stopped. Hetty came over to Percy. She and he were the same height. She took his chin in her cupped hands and looked him straight in the eye. "Now you listen, honey," she said. "I know you can dance when you wanna. I saw you with that foxy Frenchmen. No I don' care who you dance with. You got hips, you got legs, knees, feet I know you have. Hetty saw them move." She let go his chin but carried on looking straight into him. "Now there's nothing like sex can make you dance but he ain't here no more and you don't want sex with me or Miss Lyle here and you wanna keep off the coke but I wants you to move so watch me and I'll show you my trick how to do it. Okay?" Percy stood, embarrassed. "Don't worry honey I ain't gonna eat you. Not like that anyway." She let out a raucous peal of laughter. "Okay so do what I do. Lift your arms in the air. Keep your elbows bent. No, away from your sides or you look like a faggot. Now think all your weight going up through your fingertips. You too, Lyle! All your weight going flying up till your legs go empty. Now all the weight flies on up out of your hips. Okay? Now wiggle your back. Eh? Ain't it all light down there? Like you wanna take off and float. Okay so now you bring a teeny bit of that weight back. Keep your arms up. Lift your feet now lift your feet now move your feet now move your hips now bend those knees float up now press down now, sway those hips now make a little shimmy now set on off keep it up, keep it up now walk this room yeah dance this room now, move your butt now. Ain't no one looking, Okay Louis let's make this man really dance, hit it now."

Hetty had been walking, dancing in front of him. The trumpet took off up-tempo and she turned to take Percy's hands. "Come on," she said. "I don't bite. Imagine I'm the one you want. Now look at me. That's it. Now I'm your man. Dance for me, Come on honey do your dance. Do your own dance. That's it. That's it." Blood rushed into Percy's head and his legs, feet and hips broke away from his conscious brain and began to move in a dance. Hetty let go. He brought his arms up, brought them down, spun around, kicked, jumped, spun around again. Lyle was doing the same but wheeling her arms around like a windmill stamping up and down faster and faster. Then she stopped, leaned back and came up to Percy with great strides. She took hold of him. He flinched. She frowned. She spun him round, let him go, caught him and spun him again. She stood next to him. They jumped, spun round, separated, hugged themselves, swayed and spun around, careered from one side of the room to the other, turned, did it again. The trumpet sallied on jazzing it up at speed. Lyle and Percy stuck out their backsides, shook their hips, bent downward, shook their hands, stood up, hands forward, shimmied, lent back, did it again. They walked, slid, hopped, bounced. Hetty joined them, clapping her hands and shaking her hips, arms in the air. "Do your dance!" she cried. Then the music came down to tempo and she was back on the note: "C'est si bon De partir n'importe ou Bras dessus, bras dessous En chantant des chansons". Slowing down to a more sedate waltz Lyle and Percy danced bras dessus, bras dessous until the trumpet screeched out a long wavering note. They froze. Then with Hetty they sang, "Et si nous nous aimons cherchez pas la raison. C'est..." They rolled with the trumpet which broke into a long slow climax of sound, "parce que c'est si bon!" They waltzed through the last lines of the chorus until with a giant wavering screech the trumpet blew its long, long last note.

"Why thank you, my friend," said Hetty, "for that remarkable treat. Now I'm going to get you back up to the party for a glass of Champagne." She took Louis' arm and steered him toward the door. They both looked back.

"Thank you. Good night!" chorused Lyle and Percy. The departing couple smiled and walked on toward the grand staircase and out of sight.

"My goodness," said Percy. "Was that actually dancing?"

"There are more dances in heaven and earth," said Lyle, "than our dull ballrooms can dream of. Come on," she said, "let's go and get that fresh air. Unless you have to be back to work?"

"They can spare me a few more minutes."

"I do like you," said Lyle.

"I like you. I wish David were here."

"So do I. Do you think you have a future?"

They walked a little.

"If he really feels about me the way you say then I don't know. Perhaps. If we can find somewhere where men can live together. Not Tangier by the way."

"But maybe for David."

"I don't know, I don't know what it is for him. Boys, Guardsmen, snake-hipped Arab youths. Men that look like girls. Hairy brutes. We've never talked about it."

"Perhaps it isn't about sex."

"You mean a kind of relationship of convenience."

"Is love just convenient?"

"You know I hardly know him. We were together a lot at school but he was older than me and head boy eventually and there were conventions about keeping your place and not having friends across forms and years. But we were close once, yes."

"When you were abandoned there?"

"That sounds dramatic but yes."

"But you saw him in Shanghai."

"Out of the corner of my eye."

"And you were in that prison camp together."

"Yes. But not in the same Mess luckily."

"Why lucky?"

"Because if it had come out that we were..."

"Lovers."

"Friends. It would have been just as awkward as at school. I was a hotel manager, and he was Government House. Just about. You've no idea how snobby Hong Kong could be."

"Didn't the camp shake things up a bit?"

"Yes, but not that much. Not always."

"When did you know you loved each other?"

"You mean like Scarlett and Rhett against a backdrop of burning Hong Kong go-downs."

"Yes please."

"I think it was when we said goodbye."

"Oh, Percy! No night of bliss!"

"Sorry to disappoint."

"You mean you just shook hands and kept your upper lips stiff and nothing else?"

"I don't think we expected it to be such a wrench, that's all."

"Was it in a burning dockyard?"

"Not far off. We weren't long out of camp. Actually David was out and I wasn't. Then he sent a message to meet him. He was about to board a Royal Navy ship to be debriefed."

"Did anyone think it strange he sent for you?"

"There were a lot of friendships in the War. That had to end."

"I see. Of course. How romantic. What did he say?"

"He just said, 'Thank you,' and shook my hand."

"Were there lots of people around?"

"Yes."

"And he walked off up the gangplank and that was it until...."

"That night in London."

"When he picked you up off the sidewalk."

"More or less."

"Don't you want to be with him?"

"When did you become a white slaver?"

"Percy! I'm shocked. Oh dear. Is that how it comes across? Like I'm experimenting with you? I'm sorry. Really I am. I know it's impossible and yes I'm sorry to interfere. But he spoke about you with such affection. Like you're his talisman or something. Is that right? A talisman? And then I know you like men and as for him..."

"Yes?"

"I think he's a sort of Julius Caesar. A man to all women and a woman to all men. That kind of thing."

"Not a great foundation for a marriage."

"Some of the best marriages actually. Especially the honest ones."

"Honest liars."

"Something like that. Here we are back at the grove."

"So you think he should get married to a girl but carry on with me at the same time? For the rest of our lives?"

"I know. It's the sort of thing dear Noel was writing about."

"Do they bear reading?"

"That was unkind"

"You mean the actual choice isn't Amanda it's Victor?"

"No of course not. For Victor read Amanda. Sort of."

"I can't imagine him acting that one out in front of the Lord Chamberlain."

"Do you think the Lord would have cottoned on?"

"Did you know he wrote it in Shanghai?"

"Not at the Atholl Palace?"

"Nothing ever happened at the Atholl Palace."

"I met Gertrude you know?"

"You've met everybody. Even the people you haven't."

"There may be troubles ahead?"

"But while there's music..."

"And love and romance..."

"Let's face the music and. Shall we really?"

"Why not. You can just about hear the band." "

"May I have the pleasure?"

"You may."

Lyle curtsied and Percy bowed. To the far-off music of the band they took a waltz across the gravel. Suddenly they stopped. There was movement among the trees. They looked at each other and into the grove. There like a giant owl a figure in a long, flowing loose dress swooped and rushed around and between the tree trunks. It warbled a song and Percy, mome raths and tulgey woods flitting across his mind, had a strong need to laugh. Lyle reached out and put an arm across his chest as if to stop him. It was L'Alouette and she was dancing. They stood, separate, as still as the statues. At that moment a big black dog, a wolf-like big black dog materialised out of the grove and stood itself right in front of him. As Percy looked the dog in the eye it growled softly.

"Okay Buster," said Lyle, "we just wandered down here to get some air. We're gonna turn our backs now and leave Momma to her dancing. Aren't we Percy?"

She turned very slowly to face along the canal toward the house. Looking at anything but the dog Percy did the same. After a few seconds with no teeth in his trousers he assumed the dog had run off.

"Keep looking ahead," said Lyle.

They did and were rewarded by the sight of a huge burst of fireworks above Castel Beau. Partygoers were crammed onto terraces, glasses in hand, gazing up into a night sky powdered with cascading stars and meteor trails. And below that the fireworks banged, fizzed and boomed away causing all the penned dogs to bark and the people to set up a chorus of delight. The last rocket trail curved back to earth and the people, realising they were cold, rushed back inside. The party was beginning to end.

"I must get back," said Percy to Lyle.

The next morning Percy was back on duty at eight manning a skeleton staff while, fortunately, the guests slept late. At nine he allowed himself a cup of coffee in the office. There was as usual no sugar but he had, in any event, lost the taste for it in the years when he had had none. At least there was coffee again. Proper coffee not that roasted chicory powder with hot water. He sighed and studied the rota for the next few days. Was this really it, he asked himself, for ever? He'd married work young, perhaps too young. And now there was an itch of uncertainty prompted in good part by Lyle's questioning. She meant well. In fact she was turning out to be a kind of guardian angel. But she was wealthy and had choices. He had none. That was a chilling thought. To be on a track whose points were frozen careering on and on until. Until something.

Percy made a noise between a sigh and a yawn. He liked it here but did he actually belong? David hadn't shown any interest in him these past few months. Not a dickybird. Lyle said he was extricating himself from some kind of financial scrape. "But he will come, she said." Poor Jehane du Castel Beau. Went mad with waiting. Waiting for what? For love. And then it killed her.

If he were to be a hotel manager for the rest of his life then he'd end up somewhere top-notch. If he wanted to. No doubt about it. His curriculum vitae was sound. Good, even. And yet Lyle had said that David cared for him deeply. That he was David's talisman. So what? Their lives were hardly on converging paths. And there had been Lopez. Or there had nearly been Lopez. Worrying about trouble ahead he didn't like to think about Loiret. The best he could hope for there was that Lady Whatsit would take her husband to England to freeze or drench the passion out of him. Next time though. Next time a fling. Why not if he was discreet? Everyone said he was discreet. His time as a Night Manager had been his schooling in that. Oh dear. If all tracks led to a "sun-lounge" in Eastbourne having coffee, lunch, tea, supper, breakfast with dying colonels and their bridge-playing wives and widows was it worth spending the next thirty or more years as a monk? Poor us, thought Percy as he pulled himself together. Common little Tweedledum and Lord Tweedledee. Unrequited love. He took a sip of coffee. It had gone cold.

There was a knock on the door.

"Entrez," he said.

It was Lisette with a letter in her hand. "Pour vous Monsieur," she said reluctant to let the letter go.

The paper was heavy and scented with an eau de cologne. Roger et Gallet? The front read Mr Percy Lowrigg. He knew at once who the sender was.

"Merci Lisette," he said pulling the envelope out of her hand. She bobbed and left. Percy took up the letter-knife and slit the envelope across pulling out a piece of stiff, crested card that read, "Dear Mr Lopwood would you allow me the pleasure of inviting you to join me for lunch at L'Oie d'Or in Sarlat today at one o'clock?" It was signed simply, "Daphne Loiret". The rest of the card sported an address and telephone number. Nothing about either the card or the message allowed for refusal. This was the dread command alright. Percy made himself stand upright even though his knees were shaking. Knocking his thigh into the desk so that it hurt he staggered toward the door and the front desk where he asked Thierry to phone through to the number on the card and communicate his acceptance. Then he went outside for a cigarette.

The morning was golden. Gold leaves hung from trees or fluttered groundward to join the others in glowing piles. The light poured a kind of honey around the hotel garden from a sky of the purest cerulean. How strange it was that the flowers of autumn were so often mauve. Those colchicums and Michaelmas daisies. Michaelmas. Was it today? Perhaps a week or so off. St Michael and All Angels. That had been the dedication of the chapel at Yantai. Michael. So Old Testament. With his sword. And his living fire of judgement come to purge the earth of what was it? Purge this realm of bitter things. Solace all its wide dominion with the healing of thy wings. There was a flutter and all the white doves that lived on the hotel roof rose up from where they had been pecking for food on the ground and flew off to wheel around and around till they resettled on the ridge of the garages. The sun's oblique rays caught a bush in a garden bed. What was it? St John's Wort, he thought. Fixing in the yellow leaves and the red-amber berries the sun seemed to set the bush on fire. Bells sounded from across the river through the still air. Did they do Matins in France? The bush blazed on. Oh let it freely burn thought Percy let me freely burn till earthly passions turn to dust and ashes. Kindle me with ardour glowing. O comforter draw near. Out of the sun, its black fur glowing rich russet stepped a cat the likely putter-up of the pigeons. It was Mephisto, the house cat. It came and wound itself around his ankles, purring. Percy bent down to stroke its ears. Cross my path he said to it; cross my path. Obligingly Mephisto unwound himself, walked off to the right then sallied back straight in front of Percy and made off to the left the top of his tail making staccato quiverings in the air. The sun still held the bush and made it glow like an artefact and not a living thing. The golden smithies of the Emperor must have made it. A leaf fell and dropped to the ground. Some casual shout broke the silent air. "Monsieur! S'il vous plaît! La téléphone!" Cigarette unsmoked Percy went back inside.

By midday Percy had farmed out all his work to others and was getting ready. He put on his best cream-coloured linen suit with a white shirt and the cerise colour tie rippled with silver that Gilbert had given him all those hours ago. His socks were brown lisle and his well-polished shoes were tan brogues. His hair was carefully brushed and pomaded, his fingernails clean and scrubbed and his spectacles polished. He put money in his wallet. Picking up the bottle of Floris he put it down again. This interview could turn nasty and he would be a fool to hand weapons over to an adversary. "You even smell like one of those," he could imagine her saying. It takes one Edwardian to know another one, he thought. She'd have been brought up in the same code that he had learnt; that people of other "races", homosexuals, the poor of mind and bank account, men with eyes too close together, the deformed, the unlucky, the Non-U, Roman Catholics, Jews, the list went on, were all "them" while "we" had been taught from birth how to recognise "us."

Percy was only barely inside the gates. It was having been brought up starved of love, first, and his exposure to the brittle cosmopolitanism of Shanghai, so full of fakers, second, that had given him enough detachment to seem like a member of the tribe. A very junior member of the society of un-carers. Strange wasn't it that the Nazis, in the early years, before the exposure of the camps and the Japanese too with their utter contempt for the Chinese and Koreans were deemed racist while the salons, banks, clubs, parks, gardens, government and more of the Imperial British were closed to their coloured subjects. We were close, thought Percy, very close to the evil. He straightened his tie.

That had been Lyle on the phone earlier. He'd told her about his forthcoming lunch with Lady Daphne. "Put your tin hat on," Lyle had said. "And prepare to be on the menu." She'd paused. "That one's a vicious bitch. Would you like me to come with you?" No thank you, Percy had said. "Then I'll see what's left of you later. What time do you finish? Okay, come over. No it doesn't matter how late. Stay the night. Ciao."

Now put your armour on. Wrestle and fight and pray. Tread all the powers of darkness down and win the well-fought day. Hmmm. Sentiments fine for an all-boys school chapel. He didn't like to think how Lady Daphne might fight.

"Monsieur est très élégant!" said Lisette as he passed by the desk. "Bon appétit!" Actually he had none at all.

The bicycle-ride down to Sarlat had left him dusty and he'd dashed into the restaurant's cabinet to wash his face and brush himself down. As he came out he saw Lady Daphne already at a table.

"Powdering your nose?" she said. "Such a good idea."

"Good morning," he replied. "How nice to see you."

She flinched slightly. This was the sort of greeting one would give to an equal. Touché, he thought.

"One has been told that this is positively the best restaurant in town. Their speciality is pommes sarladaises. Have you tried? Oh but of course at the hotel. They're quite peasant food in actual fact. Rather like that ghastly cassoulet. Just bits of bird and some beans. Too, too funny how the tourists salivate over it don't you think?"

"Thank you so much for inviting me, Lady Daphne."

"Oh my dear not at all. One imagines you don't manage to get out much. Of course people will talk. Don't you find that delicious?"

She gave him a smile of stage coquetry.

Why you're more practised than a Geisha thought Percy.

"Will you have wine? Shall I call for the list? Garcon!" Her tone could have commanded the entire Grande Armée. "La carte des vins s'il vous plaît. Pour monsieur."

The waiter showed no sign of anything other than well-modulated servility, but it was clear to both men that this was an inversion of the natural order. "Oui Madame," he said with but the barest glance at Percy the un-man.

Lady Daphne had unveiled her pennant. Percy knew that against those who feign indifference, indifference is the weapon of choice.

"What wonderful weather," he said.

The sommelier came over with a wine list as thick and as dusty as a Bible. He handed it to Percy while glancing over at Lady Daphne. It seemed likely that she'd been here before.

"Do choose," she said. "Laurent doesn't look at it of course and he always orders the same thing. I'm sure if you asked the little man he'd tell you."

Percy opened the book and slowly turning the pages almost to the end passing the clarets and the Burgundies flipped onward to the Vins de Pays. He pointed. "Le Tour des Gendres," he said. "Le quarante-quatre. Bien chambré."

The Sommelier raised an eyebrow. "C'est bon," he said.

Percy took out his cigarettes and handed the case to Lady Daphne.

"Would you mind terribly if I smoked my own?" she said. "They're frightfully mild and my throat is so tender this morning."

They both took out cigarettes. The waiter rushed over to light her ladyship's. They both exhaled smoke.

"You were Out East," she said. "Pith helmets and stengahs and Myrna Loy and all that."

"Further East Lady Daphne. China."

"Shanghai? Was it all terribly seedy the way one hears? Not now those frightful reds are taking over. Put the lids on the fleshpots one shouldn't wonder."

"Before the war," he said.

"And were you in the hotel trade in those days?"

"I was," he said.

"The Compagnie?" "

234

"They were the competition," he said. "I learnt my trade working in my parents' hotels."

"How glamorous. Shanghai before the war. One imagines opulence, opium-dens, White Russians selling their fabulous gems to survive. Did they all troop into your foyer, Mr Longbury telling you their tales of woe?"

"We mostly catered to Americans."

"Then I imagine you must have had impeccable plumbing Mr Lingfield. Americans are notoriously hard to please."

The Sommelier appeared with the wine. He uncorked it and was about to pour into Lady Daphne's glass when with a tiny wave of her hand she directed the wine into Percy's.

Percy swirled it around and sniffed it. "C'est bon."

"Mais oui," said the Sommelier. "Monsieur a bien choisi. Une belle robe, nez puissant, cerises à la bouche."

"Absolument," said Percy.

The Sommelier smiled. Percy now had a guard of one. The Sommelier went away.

"Please do choose for me Mr Loudbrook. Laurent normally does of course. But nothing with donkey or horse if you don't mind. The war rather put one off."

"Many French ate rats."

"If one must eat rat then one would prefer them cooked en brochette."

"The Romans ate dormice after all. With honey."

"You're a classicist Mr Langshank? Latin? Or you prefer Greek?"

"Salade aux noix and then the foie de veau?"

"With pommes sarladaises? One simply must."

Percy called the waiter over and gave their order.

"One can tire of goose eventually," said Lady Daphne. "They're so common around here. And do you know that the clever locals let not a bit go to waste. Other than the head of course. They eat the liver as you know, the meat, the feet, the gizzards. Are you fond of food Mr Lethbridge? You look as though you might be."

"Yes," said Percy, "I'm helping in the kitchens occasionally. Taking lessons."

"How fascinating. We've been through no end of cooks over at Montfleury. None of them seem to come up to the standards of the belle-mere and they don't last a month. She's a great one for the rissole. Nothing edible may be wasted that cannot be minced and fried up. My stomach abhors twice-cooked food. One does rather long for a great carnivorous feast at Simpson's. Are you much of a meat-eater Mr Latterbury?"

"Is Montfleury your husband's family home?"

"As a matter of fact, yes it was. A couple of generations ago. The grandfather lost his fortune, they were in cement-powder I believe, and the place had to be sold."

"And you bought it back."

"Yes, wasn't that too marvellous? There it was on the market and it simply had to be snapped up."

"And the estate?"

"Yes, most of it actually. There had to be land because Laurent loves so much to ride. Do you ride Mr Lowstones?"

"No."

"Quel dommage. There's little more fun to be had than having a great beast between your legs. Ah. Here comes our salad. I do hope it's got some of that Roquefort in it. I do love salty cheese."

The salad arrived: escarole, roquette, walnuts, Roquefort, tiny cubes of fried bacon all dressed with a walnut-oil vinaigrette. Bowls were presented. The waiter disappeared. The salad stayed where it was.

"Oh do go on," said Lady Daphne, "help yourself."

Percy took some salad, put it in his bowl and looked at it. This was far too much like a school exeat: the over-eating, the strained smiles, finally the bloated stomach.

"Perhaps I shall smoke a cigarette. Would you mind?" Percy waited for the next traduction on his surname but there was none. Perhaps she'd run out of ideas.

"We have a positive forest of nut trees. All out to tenants of course. They make the most marvellous oil. Honestly," she let out a puff of smoke, "the food here is so rich I've put on pounds and pounds since we arrived. Thank goodness for riding. It's so toning. Do you exercise..."

"Please call me Percy."

"Why thank you." Dragon-like she blew out more smoke. "It's so strange to one to hear Percy as a Christian name. Of course we know the Percys back home. Are you related?"

"Do you ride ever day?" asked Percy.

"Oh well I try to you know but Diablo, that's his name, is such a lazy brute. One practically has to whip him into action. There are some days I think he'd rather just be ridden about by the stable hands. Of course, I don't stand for that. There's no point in owning horseflesh of that quality just to let it be straddled by little boys. Wouldn't you agree?"

"Salad?"

"I rather think I shan't, thank you. But an excellent choice. Are you thinking of going fully native?"

"I'm sorry?"

"I mean settling down here. Getting yourself a nice French" - she paused - "Wife."

"I'm not really planning ahead."

"I think that's wise," said Lady Daphne, "You never know what might be just around the corner. Garçon? Enlevez s'il vous plait. Ah non, désolée, j'ai pas faim."

The bowls were taken away but the salad left where it was. Warm plates were brought and from a silver dish great lobes of thin, supple calves' liver were served and the foaming butter poured over them. The remaining rosy juices from the dish were poured over the salad. The Sommelier came over and refilled their barely touched glasses.

"Bon appétit," he said though his words fell like an unfortunate stone into a deep cold well.

"Such fun," said Lady Daphne. "I understand you came here from London. Did you work there?"

"Yes I was assistant manager at the Sherborne."

"Oh gosh, the poor old Hotel Shub. Is it as boring behind the scenes as it is out front? One imagines poor little mousey women going off to join their husbands in India. What will they do now we've given it away? Poor Louis. He's tried so hard. And poor Edwina! What she's put up with."

"What has she put up with?" said Percy.

"It's simply what one hears you know. Not a grain of truth I'm sure. I shall leave you to guess. Daddy would kill me if he thought I'd been peddling rumours among the hoi polloi. He's frightfully strict about that kind of thing. Let's just say The English Disease."

"Gout?"

Lady Daphne gave a trill of laughter and leant back her head showing one or two pointed little teeth. Putting her hand delicately to her chest she rolled her eyes sidewards in an imitation of amusement.

"Too perfect!" she said. "I really must pass that one on to Daddy. He has to spend so much time entertaining people he'd love a new bon mot to add to his repertoire."

"Is your father on the stage?" "

"Oh too priceless!" she shrieked. "And another one! Perhaps he could recruit you to write his endless after-dinner speeches. What a scream!"

The mask of a smile moved across her face from side to side. "I should have thought Lyle Destrooper would have told you. It is Destrooper isn't it? This year, I mean? You know Ferrand was completely decapitated? The husband who was killed at Le Mans."

Percy paled.

Lady Daphne leant in and touched his forearm lightly with her gloved hand. She looked him in the eye. "Didn't she tell you?" she said tapping his sleeve with her finger. "He just came off the track and piled through a plate glass window. They had to stitch it back on for the funeral. These Roman Catholics believe you have to be buried entire you know." She leant back and paused. "Does that mean eunuchs can't go to heaven one wonders? Oh I say isn't this conversation taking the most bizarre turn? Do eat your liver. It'll get cold."

"What made you think of eunuchs?"

"Gout."

Percy did his best to eat some of the liver on his plate. It was cooked to absolute perfection tasting of milk and butter with a faint tang of something earthy like mushrooms or truffle.

Lady Daphne stood to get up. "Frightfully rude of me while you're eating but do excuse me a moment." Percy bobbed out of his chair to a half-stand. "Please don't," she said. "Enjoy it while you can."

Her willowy figure dressed today in a pale-green New Look suit, the cynosure of all the eyes in the room, her head crowned by a tiny skullcap tightly covered in primrose-covered feathers. She stepped delicately toward the back of the restaurant. Percy put down his knife and fork and lit a cigarette. He was still smoking when she came back. Once again he elevated, was flapped at, sat down again.

"Women's issues," she said. "Do I startle you? No I imagine you must be very modern. We have to be careful of taking too much exercise you know. One must look after one's seat. It must be nice to be a man and not be prone to that kind of thing. Or perhaps some men are?"

"The liver was delicious," said Percy.

"Will you stay in France do you think?" said Lady Daphne. "Are you, as they say, bedded down here?" She smelt gorgeous.

"What a lovely scent," said Percy. "If I may say so."

"Goodness me!" said Lady Daphne. "I must say I have never been complemented on my scent by a man before. At least not in public. Why you are very French already. Percy. Well," she said leaning forward again so that the fresh scent enveloped him, "since we're two girls out for lunch together I can tell you that it's been made for me by Nina. Nina Ricci. I shall have to stop wearing it when anyone can buy it of course. It's to be called L'Air du Temps. Don't you think that's clever?"

"Yes," said Percy. "Very modern."

"Well me must leave the tiring old war years behind don't you think? I'm sure everyone's had enough of it by now. The Americans have rather got it right wouldn't you say? All that youthfulness. All those low waists and canvas shoes. Everyone having a good time. All that rock and roll music and that jive dancing. Do you enjoy dancing? Percy?"

"I don't think I'm very good at it."

"So much depends on one's partner don't you think? It's rather like horse-riding. One must choose the right mount."

"Yes," said Percy.

"And be so careful not to choose the wrong one. Or one could be headed for a fall. So to speak. Dessert? So much more ethereal than pudding isn't it? As a sound. Pudding sounds so stodgy and dull. Dessert, pronounced correctly, sounds delicious. One imagines light little pouffes of choux pastry full to bursting with cream. And covered over with dark brown chocolate. All ready to be gobbled up. Goodness, I'm such a glutton!"

"Tart," said Percy. "Apparently they do a wonderful tarte aux abricots here."

"Yes of course, apricots. Rodolfe!" she said, "Rodolfe!"

"You know the book?"

"I'm not as green as I'm cabbage-looking as dear Nanny used to say. Do I surprise you?"

"It isn't an easy book."

"Too difficult for simple overprivileged women like me? What a shame? Just when I thought you were joining our side."

"It's simply that I found it very..."

"Bleak."

"Yes, a very bleak view of life and the world."

"Bleak for women of appetite."

"Yes. For women who are more, more passionate than their men." She breathed out smoke. Percy stayed silent. "Men! Now surely this is something we have in common. An understanding of men. Yes do you know I will have the tart."

The waiter, hovering having taken away the meat plates, understood. He slid away.

"This is jolly," said Lady Daphne. "Let's anatomise them; see what breeds about their hearts. Shall we say laziness?"

"I don't think that can be true of all men."

"Perhaps not in the public sphere. At home they'll expect to be waited on hand and foot. Personally, I think it's a kind of emotional laziness that affects them. They don't seem ever to consider the effect of their actions on others."

"You mean like starting world wars."

"Or finishing the coffee and not ordering more."

"Or destroying Dresden."

"Or reading the newspaper first."

"It sounds as though most of men's sins are committed at the breakfast table."

"Shall we move to the bedroom. Metaphorically. Don't worry. Having their way with women they regard as their right don't you think. As if we all lived in caves."

"Surely things have changed?"

"Oh well there was the war and women drove ambulances and dug up mangel-wurzels and riveted away and got up to all kinds of things in the blackout. But now it's over we have to go back to the kitchen sink."

"I can't imagine you at a kitchen sink Lady Daphne except..."

"Metaphorically, yes."

"Do you see yourself as part of a sisterhood?"

"I had no idea our hotels had been infiltrated by radicals. Shall we be murdered in our beds? Will the cancer stop at Italy or spread up to England?"

"Do you see women as men's superiors?"

"Yes as a matter of fact I do."

"Are there no men in your life you defer to?"

"Defer. What a servile word. Yes of course one has been brought up to show deference to one's betters. Which mostly means men. You talk in a very old-fashioned way Mr Lostboy. There are new philosophies emerging. Actually here in France. The talk in the cafes of the Left Bank is of existentialism."

"What does that mean?"

"In a nutshell? A woman's view? That the greatest sin is to put others first."

"Especially men."

"Especially men. We women must know ourselves. Respect ourselves and our desires."

"But you were accusing men of selfishness."

"That's merely being inconsiderate. They mean or at least I think they mean that freedom comes from within."

"And in the meantime you put up with enslavement without?"

"One must first find one's inner freedom before seeking freedom outside oneself."

"Don't you think this could be just a little local philosophy? A way of coming to terms with four years of occupation, collaboration, humiliation?"

"Do you always speak in threes? Perhaps, but that imprisonment may actually have opened a door."

"Into the mind?"

"Yes, if you like."

"And where does this leave relations between women and men?"

"Equal."

"But you said you think that women are superior."

"I do. And I think that after a few years of equality that will be abundantly clear."

"Do you hate men?"

"Ah the man-hater, the man-eater, the heartless bitch. Look I'm talking in threes too. Because a woman has been let down again and again by men to the point she no longer looks up to them she must be a gorgon, naturally."

"I didn't..."

"Oh there's no need. I know what people say about me. The Ice Queen. Blanche Neige my husband calls me. Ah here is our tart. You may it eat. It isn't poisoned."

On the plates in front of them sat a perfection of apricot tart. The pastry, better even than that prepared at L'Epergne d'Or, stood up to the fork but did not resist it. The frangipane filling had the slightest feel of bitterness of almonds to contrast with the unctuous flesh of the apricot. The covering glaze had been made with just enough lemon juice to correct its sweetness. A piece of it barely weighted the fork in the hand yet in the mouth it was solid, powerful.

"Frightfully good," said Lady Daphne.

They finished and looked at each other. "A digestif?" said Lady Daphne.

"No thank you," said Percy.

"Coffee?" she said.

"Yes please."

The waiter came over for his instructions.

"Imagine us talking philosophy," said Lady Daphne, "over a meal. Is this what would have been called a symposium? Where youths were corrupted by their elders?"

"They were all men," said Percy.

"Well of course. What's the fun in having sex with slaves all the time? They have to do it whether they like it or not. How much more exciting to have to make someone want it of their own free will. There aren't many men who bother with that, I think. No. Sex between men fascinates me. How does one please an equal? After you? No, after you? Am I shocking you?"

"Not at all. But you're asking the wrong person."

"Because you don't prefer men or because you haven't been to bed with enough to know?"

Percy blushed.

"You know we vestigial upper classes are much more enlightened than the commonality seems to think. We've been bred. According to strict rules. When we're not in season our men must find other ways to enjoy themselves. No one really cares with who. Or what."

"But you've married from choice, surely?"

"Freedom means the power to make mistakes."

"Are you saying...?"

"Under normal circumstances that would be none of your business but seeing as you seem to have set your cap at my husband..."

"I have not."

"Don't argue. It's tiresome."

"You mean I should defer to you? To your interpretation of events?"

Lady Daphne looked at him in silence. "Well, Mr Nethersole," she said. "Tell me your side of the story."

"Neither at the pool nor at Castel Beau did I invite Mr Loiret to swim or to dance. They were both entirely his idea."

"Yet you went along with them."

"I did."

"You led him on."

"I did not."

"You're very definite."

"And you are blinkered."

"Now that shocks me, Mr Whateveryourname is. I take exception to that. I'm not a mare in harness. You will take that remark back."

"I shall not. You've put the blinkers on yourself. You're seeing only what you want to see."

"I know what my husband's proclivities are. I know in which direction his wand points. If I've put on blinkers, Mr Langrigg, it's to avoid seeing who he's carrying on with. How low he can sink I do not care provided that he descends behind closed doors. I don't want his goings-on shoved right into my line of sight nor everyone else's at the same time. You crossed a boundary Mister Brownsword. You humiliated me in public."

"This is life, Lady Daphne, not a play by Racine. Divorce him. Let him go. Let him be where he belongs."

"With you?"

"Of course not. I already..."

"Already what? Have a lover on the side? Let me see. David Maldon. So the talk is true."

"What talk?"

"That his heart belongs to Daddy."

"That's ridiculous."

"Then why are you blushing? I didn't realise he'd lost his reputation for a little non-entity such as you."

"If I'm that little and if my entity doesn't exist then why are you so worried that I'll snatch your husband?"

"I'm not worried about that. Don't be preposterous. I've seen him take fancies to men before and they all come to nothing. No, Mister Percival, I need to see you punished. Pour encourager les autres. Ah. Here's our coffee."

They drank in silence. The rest of the room was empty.

"Here's what you will do Mister. Mister. Mister Beggarman-Thief. You will leave France. Tomorrow. You will go. And you won't come back."

"Why should I?"

"Did you know my father is our Ambassador in Paris?" Percy was silent. "Daddy can have just a little word with someone who can take away your passport. Or have you denounced to the French police as an active homosexual. You would then be deported. And imprisoned in England. Any source of money you have from England can be stopped. Your right to work in France can be taken away. Do you understand that you have no choice? Good."

"We all have choices."

"And if I were you, I'd choose to go. The hotel won't want you if your presence disgraces them. And you can be sure that any other employer would be given the full facts about you."

"They aren't facts."

"They will be. And don't bother going running to the third Mrs Heiress either. She hasn't been popular here since Ferrand died. They blame it on her. She's a pariah. Only her money is on her side."

"I could just tell the truth. That your husband chose me as his partner. In the pool. On the dance floor. Just a prelude to the swelling act..."

Lady Daphne reached out across the table and slapped him smartly on the cheek. "Now," she said, "you will leave France. Answer me."

"I will not give my thoughts away to you, Lady Thoroughbred.

Whatever I do and whatever I choose will be unconnected to you. I am a free man. A free man who happens to be homosexual. You are not a free woman. What you have been saying proves it."

They looked at each other.

"What a pity we forgot the pommes sarladaises. And such a shame that you won't be able to come back to try them." said Lady Daphne.

Percy stood up summoning all his will and strength and walked to the door. Outside the sun was shining.

Lugano, Un Biccherio d'Acqua, 1988

Un biccherio d'acqua

"Thank you I'm quite comfortable. I'm well looked-after aren't I Tonia? Yes, thank you cara non ho besogno. Where were we?

"Yes of course. Into the microphone. Could you? Thank you my dear. Yes, my name is Lyle Destrooper and I am resident here in Lugano, Italy. My age is. Oh gosh you don't want to know that do you? Oh, thank heavens. I'm not sure that I remember myself. And you want to talk about my dear friends Percy Langrigg and David Maldon. Mostly about Percy and his cooking scuola. Yes. I helped him to start that you know. Oh yes you do know. You say Tom told you? You've met Tom? Oh my goodness. Tom! Dear Tom! Such a sweetheart and so good for Percy. Percy used to call him my little fag. It had to be explained to poor Tom that it was a British private school thing. You know where the older boys made younger boys slave for them. Fagging they called it. Tom wouldn't let Percy call him that in public you won't be surprised to know. No, I'm absolutely sure not. No. Tom was his amanuensis. Tom began his book for him. We liked Tom. He was so pretty like the marble faun if you've read it. Or seen it. And suddenly one day his folks turned up from Fresno and abducted him. Just like that. Can you believe? Poor kid. What? Oh dear. Recently? Oh my. Oh not that awful disease. Tonia portami la scatola dei fazzoletti. Grazie. Excuse me. One minute. Such a cruel. Mi scusi. Un attimo. Poor sweet Tom. Grazie Tonia questa signora dice che un mio caro amico giovane e morto di AIDS. Che destino crudele. So cruel. Yes, I'll just have a sip, thank you.

"Where would you like me to begin? Ah yes, the flight from France. Well of course he went straight to Gilbert as you can imagine and told him it would be best for the hotel if he went. I think Gilbert put up some protest but apparently he was having money troubles and thought he might have to put the hotel up for sale so six rounds with Blancheneige didn't exactly appeal to him. So between them they decided Percy's departure would have to be on the q.t. and that's exactly how it was. I'd have socked the stuck-up bitch on the jaw. Seen some blood on the frosting. Kind of see myself as Annie Oakley. Did you ever see it? I saw it in London in '47. Dolores Grey was swell but you had to wish you'd seen Mary Martin. Did you know she ended up a mezzo after two years of belting out those numbers? Sure did. So you see I'd have stood up to Snow White and that pompous father of hers and told them I'd drag them all into the gutter with me. And fuck her husband too. After all what did Percy have to lose compared to them? His folks had sold all the family silver and he didn't get back-pay after the War like many of them did. He really had to work for his living.

"But yes there we were at Les Rossignols at the crack of dawn getting into the car. My it was a beautiful morning. A real Fall morning. Sun not yet up but you could see the light shining on the spider webs over all the plants. Connecting them all. Only connect. Who said that? He was one of those too you know. Had an affair with a policeman, didn't he? And it was purple. Or rather mauve. The flagstones and the gravel and the walls and all the plants in the garden had turned mauve. That used to be a good word you know, mauve. Comes from Turkish mavi – it means blue. Or purple blue I suppose. Percy loved to know about words. About their history and what they'd all been through in their lives. How life had changed them. He used to say words are like folks only he wouldn't have said folks that's just me being folksy. People he'd have said. Words are like people. They can be just one thing from birth to death or they can change as they go and take on another character. Or more than one character. Look at gay. You know 'madly gay.' Gay was like joy or joyful. Something that put a spring in your step. What does beige come from? Percy would have known.

"Anyhow. Mauve. The colour of colchicums. I had acres of them at Rossignols. All over the place in front of the house as you drove in. Out in the open and wild cyclamen under the trees. Colchis was where Jason went to steal the golden fleece. Where he met Medea. Another of my spirit-ancestors you know. I used to sometimes wear black and vamp it up for Percy with a veil or a cape or something over my head and a whole load of mascara on. "Andromaque!" he used to say. Or recite. "Andromaque je pense à vous!" Andromache, Medea, close call. Funny how dramatic he could be despite being so buttoned-up when you met him. He'd read so many plays, read so many poems. You know, he used to say, one day movies will be three-dimensional, and you'll be able to play them in your own parlour. Did he say parlour? I said yes wouldn't it have been wonderful for that little amphitheatre at Rossignols. We could have put on Racine and watched all those flaring nostrils with fire and passion all the flammes and the couroux pouring out of them. But he had them going on in his head all the time. Poems are like plays he used to say. They need to be spoken to come to life. Yes. Now that shows how Edwardian he was of course. You can't imagine people getting round the fire or the salon or whatever and reading Tennyson to each other anymore. Can you? But he did. All along the valley. Stream that rushest white. That was one of his favourites. Now why did I remember that? He'd just come out with a poem sometimes of an evening or at una piccola festa a casa mia. The best thing was he was completely unembarrassed whatever folks thought and you had to hand it to him. Dear Percy.

"Anyway, there we were in the crepuscule and everything was chilly and mauve and it felt as though a great adventure was about to begin. And it did. The air was like Riesling from a great year. The car was like a hound with a great long nose lying there on its paws all ready to run till it bust and it kind of growled a little. Not the De La Haye – I'd exchanged it with Gilbert for his Lagonda. And one of the maids, was it Berthe, was sobbing. I remember I gave her my handkerchief. Madame, she said, madame j'ai peur que vous ne reviendrez jamais. That made me shiver. It was like a little curse. Little fata morgana. A vision. Ein morgenvision. She was right of course. The staff were okay but they didn't like me in France not really. They said my money had killed him. Ridiculous but you know, shit sticks. So I didn't go back. And I never saw my colchicums or my cyclamens again. I mean what the heck we'd only lived there together a few months and it can only have been two years I lived there alone well only a quarter of the time really if you think of all the travelling but I don't know. I missed those colchicums and those cyclamens. They were like a promise of something better. You know; after. I can't say why or how. I just felt it. Still Percy had the quotation of course. "Ride together, forever ride," he said as the car pulled away and we were looking out of the windows. That became one of my favourites. It's so sad you know it can make me cry. You can't imagine crying over a poem, can you?

Thoughts that do often lie too deep for tears and all that. That was the other side of being Edwardian. Your buried life. You know that one? We had to keep it buried. And so we buried Les Rossignols and I buried Ferrand finally and Percy buried the Mirabelle and whatever ideas he'd had about putting down roots there and we had a nip of pear eau-de-vie like the farmers have for breakfast and we drank a toast to everything we were leaving behind and off we went.

"No, not straight away. I didn't want to go to the Riviera. Too many familiar faces even at that time of year. Anyway I'm super-sensitive to gossip and I could just imagine them all saying there go Dick and Nicole and laughing away behind our backs. So we went down to Perpignan. Pepinya, the Catalans called it. Practically empty. And every day we motored down around those stinking ponds etangs they call them god knows what ends up in them they're kind of like a test you have to pass to get to the beach but when you're there it's just a huge sweep of sand practically from the Camargue to Collioure. Yes we did go there but I felt like a sardine in one of their cans and everyone trying to look like Picasso and looking like a convict instead. I hated it. So we just went to the beach at Argèles and read books and swam and I said don't worry she wouldn't think of looking here so you just lie down and take a nap and maybe you'll get woken up by a prince and there was one young man used to come down for an hour a day and lie there and up would go his erection and stay there oh half an hour and then it would come down again gradually and he'd pack up his things and when it was soft he'd go. There was nothing there really. You just parked up and walk to the beach oh there was a kind of cafe how could I forget that. La Flamant Rose. No Le Flamant Rose. The Flaming Rose we used to call it but it means pink flamingo as I'm sure you know. There were flocks of them on those stinking ponds. It served only the local wine or wine from the area that rough red stuff they make. The only white grapes they grew were muscat and it made a sticky topazzy sort of wine you drink bien frappe ice cold. Or you could put out glasses and trap the wasps with it. Yes and it did serve some food fish mostly of course. They'd cook sardines over charcoal and then fillet them and you could have them in a baguette but there were always bones. Sometimes they'd cook rouget and you could actually have those on a plate – not a particularly clean one. One day they cooked a whole loup-de-mer over embers and they brushed it with rosemary branches dipped in olive oil. I remember Percy said could you buy this for me Lyle, please, and we could add a bar and run it for the tourists and I said who'll ever come to Plage Malodorante and Percy said we could call it Bar Malodorante just for fun. Now it's Canet-Plage and all built up I believe. In the evenings we'd wander round the old town where it was still so warm and eat paella and tons of fruits de mer and Percy said is honeymoon like this and I said no buster this is a whole lot better.

"But yes of course we couldn't stay there forever. 'Undern cometh after noon' was Percy's motto, so after a month or so the winds started to blow up and one day the cafe was closed so we had a pow-wow and went East. Yes, to Italy. And eventually he asked me about David as in: was it true what the bitch had said that everyone in London knew his heart belonged to a man. What could I say? I think what she said really shocked him but it was better he knew the truth so I said yes, honey, it's true. And am I the man he said? What could I say? I said I think you are.

"David? He was back to making documentaries after the studio thing went phut. He picked up work from Pathé and Movietone and the other British newsreel companies. I used to love them, didn't you? That screechy music and there's the Duke of Edinburgh or Lady Docker or Charles de Gaulle or Nehru - it was all so random you never knew what you were going to get. And the plummy voice-over like he's taking you through the race card. Out they come all the famous people or infamous and have a little trot round the ring and profile and smile to the camera please. now mosey along. we've got a famous politician waiting. He went all over the place and I believe he was well-respected in his trade and he was so dashing to look at and turned up at all the right parties. His name was always being hitched up with some society girl or actress you know The Lord and the Showgirl. Yes, just like Laetitia West. And Deborah Kerr would you believe? I sure didn't. But then some wag said his heart really belonged to Daddy, so everyone started asking who and no one even dreamt about Percy till that frigid bitch put two and two together and made a million. That was the real reason David didn't come out to France that Summer like he told me he was planning to. He didn't want to drag Percy into the limelight, so he let it go. It was better. Was David sad about it? You know what? He was probably heartbroken, and I say probably because no one knew where David Maldon kept his heart and that included David Maldon himself.

"Back to Percy. Yes. He didn't really say much in the car for quite a long time after we left Perpignan. I guess he was trying to work it all out and I just left him to it because in the end he made the right decision which was to press on with his own life and not be beholden to anyone else. Like he'd sort of taken his vows. I used to wish for him that he'd have some kind of affair and I pushed him in front of so many men in so many places and I think he had the occasional one-night stand but nothing more and I remember I kept on thinking oh Lord please don't let him fall too heavily you could just see it coming that he'd fall in love with someone totally unsuited to him but as it happened he already had. Prince David. Yep he was an Edwardian all right. A very long engagement and practically almost a virgin on the big night.

"So we pressed on that autumn and no he didn't want to go to Grasse or Menton and it wasn't such a hardship because the few fun people had left the Riviera already. And I drove and drove and it was lovely in its own way. He wanted to see the Grande Chartreuse for some reason to do with a poem I think or Ruskin or someone who'd stayed there but in fact it had all been a hospital in the war, then it was off-limits and anyway the monks had been kicked out for years. But we bought some of that liqueur and turned back South. It seemed to please him going through the passes and yes, I could see what he meant that it was like taking a dive into deep water the way you see it all in front of you if it's a clear day and down you go. There wasn't much traffic then of course. Fuel was rationed except for tourists. Italy was pretty messed-up. Those Germans were bastards what they did on their way home. They kept up the killing right to the bloody end even after their game was up. They pretty much raped Italy. No wonder it nearly went Communist. But that was Uncle Sam's big success against the reds: 'saving' Italy. Making it safe for Audrey Hepburn. Though that was a couple of years later, of course. I think we stayed in Turin and I made him go and see Portofino and he did deign to say he liked the food which was mostly fish and those awful slippery sea urchins and things with tentacles but I just kept schtumm. The wine was delightful everywhere. We had to go to the beach near La Spezia and we lit a bonfire on account of Shelley then he wanted to go to Sirmione on account of Catullus, so we headed East again.

Can you open the window, please? I'm going to have a smoke before Tonia gets back. I'll just blame you; do you mind?

"And just before we go any further can you remind me why of all the people I've ever met it's Percy you want to talk about? I mean why not JFK or Clark Gable or my first three husbands? If you want to know who was gay and who was sleeping with whom back in those days I can probably help. And I know quite a few writers. Nancy Spain, Willie Maugham, mad old Ezra, Howard Spring, Taylor Caldwell they all came to visit in France or Italy. Or England. No I'm never going back. I'm a European now. Who changed the subject? I did? Okay but now I ask you a question. Why Percy? Are you related? No. Oh to David. You're related to David? No. So why then? You read his book. His book. His cookbook? You're doing a thesis. Okay. On cookbooks? I thought you student types were all radical Marxists. What's it called? Cookin' up a Revolution? Hey now that would be swell. I'm just trying to imagine Percy Langrigg as the Che Guevara of the kitchen. Okay so he had a moustache at one stage and I even once saw him in a beret but. Oh okay. Your turn. Yes I did ask. Wait up, I just have to chuck this into that bush. Ouf. There you go.

"So you were saying you're writing about Percy's cookbook. Not just Percy, okay. And Elizabeth David? Oh yes, Percy used to talk about her. Julia Child. Of course. Big Julia. I'd forgotten about her. Percy had her first two books. Really? A TV show? In the States. Oh my. Of course yes, Julia Child. Paul. It was Paul wasn't it? Paul Child. Yes of course. Diplomatic Service? Paris in '48? Yes, it comes back to me now. I think I must have bumped into them at some kind of do. Big woman, that's right. Pasadena. Now why should I have remembered that? She came from Pasadena. Why not? Some of my best friends are from Pasadena. [Sings] 'Home in Pasadena, home where the grass grows greener.' [Coughs] You know Percy used to call her L'Impératrice? As in Riz. My, how it all comes back to me. Okay so you're writing about the David woman and Child as well as Percy? So does it have a theme this thesis? You know, a title? Not yet. Leave it to the end. That's what Ernest always said. Don't straitjacket yourself into a title. It should all become clear at the end. He was older of course, Ernest, but it's funny how Child and Percy were practically exactly the same age. And the David woman too? Really?

"Well he might have done if it hadn't been for the war. He was a dead man walking. In some ways. He said he wouldn't make his fiftieth though he did. I think that's why he loved his poetry so much. And food of course. He had to teach himself to cook. He'd never cooked before the war he told me and during it the only thing they had to cook was rice. I think he picked it up working in hotel kitchens. Oh of course. You know about all that. Did he talk about food all the time? No. No he didn't gush like that Child woman but it was very spiritual to him. I think after the war he was kinda brain-dead for a while. It had taken his parents after all. They were torpedoed in the Java Sea. Let's hope they drowned quick. There were some fat sharks in the Java Sea. Then he felt obliged to come back to London which was like living in an empty coal scuttle. It wasn't just the rationing. People slate British cooking you know but it's okay when you realise it's just a branch of German cooking with beef instead of pork. And American cooking isn't anything to write home about. That's basically German too. Read *The Joy of Cooking*? A hundred pages of baked goods. And the parents had used up all the dough. Do you get it? Dough! [Laughs. Coughs] So he had nothing. No friends. An aunt somewhere in the country, I think. That's it, the one that died and left him something. Aunt Clarice? Aunt Joyce? So, my take is he just kind of closed in on himself and made like a monk. But you know it was his tastebuds woke up first. That's how I see it. Before music, or colour, or travel or sex even. He learnt to live again through his tastebuds. He ate his way to happiness. No, he wasn't fat. Not in those days. He used to say he wasn't sure which was worse the starvation or the pilchards. You know they gave those POWs Mars Bars and tinned pilchards to fatten them up after they came out of the camps. Look close enough in *The Joy of Cooking* and you'll probably find a recipe that uses them both. And smell you know. His sense of smell was extraordinary. He could almost always identify a perfume on a woman. Or a man. It was a remarkable gift he had. Remarkable.

"Hi Tonia. No my dear we're getting along just fine. Like old friends. Would you like coffee Miss... [pause] Miss? Why no thank you dear. Perhaps some water. For us both. Acqua. Ferrarelle. Thank you. Grazie mille. She's a wonderful girl. Half Kraut you know. The mother was raped and the father was shot in one of those reprisals. They were lucky to be taken in here or they'd both have been putane by now. Buona Sera, Mrs Campbell and all that. But not funny. Not the movie either. Ah grazie carissima. La giu per favore. Grazie. Si, si, ha ragione. No, Americana. Uno scrittore. Sta scrivendo un libro su un mio amico. Non famoso. Un caro amico. Te lo dicopo. Abbiamo tutto grazie. Grazie.

"She's glad you're American. The English have been relegated. Where were we? You want to go back to '48. That journey we had. Is it significant? Well that's up to you to decide I guess so shall I just go on? Sirmione I think. Yes we were headed to Sirmione. Why? Oh Percy had this thing about Catullus. Not the sex poems. The what shall we say? The domestic ones. Like the one where he comes home to Sirmio after his exile. Was it exile? After being away from Rome on service. It was Ovid that died out there wasn't it? I think I'm right. Yes. Well Catullus did it in style by all accounts. He actually had a boat made for him to sail home in and then rowed it up the Po then another river. The Mincio? Then he had it dragged overland so he could sail around Lago di Garda in it. And he wrote this poem about how delighted he was to get home and Percy loved it and he used to recite another poem by Tennyson about having visited Sirmione – Oh venusto Sirmio! So he really had it all on the brain. It was nice. The hotels were mostly closed and I didn't speak much Italian in those days and the food around Desenzano was still pretty grim but Percy made friends as usual and we got invited in by a family and we just said we were married to make it easy. No I don't remember what we ate. Lake fish I imagine. Maybe eels. It was fun and we had the local wine. Next day I had a terrible head-ache so Percy went off clambering around the ruins to his heart's content. Le Grotte di Catullo.

"Yes. Then we got back in the car and headed to Venice. I practically had to drag Percy there. We drove fast down all those straight and empty roads and Percy timed us by the telegraph poles and we drove at a mile a minute for seemed like hours. But Venice was still pretty empty. A friend of mine had lent us her apartment so we had the run of the place. We were just over from Rialto market and I swear Percy must have swum over there in the mornings he was so keen on it. He'd have done his rounds and got back by seven. There was a cook came with the apartment. Signora. Signora. Zen. That was it. Percy used to call her the Nipponese when she wasn't around. But boy could she cook. She could create a feast from next to nothing.

Whatever Percy had liberated. She could be a bit prickly. We used to say she was like one of those shrimp from the lagoon all spiny and sharp. But eventually she let Percy into the kitchen just to watch and I think she was flattered so she let him help her sometimes. Risotto she would cook. And it was Fall so she'd do things with mushrooms and those pumpkins from Chioggia. And fish. There was always fish. In sweet and sour or fried. In saor they call them. Sarde in saor. And all those skinny prawns that are hardly worth eating. All the small fry from the lagoon. Occasionally there would be a bronzino. And eels. Percy went out to one of the islands on her recommendation and came back with smoked eel. That was good. The restaurants all served stuff brought in from the mainland you know steak for the Americans and Chianti because the tourists liked those straw flasks even when the Veneto wines could be superb."

"I remember Ernest telling me about Venice and Veneto wines. And Harry's Bar. It was just as he described it. And we just mooched around whether it was raining or not and looked at all the paintings and it was like a treasure-house. One day I think it was by the Rialto Market after it had closed. I think we went there because Percy had found a place for lunch that served the workmen and you stood up to eat and suddenly he was staring out at the water at a group of tourists getting out of a gondola at some steps and he looked as though he'd seen a ghost and I said Percy, what's the matter? and he said, that girl. Well it was a young woman and she was dressed nice in New Look and she was with a tall man, a good-looking man and a couple who spoke Italian. But she didn't look too well. Kinda scrawny. And lost. Completely lost. Like she wasn't there she was somewhere else and Percy said, that's Ray and Archie, and I said, who? and he said, she was in camp. I said, why don't you go and say hello? and he was just about to when they all got back in the boat and were rowed off. I said, we can track her down. Or try to. But he was such an emotional Edwardian. He just said it's okay he's alive. Must have survived Japan somehow. And that was it. I didn't want to make him cry.

"So after a few days holed up in the piano nobile of a Palazzo we'd begun to feel a little jaded. Even tea with Peggy didn't quite lighten our spirits though I had to complement her on two of the most gorgeous young men I'd ever seen but turned out they weren't part of the permanent collection. Percy kept having to look the other way and pretending not to notice them. Percy was more of a homely homo. He didn't like getting dressed up and showing himself off and he wasn't going to do it even for the Venier. He just went along in his usual sport coat and that ghastly pipe he'd taken to smoking but Peggy decided he looked just like Ernest and kept asking him if he were a writer which put the gorgeous young noses slightly out of joint. Then he told her about his hunt for the smoked eels and she got someone to write down the directions and then they got talking about food, solid food, and it looked like the principal boys didn't actually take any so they frosted themselves over while Peggy and Percy talked Foods of the Lagoon and had a whale of a time no pun intended. There wasn't much there at the Venier at that stage and really as Percy said it was just a nice bungalow but it had a kind of emerging taste, a different aesthetic about it. Plenty of '40s frippery but it was different. Somehow. And she asked us to meet her at Harry's but it was a week away or more, so we had to say no we were heading South.

"And we did. Is this still all relevant? Okay it's your call. We drove South around the lagoon and crossed the river and Percy I don't know how had seen *Ossessione* so we took snaps of each other outside likely-looking roadside bars. And how those roads went on. Straight as dies and those billboards flashing by one after the other. Percy said it fitted in with the Italian love of movies. Pirelli, Pirelli, Pirelli. Gave me a headache. And eventually we got to Ravenna half dead in our brains from the drive and found an okay hotel with a nice courtyard you could still eat in if you wanted to. And next day we saw the churches and the mosaics and all those Emperors and Empresses dolled up to the nines not like real Ancient Romans at all. But of course, as Percy said, he was a real fount of knowledge you know, they were more or less Greek by that time and for them Julius Caesar was as long ago as Henry the Eighth is to us. But Ravenna felt a bit lonely out there in its marshes, Percy said it was like Winchelsea and I knew that Henry James had lived there that annoyed him so we didn't stay long and off we went again but we stopped at an enormous church not far from Ravenna completely covered in mosaics and the floor I remember went up and down in waves and it got me sea-sick. So we were headed for Rome. Eventually. I should say that. Just in case you think this is going to go on for ever and Rome is where you want him, isn't it?

"What else from that trip? Let me see. Oh. Pesaro. Sitting beneath a yellow awning at the last bar on the seafront to stay open drinking Verdicchio and making up stories. Percy was good at it. He had a kind of crazy take on things and he could do an entire movie script around just random goings-on. Like someone would wander into the bar and Percy would say he's just shot his lover but no one knows yet. He's without remorse like a character by Camus. The barman suspects and he has a shotgun under the counter. Then a woman comes by selling something and she doesn't know anything. Then nah nee nah nah the police are on their way and the two men and the woman look at each other and they all know everything and the man stands up and just walks toward the bar and the barman takes out the shotgun and blasts a hole in his chest just as the police walk in who shoot the barman then the woman screams and holds her hands to her face and it turns out the barman was her son and she goes mad on the spot. You know I guess they did a lot of story-telling in that camp to pass the time only Percy can't have been all that popular you know I didn't hear anything like the melodramas he made up till I went to my first Samuel Beckett play.

"We loved Pesaro even though it was out of season. Percy practically invented neo-realist cinema under the yellow awning and we drank and smoked and drank and smoked but then we got back in the car and drove up into Umbria where it was cold and it drizzled a lot and you had to admire the Umbrians they must have been hardy wee folk like the Scots. Then Perugia. And Assisi. Now that was a spiritual experience. It even got its hooks into a flibbertigibbet like me. They said it was a cathedral no they didn't they said basilica anyway it was like a cave all dark with candles instead of fireflies and it was like being in the presence of a Mystery. Do you believe in Mysteries? I know it's hard for men to understand; perhaps they need a vagina. Yes, still with me? We motored on down to Lago di Trasimeno so Percy could see where Hannibal whupped the Romans because you know he used to say he was on the side of the Punes and yes lots of people did a double take but it means Carthaginians. Punics. He'd read *Salammbo* at an impressionable age and got hooked on all that glamour. Like Cecil B DeMille with real human sacrifices. Nor waves the cypress in the palace walk my he could channel Tennyson and Flaubert simultaneously which is an achievement you gotta admit.

"Then what, oh yes, we kind of turned vaguely in the direction of Rome but did a bit of Tuscany first. We went to Florence because you gotta and it was lovely and so calm and a bit foggy it's a cold place in Winter and it was October by now. But not so many people around and Percy was in a kind of ecstasy because he'd had five minutes on his own with La Primavera. Me I really like the Giottos especially after Ravenna and all that gold and you could see how revolutionary it was to paint little grey men in field barns instead of making Emperors out of tiny tiles. And we ate steak of course, lots of it and we learnt to say ai ferri and not to insult anyone by asking for it blue. But we took a wrong turning coming out of Florence and were heading for Bologna for a while and I was just going to turn the car round and Percy said please no not just yet just look at the woods and I looked at the woods and he looked at the woods and it was true it was like looking at Italy even before the Romans and those great waves of brown and yellow leaves completely thick together waving and moving like a living being. Dryads. Or the Old Gods. And Percy said we had to go to Vallombrosa so I turned around again and we went to this Abbey in the middle of yet more woods and it turned out that your poet Milton had written something about it and Percy reeled off a list of English poets that had been there and apparently so had Nietzsche so there you go. Then we hit Lazio and did a bit of Etruscan and then it was Rome."

"The parting of the ways."

"'Diversae variae viae reportant,' Percy said. That's from Catullus.

But not immediately. Firstly I felt I had to get Percy set up somehow and it was getting colder in Rome and the whole place was still pretty much on its uppers despite Marshall Aid kicking in. It was a kind of turning point I guess, that year. We got there after the Communist riots and at a point it did look like Italy might go Red but Uncle Sam threw money at Rome to make them go away and it looked like it was working. And it was so cheap. That was the great thing. Cheaper than Paris. So it was filling up with American tourists and new bars like Doney's were opening and Hollywood started making movies there and it was like a kind of colony for a while. But that was only just beginning when we got there. Percy had some money, finally, from his aunt but there was only so much the British were allowed to take out of the country. So we sat down and did lots of math and we worked out that on his money Percy could get by for a while without working and it was clear he wanted to stay there maybe the rest of his life. Which he did. As you know. And I had to get back to Fresno not for long was the plan but there was some family stuff I couldn't avoid and I had to go. But before I left I bought an apartment just on the edge of the Celio and offered it to Percy so he had somewhere to live. He wouldn't go there. He found that hideous Monolocale on the Labicana and clung on like a pigeon on a cliff-face. I guess it was just his stiff upper pride that wouldn't let him. When I came back – oh that was three of four years later – Rome had changed and so had Percy. One he'd taken up my suggestion to get into cooking. And two there'd been a nuclear explosion. David was there and they were shacked up together in David's apartment on Piazza Navona admittedly in separate suites but as David used to say, 'our kitchens were conjoined.' And that, my dear, is I think where you come in?"

Stanley PoW Camp, Hong Kong, August 5th 1945

Boiled Rice

"Now Mrs Porter, please. More attack Mrs Porter, please. Ah one, ah two, ah three: 'Oh a life on the ocean wave, dah dah dah dah dee dah dah,' that's right off we go. Now Mrs Bush-Patterson in you come you're the eagle: 'like an eagle cag'd I stand, On this dull unchanging shore, Oh give me the flashing brine The spray and the tempest's roar'. Now back to you, Mrs Porter, what? 'A home on the rolling deep', dear, shall we pick it up, ah one ah two ah three 'Where the scattered waters rave…' That's it. All together, keep your revels. And now, verse two, attack it, Mrs Porter, attack it. Imagine it's Yamashita. That's it, very good. 'Set sail, farewell to the land,' and off we go. Just imagine that gale abaft 'like an ocean bird set free' – that's a good thought. And the song of our hearts shall be, what Mrs Bush-Patterson? That's it: 'A life on the heaving sea' – more like the passengers, dear – and now we round off with the raving waters and there we are. Yes bravo! Well done ladies! Very nautical, all together very naughtily nautical. Thank you, yes please, do have a short break and we'll reassemble in ten minutes for Rule Britannia. Has anyone seen Britannia? Mrs Foulkes, Mr Westerly? Anyone seen Lady Considine? Oh dear can't be helped. Now Mr Westerley, a little slice of corned beef for one of those gaspers? Jolly good, yes, I'm splashing out. Can't be long now, can it? I overheard Mrs Heard do you like that overheard Mrs Heard oh and a match too. What unspeakable luxury, ah bliss, telling Mr Wicks she'd actually waved at one of the American pilots or co-pilots or something and he'd done a V for victory sign and a thumbs up at her. At least that's what she said it was. Yes, you go and smoke in peace and I shall do the same. Perhaps a short sit-down. Ah. There we are."

Everett Causey, producer, or Master of the Revels as he liked to style himself, sat down and surveyed his theatre, his Wooden "O" for what he hoped would be the last time in three and a half years. It was the Fifth of August 1945, and this must be the oh, fifth, sixth production he'd put on to boost morale even when there'd been precious morale left to boost. More than half his cast had vanished into thin air, not by death or misadventure; they simply weighed half or less than what they had back in '42. Not everyone of course. Just those without the cash or the contacts. Almost anything could be got if you had the brass whether in the back of a truck from town, over the wire or under it. Everett himself had a friend in Argyle Street where the British officers lived in so much luxury that his friend could send him the scraps. Scraps. The food here didn't even approach the level of scrappage. Rice and water. Congee. The green bits from potatoes. Who was getting the white bits? Stinking residues of fish. Still, he was dysentery-free for the moment so that was something. He could have had extra rations if he'd joined the latrine-digging-out party, but the police and rugby types always got in first. And now they were putting it on the gardens for fertiliser just like the Chinese. Now he understood why he'd never liked bak-choy.

The Chinese, thought Everett. Had anyone spared a thought for all the Hong-Kongers and that great flood of people that had arrived back in '41? It didn't come up in conversation much but he didn't exactly mix in Government House circles. Talk about Government House, thought Everett as the taste of cigarette butt began to settle on his tongue, here comes Dishy David. What did someone as dishy as David Sopley see in that scrawny little Scotsman? They'd been at school together, that was it. Mutt and Jeff, everyone called them. But Jeff dear, bless his heart, had a lovely voice and knew all the words to all the songs in the show which was just as well since they didn't have a book. Everett's hand went to his chest as his heart began to thump a bit faster. Not for David Sopley, although it could have been. No this was nicotine, burning cigarette butt and a ripple of something caused by malnutrition that made his heart race. They all had it every now and then that flutter of the bird inside its cage beating its wings to get out. Steady the Buffs. Deep breaths. Feet on the ground hands on knees look straight ahead. Ah one ah two ah three.

It couldn't be long now. Could it? American planes were over almost every day. The Nips had actually begun to take down the gun emplacements. The guns that they all knew had been put there to slaughter them if the Yanks invaded Hong Kong. It was Imperial policy. That was on record. Shoot the prisoners. Then that bungalow had taken a direct hit but the Nips knew things weren't going their way so they were window-dressing Stanley to make it look as though they were abiding by the Geneva Convention. You could tell the guards were rattled. They'd started to use the odd English word. Whatever next. Only the Kempeitai were holding out against reality.

"Oh my god." Another bomber went roaring overhead unchallenged. The sound was deafening. "When are we going to get a moment's peace to stage the show?" He must remember to have a chat with the cast about what to do when planes went over. Perhaps they could mime. That would be rather fun. We could do an entire rehearsal in mime. Just the thought of Mrs Hancock and Mr Ball miming their tender love scene made him want to cry with laughter. Priceless. It would be priceless. But would anyone be even looking at their performance with so much excitement in the air? So to speak. All the work they'd put in. The costumes, the backdrops, even the programmes all made by hand from the last set of costumes, the last backdrops, the last bits of paper and worn-down coloured pencils. Not for nothing. For us. For ourselves.

And now change beckoned. Some said that you could die if you ate too much when you were let out. Others wondered if they could stand the shock of being free. Everett had joined a group discussing Oriental philosophy. There weren't many of them in it. But it had been interesting, liberating even. Respect for the Orient and for its wisdom and all that. Best kept to oneself. Even trying out Yoga was held to be un-British. Oh good, here was Britannia probably back from a bout of the squitters. He stood up and clapped his hands.

Outside, Percy turned to David.

"I'd better go and join them."

"Yes, you run along. Mum's the word. Say nothing to anyone."

"It'll be all round camp in ten minutes."

"Can't be helped. As long as it didn't come from us."

"Of course."

"Good show."

David Sopley, thirty-three years old, tall, still blond-haired, lean as a whippet, chest concave, ribs clearly showing, belly extended, bony knees knocking together walked like an old man slowly toward his quarters. Around his waist a pair of shorts held up by a belt and on his feet, shoes made from car tyres laced up with string.

Percy turned toward the main block of St Stephen's College where the show was being staged. He too wore nothing but shorts and on his feet were a pair of brown leather brogues practically worn through. He stopped for a few seconds thinking over what David had told him; that the Americans were planning a really big show against Japan in early August. It was now August the fifth. A show that could end the war. Knowledge like this could be dangerous. What if it had come from a clandestine radio in camp? Percy doubted it thinking back to '43 and the hidden-wireless torture and executions. No it didn't seem likely that another radio could have been smuggled in. There was another possibility. David had once mentioned the BAAG, the line of supporters of the Allies stretching all the way from places like Hong Kong to the safety of American-financed Chungking. Percy could well believe that they had agents in place perhaps in Argyle Street delivering information to the well-fed British top brass, information that would have been carefully passed on to Government House people in Stanley. David hadn't ever actually admitted working for British Intelligence but neither had he denied it. If something really big were actually happening plans would be afoot, surely, to get government back on its feet again. If the gates were to open Percy doubted if he would ever, after that point, see David again.

"Coo-eee Mr Langrigg! We're ready when you are. No hurry. Take your time."

Closing the double-doors behind him Percy stepped into Causey's territory. This was the sight that met Percy's eyes: A set of bamboo rods had been joined together to make a long pole attached to either wall and suspended across the room. From the pole, secured by loops made from the same fabric, hung a pair of sacking curtains that divided auditorium from stage. A similar pole was hung just three feet forward of the end of the room supporting a length of canvas forming a backdrop painted to look like the sea with above it the words *Heave Ho Me Hearties. The Stanley Revue of 1945.* At the moment the stage curtains were open, and the cast was assembled. Upstage centre was a dais made from a tea chest painted grey to resemble a rock. Slightly concealed behind the chest was a small set of steps also painted battleship grey. Together they made the sum of properties on view. A dozen or so people sat on the parquet floor or lounged against windowsills. Almost three and a half years into imprisonment, punished by tropical disease, malnutrition, boredom and fear this was a tableau of dejected inmates that could have be found anywhere around Stanley Internment Camp that day from the rice-kitchen to the hospital, from laundry to workshops, from the living quarters to the gardens and the areas that were open for walking. Moreover it was warm and the fat, shit-fed flies buzzed around constantly. House flies, drain flies, bluebottles and, worse for being almost invisible, sand-flies that were the cause of the penny-size septic weals on the shins of many of the cast. The men were largely dressed in shorts and sleeveless Aertex shirts. The women, some wearing headscarves to conceal the fact that alopecia areata, common in camp, was causing their hair to fall out in clumps, were mostly dressed in much laundered, faded, patterned summer dresses. It pained Percy to imagine them four years ago at tea-parties, shopping, hurrying off to play tennis or swim at Shek-O wearing these same frocks, innocent of their fate.

"Rule Britannia!" said Everett Causey. "Lady Considine are you ready?"

A tall, aristocratic-looking woman with her grey hair still intact came up from downstage and arrived at the back of her rock.

"I can't stand here long, you know," she said. "One's not feeling tip-top today."

"Of course, Lady Considine," said Everett Causey. "Just a quick run-through for today. So to speak. Up the step it is. Mr Langrigg would you mind standing just there to assist if her ladyship needs you. No, just there. Thank you. Now. Cast. Positions please. Thank you. A rousing chorus if you will and please do remember it's Britannia rule the waves not rules the waves – it's an invocation you see so please invoke."

He went around to stand looking at this semi-circle of men and women all standing facing toward Britannia one arm raised in her direction. Bless 'em all, thought Everett Causey, the long and the short and the tall. If only I'd stayed in bloody Blighty instead of coming out to this hellhole, I could have been a leading light in ENSA. The travels, the food, the food, the food the food. Get a grip.

"Ah one ah two ah three When Brrrrrittunn fuh uh uh uh urst..."

They sang well. They put so much into it. He loved them. Even the little Scot with his light tenor. We all know he's one of us. Why won't he bloody-well admit it? The look on his face when Everett had made just the most discreet of passes at him. A look as though I were something he'd stepped in.

"Can't hear you Mr Langrigg!" he shouted.

"Arose, arose, arose from out the ah ha ha hazure main..."

He's always bloody picking on me thought Percy; any excuse to mention my name. Anyone would think he fancied me. Rebecca Charlton practically said as much during the last show. Oh god, what if she's right? It would explain a lot.

"Britons nevah nevah nevah Shall. Be. Slaves."

Though that's exactly what we are. Or at least those poor bastards from Sham Shui Po sent to Japan to work. Slave labour. If any of them come back it'll be a miracle.

"Well done cast. Thank you," said Everett Causey. "We won't practise our curtain call just yet. I rather think we need to brush up a couple of numbers. If you're not in them you can go, thank you. Back at four for the dress rehearsal please. Those numbers are: Has Anyone Seen and BTWS so Mrs Uttrell, please, Mrs Charlon, please. And Mr Langrigg."

That was a couple of years ago at least, thought Percy. When they had to move rooms for the umpteenth time by order of some bloody committee or other. The place was riddled with committees. Causey and I were alone for a night. What was it he said exactly? I can give you something to make you sleep? I can help you get to sleep? And I just gawped at him. He must think I despise him. What did I say? I simply can't remember. Nothing, I think. I hope. Still I've been in most of his shows. But I must have hurt his feelings. The way he looks at David. Does he think? I suppose he must. Not that I'm fooling myself that I am. The only man for him. That hurt you know. When they said he'd been having it off with that Matthews woman around the back of the rice kitchen. I felt so jealous. For a while. I don't know why. It's not as though we're a couple. Though people smile at us when we go for walks. Coming through the rye he calls it. All the lasses hae a laddie none they say have I but all the boys they smile at me when. There have been times, yes there have been times when I think he just wants people to think he's queer so he can go and have it off with their wives. But he kissed me even if it was only once and a hundred years ago. He kissed me. The chubby little Scot with the specs. Can't keep him, though. He'll be off out of those gates like a shot the moment we win. If we haven't all been machine-gunned first. And all that terrible radio episode. He must have known. They beat him up but thank the Lord that little gang had their story and they stuck to it. It was a miracle the Nips let him go. What a mess he was in. Didn't see him for a month. But he was so close to the wind that time. Him and his gang. God if we felt sick during the trials what must they have felt like. I'd have been in a complete funk in case any of them blabbed. "I couldn't help it. I'm sorry." "Never mind old boy we'll swing together." But it was a ditch of course they had to kneel over. God those fucking Nips and their disgusting swords. Medieval. And the men who cried and hung their heads down and it took three chops or more. Now if we'd been medieval like them and seen an execution at the block we'd have known to stick our necks out as far as we could and stretched out our arms backwards to make it quick. And here we are in St Stephens where they showed their true colours. At least I'd already seen it. Those lads who were bound together with wire then bayoneted then set alight with gasoline. On the cliffs up behind the hotel so they fell down not all of them dead. He's here, somewhere, the one that got away crawling over the beach in the dark.

"Tickety-boo are we Mr Langrigg? What would we have done without all those tunes you keep in your head. And all those words! I'm really most grateful to you. I know you think I'm a funny desiccated little stick and a complete nobody - no please don't interrupt - you know how bloody snobby this place is but in case we do get out alive and in case we never see each other again then let me say what a privilege it has been to work with someone as dedicated as yourself You have the professional spirit Mr Langrigg and that is the highest compliment that Everett Causey can pay. I'm sorry we couldn't have had a closer relationship perhaps over the past three years but of course we're worlds apart and I'm just a queer little chap who pops up in Music Hall at the China Fleet Club marooned on this excuse me godforsaken island and you were born out here somewhere and you have friends at Government House."

He paused and looked at Percy.

"Did you see *The Cheerio Club Revue of 1940*? No? My Pièce de Résistance. Most of those grandes dames de la charité are in here but have I had a single cup of what they call tea off any of them? Not on your nellie. Never mind I can see their minges through their bloody old tea frocks they still treat me like a servant. But you Mr Langrigg you're proper old-fashioned in a good way. You remind me of my Uncle Albert that drowned at Dunkirk. Now he never married but he always had a good word to say for everyone and he shook the hand of a lord or a lady same as he did the lamplighter. Now he was a coachman first, then a chauffeur when they took to motors and he'd been in the first war and he used to say we're all cock and balls lad when it comes to it all cock and balls. So there. Well it's been nice talking to you. If we ever get back to London you can find me at the Cock Tavern Euston Road most Sunday mornings. They do roast potatoes at the bar. Now, Mrs Uttrell, you're in fine voice today but could I hurry you a bit down to the deep rolling sea you're looking for your true love after all not a dropped stitch. Once more from the top, then Mrs Charlton. Mr Langrigg, you're next."

Felicity Charlton clad in the regulation much faded summer frock came over to sit next to Percy.

"Tiggy's in good voice today don't you think?"

"Yes," said Percy.

"If you close your eyes you really could think it's Kathleen Ferrier there, couldn't you?"

"No."

"Have you actually seen Kathleen Ferrier sing?"

"Yes."

"Oh come on William Wallace, do brighten up dear. You know," she moved closer to him sliding along the wooden form, "you know they're saying the Americans are going to teach the Nips a lesson they'll never forget. And it's going to be soon."

"I hadn't heard."

Felicity Charlton drew back in an ingenue way then leant forward closer to him an elegant wrist poised on the wooden bench, a shoulder raised.

"You're a little liar," she whispered in his ear. "Everyone knows. Know who told me?" Percy sat still. "Flora Matthews. Your bum-chum David Sopley told her behind the rice-kitchen." Percy turned bright red but kept still. "It's all right dear." said Felicity into his ear. "Everyone knows and nobody knows." She drew away slightly and adjusted her frock over what was left of her breasts. "But look at poor little me. Just a single girl with no provider hoping to last out another few weeks. Know what else Flora Matthews told me? Can you guess?" She opened her eyes wide, and smiling, said, "He did it to

267

her up the backside. She nearly screamed it hurt so much. She offered him a condom but he wouldn't take it. Is that how you boys play? Do you like to be rough on the outside and tender on the inside? Is that it?" Percy stayed silent. "Well you're not very talkative I must say."

"Must you?"

"It speaks."

From out there in the parallel world Percy heard Everett Causey suggesting that Tiggy Uttley have some water for her vocal cords. Felicity Charlton had laid a fingertip on his arm and was beginning to stroke it very lightly as though he were a suspect cat.

"You know your man's going to be on the first boat back to England. He's hush-hush you know. They'll want to debrief him. Or whatever they call it." She gave him a lewd smile out of her shrunken, starved face showing her discoloured teeth. "And what will poor Robin do then? And poor me all alone too without a husband." She paused. "I saw you that time you know."

"What time?"

"The time that David Sopley was about to fall back into the latrine pit. There you were, you little Scotch Terrier to save him. You simply hugged him to your breast and pulled him out. There you were gazing into each other's eyes like Rhett and Scarlett while Atlanta burnt to cinders all around. Oh my! What a touching scene. Nothing to say? Well I have a little proposal for you Mr Scarlett Langrigg."

"I don't want to hear it."

"Now don't get angry with me or I shall scweam. Everett's looking at you. He fancies you, you know."

"I've heard enough."

"Oh Percy! How could you use a poor maiden so? Now listen," she said, "to this. My plan is we should join forces when we get out. You know, allies. We could even get married." She continued to stroke Percy's arm. "Then you could get a job in a nice hotel somewhere. London! And you could take it up the backside from whoever you liked and so could I and we'd be such fwiends. Wouldn't that be too divine?"

"Thank you, Mrs Uttley now please go and rest your voice, till dress rehearsal. Mrs Charlton, Mr Langrigg please. How nice to see the two of you getting into character. A proper couple of red peppers, I'm sure. Now let's have a bit of that spirit in your number please just focus on that bone. Of contention. You're friends, you're colleagues, you're partners, you're a double act and you're sick to death of each other. But only on the stage of course," Everett Causey coughed. "Dear me, can't seem to shake it. One had the rare privilege of seeing Mr Coward and Miss Lawrence perform it on the stage at the Phoenix in '36. So in tune with each other they were like an old married couple. Think you can do the same? After all," he coughed again this time for a little bit longer. "After all this is going to be the last Everett Causey production at St Stephens, a veritable Cheerio Club and no mistake so I hope you'll do me proud. Now," he said, looking round "As to the hoofing, you've been proper troopers both of you despite any disadvantages you may have had. Size isn't everything after all and in fact small feet are better than large in the circumstances. We've kept the what-I-call-routine simple but as you know nothing gets them going like a bit of dancing so do your best. Everett has a gift for you to help you find your energy tonight." He rustled in the blue canvas bag he always kept with him. It looked rather like a Yantai School satchel to Percy. From inside it Everett produced two bars of Hershey chocolate.

"Good lord Everett," said Percy, "Where on earth did you get those?"

"Yes indeed," echoed Felicity. "What on earth did you have to do for them?"

Everett coloured and coughed and looked away. Percy gave Felicity Charlton a look of pure loathing. She smiled back.

"Thank you, Everett," said Percy, "For these and for everything you've done for us. For morale."

"Three cheers," said Felicity Charlton.

"What are you going to do when it's over?" said Percy.

"Oh lord knows," said Everett. "Head back to London I shouldn't wonder. And you?"

"Probably the same," said Percy.

Felicity Charlton gave a faint snigger.

"And you, Mrs Charlton?" said Everett Causey, "Why don't you keep some of this bunting to put out when your husband gets back? After all my dear we all know you've made something of a pastime of putting it out over the past few years. You really should show your husband the skills you've acquired. And bunting is so handy. You can put it out anywhere as I'm sure you know. Now. Positions please. Mr Friedman on the piano Has Anybody Seen Our Ship. Please. That's it, Mr Friedman in your own time."

Percy broke off a piece of the chocolate, ate it and put the rest back into Everett's satchel for safe keeping. Although he couldn't bring himself to look at Felicity Charlton he knew she was there behind him stretching and limbering up for their routine. Really but the woman was made of brass: brass neck, brass cheek. Everett was right though; his disliking her would certainly help put some red pepper into the number. Time to put off his dour Scotsmanship. He loved performing. Here on the stage the rules were different. Height, looks, even his eyesight didn't matter. He could just about get by without his spectacles and in some ways seeing an audience blurred made it less intimidating. David had mocked him of course but Percy loved the sense of belonging, the flimsiness of the sets and the paucity of the props. By taking on other roles he'd found that he'd for the first time come truly face to face with himself. Could good things have come out of this evil time? It had been like school in so many ways. Didn't they say that a boarding school education prepared you for prison? After it was all over would they get together and talk about The Stanley Years? Or would they just want to forget? He'd started to make a collection of mementoes; revue programmes, notes from the outside, cancelled IOUs. Oh god the IOUs, the camp currency. What did that ubiquitous system say about us? That we trusted each other? That we always believed the war would end in our favour? Or that the circumstances made gamblers of us all? Felicity Charlton touched him on the shoulder.

"We're on," she said.

The piano began plonking out the opening chords. How lucky they'd been not only to have a piano but also a piano-tuner in camp.

"One two three four," said Everett Causey. "Ah one two three four and..."

"What shall we do with the drunken sailor, so the saying goes. We're not tight but we're none too bright...." It was extraordinary the way Felicity Charlton transformed herself into a passable imitation of the great Gertie. Looking at her you realised she had the same large nose, the same tenacious tilt to the head as if she were slightly short-sighted, the same seen-it-all eyes and wide mouth. Of course Gertie had known hardship before fame; growing up in Lambeth, drunken, dissolute father who'd walked out on them, a performer in the hard-knock school of pubs and music halls looking for her way onto the variety stage. Felicity Charlton had it all to a tee down to the rather tough, grating cockney that Gertie would use if she needed to remind anyone of her slum credentials. And Felicity could move. He felt her ribs and through them her heartbeat as she fell into his arms and he pushed her away. "We've lost our way," – quizzical look at each other, pause – "And we've lost our pay" Hold. Both spin. Turn back to face each other. Slight stagger. Lean in. Hands on each other's shoulders. "And to make the thing complete," - Pause. Face audience - "We've been and gone and lost the bloomin' fleet!" Down centre stage for the chorus. "A lady..." – here they'd developed a little turn of their own. Everett hadn't liked this bit of business but they'd managed to get Friedmann on side. The playing stopped. They looked at each other. Felicity threw her head back, picked up the hem of an invisible skirt, made a moue at the audience and struck a cabaret pose. Percy did the same. Anything for a laugh. They looked each other up and down. The piano came back. "A lady bold as she could be." And so they went on. The other cast liked this number. They'd have the audience in stitches.

Out of nowhere came the immense roar of an aeroplane flying low over Stanley. The whole room seemed to rattle in time with its engine. Or was that its machine guns? It was. The Americans had been strafing the Jap positions on and off over the past few days. From close by they heard shouts in Japanese and the sound of rifles being discharged as the guards fired up at the Grumman Hellcat. Percy, Felicity, Everett had all instinctively thrown themselves to the floor. Mr Friedman had chosen the piano keyboard for cover and was curled up on the pedals. Only Millicent "Tiggy" Uttley stood firm and upright as the noise stormed around her.

"Come on!" she yelled, looking out of the windows and raising a fist, "Come on you Yanks. Cut the little fuckers in half!" She was trembling so hard, Percy noticed, that she had practically levitated above the parquet. "Blow their fucking turnip heads off! Come on!" The plane roared away. The rifle fire continued uselessly. Tiggy Uttley took a deep breath. "Oh dear," she said "I do hope they don't come back while we're on. Wouldn't that be a bore." She looked around her. "Yes dears?" she said, "One does get rather carried away. Shan't happen again. Just wanted to take a peek at your number. I'll be off now."

"Positions please," said Everett Causey. "Everything all right, Mr Friedmann? Good show. Off we go."

"What shall be done with the girls ashore," – pose and wink from Felicity. "Who lead our tars astray?" Felicity held her stance, looked him up and down, faced the audience and rolled her eyes. On they went working together like a real team. As though they really were the Red Peppers. As though this was the real *Tonight at 8.30*. It was a revelation. It was a proper piece of theatre. Perhaps one should have more respect for Felicity Charlton. The men here ran everything just as they had before. It was true; she had no one. Her husband had been carted off from Sham Shui Po to Japan. Girls like her were shunned by the British society matrons inside just as they had been outside. So she'd set her cap at David? Good for her. At least she had taste. So what if she was just a steno? Why on earth did things like that still matter? "But the captain pulled his cracker," Pause. They looked at each other. Felicity smiled. Percy smiled back. Turning to face the audience they both leant forward slightly, widened their eyes and hid their privates behind their hands miming an "oooh". "And we cried," Percy in falsetto "Oh dear!" Together; "Has anybody seen our ship?"

Dum-dum, dum-dum; dum-dum, dum-dum went the piano. Off they marched around the stage mock-purposefully. The intro was perfect for stage business and Percy followed Felicity's inventiveness. As long as the dum-dum, dum-dum went on they could do what they liked. All it took was a wink at Mr Friedmann from Felicity and the melody would begin again. Everett Causey was by this time sitting down on a chair in what would be the front row. Felicity careered around the stage taking long marching steps and Percy followed. Suddenly she took a dive at Everett and ended up on his lap, legs crossed. Drawing a finger under his chin she made him blush. Percy stood still.

"That's right dear," said Felicity leaning back and looking at Percy. "You stand to attention too. Or is that where you put the telescope?"

Leaping out of Everett's lap and before he had a chance to speak she signalled Mr Friedmann to start the next and final chorus; "Has anybody seen our ship the HMS Suggestive?" Here Felicity prettily held one hand to her mouth and one on her crotch. On they went, singing well, singing together. On the line, "The world forgetting by the world forgot" Felicity stepped forward and touched Mr Friedman on the shoulder. Startled he stopped playing.

"That's right," said Felicity in her best Gertie Cockney, "But it ain't either, is it?" She looked challengingly straight at the absent audience. "It may have felt like we've been forgotten but not anymore. They're coming to let us out. Maybe next week. Maybe next month. But we're going to be free. Only thing is ladies and gents and sirs and melords and what-not we never forgot our little old Hong Kong world did we? We carried on being the same old snobs as we ever used to be. So what if we all looked the same, smelt the same, shit the same and starved the same? Some of us made sure we never let the lower orders forget they were different now, did we? So before we all fuck off back where we came from let me say one thing to you this evening. Enjoy the next few days till the gates open because I can tell you when you get out it won't be your exclusive world no more. The Japs have done in three and a half years what it's taken centuries for people like me to try to do and not do. Those turnip-heads showed us that it's not about what you got in the bank it's about what you've got up top. And down below. And they helped us see that a woman can do as much as a man or more. So when you get back to England or your house on the Peak you remember what Felicity Charlton told you that day when the war nearly ended. And you wake up. You lost Hong Kong thanks to your toffee-nosed top brass and next you're going to lose your sodding Empire. And you better get used to it. That's all, Folks!"

Silence.

Then Everett Causey started to applaud. And Mr Friedman. Percy, too. Only Tiggy Uttley stood still with a look of absolute disgust on her face. She turned to face Everett Causey and the applause died away.

"I'll sing tonight because I've given my word and an Uttley never breaks it. And also because of what we owe to the brave British soldiers and nurses of the Empire who died in this very building. This very room. But let me tell you, you bunch of tramps and degenerates. And Jew. None of you will ever play Bridge in this camp again."

"You still here?" said Felicity Charlton.

Tiggy Uttley looked at her with exquisite hauteur and left the room.

"Well dear," said Everett Causey. "You're a firebrand and no mistake. Brava my dear, brava. Word'll be round the whole place in five minutes. Maybe they'll boycott us? What if we don't have a House tomorrow?"

"We will Mr Causey, we will," said Felicity Charlton, "even if it's only to see what all the fuss is about."

"It's all about you, dear," said Everett Causey, "you've gone and thrust yourself into the limelight. Admirable. Gertie herself would approve, I'm sure." There was a silence.

"Do you really believe in all what you said?" said a voice from the piano.

"Yes," said Felicity.

"Good," said Mr Friedmann.

"Does this make us all traitors?" said Everett Causey. "Shall we be hung?"

"They'll say I've let the Empire down but it's really just them I've had enough of," said Felicity. "They're finished anyway."

"Where did you get all these ideas?" said Percy.

"You mean I must have got them from someone else? A man? Oh yes, I once loved the most shattering physician. Quite the best looking doctor in the state."

"Selangor?"

"Cole Porter."

"Let me finish. Yes I did once know a Cambridge boy. Very bright and a red-hot Socialist. We went to one of their May Balls. He'd read Karl Marx and he'd been to Russia. This must have been in '39. He told me to throw off my chains."

"But you just threw off your clothes."

"You'd have done the same Everett dear. He had the body of an Adonis, and his mind was pure Plato."

"You mean he just wanted to be friends?"

"Yes. Something like that. Anyway, he got me thinking. About history. And my place in it. And how I needed to understand the events that had shaped me, funny way he put it, if I was ever going to understand myself. Can we sit down? It's hot and I'm hungry."

"The chairs haven't been brought in yet."

"There are two. One for you and one for Mr Friedman. Percy and I can sit on the floor can't we, Perce?"

Percy and Felicity sat on the floor backs against the wall.

"You were saying?"

"Yes indeed. Rattling on I was about the individual and society. Oh," she made a tiny belch. "Sorry. All that smoked salmon not agreeing with me."

"This has been the perfect Marxist experiment," said Percy. "Look how when everything else is stripped away you see what really makes us tick."

"Consciousness," said Mr Friedman. They looked at him. "It is the consciousness of the worker that creates history. Only when we arrive at individual consciousness can we make the supreme sacrifice and give it up to the collective consciousness. Then there will be true Socialism. But don't ask me no more. I am an anarchist."

"Don't look at me," said Everett Causey. "I'm petty bourgeois and proud of it."

"Imagine if the Nips had actually tried to re-educate us politically as well," said Percy.

"As well as what?" said Everett, "starving us?"

"Well yes, actually. This was all meant to teach us a lesson."

"In?"

"Humility. Obedience. Something closer to those medieval Japanese codes than Communism."

"Next you'll be saying they've done us a Christian charity by taking away everything we own."

"Well in a sense they have. No really. I mean it. The rich man getting into heaven. Well after three years and more in here we're thin enough to get through the eye of the needle. Perhaps Mr Friedman's right. The ultimate goal in life is to give it away."

"Whoever shall save his life shall lose it. Whoever shall lose his life shall save it?"

"Something like that."

Felicity was drawing patterns on the parquet with her fingertip.

"People were nice to each other, you know. Tell no lie. Some people. More than they used to be out there before. Some people done me good turns. Someone made me a pair of shoes. I got a tooth pulled out. Look how everyone's helped get the shows together. All that begging, borrowing and stealing to make the costumes and the props and the programmes and what-not."

"And classes," said Mr Friedman. "I give piano lessons. No one come to my lecture on Anarchy."

"But it wasn't pure charity, was it?" said Percy. "I mean all those IOUs. Some people could make a mattress out of the number of chits they've extorted."

"There's a rumour that all chits will be cancelled once it's over."

"Hurrah."

"When we all get back to normal."

"But wasn't it normal in here too? I mean not what happened in this room, not the executions and all that ghastliness but when it's over and people ask us what went on here what are we going to say? What will people have written in their diaries? Mr Snell executed today for operating a wireless set. Funked it at the side of the ditch, didn't stick his neck out properly, had to be shot. Went home and had tea. Evening Bridge Club with Dotty and Dolly and poor Mrs Snell. Simply didn't know what to say. Lost by three rubbers. Mrs Snell most apologetic. Lady Bottomley shared her can of corned beef. Weather frightful."

"Like the shows," said Everett Causey. "They must go on, you know. They did go on. It's what people do. They go on."

"But they didn't have to go on being snobby and hateful about single girls or Eurasians or Jews or poofs but they did. They kept their prejudices longer than their teeth or their hair."

"And I have a horrible idea this is all going to be made to look like a fine example of British Pluck. You know, how we kept our senses and our dignity when all around us were losing theirs."

"The Americans made a much better job of it than our lot ever did. They really worked together. No bitchiness. No backbiting. I really missed them when they went." Felicity paused. "And here they are coming back to save us. Who's fighting the Nips? Not us."

"In Burma we have."

"Only because they were trying to get into our precious bloody India. We gave them Hong Kong, Singapore, Malaya but when they tried to roll their tanks onto the polo pitch that was really going too far."

"There's a man in my room with a flag under his mattress. I know. Would you believe it? Silly fool. What if the Japs had found it? We'd all have been for the chop. But he's quite a sweetie, really. He's got this idea that the Americans or the Chinese are going to try and take over Hong Kong so the minute the gates are open he's going to Government House to find a flagpole and fly it so they can't have it. Maybe he's a bit cracked. I don't know."

They paused and looked out of the window. Conscious of hunger, of the physical ills that afflicted them, of the state of their shoes, their hair, their teeth, their bowels. Consciousness over the past three years had also become imprisoned. Hard to think in abstractions with the weight of mortality pressing on the mind almost every waking second. Even in their dreams they were caught in ever more complicated traps.

Another American plane roared overhead firing its machine guns at the Jap emplacements and again with cries of Banzai! the Japanese responded with rifle fire.

"They'll never give up," said Everett Causey. "McKay told me. He's Police you know. They have to die for their Emperor right down to the last single one of them. If the Yanks make it to Japan there'll be a bloodbath."

"And that includes us."

"He didn't say so."

"He didn't have to."

Everett looked at Felicity Charlton. "Why didn't you leave in '41? Most of the wives did."

"Oh I just wanted to keep the home fires burning."

"I think you're very pretty."

"Thank you, Everett, dear. You're too, too sweet."

"It was to save their commercial interests," said Mr Friedman. "They want their banks and their godowns back after the war. The soldiers were a sacrifice. We are all a sacrifice. This is all I will say." There was a silence.

"Friedmann, you're a dangerous agitator," said Percy.

"Thank you," said Mr Friedmann.

"You're Russian, aren't you?"

"I am Latvian."

"Are you one of those dreadful communists, Mr Friedmann?" said Felicity. "Are you trained to murder people in their beds?"

"It is my family who were murdered, Miss Charlton," said Friedmann. "I am the only one left."

"Oh I'm so sorry Mr F," said Felicity getting up from the floor to go across to him and kiss him on the cheek. "I'm so sorry."

"It's all right," said Mr Friedman. "Don't be sad. Listen. I make you my daughter! You're clever, like my Irina. Always questions, questions, questions. Irina also did not think much of men. I am glad of this. When they raped her, her mother and her sisters she was not surprised. Of this I'm very glad. But her mother, she died of shock. So I was told."

"How did you get here, Mr Friedman?" asked Everett.

"Oh I walked Mr Causey. I walked, I rode in the backs of carts, in the wagons of trains. Some people helped me. I came to Vladivostok and then to Shanghai and then to Hong Kong. I arrive seventh December 1941."

"What's your profession, Mr Friedmann?" asked Percy.

"You mean what was my profession? I was an astronomer. In Moscow. My family were in 1940 in Riga."

"But why did you leave Russia? Surely you'd be safe in Moscow?"

"From the evil of the Generalpan Ost no Jew is safe. I had lost my family and my mind. I decided to follow in the footsteps of the Whites and go to China and begin again."

"Your English is very good," said Percy.

"Other people here pick up cigarette butts; I pick up words," said Mr Friedman.

"And you play the piano like an angel," said Felicity.

"Thank you, my dear," said Mr Friedman. "Now," he said, "will you become my daughter?"

"I will, Mr Friedmann," said Felicity. "I will. Felicity Friedmann. I like it. Where shall we go when this is over?"

"To America," said Mr Friedmann. "Is there anywhere else?"

"You won't get in if you're an anarchist," said Percy.

"Then I am not and never have been," said Mr Friedmann.

"It's getting like a fire sale," said Everett Causey. "Everyone's having a clear-out before the grand finale. Swapping addresses I wouldn't wonder. Little bits of last-minute toadying. Makes you sick."

"You mean you'd rather stay?"

"No of course not. I want a decent dinner like everyone else. But it has been sort of safe here. Before, you know, before the war things were a little bit tricky sometimes. Now when we get out. If we get out. Well to be Jack Blunt I'm not at all sure what I'm going to do."

"You'll get a passage back to England. Everyone says that."

"Oh, England," said Everett Causey. "Land of Hope and Glory. My arse. I ran away from that years ago; didn't take no Jerries to chase me out, begging your pardon, Mr Friedmann. On the other hand if I'd stayed I'd be bloody ENSA by now and no mistake. Still..."

"What, Everett?"

"I'd never have met the love of me life, would I? Stupid bastard only got a bayonet in the guts though didn't he. I'll never forgive him for that see if I don't."

"Not here, Everett? Surely not here? Oh god Everett how can you have stood it?"

Felicity had gone to stand by him, holding his head to her breasts. Everett patted her arm and detached himself.

"Last thing he said last time I saw him was 'be brave'. I didn't know, you see, until we was told we were coming to Stanley, then one of his mates said, 'I'm going to tell you the truth, Everett. Don't think I approve of you and him being you know what but you've got to know before you get there.' That's when he told me about the massacre and how they didn't stand no chance from the Nips and how it were the nurses as well and they tried to burn them all even the ones that weren't completely dead and how they chopped off noses and ears and arms and legs. And I know it was out there outside that window where that black patch was they did the burning. I found a cap-badge you know. Lots of people found things. It was his regiment. Might have been his. I just hope it was quick for him. I spent three and a half years hoping it was quick. But one night I saw him, you know. Underneath them trees. He were just standing there and smiling and he talks and he says, 'Everett, it don't hurt no more. I'm here waiting for you, Everett.' Then he sods off just like that. No change there then."

"What was his name?" said Percy.

"Lionel Green. Sergeant Lionel Green. Middlesex Regiment. From Acton."

"Lionel. Your friend. Would you like to tell us about him?" said Felicity. "It's just us and we'll soon be at the four corners. However private it is we'll never tell a soul."

"Yes," said Percy, "tell us."

"Well," said Everett. "'E was my friend."

"What was he like?" said Felicity.

"Well," said Everett, "now you're asking." He smiled. "He was quite tall and sort of beefy. Not fat. But big. He had a moustache. He told me it was obligatory for Sergeants to have a moustache. We were the same age born in '97. Small world, innit? He was apprenticed to a carter but joined up in '15 and got posted to Mesopotamia."

"We lost a lot of people there," said Percy.

"Yes they did," said Everett Causey. "Them bloody generals, Kitchener worst of all." He gave a dramatic sniff. "Of course, I couldn't join up on account of me rickets having left me a bit lop-sided, but I ran away to the Theatre. Backstage at the Coliseum. But this ain't about me. He managed to survive the heat and the flies and the bloody bungling somehow and then afterwards he got posted to Palestine; he loved it there he said. I think that might have been the boys. Then after a bit he got promoted Lance Corporal and went out to India with the Middlesex. Allahabad he was. Said he loved it there, too. I think he must have had a bit of Gyppo blood in him or something 'cos he loved all these foreign places with sand and sacred cows and what-not. Anyway come '36 he was in Colombo helping run the tramways. Never left the army. Never wanted to. Said he was married to it. Anyway they made him Sergeant and he thought he'd gone to heaven drilling all those soft white recruits out from England and waving his knob-head stick around. And he got invited to join the Freemasons and really that was life complete for him. He'd never got married, no kids, that was unlikely he said. Said he'd planned to retire to The Himalaya, that's what he said, and get up every morning and see Kanchenjunga and he wanted to die like them Hindu and have his ashes dumped in the river."

Everett Causey paused. Felicity gave his shoulders a gentle squeeze.

"Did he have family in England?" said Percy.

"Oh yes he did," said Everett Causey, "but they disowned him on account of him being found in the straw taking it up the arse from the carter and showing every sign of enjoying it. That's when he joined the Army and he never talked to them again."

"That was sad," said Felicity.

"Maybe," said Everett Causey. "So there he was in Colombo married to the Army, drilling young boys and rolling up his trouser leg on Saturdays swigging pink gins and playing cricket and havin' a whale of a time when there was a riot on one of his blessed trams and him and his boys 'ad to come down and whack the buggers back into line and that was when he found me. I was hiding under the seats. I was lucky they didn't torch it. Anyway, well he drags me out and sort of dusts me off and says what was I doing there and I says, 'havin' a look round the town on me day off,' and he says, 'day off what,' and I says, 'Don't yer know that the Gaiety Galore's in town at the Elphinstone two weeks starting tomorrow?' and he says, 'You don't look like an actor,' and I says, 'No call to be rude and anyway I'm stage manager and it's my job to work with the local am drams for the support acts.' So he pulls me up and I wobbles a bit and he says, 'What's wrong with your leg — Jerry bullet?' and I says, 'No, I got left out in the rain by me mum.' So he says, 'Take my advice, stay off the trams the next few days where you going. I'll give you an escort. Galle Face?' he said and I said, 'It's a bit soon and anyway my mum…', 'What left you out in the rain,' he said, 'My mum,' I said, 'said never to go with a soldier.' 'Well,' he says, 'sorry mum, but you're with me from now on.' And that was it. He took me back to the hotel and it weren't the Galle Face, of course it wasn't, it was some dive and he inspected me kit and carried out some drill and made me a recruit. Are you sure I should be telling you all this?"

"Haven't you told anyone else about Lionel?"

"No course not. I'm already an outcast without being cast out any further thank you."

"But you're telling us."

"Well like you say we'll be out of here in a month at most is what they're saying and I like you. You're the nearest to family I've had these last few years so yes, I'm telling you. Before we forget. I hope you won't forget."

"I won't forget," said Felicity. "I'll always remember you and Lionel."

"Me too," said Percy.

"Es ari," said Mr Friedman.

"Thank you," said Everett Causey.

"So we had our two weeks in Colombo and then me and the troupe went on to Madras. God we used to wish for a typhoon when we was on board so we could stop bloody rehearsing all the time, then the Gaiety in Calcutta, then Rangoon and there was a letter from me there from Lionel saying he'd follow me to the ends of the earth where was I going next, so I wired him, 'Singapore then Hong Kong,' so there was a letter in Singapore saying, 'don't leave Hong Kong am coming to get you.' And he did. Got a transfer. That was '37 by then and I got a job. Sheer luck that was; it must have been meant. At the China Fleet Club managing the London shows and all the amdrams like the Cheerio Club and I loved it. We had a flat in Wanchai and Lionel told them I was his crippled brother and he needed to look after me and they somehow swallowed that and let him alone and the Chinese didn't mind and we just kept out of people's way and Lionel was really good at cricket so they didn't want to lose him. Then when things started to look bad he told me to leave and go to Australia and I said, 'not with them spiders and snakes,' and I stayed. So then he got made an instructor for the Hong Kong Volunteers first of all and he was up on Tai Tam when he got shot in the arm. That's how he ended up here in Stanley. That's what his mate Chalky told me anyway. Then when the Nips broke in he tried to hide one of the younger ones under his bed but the Nips bayoneted right through him and nicked the nipper and he cried out so they found him and bayoneted him too. Then they dragged the bodies out, chopped up the survivors while they were still alive and burnt them like I said before. RIP Lionel Green and the nipper whatever your name was."

There was silence.

"What are you going to do when it's all over?" asked Percy.

"You know what, Perce, since we've been talking the penny dropped and I'm going to stay put. They might re-open the Club. It's worth a chance so I'm going to stay here. With Lionel. He never wanted to go back to England so maybe this is him telling me something. What do you think?"

"What are you going to do?" asked Everett Causey. "You know. After."

"I shall stay on a bit," said Percy, "if I can. I must try and find out what happened to my parents. Where they are."

"I'm staying in here till it's safe to go out," said Everett Causey. "Till the flag's flying again and even then I'm not so sure. You know what they say about what's going on out there. How the Nationalists are fighting the Communists and the Nips will carry on killing till the last man and how if the Nats or the Commies or the Nips don't get you if you look at someone the wrong way out of your white face and they're a Triad they'll slit your throat from ear to ear. There's still a whole army of Nips out there you know."

Percy had heard David say pretty much the same things about the state of Hong Kong and what was left of it. How the suffering was likely to continue for the Europeans and the Chinese even in the unlikely event that Japan were to surrender without a bloodbath. That revenge killings, looting and starvation would be hard to bring under control.

"Anarchy," said Mr Friedman. "You British are broken. You cannot hope to take back charge without your navy. And where is it? Does it even exist anymore?"

"There's the Indomitable what's been flying planes over," said Felicity loyally. "And the Royal Australian Navy."

"And how long will it take them to get here? Three weeks? Maybe Hong Kong will become American? Maybe the Chinese will walk in and take it. Where is your London calling? It is a very long way away. Many things could happen before you British come back. If you still want to, of course."

"They wouldn't just leave us," said Everett Causey. "They wouldn't. They know we're here. Mr Churchill said so. They'll send ships for us and food and medicine. The Yanks will have told them they've seen us. They've flown right over us. They've chucked chocolate at us. And they made that V-sign at Lady Considine."

"Do you think we'll ever see each other again?" said Felicity. "You know, after we've all been docketed and ticketed and de-loused and loaded up with tinned mutton? Won't we just be ordered about and told to go here or go there or get on this ship or that ship? Do you think we'll have any choice? I mean, will they really let me go with Mr Friedmann to America?"

"It'll be difficult if you don't have relatives there."

"So Mr Friedmann, what will we do instead?"

"We will get there," said Mr Friedman. "I have relatives. They went in '38. And we will say you lost your passport. There will be ways."

"And if not?"

"Ach, my dear then I will play the piano and you will act and dance and sing and we will set off by every night club from here to

Manila to Hawaii to San Francisco and on every boat we will sing and dance our way to the promised land. Have no fear."

"And what about your friend?" said Everett Causey to Percy. "Mr Sopley. You was at school together wasn't you? He'll be one of the first out of here. What you going to do then?"

"What I've always done," said Percy. "I'll look for a job. Go back to work. Maybe have my own hotel one day."

"Sounds more like Monopoly than a burning ambition if you don't mind my saying so. Most men would say I'm going to settle down, find myself a nice wife, have kiddies. Don't you want all that Mr Langrigg?"

"Perhaps about as much as you do Mr Causey."

"That ain't a proposal, is it? Look. We're friends. Would it hurt to be honest? For once? You're not the only couple in the camp you know. 'Course no one actually sleeps in the same beds but boys will be boys and all that. I mean look at Adams and that policeman what's his name. They go about pretending they're deadly enemies and do all what they can to make it look like they've got a feud going on but it's all hogwash. They're devoted to each other. Never met before they came in here neither. And it ain't all men of course. That Her Royal Highness Uttley gets her fancy tickled regular as clockwork by her chum Cynthia. Same as it's ever been ain't it? There's none so blind as him what will not see or don't want to look at what's right under their noses and I don't mean their fannies or their percies, sorry no offence."

"O ye'll tak the high road and I'll take the low road and I'll be in Scotland afore ye," sang Felicity. "But me and my true love we'll never meet again on the bonny bonny banks of Lock Lomond."

"It is not lock," said Mr Friedman. "It is loch as ach zu liebe..."

"Yes, I'm very attached to David Sopley. Of course. He's been like a brother to me since we were at school. We were as good as orphaned you know. And yes, we've looked out for each other while we've been in here."

Everett Causey raised his eyebrows and put his hand on Percy's knee. "Now you listen to me Mr Percy Longwords. No. Just listen to me just once. It could be weeks before we're let out or hours before we all get the bayonet or whatever and here we are in no-man's-land between yesterday and tomorrow and you know what here we are behind all this wire but this could be the closest we'll ever get to freedom. Real freedom. In a funny way. So let Everett Causey tell you a few home truths you might want to listen to."

"Oh early one morning just as the sun was rising I heard a poor maid in the valley below."

"What is a valley below?"

"You see where the hill goes down to the prison then up again the other side? Yes? Well, it's a valley and it's below us so it's a valley below."

"Thank you my dear."

"Oh never leave me, oh don't deceive me, how can you you-hoose a poor maiden so?"

"How are you going to feel when BAAG or whatever come and take him away before any of us gets let out? Everett Causey knows about BAAG the China Fleet and that kind of thing. I ain't so green as I'm cabbage looking as me old mum used to say. They were talking about him at the Cheerio Club back in '41 – oh that dishy looking new Government House fellow – but he's MI6 didn't yer know. He come here to spy on the Chinese. Not the Japs mind, the Chinese. 'Cos he speaks Chinese don't he? Do you speak Chinese?"

"Yes I do. Cantonese."

"Yes, well he were unlucky weren't he; caught like a rat in a trap with the rest of us when he had a ticket booked for Chungking. People say he had to bury everything toot sweet or the Japs would have shot him for a spy. But you know all this don't you?"

"Everett, I admire you I really do. But I'm not sure I should..."

"Be honest?" Everett Causey squeaked so loudly that Felicity Charlton looked around. He began to cough noisily.

"Are you alright Everett?" said Felicity Charlton. She started toward him but Everett waved her away through his coughs before eventually spluttering out:

"Yes thank you, my dear. Just the old camp croak."

Felicity smiled and turned back to the piano and Mr Friedman.

"You know Percy, this Empire of ours has done you no good. You can't be honest about yourself or your feelings at all can you?" Everett coughed a little more before recovering. "You're so constipated in your 'eart it's going to burst one day and you'll drop down dead. You really are a knight of old and no mistake. Honesty. Alright. Honesty. Is it honest to shag whoever you like even when you got ties so to speak? Well I'm going to guess you'll say no and you'll be right. But you know your David ain't been how shall we say exclusive with you. You do know that don't yer? Course you do. Everyone does. So now I'm going to ask you a big old question. How do you feel about that?"

Percy was silent.

"You ain't got a heart of stone now Percy, have you? Ask yourself, how do you feel?"

"What he does or may do is nothing to do with me. He's a free man."

"Oh but you ain't are you, Mr Scotsman? You ain't free because you loves 'im. That's how the world will always go, Robbie Burns. When two people are in love one will love more than the other. One's going to care more than the other, you see. Don't them poems of yours tell you all about that? All that blinking heartache? Or was all that a bit too obvious for your Lord Tennyson? Mind you he had to be just a bit queer, didn't he? I mean he was in love with that man in that poem we had to learn bits of at school what was it called?"

"*In Memoriam.*"

"That's it. That's the one. About the chap who died. His lover..."

"We don't know that."

"We don't need to. It's as plain as a pikestaff. Maybe that's what he 'ad. Bit of a nice pikestaff."

"The poem is above all that."

"No, it ain't. See you can remember great chunks of it I've heard you, but do you feel it too? Let your heart become an April Violet, Percy dear. Go on, bud and blossom like the rest of us. Liberate yourself and Everett Causey won't be needing to liberate you before the Yanks get here and it's too late."

"I do. I do. I feel."

"You feel what?"

"Love."

"See," Everett Causey patted Percy's hand. "World ain't come to an end, 'as it? We choose our own chains, don't we? It'd be a shame if you stepped out of here straight back into prison. That's what Everett Causey thinks."

"You two having a nice heart to heart? Got all your plans sorted out? Don't tell me. You're going to elope to Macau and set up a hotel with a casino and make oodles of money and live happily ever after."

"What are you talking about you wicked girl?"

"Of course. I forgot, his heart belongs to Daddy. On the subject of daddy, Mr Friedmann, I really think you should go back to your room and have a little lie down. All this rehearsing has been too exhausting. Still, did you notice?"

"Notice what?"

"No bloody tone-deaf Japs telling us to shut up. Makes a nice change. Yes, off you go dear. And you too Mr Causey you should take forty winks, too. We need you on top form tonight don't we Mr Langrigg? Toodle-ooh. So that just leaves you and me Percy. All alone."

Felicity Charlton went over to the piano and stood over the keyboard. As the sun came into the room it showed her figure, slim. boyish, naked through her cotton dress. She leant forward, placing a finger on a key. Her hair fell forwards over her face and with the other hand she pushed it up, her shoulders tilting back as she did so. Percy noticed how young she was. Twenty-five perhaps? Stretching out the fingers of her right hand she brought them down onto the piano. C, E, G. C major.

She sang; "Love's always been my game, play it how I may. I was made that way. I can't help it."

She stopped.

"Are you in love Mr Percy Langrigg? With him? Are you in love with each other?"

"I think so," said Percy.

Felicity Charlton turned round and looked at him.

"My goodness Mr Langrigg. The truth. It's as well the balloon's about to go up because if you ever breathed that out loud to anyone else you'd never play bridge again anywhere. Exciting times. Don't you feel it? We can say things because soon it'll be cheerio and we won't ever see each other again. Soon there may be food. Imagine it. And tea. Coffee! Look I've got my chocolate bar that Everett gave me. Shall we share it?"

She broke the bar in pieces and waved one at Percy.

"Come on. Open wide."

The sound of slow applause came echoing from the double-height ceiling and across the mauled parquet. Felicity dropped backward to sit on the piano keyboard with a loud, atonal plonk. She was looking in the direction from which the clapping was still coming. Percy stared straight ahead over her shoulder and out of the window his head reeling from the sugar.

"Well look what the cat dragged in," said Felicity Charlton. "If it isn't our man from the ministry, Mr David Sopley himself. Look Percy, it's your special friend."

The applause had stopped.

"Have you finished?"

"No, I hadn't actually, Mr Sopley."

She climbed down from the piano keyboard with another crash of the keys.

"Well, I'm going to skip along and have a little rest before dress rehearsal. Then I'll have filet mignon and Champagne in the dressing-room. Sounds boring I know but it gives a girl a lift. Toodle pip."

Head held high she walked out of the room and into the afternoon sunshine.

"You weren't in the rice kitchen. They're looking for you."

"I'll go now."

Percy sat down on the piano stool. "On second thoughts they'll have to do without me for once," he said.

"But you're the champion rice-stirrer of the camp. No one quite makes a congee like you do. Cigarette?"

"Old Gold? Where on earth did you get them?"

"Passing plane kindly dropped them practically at my feet."

"Who did you have to kick aside?"

"D'you think I'd stoop to that?"

"It sounds as though stooping's pretty much your thing."

"You don't want to to be taken in by her."

"I like her."

"You mean you feel sorry for her. There's an entire club of chaps and some women who feel sorry for Felicity Charlton. Subscription's quite reasonable. Just unswerving loyalty, a few black-market purchases and a promise to look after her when the war's over."

"She's still just a girl. She has no family, no husband..."

"Last reports from Nagoya say Tommy Grinter's still alive."

"Who's Tommy Grinter?"

"He was ADC to the Governor. Charlton was his steno. Governor completely disapproved but Grinter was determined."

"So she was fishing fleet?"

"And he was twenty years her senior. Apparently wanted to do some good with his money so he'd changed his will the day before.. All his pension'll go to her if he doesn't make it back. She'll be set for life. Cigarette?"

"Oh yes, of course, thank you."

Percy took the cigarette and held his head in closer to David to get a light for it. David was leaning over him and despite the sourness of the smell they all carried around with him there was still the faint lingering scent of the David he'd always known that carried across the short distance to enter his nose, his brain, the place where only life-long bonds are made and stored.

"I'm sorry," he said.

"Don't be. She led you on. She can't help it. It's all rather impressive really in a Darwinian sort of way. She's spent the last three years trying out most of the men in camp to select the perfect mate."

"Isn't that what men always say about women?"

"In this case it's true."

"I think she wants you, David."

"She knows she can't have me."

"Perhaps that makes her all the more determined."

"I rather admire her. The girls had the worst of the shock I think when we were all herded in here. The single girls I mean. Used to depending on men for pretty much everything."

"You mean the unmarried ones."

"Not just them. All the widows and girls with husbands in other camps too. It must have been hell for them. They had to learn how to survive."

"But there are so many women in here looking after each other."

"Even so. They had to toughen up or die. I feel sorry for their chaps when they meet up again. Can't see them going back to warming slippers and making cocoa."

"Perhaps that's just what they're longing for?"

"Perhaps. Until it actually happens."

"Is it going to happen?"

David took a drag from the luxurious cigarette and looked around the room. It appeared that they were on their own.

"What I told you. It's happening tomorrow. The mother of all bombs is going to be dropped on Japan. If that doesn't bring them to terms there'll be another. And then another till it works. It's hideous but the Americans don't see any other way to get them to stop. The only alternative is hand-to-hand fighting the whole way from Okinawa to what's left of the Imperial Palace."

"What's left of it?"

"Of course you wouldn't know. The Americans bombed it and practically burnt it to the ground back in May."

"So, they're getting a taste of their own medicine?"

"The Yanks have been practically carpet-bombing their cities all year but it hasn't forced the surrender. Their top brass are terrified that if they have to repeat Okinawa on Kyushu, Shikoku then Honshu there won't be a Nip or a Yank left alive."

"I've got to ask you, do they know we're here?"

"Oh yes little one, don't worry about that. We know. The Yanks know. Trouble is getting it into the Nips' heads the game's up. So it's these bombs or the Russians or both."

"It's not over yet?"

"No, my sweet, it could fizzle on for months even if they do officially surrender."

"What will happen to you when it's all over?"

"No change really from the last time we talked about it. I'll be out pronto to link up with BAAG and give them the gen on all the POW camps around Hong Kong. Then I'll come back and do whatever I need to do to help Gimson step up and take charge. Tell him who to talk to. Who not to. Let him know how the land lies. It's going to be dangerous if the Japs give up. Not all of them will and there are thousands of them here. Then there's the Chinese wanting to get their hands on the place. And then there's the local Triads. God knows if there's any money left in the kitty to buy them off this time. It isn't going to be much fun."

"Will I see you?"

"Doubt it old boy. You get yourself back to England."

"I'd rather go back to Shanghai."

"Don't be an idiot. There's another war about to start between Chiang Kai Shek and this man Mao the Commie Generalissimo. The place is going to tear itself apart."

"Then I'll stay here."

"They won't want you. Whole place has got to be rebuilt."

"The Repulse Bay may open up again."

"It may but it won't have any guests for a while. Really. Go back to London. Find that aunt. Stay there till I come and find you."

"How will you find me?"

"How have I always found you?"

"Chance. Will we be together after that?"

"One day. We'll see. One day when I can decide for myself how my life goes. In the meantime you make your own decisions. Do what you have to."

"'Marianna in the Moated Grange.'"

"The rusted flowerpots. Just don't end up like her. Enjoy your life."

"You're my life."

"No I'm not. Don't be so ruddy sentimental."

"God it's like end of term, isn't it?"

"You mean back at Yantai? 'Lord dismiss us with thy blessing and all that?'"

"'O dulces comitum.'"

"That's not what you were calling them a minute ago."

"'O dulces comitum valete coetus, longe quos simul a domo profectos.'"

"'Diversae variae viae reportant.' You can just hear their leather sandals slapping on the stone roads getting further and further away."

"'O hark, o hear how thin and clear,'"

"'And thinner, clearer, farther going,'"

"'O sweet and far from cliff and scar,'"

"'The horns of Elfland faintly blowing.'"

Percy looked at David's face and saw the scars there, the cuts from the rings and the bruises from the knuckles of the Japanese who'd made him stand still, crouched down and leapt up to hit him in the face, over and over again, just because he was tall. And foreign. And a captive. Oh David.

"'O love they die on yon rich sky...'"

"'They faint on hill or field or river...'"

"'I'll wait for you for ever.'"

"Don't."

"You said I should."

"It's just a dream."

"'Dies at the opening day.'"

"Don't be morbid for god's sake."

"You said you'd come and find me."

"'Whistle and I'll come to ye my lad?' Don't be sentimental little Perce. Work hard. Love well. Perhaps one day in the future our paths will cross. Perhaps the future will be kinder to queers like us. When we're old and no one cares anymore."

"You mean a bungalow in Bognor?"

"Mon repos."

"Glenhomo."

"Puck's Bottom."

"Bell's End."

"Percy's Bush."

"Ball Hall."

"Seamen's Rest."

"Rimmers' Cottage."

"Done Goblin."

"Fairy Dell."

"Homo Sweet Homo."

"I'll hold you to that."

"You'll hold me now. Come here."

David grasped Percy's hand and led him to a corner of the room in behind the stage curtains. "Holes in corners," he said. And he looked down at Percy and said, "now kiss me." Percy reached up and put his hands either side of David's face, that gaunt, stubbled, scarred face and brought it down to his. David opened his lips and Percy put his over them pulling that head down and gulping in David's air that smelt of smoke and sourness. David put his hands round Percy's waist and leaned further and deeper into the kiss. They both stiffened and David pulled them closer together still. Percy felt the stubbly nape of the taller man's neck. David cupped what was left of Percy's buttocks with his hands. They stayed, breathing into each other for a minute, perhaps a little more. David stepped back, broke them apart. They stood, looking at each other, hands at their sides.

Had they come all the way for this? he asked

"Yes," said Percy.

"I must go," said David. "No dull sublunary lovers' love, mind."

"Not a breach but an expansion."

"Indeed. Like gold to airy thinness beat. Now bugger off and get that rice cooked."

"All right," said Percy

Rome, Ostia Antica, August 1951

Saltimbocca alla Romana

Percy couldn't remember all the details of the night before but as the hot, crowded train rocked and bumped its way from Termini to Lido di Ostia he felt seasick for the first time in his life. It was Ferragosto and the carriage was packed. With girls in polka-dot sundresses and their white-clad boyfriends shouting, laughing, flashing teeth and smiles. With Roman matrons dressed in black or dark blue with their broods of children and unshaven husbands carrying baskets of food and bottles of beer. And the chatter was ceaseless. Ceaseless and voluble it ebbed and flowed around the carriage like those little waves that kiss the Mediterranean sands in Summer, roll away and leave no impression behind them. They talked of friends and friends of friends, acquaintances, and acquaintances of acquaintances, of jobs, money and the difficulty of putting food on the table. They talked about relatives and relatives' relatives, of affairs and scandals, of cheats and of saints pausing briefly to admonish a child or command a husband. Percy's stomach heaved with nausea. A rush, a flood, an ebb, a retreat a peristaltic wave oh god he was going to be sick.

How on earth could David stand it? Where was David? Oh yes, there, by the window chatting to the man next to him over an article they were both reading from somebody else's newspaper. Why couldn't they have come by car? David had insisted that the only way to really enjoy a Sunday in Ferragosto was to join in with everyone else and take the train. He'd been too hungover to object and had merely lain in bed while David went out to see what he could find by way of a picnic which turned out to mean some greasy ham, bread and tomatoes. Lain in bed. Yes. Oh the stupidity that had made him get drunk and be suffering on the first morning in his life that he'd woken up next to a naked man. A naked David in his bed in his apartment.

Now here they were, Percy and David, together, rattling down to Ostia. How many stations had they passed? Percy couldn't see the map of the line to check where they were or how many stops to go.

A bell clanged and the train jolted over a level crossing. Behind the gates were packs of people on bicycles, young men and women, more polka-dot dresses tied up behind the nape of the neck, cork-soled shoes, sunglasses and sun hats. The boys wore shorts that clung to their upper thighs and scraps of shirts open to the navel to reveal tanned skin. On their feet were stained white plimsolls. Behind the ranks of cyclists were other ranks of mopeds, motos, motors revving and coughing, smoke billowing, boys and girls on pillion, heads all turned chatting to other heads and laughing mouths under scarves or caps on the backs of the other motos. Behind them again were the cars, big family cars, tiny Topolini all crammed with people, chairs, tables, baskets of food, children. All of Roman Rome seemed to be careering toward Ostia today. The train screeched to a halt and people and packages were bumped around together. "Come on old chap," said David, "here we are."

It had been David's idea to get out of town but only as far as Ostia Antica. "Roman ruins," he'd said. "Great big pine trees, lots of shade, you'll love it."

Percy scrambled toward the open door of the carriage with mumbles of permesso and senta, scusi and mi dispiace and sorry. When he got there he stumbled and fell down the step. He heard a collective gasp from all the faces at the windows and then, as David, having set down the picnic basket, neatly broke his fall and swung him to the ground there were cheers and wolf-whistles and shouts of bravo and bace, bace and other Roman things he couldn't work out such was the banging in his head. Someone threw his hat out after him. His London Panama hat. As the train pulled away South the level crossing gates opened letting the flood of people and machinery roar off down the road until gradually the rustling quiet of an August mid-day began to redescend on the little, pine-fringed station.

"All right?" said David.

David led them toward the creaking little bridge that took them over the line and into the excavations. Following a path they came to a gate and a ticket collector's hut.

"You won," said David, pointing at the sign that said Chiuso per Restauro.

"Bollocks," said Percy. The next thing he knew he was at David's feet vomiting and vomiting then reaching and croaking.

"Mind my shoes," said David. "They're Trickers."

"Sorry," said Percy, finally, once his guts had stopped emptying themselves into the long grass. "Just not used to it."

"No indeed my little monastic friend it would seem not." He sent down a hand that Percy grabbed and let himself be hauled to his feet. "Come on," he said, "onward goes the pilgrim band."

"But it's chiuso."

"Of course it is."

"Can't you read what it says?"

"Yes. It's Italian for Buggered off to the Beach."

"It's locked."

David pushed gently at the gate - it swung open.

"We shouldn't do this. We could be fined."

"Yes," said David, "that's true. Come on my mouse of virtue, this way."

Within a minute the ticket kiosk had disappeared behind the screen of tall, chattering bulrushes that marked the beginning of the excavations. Over and over again they told their story of ancient rivers and waterways, and their job was not to let people forget that this had once upon a time been a port, perhaps even the biggest port in the whole Roman Empire. The men"s feet found stone. A wharf.

"She holds the gorgeous East in fee," said David.

"That was Venice," said Percy out of a dry mouth and with pain rocketing around his head. "Shelley."

"Byron. Childe Harold."

"That's the sea Cybele fresh from Ocean you're thinking of. Actually, it's Wordsworth. Extinction of the Venetian Republic."

"You win. Look can I have some water? I'm parched."

"We'll sit down in a minute when we've found somewhere nice."

"Nice."

"Yes, nice."

"This isn't Hampstead Heath."

"No. It's foreign. We're foreigners. And trespassers. But here we are, eh? So let's have a nice time."

"Ugh," said Percy.

"Are you going to be sick again?"

"I don't think so. What on earth did you make me drink?"

"Nothing that you didn't demand."

"Why didn't you stop me?"

"Because you were on such good form."

"What did I say?"

"Ah, well, we'll get on to that later. Where's a good place to sit?"

Away from the excavated area of wharf and the stumps of walls of what had been offices, wineshops, ancient Roman snack bars catering for sailors, dockers, prostitutes and Roman officials they forged through undergrowth into what had been a street, one among hundreds. With the Ostia road away from them across more ruins and a large field planted with maize they stood, shoulder to shoulder taking in the size of the port around them, flattened but still huge, empty of people but full of the sounds of crickets, birds and the rustling of rushes that mimicked the swish of the long-disappeared sea. "Come along," said David. "Chop, chop."

David carried the picnic hamper. Percy followed, Panama hat on the back of his head, linen jacket over his shoulder, plimsolled feet scuffing the stones, sharp marram grasses getting into the lace-holes and sand creeping in everywhere. David sauntered, head covered in a neat linen peaked cap, expensive sunglasses over his eyes, tatty but expensive white trousers, those English shoes. The eternal public schoolboy thought Percy. He felt like Tom Brown trailing after the sleek, slim Scud. And yet, he reflected, as he tripped and stumbled his way through the ruins of the port, he had pleased David last night. Pleased him with the last of the energy and euphoria of a night on the town, the final hurrah before lapsing into unconsciousness and self-inflicted pain.

An insect whined toward him and he slapped the back of his neck. A cigarette would sort them out. But, oh hells bells, the thought of a cigarette made his stomach heave and he wobbled as he walked.

"Come on you," said David. "Ave, Parsifalus Dorsolongus, tu tamen ebrius est?"

"Cod Latin," said Percy. "How much further?"

"I was heading for that bit of ruin over there. We can park our things and go and have a shufty around."

"We can park our things and lie down until the place stops moving up and down."

"Still under the weather. Well, I'm not surprised. It's what happens when monks forsake their vows."

"Why this is Hell nor are we out of it."

"Come on old chap it's our first day out together and free since oh, let's see, 1924? Crikey, a twenty-seven-year engagement. We both deserve medals."

"For?"

"You know I really can't decide between complete stupidity or persistence above and beyond. Look, how about here?"

David stopped in the centre of what might have been a room, its walls now reduced or restored to a height of about three feet. Grasses and the dead heads of wildflowers rustled in the corners but in the centre was a patch of something like lawn studded with brown pellets.

"Rabbits," said David.

"I'm going to be sick." Percy turned away and staggered out of the room, across a courtyard, into a street and when far enough away from David that he hoped the stench wouldn't carry collapsed down onto his knees and vomited into a bush. Then he rolled over to look at the sky. A Japanese soldier was standing over him, rifle raised above his head, bayonet hovering over his stomach. Percy gushed sweat and turned freezing cold. He opened his eyes and found that now he was lying on his side with his cheek on a patch of moss growing out of sand. He was Gulliver and he was lying across an archipelago of soft tropical islands. An enormous bird, a roc, descended then turned into a butterfly. Ants crawled over the sand like elephants crossing a plain. There were giant, towering trees. Everything beyond them was blurred. He moved his head and looked up a little. The trees were euphorbias and their dead flowers rustled. The woodspurge has a cup of three, he thought.

"Come on Lazarus," said a voice. "I've opened the wine."

"I don't think I should," said Percy, back in the room from which he'd fled. "I really don't."

"Come on. Hair of the dog that bit you."

"What is it?"

"Frascati of course."

"Warm Frascati?"

"Not hot."

"Oh god. Must I?"

"You must." David handed him a tumbler full of pale gold liquid. "The true, the blushful Hippocrene," he said.

Percy took a sip. "Could have done with another few hours in the deep-delved earth."

David brought his glass close to Percy's and clinked the two together.

"Cin," he said.

"Cin," said Percy and he sipped. The sugar rushed through him and he instantly began to feel better.

"There you are," said David. "Brought the colour back to your cheeks." He took out two cigarettes and handed one to Percy.

"I don't think I could."

"Probably wise," said David putting one of the cigarettes back into its carton, lighting the other and reclining full stretch on the grass with a cloud of smoke spurting from his nostrils.

"'Fire, fire,'" said Percy. "'O Troy's down. Troy Town's on fire.'" The smoke went up toward the umbrella pines.

"'Its little smoke, in pallid moonshine, died,'" said David.

"David?"

"Yes, little Perce?"

"Look, I know you've been with lots of men. And women."

David raised himself up slowly onto one elbow. He peered at Percy over his sunglasses.

"You think I'm a monster of selfishness, a roué, a practised lover, a cad, a debaucher, that I'm shameless, a philanderer. Why not go a bit further and call me a whore?"

"Are you? I mean do you do it for gain? Of some kind. Sometimes?"

"You mean to help my career?"

"Yes."

"I have done."

"With men as well as women?"

"Yes."

They were silent.

"Look here, little Perce. Look at me."

Percy looked at the long, handsome face, the strong chin, the tawny, receding hair and the puckle of little scars across cheeks and forehead.

"D'you remember when I found you with that schoolmaster on the last day of term?" Percy was silent. "I know you do. Do you know how many times he'd done it to me? Like that and up the backside? His pretty boy he used to call me."

"You were beautiful."

"Best not to be I think. I'd rather have been plain."

"Like me. Fat and spotty and wearing glasses."

"He has a daily beauty in his life that makes mine ugly."

"That's exactly what I used to think about you."

"You can't wish you were someone else. It isn't a good idea to have heroes."

"You were my hero."

"Thank you."

"And you still are."

"Percy," said David softly, "you really mustn't think like that. Heroes disappoint. It's in their natures. They have feet of clay."

"I think all this is about letting me down gently. Isn't it David?"

"Cigarette?"

"No. No thank you."

"You're just too bloody polite. Why thank me when you know I'm just trying to change the subject? Why give me the upper hand all the time?"

"Because I love you."

"I envy you your ability to be emotional."

"And I'm being an emotional fool over you."

"Trouble is, Percy, I'm not really alive. I'm dead already. Emotionally speaking."

"For goodness sake."

"Aren't those always the best horror stories the ones that are told in the brightest sunlight?"

"It was noon. The sun fell on my head. And it was not an hour in which we think upon the dead."

"Exactly. I mean here you are on a hot day in August out in the open air, in the sunshine, large as life telling me you're Nosferatu. Give me that cigarette. And a drink."

"That's better. Assert yourself. Take charge."

"Lay hold of life and it shall be."

"Thy joy and crown eternally."

"Don't come after me into the dark little Perce. Light me a gentian. Light me a torch. Who was that? No, don't. I want always to think of you up there on the surface being happy. Don't come looking for me and don't try and come down and rescue me. I'll always look back. If

I get offered the forbidden fruit I'll eat it. You know that. Come on. Don't be glum."

"I'm not glum. I'm just feeling a bit lost."

"Find yourself. Gnothi seauton. You know the drill. You know why they call it making love? Because you don't have to be in love to do it. It's like two scouts with a piece of wood. Keep rubbing away and there may be a spark eventually."

"Which you'll try to put out."

"I'm asbestos, Percy boy, but you're a conflagration waiting to happen. Here's your cigarette. Be careful not to set light to the undergrowth. It'd go up as quickly as you."

"Whatever happened to Felicity Charlton? I last saw her standing on the steps at Stanley jetty waiting for one of those Australian corvettes. The Launceston I think it was. Waiting to go out to the Empress of Australia."

"Was that Jew with her?"

"You mean Mr Friedman? No, he'd decided to go back into town for something or other back at his old flat. Disturbed some looters and got a knife in the ribs."

"Whatever happened to Laetitia?"

"Didn't Lyle tell you?"

"Not really."

"You were the last of us to see her. Wouldn't let me into the flat. Didn't call. Next thing I knew I heard that she'd got on a boat for New York and was shacked up with a musical producer. So began her glorious Broadway career."

"And you haven't heard from her since?"

"Not a dicky-bird. And I rather admire her for it. Le jeu d'amour et du hasard and all that. She won. Jolly good luck to her."

"But you lost your main asset."

David laughed. "Now you're catching on. Yes, I lost my star so all the projects and all the backing went down the drain. Lucky to get out with my shirt. Or some of it."

"You don't sound particularly aggrieved."

"I'm not. I wasn't. We were all making good films. Denham, Pinewood, us. But there wasn't the money to compete with the Americans, so it was going to be a decade of low-budget movies made from war memoirs and I didn't want that. I didn't want to look back."

"Lyle said you went to France."

"Yes to see if things were any different. There was some talk of a new way of doing things but it looked exactly like the old way. At least to me. With the exception of Tati of course. But even that was vaudeville. And those turgid melodramas the rest were churning out. Ghastly. Provincial. Just like ours."

"Lots of people went to see them. I went to see them."

"Which?"

"Oh gosh. *Le Colonel Durand. Ombres sur Paris. Manon*."

"All pretty stock stuff. Historical dramas. Doomed romances."

"Yes. But there was *Mr Hulot*. That was extraordinary. French but could go anywhere we thought."

"We?"

"Lyle of course."

"And you know what happened next? Tati made *Le Jour de Fete* in '47 and couldn't get a distributor in France. Not one. First showing was in London this year."

"*Les Parents Terribles*."

"Interesting, Cocteau. I went to see him down at Cap d'Agde. Plenty of ideas but *Les Parents* was too stagey for my taste. He's like a French Noel Coward in some ways. A dilettante in others. It takes more than that to start a movement."

"*Les Voleurs du Bicyclette*."

"Now you're talking. That's why I'm here. Do you know what's going on here? In film?"

"Well everyone's talking about Cinecittà and my neighbour was coming back with her shopping the other day and ended up being filmed. She had to walk to the corner over and over again until she was dizzy and told them she'd had enough."

"Who was filming?"

"A sort of wild man with crazy hair."

"Federico Fellini. He's the rising star you know." David paused. "But you've met him."

"No I haven't."

"You jolly well did you know. Last night."

"Oh no."

"Oh yes, little Perce. In fact he owes you a debt. You did him a favour."

Percy brought himself up to sitting, hands clasped around his knees. "What?"

"You don't remember."

"Of course I don't or I wouldn't be asking."

"And you did me something of a favour, too."

"Oh good. Do go on."

"Do you remember being on the Via Veneto last night?"

"The Via Veneto? I never go to the Via Veneto. It's all the flash harries and their molls."

"Precisely. See and be seen. Especially after eleven at night."

"How on earth did we get there?"

"We walked. Corso. Condotti. You made me go that way and gave me a lecture on Keats outside the Caffè Greco. In fact you wanted me to go on a tour with you. Casa Rossa, Piramide di Sestio. Borghese gardens."

"In that order?"

"Well I agreed to the gardens and got you as far as Largo del Tritone but you had to go to a bar for a caffè corretto."

"Corretto with what?"

"Oh grappa, I think."

"No. I loathe grappa. It makes me ill."

"More of that later. I didn't know what had happened to you. You were like a thing possessed. As if you were on Benzedrine. You were buzzing like a little scotch fly."

"I don't go out much. Must have been the excitement of seeing you. Did you really save me from a flying ashtray?"

"That was much earlier. At least three negroni earlier."

"But I never have more than one."

"You're getting rather set in your ways, aren't you?"

"Don't mock. I've been doing perfectly well up to now."

"And you told me about all your plans."

"Do I have any?"

"It appears you do. You want to write a book about Roman cooking. Cooking by ordinary Romans that is. And Lyle's going to help you out and put up the money to get it published."

"Really?"

"That's what you said."

"It isn't such a bad idea."

"You've always had a thing for food haven't you? The jiaozi feasts at school. And you were a wizz at remembering recipes for those camp journals. How to make beef olives and all that kind of stuff. Your imaginary feasts kept us going, little Perce. *The Stanley Cookery Chronicles*. And now *The Roman Cookery Chronicles*. No gravy or custard I imagine."

"Lyle thinks I should give cookery lessons to rich Americans."

"There are plenty of them about."

"She thinks I need to do a book."

"She'll know some publishers."

"Apparently she does."

"Now on the subject of rich Americans. We've dawdled long enough over two or three caffè corretti in the Tritone Bar. We have to head up to the Via Veneto."

"Do we really?"

"We do. This is a story that I think even you would be pushed to make up, little Perce."

"Does it account for why I feel so ill?"

"That's for you to decide. Shall I begin?"

Percy was silent.

"First we went to Rosato's. Then the Café de Paris."

"Oh no. I don't go to places like that. I can't afford them for a start. And I'm on my own. No one goes to places like that on their own."

"Truman Capote did."

"Who?"

"*The Roman Spring of Mrs Stone.*"

"Oh yes the church domes looking like the tits of recumbent goddesses or something. Lyle thinks he's wonderful."

"She's probably met him."

"She knows all those expat American writers looking for some Italian inspiration."

"By which she means sex."

"Yes. She said sex."

"So that was you being coy."

"Tennessee Williams. And someone called Gore Vidal. Gore Vidal."

"Guess which of those sex-seeking Americans we met last night."

"No. No, I wouldn't."

"In that case I'll spare you. Let's just say that there is out there a young American playwright toying with the idea of recreating the myth of Oedipus on the Mississippi. One day. Partly thanks to you and your lecture on Greek Tragedy over a grappa at Doney's."

"Oh no. Was I going on and on?"

"Yes, but in the most wildly wonderful way. Eyes aflame and that kind of thing."

"Oh dear."

"Well he stayed to listen for an hour at least so he must have been interested. So was the man at the table behind him."

"Please; no."

"Yes. Orson Welles. And he didn't seem at all put out when you started chuffing on about how Rome was being colonised by American so-called actors and their twice-named actress chums."

"Gosh how rude."

"No, I think they liked it"

"They?"

"Actually I think Joan Fontaine might have been slightly out of earshot."

"I feel cold."

"And luckily there were no close friends of Tyrone Power or Lynda Christian in that evening or they might have taken issue with your feelings on the wedding of the year."

"Some relief."

"But you must remember your success fou of the evening?"

"You may not believe me but I actually remember nothing of this. Whatsoever."

"That's a pity. And an even greater pity there was no one there to film it."

"Deal the blow."

"Hedda Hopper."

"Who?"

"The American journalist. I think you may have signed her up to one of your cookery classes."

"Thank goodness Lyle wasn't there."

"You know at one stage I was ready to put in a call to the Pelicano at Porto Ercole and get her down to see the real Percy. You're pure TNT under the skin you know."

"Then you finally did the decent thing, stopped enjoying the spectacle at my expense and got me home. No. To yours."

"Well you know I was just about to but..."

"I sense worse coming."

"When who should turn up but Federico Fellini himself and it was the God-given opportunity for me to finally collar him. He had someone with him who spoke English, thank goodness. What a turn-up for the books. I've got a meeting with him next week and it was you who put the clincher on it."

"Did I put a loaded gun to his head and force him to agree?"

"No but you did the next best thing."

"I can't..."

"You announced you were going to be sick, stood up, walked backwards over one of those hedges in pots, fell over, dragged a couple of photographers with you and were violently sick over both of them. Much shouting. Much disgust. Molto schifo. They had to get onto their motos and go home to get changed. Peace reigned. No cameras flashed. I got you up again and dragged you away while the applause was still ringing in your ears. Not just the guests. The maître d' and all the staff came out to cheer. You have a note promising you free dry-cleaning at a place a brother owns and a free grappa at Doney's every evening for the rest of the year. Even Fellini cracked a smile at one stage. Well done, Perce."

"Well at least I understand why I feel so awfully ill."

"Lunch?"

"You're a bastard, David Sopley. An out and out..." David had rolled over and pushing Percy to the ground lay on top of him. "That hurts. I'll be sick again." The brims of their hats met.

"I don't think I'm going to French kiss you just at this moment. You need some water. Or a drink. Here," said David, rolling over to lie next to Percy," "have a nice Frascati."

So they lay next to each other, close, touching, for what might have been an hour or even two. With their hats shading their faces they slept, these two lovers in Rome. Shoulder touched shoulder, hip hip and hand hand. At one stage David began to snore. Several times a hand twitched and came out to swat away a fly or a mosquito. All the time they seemed insensible. Butterflies flew down to inspect them. Birds chirruped in the stone pines and from all around the ruins of Imperial Ostia. A light breeze blew, and some pinecones fell onto the carpet of needles under the trees with barely a sound. Marram grasses and the brown, dead flower heads of Roman herbs swayed gently. Across the field of maize the road to the sea had gone silent during the siesta hour.

Percy woke up and said, "'Over the tender, bowed heads of the corn.'"

"I don't think it was Indian corn he was talking about," said David.

"'Pray but one prayer for me 'twixt thy closed lips.'"

"That you may live long and be happy."

"'Speak but one word to me over the corn.'"

"Lunch," said David.

The damp cloth wrapped around the bread had long dried out and the wax paper surrounding the sliced salami and the etto of prosciutto crudo was greasy with fat. But the chubby tomatoes had loved the warmth and they and the figs had plumped and sweetened. From the basket David pulled a bottle of Rosso Lazio and groped around behind a wall-stump from where, in a shaded clump of grasses, he dragged a bottle of Fiuggi still relatively cool. They poured out whatever remained of the Frascati and refilled with the red.

They sat with their backs to a low wall looking around the ruins.

"Got the place to ourselves," said Percy.

They ate, drank more wine then lay down to doze.

"Were you going out with him? Or both of them?"

Percy was more than half asleep. "Mmmm?" he said.

"The tall Spanish-looking one and the mad little Illyrian."

"Croatian."

"Same difference."

Percy sat up. "How the bloody hell did you know he was Croatian?"

"I asked a chum from the old days to do a little checking up on you. This is after you'd gone to France of course. They asked some questions at the Sherborne and everything rather fell into place. He's in prison now you know."

"Smetka?"

"Yes. He'd been robbing the old lady blind since he'd been the manager. You know, fiddled receipts, double books all that kind of thing. It's a wonder no one had cottoned on before."

"It all came out in the papers?"

"Most of it."

"Most?"

"He was a commie agent. But you must never tell anyone. Ever."

"That accounts for the hotel school in Switzerland."

"Except it was Moscow."

"Good lord. And the stuff about him in the war? The rumours."

"All true."

"You mean he was a guard at those camps?"

"Worse. He was a commandant."

Percy shivered. "And we all worked with him. Sat next to him. With all that blood dripping from his hands. How did we not notice?"

"You don't. Believe me."

"All the same, In hindsight..."

"And the Spanish cook?"

"Chef."

"As you wish. Were you lovers?"

"David, no!"

"But not from want of trying on his part I imagine. And I think you would have been if the mad Illyrian hadn't turned up and spoiled everything. I'm sorry about that."

"Lopez is. Was. Is a kind, friendly man."

"Is."

"Oh good."

"At the Dorchester in fact."

"Good for him. He deserves it."

"Living with the same chum I asked to check up on him. Strange world. Cigarette?"

"Yes, why not? Thank you."

They smoked companionably. A lizard ran across to within six inches of Percy then turned and ran away sliding smoothly into an almost invisible crevice.

"Thank you for all that."

"All what?"

"Getting Laetitia away from the house. Disappearing off to France. It can't have been easy for you."

"That sounds such a cant phrase. In fact it was easy. Easy and timely and necessary. I'd hated London You know we should have declared an independent Hong Kong after the war and to hell with the Empire."

"You heard Grimson's farewell address?"

"No but I heard about it. People were calling him a bloody radical and a Chink-lover. Charming stuff like that."

"But you'll have agreed with him."

"Yes I did."

"So all that time you were a closet Red."

"You mean I supported Hilda?"

"Did you meet her?"

"Yes as a matter of fact yes. In Stanley before she and Selwyn-Clarke were sent to Mai Ta Wai. And she came to the hotel in oh, must have been '39 or '40. Wanted to see how we were treating the Chinese staff."

"Red Hilda the Roedean Radical."

"It doesn't become you to mock. She was a brave woman. And she came from a perfectly ordinary background. You know she went off to Canton to avoid being forcibly evacuated."

"Well we're not sure it was Canton or indeed where she went."

"Nevertheless she had the whole British Empire against her."

"And Madame Kai Shek on her side. If she'd managed to undermine Gimson the Chinese would have been in like a shot."

"I suppose so. But going back to London. London was just so. Just so..."

"British."

"Yes, that's it. We British have a terrific talent for denial. We went round the world like snails with our houses on our backs."

"Half-timbered."

"Preferably."

"Do you think we did? You and I?"

"I think we had it rather differently. I think we got closer to the other side than many or most."

"Because we were there as children?"

"Yes."

David paused and poured for them both. "And look at you. You absorbed Shanghai, Hong Kong. Then London, the wilds of France and now you're going native in Rome. You'll have to tell me more about this cooking thing."

"And you? Isn't there something you really want to do?"

"You know, Perce, if I could I'd like to go to University and study Chinese. Don't laugh. Really study it. Someone once gave me a book of Arthur Waley translations. And I bought that Helen Waddell that came out a couple of years ago. You know Percy the great torrent of passion under some simple-sounding lines about a placid pond and a drop of rainwater. The Huns on the horizon a metaphor for life. The whole of China, the same. And death. Li Po. Tu Fu. Rivers of ice. Dragons across the mountains. Always on the frontier. Life as a frontier. The soul like a flag in the wind. I'd like to read them in the original. All of those T'ang poets. They say classical Chinese is all about interpretation. It's a sort of game with pieces that can mean this or mean that and it's all to do with where you put them down as to what sense you make of them."

"Something like that came out last year. I read a review in someone's copy of *The Times*. It's called *Magister Ludi* by a German with a name I can't remember. Anyway, it's about a game with glass beads that can go on for ever and ever with no winners. I know it's not very like what you're saying but..."

"Yes, and to read books too. To go back to books. You know what, Perce? All those poems of Morris and Rossetti and Tennyson we used to love I'd like to stand at street corners and recite them to whoever goes by."

"You'd get arrested."

"Or put in an asylum. But they need to be spoken out loud."

"We do it a bit."

"Yes, it's our game and I enjoy it. But it's like taking one page out of a diary and missing a whole life."

"You could join a long and honourable tradition of English aristocrats going mad. They'd take you away very gently I imagine."

"Perhaps it's why I love films and filming so much. They were all very visual the poems we read. They were scenes. Brightly lit scenes. Little episodes. But completely lived. A good film is like that. A story made up of bright scenes and episodes."

"So you're going to make films in Rome and not go to University to read Chinese."

"Films first, Chinese later. I'm still only forty-something like you."

"Where did you learn to make films?"

"Before I got packed off to spy on the Chinese you mean? Let me tell you a secret. I didn't have a bloody clue about films. I learnt it all after the war. Back then I was entirely dependent on the crew. I was just there to speak Chinese and spin some yarns while the boys got the battalions or the ships or the guns or whatever into shot."

"What happened to them?"

"Got them all out on one of the very last boats."

"But you stayed. Why?"

"BAAG."

"But you were a civilian. Did you volunteer to stay?"

"Yes. At the beginning it looked as though we could get people out. But it was only a handful. So I ended up in Stanley all eyes and ears."

"You passed on information?"

"And got information via some of our Chinese. It was all tricky. And I'm not sure that I was much use until the end when I could tell the powers how many we were, what condition people were in and all that. So not much really."

"Is that why you kept your distance? I couldn't work it out."

"I couldn't risk bringing you down with me if the Japs cottoned on to us. They'd have beaten the hell out of you and then cut your head off. I thought if we were friendly we'd become too friendly and be a talking point, too. Not to mention me being Government House and you a hotel receptionist. You remember the gossip?"

"It was what kept us going wasn't it?"

"Now out of all that muddle here we are the filmmaker and the cook. Who'd have thought it? Drink?"

"I'd rather kiss you."

"You know we can't keep going like this?"

"Why not? Why couldn't we just live together?"

"A chorus of disapproval. Ostracism."

"You mean not being invited to British matrons' drinks parties and Embassy bashes? Is that what's most important to you?"

"Yes, Perce. I'm deeply shallow. I need all that and I want it. And anyway, what would I do living with you? The washing-up?"

Percy was silent and stared fixedly at the ruined walls in front of him. He got up. "I'm going for a walk," he said.

He walked out of sight of David Sopley and lay down on his side on the ground in some ruined room. My eyes wide open, he said to himself, have the run of some ten weeds to fix upon. The feeling of cold had come back. He shivered in the August sunshine. I am not happy. It is noon. The sun falls on my head. It is not an hour in which we think upon the dead. Should have brought my hat. I feel dead. Have we come all the way for this? To part at last without a kiss. Oh god I feel awful. Lucky I'm not a Via Veneto person because I'll never be able to show my face there again. But David would be there every night. Drinking and chatting up American film stars. Flirting with the women. Touching the men under the table. What if he gets a job at Cinecittà? I'm sure he will. Working all hours. The parties. Fellini. People say his film's no good. He's going to go bust. There are others. De Sica. Not to mention the Americans. Hollywood on the Tiber. It's him. It's what he does best. Being a part of things. Fast living my mother would have said. They say she's fast. I know he's fast. And me? God but I'm slow. Slow to catch on, slow to catch up, slow to change. The tortoise and the hare. Living together? Put myself in a suit and go along with him to the receptions? Lady Maldon? That's what they'd call me. O here comes Lady Maldon with her recipe for carcioffi a la Giuda. Sweet but quaint. Can't think what David sees in him when he could have had his pick. He's picked at me. And me. And me. And him. You can't imagine him being home for dinner at eight every evening. He doesn't touch his food. He just drinks and smokes. But he's eaten me and enjoyed it. And me. And me. And him. He'll eat anyone.

Oh Lord. If only Lyle were here. Send me Lyle. She'll know what I should do. Start the cookery school. How to trim an artichoke. Have a basin of acidulated water ready. That's water and lemons. Like the old woman by the fountain with the great heap of artichokes. Out comes the knife and all those spiky leaves and that hairy choke away they go. Just one or two cuts and plop into the water goes the heart. Here's the knife. Show me how you can do it. That's it. One cut and off with all the foliage. Two cuts and out comes the hairy choke. Don't choke. That's my heart you have in your hand. Plop. In it goes to the water. Raw. Onto the next one. Heart after heart after heart bobbing about together. Are you jealous? Do you want to be the beau of the ball? Yes? Everyone will love you. It's easy. See take this knife, cut your heart out and pop it into that basin of water with the lemons in it. That's all. Adoration guaranteed. There's only one catch. What's that? It's simple, silly. Without your heart you won't be able to love anyone else. Ever. Not even yourself. But you'll be in all the magazines. Life. Oggi. Paris Match even. There you are with Orson Welles. Ty Power. Rita Hayworth. Who's that dumpy little chap in the background? How did he get in? Is he a friend of yours? No, I didn't think so. Who's he with? Gate crasher. I'll get him chucked out. Silvio!

Lyle!

A wave of nausea flooded through Percy and he rolled onto his back to try and keep it down. He must have drunk at least as much as me. Why isn't he sick as a dog too? It just shows. I can't keep up. Run the straight race through God's good grace. I'm just not fast enough. Not fast enough.

Gold wings across the sea. I pray thee kiss my lips. Percy opened his eyes. Something was there between him and the sun glowing and golden. It moved. It was David with the light shining through his yellow hair. Bonny Bobby Shafto.

"You feeling all right, old man? Come on. Best stand up. Here. Take my hand. That's it. You need to move. Come on. Let's walk this off. Off we go."

Percy took the hand that was offered and let himself be hauled to his feet. "I hope I'm not going to be sick."

"Don't you need an audience for that? Come on. I'm only joking. What do you know about Ostia? Tell me." Tell, tell, tell, tell. Told, told, told, told. Telling and being told. For whom does the tell told? Should not have had that wine. Should have kept out of the sun. I told you!

"This way," said Percy. "I think that may have been the main street over there."

As the noise of crickets rose from one crescendo to another and the sweet, piney breeze blew through the trees the world gradually ceased to whirl and the ground stopped its lurching. As the scenery steadied - Everett Causey would be having a word with the stagehands later – he began to get his bearings. Street. Decumanus? Cardo? It was broad, anyway. Poor old Ostia. Silted up and eclipsed by the Port of Rome. A literal backwater by the second century. Was that what had saved it? Where was the Port of Rome? What could you see of that? Nothing. But here was good old Ostia showing its bone structure to tourists, anno domini 1951. The street soon disappeared into thickets of tall grasses, rushes and scrubby bushes; tamarisk and what looked like goat willow. Behind him was the paved area with the shops and godowns. Percy pressed on South and Westward. Sand sifted softly across the dark stones of the excavated roadway re-staking its claim upon them. Beyond some pines and to their right emerged the distinctive shape of a theatre or what was left of one. They walked toward it across the low dunes and thorny scrub. David cursed as a low bush scratched his bare ankle. Of the tiers of seating almost nothing remained. Only a few arches still stood marking the entrances to the steep, curving walks that took the crowds upward to the terraces and the vomitoriae.

David shuffled through sand and out onto the orchestra.

"'Friends, Romans, countrymen!'" he declaimed predictably, one hand raised to the audience the other holding on to his toga clasp in the approved Ciceronic style. "'Quo usque tandem,'" he went on "'abutere patientia nostra O Catalinam?!'"

"I think that show would have been given in the Senate House in the Forum," said Percy.

"It was such a hit it could have gone on tour in the provinces," said David. "Starting here with a trial run before heading off to the Massilia Palais."

Percy got up walked over and stood next to him.

"Look at us," said David. "Laurel and Hardy."

Percy put his left foot forward, leant back slightly on his right leg, grasped the imaginary toga clasp, raised a hand and began; "To nouns that cannot be declined."

"Oh I love this one," said David, "May I join in?" He joined in. "The neuter gender is assigned."

Percy: "Examples fas and nefas give,"

David: "And the verb-noun infinitive."

Percy: "Est summum nefas fallere."

Raising their voices they finished together; "Deceit is gross impiety!" Percy laughed. David coughed.

"Go and lie down over there," he said, "on the posh seats. Go on, sprawl."

"Who am I?" said Percy.

"Wait and see."

David wandered up and down the stage once or twice miming

grief and despair raising his hands high to the heavens, clasping them together, dropping them down to hit himself in the chest on an imaginary breastplate at which point he bowed his head low. Raising it he turned toward Percy and fell heavily onto his knees in the sand. He stretched his hands out once again this time to Percy.

Percy said, "If you're about to say what I think, shouldn't you be reclining somewhere on a dais?"

"Spoilsport. And there isn't a dais. You'll just have to balance the lack of props with the electrifying majesty of my performance. Just think of the Stanley Players. Are you ready?"

"I'm Dido, aren't I?"

"You are. Now recline with rapt attention and hearken to my tale of woe. I shall begin." And here he stood up and began to walk around his sandy stage pointing at absent figures one by one while looking intently at Percy:

"Conticuere omnes, intentique ora tenabat,"

Standing quite still he pointed at an invisible figure a yard or two in front of the posh seats where reclined Dido.

"'Inde toro pater Aeneas sic orsus ab alto..'"

Then he walked forward smartly to where that figure might have been and, pulling himself up to his full height and puffing out his chest continued:

"'Infandum, regina, iubes renovare dolorem…'"

He dropped his head down to his chest in a gesture of grief.

"'Quis talia fando…'"

"'Myrmidonum Dolopumve aut durentes Ulixi temperet a lacrimis?'"

He wiped the back of his hand across his eyes.

"'Etiam…'"

He looked upward:

"'… nox umida caelo preacipitat, Sudenteque cadentia sidera somnos…'"

Barked, "Sed!", then gruffly, "si tantus amor casus cognoscere nostros…"

Finally he took a deep breath, held it and breathed out slowly,
"'Incipiam.'"

Percy sat up and applauded. "Good lord," he said, "that was a feat. I feel more like Augustus than Dido. Was that of all your Latin?"

"We started at book two. We were all threatened with a beating if we didn't learn the first verse and so I did, walking round and round the school for hours until I had it by heart. I think I must have been ten or eleven."

David came over to sit next to Percy.

Percy said, "You know you've always been a bit of a performer."

"Says the second Wolfitt."

"Why didn't you join us in the Players?"

"I'd have been a bit too close to you Percy. If people had seen we were chums. You know."

"The gossip mill."

"Exactly. Kiss me."

Percy brought his mouth toward David's. Their hats fell backward onto the crowns of their heads. David cupped his hands around Percy's face and pulled it gently closer and closer. A minute went by. David dropped his hands and sat back upright. "Come on Cicerone," he said. "On with the tour." They stood up.

"I've no idea where we're going," said Percy.

"Nor me," said David. "Imagine we're a couple of knights of old out questing."

"For what?"

"What?"

"You have to quest for something. A quest has to have an object."

"The holy grail, then."

"This thing about love, Perce... Are you sure it isn't just a schoolboy crush that's gone on a bit too long?"

"I suppose it could be." Percy turned to face David. "The thing is I don't want it to end. Ever. If a crush goes on a lifetime couldn't one do the decent thing and call it love? Perhaps that's what love between men is. A crush that lasts."

"Can crushes last? Don't they come to an end about eighteen?"

"Something we grow out of? Like spots."

"Probably."

"Not love then? What if the crush went on beyond the age of eighteen? What if it were returned? Would that be love? Or is it that male crushes are tolerated up to the age of eighteen, not beyond, only on the basis that they're not reciprocated. Also, once you're eighteen your love glands develop and you can only fall for the opposite sex?"

"You want me to say the word, don't you? You're going to argue it out of me in your best scholastic style."

"It's not that."

"What is it then?"

"I want to know if you're capable."

"Not me. I'm a monster. The Minotaur. The Tin Man. Help me find my heart, Dorothy dear."

"You don't understand. I want to know if you believe that grown men can love each other. Do you believe in love between men?"

"Why is that so ruddy important?"

"Because no one wants to admit it's real. All anyone talks about is the mechanics. The sex. You know yourself, don't you? When people talk about men and men it's always about who does what to whom. People are so prurient if they're not downright jealous. You never hear about love. It's all about the acts. They're criminal because it simply cannot be accepted that they come from love. It's alright for men to philander and be adulterers with women and it's accepted that women can so-called whore themselves because it's all the other side of a coin that bears the stamp of love on its face. But for men and men or women and women the face on the other side is the devil called lust."

David took the hat off his head, straightened the brim and put it back on again. He reknotted the tie around his waist. He looked up at the sky and down at the sand which he pushed about a bit with the toe of his shoe.

"I like the sex."

"You like it like a woman."

"And you with your vast experience."

"I'm not judging. I was surprised, that's all. Then I remembered what was said about Julius Caesar."

"That he was a man to all women and a woman to all men."

"I won't think about who's the man and who's the woman. Who's the bull and who's the cow. We should be able to leave that behind. Leave it all behind and let our inner natures free."

"But if you fuck me doesn't that make you the man?"

"No I don't think so. It just makes me the one who's, as you say, fucking you. If you want me to and I want to then... then we need to get the words out of our heads and just get on with it."

"Coming from the wordsmith."

"Words are labels. I'm talking about the point where the labels don't matter anymore. Worse than that. Where labels actually do damage."

"Damage?"

"Well, if people say this is what men do, this is what women do, this is the only way it can be and yet there are many, many more ways of being then just talking about roles, taking on roles, then applying labels is false. Worse, it's destructive."

"You really are something of a radical."

"I just don't like false truths. It's not true that a man has to insert a penis into a woman any more than a woman has to be penissed by a man to have an act of sex. Proper love has to be mutual, doesn't it? Then shouldn't sex be the same?"

"Proper love. Eros fucks Agape."

"Or the other way round. Or better still Eros and Agape both have a climax from doing the things or being done the things that please them best."

"Being done."

"You see there isn't a tense for it let alone the persons. You have to choose between passive and active. There's no collective. It's where language falls down. It's something language won't let us describe."

"It's taboo."

"It's outside our vocabulary. Even Lawrence couldn't say it, describe it, though he bloody well tried. Some people think he's little better than a pornographer, but I think he was trying to understand sex from both a man's point of view and a woman's. Simultaneously. When they find those two at the bottom of the lake after it's been drained they're entwined. They've become one person in death."

"Le petit mort and le grand mort together"

"Yes I think so. I think he was both Lady Chatterley and Mellors. I think he was jealous of a woman's climax and he wanted to climax as a man. But passively. Without shooting. He wanted something longer and deeper. You know he was always on about dark places and dark sensations."

"Can't say I do."

"It's all over his writing. I think he wanted to be stimulated in his arse. He wanted to have a cunt too. I think he thought that's where a man's true erogenous zone really is. There's a bit in one of his books about taking a long car ride over a desert road and how the bouncing up and down stimulates him inside. Though he doesn't put it quite like that. Coming and shooting are just too Darwinian. He wanted some kind of deeper pleasure."

"I know."

"You know?"

"Yes and I can show you. We could try it now."

"Here?"

"It's my best offer."

"We could be arrested. Beaten-up."

"We could say we were recreating an ancient rite."

"The house of Attis. I've just remembered. A house has been excavated and it had a statue or head of Attis. I think it may be over there. We should go and look."

"Shhh little Perce."

He put the forefinger of his right hand onto Percy's lips. "Look here. Love. Yes, all right. I love you. I love you beyond the fucking and the wanking and everything else. You're like a part of me but no, I don't think that love between men is the same as love between women and men. I think it's too full of dross to be pure. Or that there's simply not enough that's pure in it to make it reliable. I think it's about us chasing a different version of ourselves through man after man after man. It's wanking in front of a mirror. There can be love in there but it's ten percent love and ninety percent lust. That's what I think. With you and I it's different. Please god save me from sentimentality in what I'm about to say. Look Perce, I know your secret. You know mine. I know why you're such an entertainer when you want to be. Why you remember the words of songs and why you never let a conversation lapse into silence. Don't leave me. That's what you're saying, isn't it? Don't leave me all on my own. I'll carry on entertaining you so you won't want to leave. We're completely the same. Afraid of being abandoned like we were at Yantai. Or even earlier. So I do it with sex and you do it with words but we're both just trying to stop the inevitable. Change. Parting. Going, Leaving. What's that German song? We did it once on school presentation day. Everyone in the world must part. Muss scheiden. I can't remember and don't tell me if you know. I can hear it in my mind. But this is what I've learnt. Don't be afraid. There's nothing to fear. Nothing. We've survived this far, haven't we? We've been lucky. Others weren't. Entertain for fun. Don't fear happiness. Most of all, don't depend too much on anyone else. At least, not for love. Look into the mirror and look straight back at what you see. It isn't your enemy. It's not a succession of lovers. It's you."

"Are you going to stay?"

"Perce, really, what does it matter? I could be here for a week or a day or a decade. I don't know. I don't want to know. I refuse to know. So do what Lyle says. Do your cooking and your writing and do it bloody well. Stop stuffing your head with books. Don't just quote lines. Write them. Commit. I can't commit. You do it for me. If you want to be happy then match the love you want to the love you get. Do you see? Come on. Don't be sublunary. Look after yourself and you look after me too. Come on Perce, my talisman, my walking, talking Oxford Book of English Poetry. Tell me about Attis since we're clearly going there for cocktails."

Percy was quiet for a moment then said, "Over there," pointing to the perimeter of the excavations on the South side, up against the fence. He set off, David following. "Attis," he said, was..."

"Would you like to come and live with me?" said David.

Percy stopped dead. "I thought we weren't going to make any plans? I thought that was verboten."

"I didn't say that, did I? I said I didn't know how long I was going to be here in Rome but for as long as I am would you like to live with me?" There was a silence. "Cat got your tongue?"

"Do you really mean it?"

"Have I ever told you an untruth? I'll try not to be offended."

"I'm sorry."

"Don't be."

"What will people say?"

"They can say what they like. This isn't London. We'd be carrying on a grand tradition of English homos setting up in Europe. You haven't seen my apartment. It's huge. You could have your own wing of it for propriety's sake. In fact, it's like a stage set. You could do those cookery classes. And remember we have a guardian angel to look after us."

"Lyle."

"Yes, Lyle. No one argues with money. Or an English title come to that."

"On that subject, what about your home? What about that house and that estate?"

"I'll let it out. Or sell it. What's left of it. I don't want to be tied to some gloomy damp building in England. It isn't my home after all. I mean, is it?"

"But it's your inheritance."

"The Maldon dynasty ends here. Like it or lump it. I do like it. I can't bear the idea of aristocracy."

"Now who's the rebel?"

"It's over. All that. It was over before the War, but it wouldn't die. Had its tentacles into everything and they kept on twitching even after the brain was dead. There's been a change in English politics. It'll take another hundred years, but they'll get the old guard out eventually. And as for people like me; best we just shuffle off. Have you seen a television?"

They bumped into each other as Percy tried to steer them down a sand-covered road.

"No," said Percy. "Heard about it though."

"The age of listening is over. People are going to want to see things. In their own houses. Via a television. The bloody old BBC are going to try to turn it into a middle-class preserve to patronise the lower orders. But it's going to be the most democratic medium ever. It'll be bigger than film one day. You wait."

"So why didn't you stay in London and try to get into it?"

"All in good time little Perce. Remember I've lost my shirt and nearly lost my name, too. Television's run by older chaps. Even older than me. I think I can have five years of fun before heading back."

"Why Rome?"

"London was closed. Paris was deadly dull. I'm not flavour of the month in Hollywood and anyway, you've heard of the Hollywood Ten?"

"The so-called Communists?"

"Yes and it's about to get worse. There's just been another list published. More than a hundred this time. Even if I did get back in there I'd have to keep my gob tight shut."

"But still, why Rome?"

"Are you fishing?" Percy made a face of unconcern. "You are. You're a terrier for the truth, aren't you? All right, yes, Lyle did wire me to say she'd got you here out of harm's way. There. But it's also a wonderfully exciting place at the moment. For film."

"Hollywood on the Tiber?"

"I said that did I? Well yes, there is that. And I think it's only just begun. Italy's cheap, good technicians, sunshine. But for the Americans it's just another backdrop for romantic comedies. It's the Italian directors you should be looking out for. They're doing something really new. Telling real-life stories with actors and ordinary people. About ordinary lives. Out in the open. Everything open."

"Open city?"

"Yes, that was the beginning. Or the re-beginning after the war. You saw *Ossessione*? They say that started it and that was '42. You've heard of de Sica. Look out for De Santis, Lattuada. And Fellini, of course. Who you've met. And *Riso Amaro*. De Santis. Have you heard of that one?"

"Not only heard of it. Lyle took me to see it."

"What did you think?"

"Well Lyle thinks it's a work of genius."

"And you?"

"I thought it was a bit melodramatic."

"Films are melodramas. That's what people want. But the interesting thing here is that if you act out a turgid tale under the bright light of day, stripped bare of colour and Hollywood junk, with a mix of actors and locals you can see the universality in it."

"Like Ancient Greek drama."

"Well yes, very like Greek drama. Well said. And you know what? This style may not last long but you mark my words, give it another ten or fifteen years and it's going to pop up again. Where? On the bloody television!"

"I think we're here." Said Percy.

They stood under the hot sun, hats tipped backward, looking through a wire fence into what could have been taken for an abandoned cemetery. Sand blew and drifted up against stumps of grey wall. The papery remains of asphodels rotted down in corners with brown and wilted euphorbias. Marram grasses rustled, broom seed-heads popped and finches flew down to take the thistledown.

"Look at us," said David. "We're on the outside now."

They stood in silence, sweat running down their faces.

"And who was Attis?" said David.

"A beautiful man who castrated himself to please his mother."

"Who was this mother?"

"Cybele. She may have also been his wife."

"Murky. Cybele as in corn and harvests?"

"In some myths he's resurrected in Spring."

"Like a sort of male Persephone?"

"I suppose so. The cult had priests who castrated themselves."

"Castrating yourself to please your mother? Sounds like some men I know. Metaphorically speaking."

"Apparently before he was Hellenised the original Attis was hermaphrodite, but he cut off his balls..."

"To please his mother."

"In the original story it was to assuage the wrath of the gods. He was too beautiful."

"What was he doing in Ostia?"

"It's thought he got here by mistake. A whole load of statues were excavated around here. The Attis one right where we are now. That was nearly a hundred years ago. But it's thought the statues came from Rome and were just abandoned here. Or hidden."

"So he's a refugee?"

"Yes in a sense."

"What's he look like? Is he dishy?"

"You could say so. Quite a full face. A bit chubby even."

"Don't castrati put on weight? Like neutered tomcats? So there's no point wandering around these bits of ruins? If it wasn't his temple or monastery or anything."

"No. And I'd like to lie down again."

"Still feeling off-colour?"

"Yes."

"Can't have that. Let's get back to our vestibulum."

"Triclinum."

"You'll feel better there."

They walked slowly back to their picnic place, Percy visibly wilting. Every now and then they stopped under a pine tree for shade. Percy drank in the scent of the pines and felt it restored him. A little. David, who gallantly held on to Percy's elbow when they had to navigate the low dunes or patches of grass pitted with rabbit burrows, contented himself with looking around him much of the time. His eyes seem particularly drawn to the banks of rushes and tall bushes that lined the site.

Percy stopped again. "He wrote a poem you know. About Attis."

"Who did?"

"Catullus."

"You and your Catullus. 'Odi et amo. Quare id faciam fortasse requiris. Nescio quis, sed fieri sentio et excrucior.'"

"You put in an extra quis. It's just nescio."

"We didn't do the Attis poem did we?"

"Carmen 63. No. Not suitable for schoolboys. Far too. Far too... complicated."

"So he doesn't just chop his own balls off?"

"Yes, but it's much more than that. If I remember rightly."

"You remember everything."

"He castrates himself right at the beginning of the poem and after that it's more him thinking about what he's done to himself. Wondering who he is. He's not a man. Not in the usual sense. But is he a woman? It's tricky. He remembers being a popular lad at the gym and he says, it's difficult to translate, he says he could have done anything a man could have done or a woman could have done..."

"There's something to think about. I can see why we didn't find that one in the set texts. How does it all end?"

"He gets chased off into the mountains by his mother."

"That bitch again."

"It isn't expressly said so but it seems as though he was so beautiful that she was jealous. Didn't want him around."

"Whew. A field day for the psychologists. Look, here we are. Why don't you have a bit of a lie-down?"

"Are you going to come and lie down with me?"

"No Perce. You have a snooze. There's water left. I'll come back in a bit and wake you up."

"What are you going to do?"

"Just have a look around. See what we haven't seen."

"Will you know what you're looking at?"

"I think so."

Percy found the bottle of Fiuggi and drank deep. Putting it back in the shade he lay down on some rabbit-cropped grass as close-cut as an English lawn and put his hat over his eyes. Sleep didn't come. The sun burned its way through the fabric of his hat and poured white molten metal into his eyes. Closing his eyelids merely tempered the glow to red.

Suddenly he was aware of someone standing close by whether by sound or smell he didn't afterwards remember. Hell, he thought, this is where I get robbed and carved up. Where the bloody hell is David? Slowly, very slowly, he removed his hat from his face and, lifting it in front of him so that the brim screened his eyes he looked over to his right. There, planted on the turf were a pair of dirty plimsolls, the slip-on kind and out of them grew a set of bare ankles. A man's ankles. The ankles of his murderer. And should he survive, what would he say when asked to identify his attacker? He had slim, brown ankles, officer. Come on, he thought, you knew the Japs would come for you eventually. Sit up. Get up. Face him. Get it over with. He put out his elbow and started to lever himself up. The ankles disappeared under the hems of a pair of white or white-ish trousers. The legs were slim. Putting out a hand, palm down on the ground and into a yielding pile of rabbit-droppings he pushed himself up, awkwardly, to a sitting position. The man hadn't moved. The brim of Percy's hat only allowed him to look up as far as the crotch of the white trousers. They were bulging with a thick, hard erection barely contained within them. Percy reached up to his head, took off his hat and laid it on the grass beside him. He looked up further. The man was a youth, a youth wearing a red shirt unbuttoned to the navel showing a smooth, tan, youth's chest. He was slim. He didn't look like the sort of youth who would beat him up. He looked too delicate. A knife no doubt was about him somewhere. Percy risked looking at his face. With the Japanese guards that was something you never did. Ever. But some instinct pulled his eyes upward and he found himself looking at a beautiful young man with a face as classically perfect as the statue of a young charioteer he'd seen... where? So what next? The youth, some street-hardened criminal, would simply walk around behind him, grab his hair, jerk back his head and slit his throat. His oesophagus would fill with his blood and he'd drown in it if the shock didn't stop his heart first. He briefly imagined the youth wearing the

Phrygian cap of Attis and of Mithras, the slayer, the cutter of bulls' throats. The youth's hands went to the waistband of his trousers and Percy knew he was about to get out the knife. He even saw it, keen, slim-bladed, glinting in the sunlight. But no. Here was something strange. The youth smiled at him. Not a dangerous smile. Could he call it playful? Then he undid the top button of his trousers, then the next, then the next. He was wearing nothing underneath the trousers. No underpants. His cock sprang out of hiding, the foreskin well rolled back to reveal a very rosy, very perfect helmet that bounced up and down in front of Percy's eyes. At the opening of the urethra was a bead of clear liquid and at base of the shaft was a small clutch of bright, tawny bush.

The youth spoke. "Ho'n bel cazzo, no?"

Percy smelt the smell of cock, of young cock, sweet and stale at the same time from the sweet juice and the stale clothing and sweat. In any other circumstance he'd have simply taken it in to his mouth but here, here in some ruins on the edge of Rome with a complete stranger it seemed not attractive, not desirable, not mutual but merely pornographic. This might be the kind of thing that David dreamed of but not him. Not like this. Where was David? What would he think if he turned up now and found him like this? That he was willing, wanting? The youth's hand went around behind Percy's head and pulled it forward. "Fallo o ti taglio lo gola."

So this was it. Better than having his throat cut. Percy opened his mouth and felt the cock pushed into it right to the back of his throat so that he gagged. With all his strength he pulled his head back far enough so that he could breathe. And speak. "sto per vomitare," he said. The youth looked down at him. Now his beauty was cruel. He shrugged and pulled Percy's head back onto his cock and began to fuck his mouth.

"Succhiare," said the youth. Percy obeyed. Now the youth had both hands around behind Percy's head and was beginning to arch the small of his back. Just as Percy thought to himself "soon" the flood of semen began. And went on. And on. Percy had to drink in gulps as though he'd put his mouth to a tap of warm water. His stomach and oesophagus heaved. The youth held him in more tightly. "Uh," he said. "Uh." The pair remained there, still, frozen, for perhaps thirty seconds before the youth let Percy go, pulled out his penis and began to button it back, now wilting, into his trousers. He looked at Percy. "Sigaretta," he said. Percy groped about around his jacket looking for the packet. Please God, he thought, don't let David have taken it with him. He found it and proffered it to the youth. The youth took the whole packet. "Fiammiferi," he said.

"Non credo...." said Percy.

The youth's hand flashed out and hit the side of Percy's head with a smack. It hurt. It shoved his glasses to the other side of his face. This beautiful youth who looked so Italian must be Japanese. It was the only explanation. "Fiammiferi," it said. Percy, hands shaking, began to fumble through the pockets of his jacket. Please let there be. His fingers closed on a book of matches. Thank god. He took it out. Doney, it said on the cover. He handed it up to the youth.

"Doney, Allora, sei Americano?"

"Inglese," said Percy.

The youth looked at him with his beautiful smile, spat on the ground then slapped Percy on the other side of the head. His glasses fell off altogether. As he bent down instinctively to retrieve them the youth said, "Tuo amico."

"Si," said Percy.

"Si ti sbrighi puoi vederlo prenderlo su per il culo laggiiu tra i cespugli."

"Grazie," said Percy.

"Niente," said the youth.

Now, thought Percy, and braced himself for the downward chop of the sword. Please let it be sharp.

"Ciao," said the youth who turned and sauntered off toward the biglieterria stopping only to put a cigarette in his mouth, light it and take a draw before he began to diminish in Percy's sight his buttocks riding up and down, up and down within the cheap cotton trousers. Percy threw up again on the spot.

Still there was no sign of David. At least he didn't see that thought Percy, still trembling with shock and anger. Had there been a blinking neon sign on his head saying, "Rape Me?" Had the youth and even other youths been observing them, waiting for their moment? And why were they even here if it wasn't to rob tourists? The cold shock descended on him. They were here for sex. Sex with foreign men, rich foreign men in a world where rich meant American and English translated as poor. Both sides of his face smarted. He took off his glasses and looked at them. They were slightly askew. He'd have to take them to an optician. What was the Italian for optician? Ottico. That was it. Il Ottico. The act of searching out a word calmed him down. Still on his knees he began to look around for the bottle of mineral water and then stood up, carefully avoiding his latest pool of vomit. Wouldn't it be funny, a positive hoot, if this room were the vomitorium of the house for the voiding of swan, garum, dormouse in honey. His head swam and the back of his neck ached and he staggered slightly. There was the bottle behind that bit of wall. Everything was as it was before that nuclear bomb had been dropped. Funny how the scene all around him was the ghostly ruins of buildings, the mere imprints of their structures, but he was still standing, still alive. Sitting down on a stump of wall he found he was crying. Shock. That was all it was. Shock. Pull yourself together. But it seemed so unfair. He searched his memories of midnight sessions alone in bed with a head full of sexual fantasies to see if such a scene had ever been acted out. Ever been willed, ever desired. The act, yes, many many times. But the circumstance? The surprise, the force, the rape? Was that the right word for it? The back of his throat was sore and his cheeks ached. Had he been raped or merely been taken advantage of, his proclivities and secret desires, secret even from him having been so clearly on display? If he had been a normal man, a woman-loving man would the youth have still taken him in that way? Would he have fought off his aggressor with the full self-confidence of a heterosexual man? Or would his heterosexuality already have shone out like the beam of a lighthouse warning the youth to stay away? Had he invited it? Worse; had he deserved it? He swilled what was left of the water around his mouth to wash away any remaining trace of semen and spat the lot onto the ground. He passed the back of his hand over his mouth and then belched loudly as the semen started to be digested. It could have been worse. He was sure the young man would have had a knife. Positive. All these street ragazzi had knives. If he'd struggled he'd have been cut or worse, raped.

He bent down to pick up his hat and jammed it on his head. Not for ever by still waters. Where was David? What if the knives had come out for him? The thought of David lying bleeding to death among the undergrowth invaded his imagination with a rush of realism. This was one of those brightly lit scenes that David had been talking about. A scene to go into a film. A black and white film. A newly realistic film.The English Lord collapses to the ground. Cut to the blade of the knife. To the smile of the first youth. To the horror in the eyes of his accomplice. Pan out to see the knife's trajectory into the bulrushes. See how it catches the light like Excalibur returning to the lake. The two youths look at each other. "L'hai ucciso, Salvo," says the accomplice. The smile on the face of the other broadens. "Lo ha chiesto," he says. "schifoso frocio."

Ten miles away in the kitchen of a Roman tenement building a Roman mother is rolling saltimbocce. She is placing a leaf of sage onto each very thin piece of veal. As she rolls up the parcel to tie it with kitchen string she smiles to herself. This is a meal they really cannot afford but today is the name-day of her Salvatore. Her beloved son, man of the house now that Gino is dead. There is nothing she will not do for him. She adores him even more than his many girlfriends and the boys who always seem to be drawn to him like moths to a flame. He is so graceful, so beautiful. And he has a good job at the macelleria from whence came the veal. He is so good with his hands. From outside the window comes a sudden flash of light, a reflection from a window opposite being closed perhaps, or a mirror being moved. A very bright flash. It catches the silver metal crucifix hanging on the wall in the kitchen. She looks up and sees the face of Christ contorted with grief as though the effort of sparing a sinner is almost too great for him. Her hands leave the chopping board and the saltimbocca and spring to her face. "Aieeeee!" she cries at the very moment that the tip of Salvatore's blade sinks into the Englishman's throat and is drawn swiftly from one side to the other. From the abattoir nearby beside Monte Testaccio comes a bellow from an animal meeting its end. Mother falls to her knees on the kitchen floor. "Lui è perso," she says as she crosses herself. The crucifix appears to speak. "Sono il bon macellaio," it says. Mother falls down in a dead faint as the music crescendoes. Fin.

Where the bloody hell was David. He remembers what the youth had said. So he, Percy, had been right. There were others; a gang of them perhaps. Heaven knows what had been going on. He turned and looked into the middle distance at the wall of rushes like a line of hoplites carrying their pointed spears erect. David must be in there. Wasn't that what the youth had been saying? He started to walk toward the green, gently swaying barricade On he went over and around walls, impluviae, bases of fountains, triclinae, atriae. Along alleyways, through doorways, into wine shops, brothels, family homes, butchers, bakers and across domestic shrines. Lares and Penates, he thought, forgive me. As he got closer to the tall rushes he thought he heard a laugh. Ridete, it came to him, ridete quidquid est in domus cacchinorum. Was that David's laugh? Please yes let it be. The sun was bright above him. Please don't let him have been murdered. This is Jehane by her face. You see a slain man's rotting feet. No. Not death. Not here. Hadn't they cheated it by surviving all those things and all those years? To die here? No. It was absurd. He would find David and restore him. Raise him up. But what had David said? What was it? "Don't follow me." That was it. "Don't follow me." Like a reverse apostolic command. And yet Percy can't stop himself. The dark tower is around here somewhere and yes I must see it. The dark tower or the door to the underworld. He is following. I am following. He will bring David back. I will bring David back. He's breathless and fighting back waves of nausea but he's still staggering along as fast as he can through the ruins, the sand and the scrubby weeds. He kicks up plumes of sand as he walks, plumes that rise up above his heels like the wings on Mercury's sandals. The sun is practically blinding him. His glasses are askew on his face and smeared with oil from his fingers to which sticks the sand. He looks half-comical, like Badger rushing into battle with the Weasels. The Weasels are tall and willowy and malevolent, but he rushes at them and they are metamorphosed into bulrushes condemned to snidely whisper and lithely sway into eternity. He holds his shield-arm up to his face to protect himself as he crashes into the enemy phalanx. Blades swish and quiver around him and their sharp edges cut his forehead, his forearm. He careers on now like a boar rushing at the spearmen. Where is the one who will bring him down? He stands in rage, imagining men. His blood fizzes and sings of the beast that gives the fatal wound. Where is he? I will stare upon his blood-bedrabbled breast and sing my malediction with the rest.

Percy blunders and crashes into a clearing among the reeds, all taller than a man. It is out of the wind here, sheltered and very warm. There are three men here. All naked. What is this? A Calvary? The flaying of Marsyas? He stops at a half-crouch, panting heavily. One of the men is bending down, the muscles of his skinny shanks and long, Joshua Reynolds calves all tense beneath the white skin. He has long, elegant feet the toes of which are curling, gripping at the sand. He is in profile to Percy. Percy sees his cock, substantial but flaccid and a heavy ballbag dangling underneath his bent belly like udders. Behind him, on tiptoe, a young, tanned man is thrusting his penis into the cleft of the bent man's arse. He looks at Percy and stops, penis full into its sheath. He is dark-haired and very, very beautiful. The other man is taller and lean like the rushes or an Athenian soldier. He is naked, too. He has dark hair on his head, a dark bush and a trail of dark hair ascending from the bush to his navel. His penis is inside the mouth of the bending down man. He turns and looks at Percy and says, "Sei troppo in ritardo" and gives a great thrust into the man's mouth. His legs and buttocks begin to shake, The other young, brown man throws his head back and makes a guttural noise. His heels are off the ground and he looks as though he's dancing a gallows jig, a Matilda waltz. His body arches against the bent man like an English bow. He thrusts and quivers and then leans forward onto the bent man, hands either side of the man's waist. "Fottimi," he says. "Amo le domeniche." The figures pull away from each other. The penis of the man who was in the mouth is still stiff. "Bravo ragazzo," says the other whose penis is quickly turning flaccid. The two tanned men look at each other over the body of the still-bent man. "Grazie signore," says one of them. "Mi piace il culo Inglese." They laugh. "Ti piace lo cazzo Italiano? E il migliore al mondo, no?" They laugh again, tall, bronzed, perfectly proportioned. The man between them is still bent over and they look like two ancient Greek lads either side of a marble altar. Then the man turns his head and looks over toward Percy. No, thinks Percy, this is no fabulous symbol here. It is my heart's object and its torturer.

It is David.

David speaks. "Grazie ragazzi," he says and stands up.

One of the lads goes off to a pile of clothes and pulls out a pack of Nazionale. He proffers the packet to David and to his friend, both of whom take one, before he picks one out of the pack with his teeth. Stooping down again for matches he stands or springs up and lights the two other men before lighting his own. The god-pleasing smoke ascends to the heavens. David is looking at Percy.

"Ma dove Salvatore?" says one of the youths. "Ha perso un buona sessione."

"Gli piace cacciare da solo."

"Pensi che abbia preso questo?" says the youth waving his cigarette in Percy's direction. "Fottera qualunque cosa."

And they both laugh.

"Qesto e tuo zio?" says one to David.

David ignores them. They look at each other and shrug. David and Percy stay silent and still. The two young men start to put on their clothes. All they have is shirt, trousers and shoes. They tuck their shirts into their trousers, cigarettes dangling from their lips. They start to leave the clearing, arms around each other's shoulders. They look at David.

"Ciao," says one.

"Zenk you," says the other.

"Fuck you," says the first one. They look at each other and laugh before disappearing through the curtain of rushes, hands now at each other's waist. They don't look back but their passage is marked by the points of the rushes waving and trembling and sighing, gently.

"Don't you think you should get dressed?" says Percy.

David looks at him. His smile is there but secret, shifty, guilty. A few seconds pass. David, thin, white, naked, one hand on hip the other holding a cigarette stands like a statue. He finishes the cigarette and throws the butt down onto the sand where it lies emitting a thin, perfectly vertical little trail of blue smoke.

"Well," he looks at Percy, "what can ail thee knight...."

"Shut up," says Percy. "Shut up and get dressed. We're going home."

The carriage of the train is full of warm bodies, bonhomie and a torrent of conversation. So full is it that Percy and David haven't been able to find a place to stand together let alone sit. Percy has the empty rattan basket that had contained their picnic. He does not look at David. David looks only at him. A man in a stained shirt with braces holding up baggy trousers grasps him by the buttock and squeezes. No one can see in the melée. The man is very close and is breathing wine and garlic into Percy's ear.

"Buon Ferragosto," he says.

Percy leans very close and whispers into his ear "Va fa'n culo."

The man releases his hold and makes the sign to ward off the evil eye. Percy looks round.

David is smiling at him still. "Bright star," he says.

Antico Caffè Greco, Via Condotti, September 1953.

Crostata dell'albiccoche.

It is 11 a.m. Two women are sitting at one of the tables toward the back of the cafe. Here brass sconces contain clear candle-shaped light bulbs that emit a feeble, flickering brightness perfectly suited to the lugubrious feel of the space with its small, marble-topped tables, dark bentwood chairs, dark floor, heavy damask wall-covering and large, gilt-framed, highly foxed mirrors. It's late Eighteenth Century with a little electricity. Outside, beyond the front room the sunlight coming through the windows looks as blue as a sapphire by comparison. Here though, within, centuries of serving coffee and tramezzini to the fashionable has created the perfect atmosphere for refined, knowing chatter. Today most of the clientele are tourists though of this most the most would rather die than describe themselves as such. They are visitors, short-term residents, they know Rome like the backs of their hands. Their Rome, of course, is not the Rome of the average Roman. They won't venture out beyond the perimeter of the old walls except by motor car on a trip to Nervi, Frascati, Tivoli. Theirs is not the Rome of Nuovo Realismo and Communism. It is the American Rome of *Thee Coins in a Fountain*. Its presiding image is not a she-wolf suckling twins. It is Audrey Hepburn on the back of a scooter having a Roman holiday.

At a table for two beneath one of the dimmest of the dim sconces sit two women. Americans. Let's say this from the start. There is nothing wrong with their being Americans. In fact if one were to be an American at any stage in the history of America then their being American women and wealthy in 1953 in Rome puts them at the finest flowering of American-ness on a par with the heiresses of Henry James. America exists to make money and its greatest cultural achievements exist in knowing how to spend that money well. These two women are perfect examplars of that culture. American has won the war and is winning the peace. It has routed the Communists here in Italy by the judicious spending of vast quantities of money and into this bucket drop many more millions of dollars from its filmmakers, its actors, from second and third generation refugees sending back their remittances and finally from the dowagers of the Roman social scene.

There they sit, smartly but soberly dressed. The light glances off the lacquer in their hair, hair that has been magnificently but soberly coiffured. Their hair is plain. Dyed perhaps but plain. How unlike the hair of Lollia Paulina covered with a net of jewels worth as much as the economy of an entire province of the Empire here in Rome, not far from here, two thousand years ago. Those brilliant jewels flashed out the end of a Republic and the beginning of an Empire. Here in the Caffè Greco it's left to hair lacquer to signal the world-dominance of a Republic that is managing to remain a republic while still accruing an Empire at the same time. Some lessons from history have clearly been learned.

One of the women takes out a powder compact and flipping it open examines the end of her nose.

"Am I boring you dear?" says the other woman.

"Why Esther no," says the woman who is not Esther. "I just wanted to check."

"Lissa, my dear, do you have an assignation? Am I here as your stooge?"

"Of course not," says Lissa.

"Your chaperone then?"

"Neither. Positively neither. I'm sorry. I wanted to check my make-up. I am putting my compact away now. There."

The compact closes with a click and Lissa return it to her bag.

"May we begin again?" says Esther.

"I'll drink to that," says Lissa. "Let's order."

"You're not really going to drink at this time of day?" says Esther.

Lissa shoots out her wrist and looks at the face of an elegant but not ostentatious watch. "It's one minute past eleven ay emm," she says. "Sergio told me that only tourists drink cappuccino after eleven so that's out. Do you know what they do in Venice?"

"Go about in gondolas don't they?"

Lissa wrinkles her nose. "They have a drink at eleven," she says.

"Ay emm." Esther raises her eyebrows. They are beautifully maintained. "You know they call it an ombra. It means shadow. It's a kind of pick-me-up. Chester and I were once in a coffee bar just off the Rialto. It was exactly this time of day. There was an old lady standing at the bar. You could stand or sit down but only tourists sit down. She ordered an ombra and a tramezzino. I heard her. The waiter pulled up a bottle from a kind of hole in the bar. I guess it went down into a refrigerator compartment. He poured a glass of what looked like Champagne but it's a kind of sparkling white wine they drink over there."

"Prosecco."

"Yes. And the sandwich. It was the tiniest sandwich I've ever seen. So white and cool looking. And the old lady ate it standing up and had her glass of wine too and it was still only eleven-fifteen."

"Do you propose drinking wine now?"

"No I don't think so. I'll have a soda. They'll have soda won't they?"

The waiter clad in black trousers and a white cutaway jacket comes over. "Signore?" he says.

"Portami un caffè en un bicchiere d'acqua," says Esther in a grammatically correct but slightly drawly Italian that neglects to pronounce every consonant.

"Soda," says Lissa. The waiter smiles, bows and withdraws.

"That means you'll get Coca Cola," says Esther.

"It's so dim in here no one will see," says Lissa. "Besides, it's warm, don't you think?"

"And stuffy," says Esther.

"I almost had a glass of wine," said Lissa. "When we were at Porto Ercole the waiter was from Jesolo. That's over on the East Coast. He told me about the wine they make there. It's called Verdicchio and it comes in green flasks."

"Like Chianti."

"Thinner and without the straw. He told us that there's a saying that you can't drink a glass of Verdicchio without smiling. It's the happiest wine in Italy he says."

"My," says Esther.

The waiter returns holding a tray freighted with two glasses, a little cup of coffee and a bowl of sugar. Deftly moving aside a pair of elegant leather gloves he smoothly places cup and glass in front of Esther, glass in front of Lissa. "Grazie," he says and withdraws.

"Such perfect manners," says Esther.

"With them it's a profession to be a waiter. A good one. Once a waiter, you're a waiter all your life."

"Actually, I'm hungry," says Lissa.

"Didn't you have breakfast?" says Esther.

"No, I can't stand breakfast," says Lissa. She reaches into her bag and pulls out a pack of cigarettes. American cigarettes. She offers the pack to Esther who declines with a moue of disapproval.

"No thank you," she says. "I simply don't believe doctors telling you it's good for you."

Lissa places a cigarette in her mouth and within a second the waiter is there with a light for it. His hand is shaking slightly so she gently touches his wrist to steady it and brings her mouth close to his hand to catch the light. The flame bends toward the tip of her cigarette. She draws and leans pack puffing out a delicate cloud of smoke. "Grazie," she says. The waiter merely smiles and bows before disappearing once more.

"That was forward," says Esther.

"Don't worry dear," says Lissa. "He's one of those."

"How do you know?"

"You should see the way he looks at Chester. Like a dog wanting to be whipped."

Esther pulls a face at her friend's salacious remark, then smiles graciously to signal that she's let the incident pass by. She exhales smoke.

"On that subject. More or less," she says. "Are we going today?"

"Why not?" says Lissa.

"But you must have heard?" says Esther.

"Everyone's heard," says Lissa. "People can't stop talking about it. Even the maid this morning was full of it. Had we heard about the Milor Inglese. And anyway, Lyle phoned me just before I left saying I had to go and I was to tell you you have to go too. To support Percy, she said. On the subject of pet dogs."

"Why Melissa that was mean."

"Well he is her pet. Everyone says that."

"No reason you should repeat it. That kind of talk does not become you dear."

There is a rush of air and conversation from the front of the cafe, a rustle of quality clothing and a waft of Shocking: Martha Dearborn.

Martha Dearborn, dressed in a shirt-waisted frock of blue houndstooth silk, with dark blue collars and cuffs sporting white buttons and cinched at the waist with a wide leather belt of dark blue, dark blue courts on her feet and on her head a Juliet cap made with a swirl of dark, blue-dyed feathers enters the back room of the Caffè Greco with a chunky brown dachshund on a lead trotting behind her. "Hello my dears," she says. "Am I late?"

"Not at all," says Lissa. "It gave us time to talk about you."

Martha throws her an old-fashioned glance. "You're a tease, Isn't she Fritzy?" she says to the dog. Fritzy sits down and the waiter brings him a bowl of water and a sweet biscuit on a plate both of which are set down on the floor in front of him. Fritzy gives a muted growl. "Thank you, Angelo dear," says Martha Dearborn to the waiter. "Bad boy Fritzy to growl at nice Signor Angelo." She looks up at the waiter. "It's this weather," she says, "It makes him crotchety. Now. What shall I have? What are you girls having? Oh. Coca Cola. Well now let me see." She pulls of her pale blue gloves that reach half way up her forearm and sets them on the table. "Angelo porta mi un cappuccino e uno morsel of that apricocche crostata with the pasta frolla. I simply can't resist."

"Si signora." Angelo moves away and the dog gives one more little growl before retreating under the table.

"You can't take that creature with you to class," says Esther.

"Fritzy can wait in the courtyard."

"Last time he barked through the entire class and it was most distracting."

"There will be other distractions today," says Lissa. There is a brief silence as the three women prepare to tackle the main item on the agenda.

"Poor, poor Percy," begins Martha. "The poor lamb. I think he's so brave to take a class today. Really I wasn't expecting it until Lyle called up and told me it was definitely on and that she wanted us all there. For Percy's sake. And of course I do so agree. Don't you?"

"It seems just a little too like a wake for my taste," says Esther.

"Does that mean there'll be something to drink?" says Lissa.

"Ah Angelo, grazie bellissimo!" Angelo puts a cup of frothed coffee, a plate with a piece of apricot crostata and a fork down in front of Martha Dearborn. "Delizzimoso!" she says.

Angelo retires. Martha wields the fork straight into the apricot pasty. "Closest you can get in this town to a Danish," she says as she raises a forkful to her mouth and greedily gathers it in leaving her lips dotted with crumbs. "Divine," she says through her food. Esther looks away.

Lissa lights another cigarette, exhales and says, "so what did Lyle tell you?"

"Lissa please let her finish eating," says Esther.

"Everything," says Martha spraying crumbs all over the table. "Chapter and verse." Tonk goes the fork on the plate as Martha spears right through the last piece of crostata before raising it up and rapaciously clearing it into her mouth. "That pastry!" she says. "So leggeretto." Esther hands her a napkin from the stainless-steel holder on the table. "Oh my," says Martha. "Aren't I the messy eater! Covered in crumbs." She starts to wipe her dress free of bits of pastry disturbing the dog which shifts uneasily under the table. "He knows you know," she says. "He knows there's something wrong. Dogs do, you know. They can sense things."

"Perhaps the spirit of Lord David is in here right now. Amongst us. Waiting for the third day," says Lissa.

"Melissa Bouchet!" says Esther. That's downright blasphemous. And you know it."

Lissa swirls the last of the Coca Cola around in her glass and appears to be studying it intently. Then she says, "Personally I always found him a bit of a jerk." Esther breathes in fiercely through her nostrils and Martha's face glazes over. "I mean, just because he was some kind of English aristo that's no reason to make a saint of him. I mean so he played around making movies. Chester says he'd have never cut it in Hollywood."

"And Chester would know of course." There's a silence. Martha raises the cup of cappuccino to her lips and starts to slurp from it, noisily. Esther grimaces.

Martha puts the cup down. "Well I don't know about that. They say he's really helped get that Fellini on his feet." She has a moustache of coffee froth on her upper lip. "They say he didn't want to go to Hollywood. He preferred Europe."

She licks her upper lip with her tongue.

"Couldn't," says Lissa. "Not commercially-minded says Chester."

"Says Chester!"

"And he was a red."

Esther and Martha look at her in shock.

"But he was a Lord!" says Esther.

"And a commie," says Lissa. "And a spy for the British."

"No!" says Martha. "But he had such nice manners! So Edwardiman as Lyle says. It's just not possible. I mean I can't think of him as some kind of scarlet pumpernickel I really can't."

"Well it's true," says Lissa. "We had people on him. He'd never have gotten into the States. He knew it. It was all face with David Maldon."

"But he was always so charming!"

"Exactly."

"Well Lissa. You and your direct line to the White House. What next? He was a criminal?"

"Shhh," says Martha to Esther. "Walls have ears."

"In a way he was," says Lissa. "That's what got him killed."

Something has gone out of the day, the air, the atmosphere in the back room of Antico Caffe Greco. Perhaps it's simply that a cloud of illusion or delusion has left the space and gathered in a dark mass before rushing out of the door as someone leaves. The three women around the table have slumped a little into their chairs.

"I want a drink," says Lissa. "Anyone else?" Silence. Lissa beckons over the waiter. "Tre bicchiere di Champagne. Francese. No. Aspetto. Una bottiglia. Grazie."

Angelo's eyes open a little wider and he goes off to fulfil the command. There is a flutter of talk at the waiters' station.

"What are we celebrating?" says Esther. "No man is an island you know."

"I adore Heminghauser," says Martha. "For Whom the Bells Tolled. Oh! A classic. No but really. Lissa. Champagne at this hour? Oh I know. I know."

"You do?"

"Yes I do."

The waiter comes over to clear their table of cups, glasses, plate, wipes down and comes back with a bottle of Mumm and three glasses.

"Oh we drank this all the time in Paris!" trills Martha.

"I prefer Heidsieck," says Lissa.

"Get them to get me a glass of mineral water," says Esther.

"No," says Lissa. The bottle is opened and Angelo pours expertly and carefully. He puts a glass in front of each of the women, bows and smiles.

"Auguri," he says and retreats.

"How goory?" says Martha.

"Auguri," says Esther. "He thinks one of us must have a birthday."

"Now I know what Lissa's going to say," says Martha sweetly. "Go on dear."

Lissa raises her glass and so do the other two. They clink in the middle of the table. "L'chaim," says Lissa.

"L'chaim," says Martha.

"Is that Jewish?" says Esther.

"Just say it," says Lissa.

"Lock hime," says Esther.

"There you are," says Lissa. "Attagirl."

"What does it mean?" says Esther.

"It means 'to life,'" says Martha. "It's sort of we're sad but life goes on."

"Life is everything," says Lissa.

"Until you're dead," says Esther.

"How did he die?" says Martha. "Does anyone actually know? I mean did he take a fall like it says in the newspapers. I mean why take a walk around there anyway at that time of night? You often see men walking in the Borghese Gardens when it's dark. Why couldn't he just have taken a walk around there?"

"Out hunting most likely," says Lissa.

"Hunting?" says Martha. "You mean with a gun?"

"No," says Lissa. "With a bow and arrow."

"With a? You're mocking me aren't you? You always do. Silly me and I fall for it every time. Silly, stupid Martha. Always the patsy. Lissa Bouchet why don't you put your claws away for once. You'll turn into a Goatee and the wind will change and you'll be stuck there with a face like a Mormon. For ever."

"Harpy," says Esther.

"Gorgon."

"Are they having music this morning? How very civilised as David used to say. Used to say!" Martha gets out her handkerchief and blows her nose with sufficient force to alarm Fritzy under the table. He starts to bark.

Angelo comes over with an expression of concern. "Va tutto bene?" he says.

"Si," says Lissa. "Spiacente. Siamo parlando di un amico morto improvvisamante. La signora e... angioscata.

"Ah. Mi dispiace molto. Un amico morto. Giovane?

"No," says Lissa.

"Ah," says Angelo, understanding crossing his comely features. "Il signore Inglese. Voi ho gia visto qui con lui. Un vero gentiluomo. Mi dispiace moltissimo. Era qui con un amico la scorsa settimana."

"Un uomo di mezza eta. Scozzese."

"No. Un giovane. Italiano. Solo nelle ultime settimane. Prima c'era un altro uomo. Ha portato qui molto amici mascole. Qualcosa da mangiare? Dei tramezzini?"

"Grazie. Non abbiamo fame."

"Ovviamente. Siete tutti addolorati per il vostro amico. Mi dispiace molto. La Champagna. Pensavo stessi festeggiando qualcosa. Mi dispiace. Sorry. Very sorry."

"It's all right." Says Lissa. "Really. Veramente."

Angelo bows and melts away. There is more soft chatter at the waiter's station and a mix of glances are thrown in their direction.

"What did he say?" says Martha.

"Lots of young men? I don't believe him" says Esther.

"I think you'll find it's true," says Lissa.

Martha sighs. "Okay so split the beans."

"He was a faggot," says Lissa.

"Well I think we all know that already," says Esther. "He and Percy did live together after all."

"They had separate suites," says Martha "That apartment is practically a palazzo. I said to David people will think, you know, and he said, "We have merely conjoined our kitchens"."

"That is the kind of thing he would say."

"He spoke beautifully. Like that Lord Shelley. Poetic."

"I don't think he and Percy actually slept together you know."

"Well that's a relief."

"You mean you don't have to go on trying to work out who did what to whom."

"That's a frightful thing to say. As if a woman would have any idea what two male homosexuals do to each other. For goodness sake. I was at Bryn Mawr."

"So you have a better idea of what girls do to each other but let's not dwell. Why do you think they didn't sleep together? Are you sure?"

"Well, it just goes back to something Lyle said once. It made me sad."

"Yes?"

"Well, she said that they were truly in love with each other and always had been..."

"Love!"

"Yes, love. They loved each other. I think it's so wonderful. So ancient Greek."

"And. Or? But?"

"And they'd never let any harm come to the other. If they could help it. Oh! Poor Percy must feel so wretched that he wasn't there to save his...friend."

"Thank you. His friend."

"But."

"But. Now I'm just telling you what Lyle told me..."

"So go on."

"Don't be so abrupt!"

"It's alright. Lyle said they were just too different. In that way."

"In what way?"

"In whatever way men like to be. When they're with men."

"Or too much the same."

"What does that mean?"

"No. Lyle said different. She said different. She said they had different ideas about it."

"About what?"

"Ess Eee..."

"Eating? You mean David didn't like Percy's cooking."

"She means Ess for sex."

"Oh!"

"Oh indeed. It always has to come back to that. Anyone would think our whole lives were built on it. As if it were the only thing that mattered."

"Some people might say yes to both."

"You're referring to all that subconscious nonsense aren't you? Or that awful salacious book. Why someone was talking about it the other day at a cocktail party now where was it? Lyle's? The Merrimans? Oh yes, Contessa Barberini's. It was at Graziella Barberini's. What wall-hangings! Yes, someone brought it up in conversation and Ike said well I never expected to hear That Book that was how he said it, That Book. I never expected to hear That Book referred to in polite conversation. Whatever happened to privacy he said. That Book is a commie plot he said to weaken the moral fibre of America and whatever next he said will we all know everything about everybody? I mean he was riled. It's pornographic. That's what he said."

"You mean there are pictures in it?" said Martha.

Lissa began to laugh. Putting her glass down on the table she tilted her head forward into the raised palm of her right hand and laughed looking down at the floor. The other two women looked at her.

"Are you going to be sick?" said Martha.

"Was it something I said?" said Esther.

"No," said Lissa raising her head and looking up again. "I mean yes, but it doesn't matter."

"I'm always putting my finger in it," said Esther.

Lissa got up smartly from the table and rushed off in the direction of the powder room, hand clamped to her mouth. Abruptly she swivelled on a Ferragamo heel, darted back to the table, collected her bag and rushed off again.

"Anyone would think she were pregnant," said Martha.

"Oh Martha!" said Esther. "We should never joke about the creation of life. They haven't been blessed. We should feel some pity for them."

"I feel sorry for Chester."

"What do you mean?"

"People say she won't let him."

"Other people say he's not interested."

"What?"

"Yes. Elise Merriman told me he's just a disaster in the bag."

"Sack. And anyway, that was no business of hers to repeat that kind of thing. And how would she know? Oh my lord this town is getting too much for me. Everyone knows everything about everybody.

Ike's way out of date. It's enough to make you want to go and live in Canada."

They sat in silence contemplating Muskoka out of season.

With a click of heels Lissa walked back into the room. Her eyes were dry and her make up perfect. Angelo rushed forward to pull out her chair and then help her get back closer to the table. She looked up and gave him a smile. "Grazie," she said, looking at him.

"Signora," he said and blushed before moving away.

"Really Lissa," said Esther. "You must not flirt with waiters. It isn't done."

"I've said before," said Lissa. "He's not interested in women."

"Gracious here we are again back at that unpleasant subject."

"You're like a dog with his bone," said Martha. "Oh Fritzy-witzy are you feeling neglected? Here, have some nice water." Fritzy retreated further under the table.

"So, Esther," said Lissa, "you were saying that Percy and David didn't fuck."

"Oh my word!" said Esther. "How could you?" Her face contorted. "In public!"

"Come on Esther drop the pretence, please. You know you're just as interested as we are."

"Exactly," said Martha, against Lissa's expectations, "so why go on beating your bush?"

Lissa sucked in her cheeks as though she'd eaten ice. Breathing in deeply through her nose she turned to Esther and said "That's right. Martha's right. Come on and drop the high moral tone. You're as fascinated as we are, aren't you Esther Somersby?"

"It's really none of my business what people get up to in the privacy of their own homes. Even faggot people."

"Are you a faggot-hater? You know, burn them at the stake?"

"Ike says it was the one thing Hitler did right, locking up the homosexuals. He says it's a disease."

"You mean it's infectious? You mean if Ike came to one of Percy's classes he could go home a homo?"

"Don't be ridiculous. You know that's not what I'm saying. I'm saying it's against Scripture. It's against God's will for men to fornicate with men. Really I never thought I should have to say such a thing out loud in company."

"Where does it say that?" said Martha.

"I can't remember," says Esther. "For us it's in Leviticus. He says it's arayot. And you can be put to death for doing it."

There is a silence.

"Is that just men and men or women and women too?" asks Lissa.

"Oh you know I don't know. I never heard about the rules on Thespians. And anyway, Rabbi says Jews just don't get homosexual. It isn't in our nature. Is there any more champagne?"

"Cameriere?" says Lissa and after a series of signals another bottle is brought to the table.

"We really shouldn't be doing this," says Esther. "We'll turn up drunk to the class."

"What is it this week?" says Lissa. "Should I have brought something?"

"I hope it isn't testicles again", says Martha "Maybe it didn't help not knowing what a haggis was."

"It's lambchops scottaditto," says Esther, "and no."

"Of course," says Martha, "with Percy being Scottish and all."

"Scottaditto," says Lissa, "means burn your fingers, honey. Scottish is Scozzese."

"Scozzese. Should I have brought some special gloves? Oh my. I only have these."

"It's just a name," says Lissa in a kindly way. "You cook very tiny cutlets and pick them up by the bone-end to eat them. They should be so fresh from the oven you burn your fingers. That's where the name comes from."

"Jewish food," says Martha. "It's everywhere in this town. Next it'll be gefilte fish."

"We already did that," says Esther. "Weren't you there?"

"That was salt-cod," says Lissa. "What they call stoccafisso. Made into balls and fried."

"I remember the balls, "says Martha "But was it salt cod?"

"I don't think I could eat a lambchop," says Esther. "I don't think I could eat anything. Imagine how Percy must feel? Couldn't we just phone him and say it's too much; we'll come and see him next week."

"But Lyle said..."

"Well, if Lyle says then it's gonna end up in the Talmud for sure."

"Don't you have any respect for any religion? Oh, wait I know.

You're a cynic. Have I got something right for once? I do believe I have. You don't believe in anything, and you don't want anyone else to either, so you just mock everyone. You're a mockingbird! Yes, that's what you are a mockingbird? Heavens? Am I drunk?"

"In vino veritas," says Lissa, "say what you like."

"We did ancient Greek philosophy at Bryn Mawr," says Esther. "The Cynics are badly misunderstood."

"Oh dear," says Martha. "Have I got the wrong end of the prick as usual?"

"You're fine," says Lissa. "Here let me top up your glass."

She refills and Martha drinks and slurps. "Here's to Scottie dogs!" she says. "Dotty Scotties! Oh and Daxies of course!"

"Someone got their fingers burned," says Lissa.

"Someone was playing with fire," says Esther. "Would Fritzy-Witzy like another bisky-wisky? Lissa, could you ask that faggot to bring Fritzy another biscuit. Why are faggots always so nice looking? I think he's nice looking, don't you?"

"As a matter of fact, I do," says Lissa who signals for Angelo and asks him for another biscuit for the dog.

Angelo comes back with a sweet biscuit and attempts to hand it straight to the dog. Martha intervenes just in time before Fritzy's teeth clamp around Angelo's hand. "You probably taste better, too," says Martha, dropping the biscuit on the floor.

"Niente," says Lissa to Angelo's puzzled face. "Niente." Angelo moves away.

"You were saying?" says Esther to Lissa. "Playing with fire? You're talking about David?"

"It isn't as if it's a secret. I mean Lyle told me Percy only agreed to go and live with him if they had a separate suite of rooms. He knew what he was like."

"What was he like?"

"Oh Martha really. You want all the gory detail? Yes you do. Very well. David was promiscuous. Somewhat."

"Aren't all faggots promiscuous? Hunter says they're all sex mad and one day they'll get a disease that will kill them all and it'll be their own fault."

"They also say that men who are the biggest faggot-haters are usually faggots in disguise."

"Lissa! Take that back. Ike is a full red-blooded heteroseminal male."

"Doesn't he have a man for a secretary?"

"So what are you suggesting? Lissa are you saying my husband is having an affair with his secretary? His man-secretary?"

"Martha calm down," says Esther. "You mustn't take Lissa so literally. You know she likes to make mischief. Don't you Lissa? I think you should apologise to Martha Lissa. Right now this instant. People are already beginning to look."

There's a short silence.

"Martha I'm sorry if I upset you. I was just trying..."

"Well don't." says Esther. "Don't try any further."

"Martha was asking me about David and I'm trying to respond."

"Yes, but if you go off on a tangent again with your little theories I shall leave. Is that understood? Lissa?"

"Yes. As I was saying David was a promiscuous faggot and Percy was not a promiscuous faggot and Esther you are not to pass any of your judgements. We're not in Oklahoma now."

"I'm from Connecticut." Lissa gives a little snort.

"Who was he promiscuous with?" says Esther. "I mean he was the only faggot I knew but then Ike says they're everywhere like Commie infiltrators he says..."

"We can guess what he says, dear. There's no need to repeat." There's a pause. "Would you like me to carry on?"

Esther nods.

"Funny how us girls get so riled when we talk about faggots," says Lissa. "Maybe they do pose a threat like Ike says. Should we be worried? Do you think there are simply thousands of them here in Rome all ready to try and take our husbands away from us?"

"They're not having Hunter. And anyway, they can't offer what a woman can. Men want soft and gentle, and they want a woman to look after their household and goddammit have babies I mean aren't we missing the vital difference? I mean can men get pregnant?" Esther laughs a shrill laugh.

"There may be as many men don't want children as do," says Lissa.

"So, faggots are doing their bit to keep down the population? We should give them a medal?"

"Why are you so cross about what these men do in private? What have they done to you? I mean why do you take it so personally?"

"Well it's an abomination for one thing and for another..."

"Yes," says Lissa.

"Well they can't be soldiers can they they'd run away and they can't be teachers in case they interfere with boys and they certainly couldn't run a country or I don't know a battleship in case they start to cry or have the vapours when the going gets tough. I mean a faggot president? I'd as soon have a woman president as a faggot president. Can you imagine the White House filled with little dogs and reeking of eau de cologne? We'd be a laughing stock. And anyway they don't always keep it private: what about those two who said they were going to get married? I mean like Tyrone Power and that sweet Linda Christian?"

"Oh that's so romanesque."

"Grotesque?"

"Oh yes of course. Grotesque."

"They just show the worst side of humanity you know like the way things would be if we didn't keep a hold of ourselves and have morals and know what's right and what's wrong. They're the enemy within just like the Commies in Hollywood and that's not Ike that's me."

"So who fucked who do you think? You'd imagine David on top but perhaps that's only the British class system. Maybe Percy was the man? Gosh can you imagine? Bend over my Lord. Just a little bit more..."

A couple, a man and a woman, probably American, have come into the half-darkness of the back room of the cafe to look for a table. Hearing Lissa the woman, smartly dressed in a black and emerald-green silk New Look suit looks at the three, turns and leaves the room with the man in tow.

"You see," says Esther. "Enough champagne both of you. No Lissa. Not another bottle. You'll get us thrown out if you talk like that. What on earth has gotten into you? Oh my dear, don't cry. Listen. David was strong and funny and beautiful, and we'll all miss him. Were you a little in love with him? I think we all were, weren't we Esther?"

"He should have been in Hollywood," says Esther. "she means that well, don't you dear? She means it well, Lissa, I know she does and it's a shock. Yes it's an awful shock to hear someone you know has been, well, murdered. You can't say it any other way. It's like a great wrecking ball isn't it smashing all the nice things in life aside. Oh dear."

"Are you crying too?" says Esther.

"I feel very sad," says Martha. "You know he survived the war in some kind of awful Jap prison camp."

"With Percy."

"Yes with Percy. And he'd had financial troubles in England not his fault and he was just getting some work here with that director. Oh gosh. Name ends in lini like Bellini." "Rosso?" "Fell. And apparently he was quite gifted and he found Percy here by complete accident and they sort of lived together and he gave Percy the run of his kitchen to do his cookery and it all looked so good for him."

"How did he die? I mean; actually."

"Do you really want to know?"

"Yes. Where, when and how. And why. And I know you'll know. That husband of yours knows everything. Is he CIA."

"If he were, Esther dear I surely couldn't tell you and anyway David is, was, British so how would Chester have the gen?"

"They say David was a spy."

"No!"

"Yes. They say he was working for the British and us too, keeping tabs on all the arty Communists for them."

"David?"

"Yes David. I mean he was a spy before the war."

"He was what?"

"Didn't you know? He was on his way to where were the Chinese the good ones? Chungking. He'd been sent there by the British to find out if they were going to try and invade Hong Kong. That's almost funny isn't it when you think what happened. Then the Japs invaded and he was stuck there. And that," says Esther, "is what you call a failure of intelligence. Big time." She burps discreetly.

Martha is silent, flummoxed.

"I'm surprised Lyle didn't ever mention it." Lissa says

"You mean 'Hey, Dave's a spy. He's keeping tabs on Eytie Commie Faggots to help save the Free World', that kind of thing?"

"Poor David," says Martha.

"What do you mean?" says Esther.

"Having to keep so many darned secrets. So being one thing to one person and another to another and making sure he never got his wires crossed. Like a tightrope act."

"Maybe being a faggot helped. I mean hiding bits of yourself away all the time."

"You think he was murdered for being a spy?"

"Shall we have more coffee?" says Esther.

"I'll have a Negroni," says Lissa.

"I'll have what she's having," says Martha. "Make it a double." This time it's Martha who summons Angelo and they sit in silence until Esther's coffee and their drinks are served. "Has anyone noticed the time?" says Martha. "We're already late."

"I don't think I want to go today," says Lissa. "I don't think I could stick a knife into anything today." She looks at Martha.

"That was it, wasn't it?" Martha says. "He was stabbed."

Lissa looks down at her coffee. "They cut his throat," she says.

Martha gets up and rushes off to the Ladies" Room. Click click click go her heels. She's left her bag behind. Lissa reaches into it and fishes out the pack of cigarettes and the shagreen lighter. She and Martha help themselves, light up and smoke.

Esther puts cigarettes and lighter back into Lissa's bag. "I thought shagreen went out before the war," she says. "It's some kind of skin, isn't it?" she says. "I don't like the feel of it. I don't like touching skin."

"I thought you didn't smoke," says Lissa. They smoke in silence until Martha gets back.

"So that's the how," Esther says. "We have three more to go."

"It happened was round the back of the Campidoglio," says Lissa. "The Capitoline."

"Where people were killed by being thrown from the top," says Esther. "In ancient times."

"Thrown off the top of a rock? For being faggots? I mean chemical castration yes but no I don't go for that at all."

"In ancient times," says Lissa. "Criminals. Not faggots. I mean not on purpose anyway."

"So David was rock-climbing? In the dark?"

"Martha really," says Esther. "This isn't something to make a joke out of."

Martha holds up her hands. "My life!" she says, "I wasn't joking. I mean, really, what was David doing there."

"Looking for men to have sex with."

"On a cliff? Are they monkeys? Seriously," she says, "I thought that's what the Villa Borghese gardens were for. Oh wait, I know. Too nice. Too smooth. David was looking for some of that rough trade. Am I right?"

"It looks that way. That's more or less what Lyle said."

"May I have a cigarette?" says Martha.

"Sure," says Lissa. "I'm having one." They all take, light and breathe out a communion of smoke.

"So we have the How and the Where. We need the When and the Why. Lissa?"

"I can tell you the When. It was at about midnight. But as to the Why well I'm no Agatha Christie but Chester has some suppositions."

"I prefer pills," says Martha. "I told the doctor I aint gonna take nothing up my ass."

"Suppositions, dear, not suppositories," says Esther and takes a last drag of her cigarette. "Have they caught anyone?"

"No," says Lissa, "not as far as I'm aware. It'll be some pretty little rent-boy from one of the suburbs."

"Maybe David had cash on him." "The papers are saying his wallet was still there. Untouched."

"Maybe it was a vigil what's it."

"Vigilante."

"That's him. You got it. Maybe it was a faggot-hater trying to clean up the public parks. Do you think it hurt? I mean d'you think he suffered? If someone came at him from behind..."

"I thought that was the idea." says Esther.

"If someone came at him from behind," continues Lissa, "by surprise, or if he was expecting, you know, sex of some kind. And if the knife were sharp and the other person knew what they were doing then I think you probably die of shock."

"Instantly?"

"Who can say dear. I'm not a pathologist."

"Oh God," says Martha.

"Did they find the knife?" says Esther.

"Apparently yes," says Martha.

"So there could be fingerprints. Or shoe prints? Or someone could have seen what happened and might come forward. D'you think we should offer a reward? A reward for information?"

"That's a lovely thought dear but the police would have every crank in Rome on their hands and d'you know what? I don't think it would be kind for Percy. I mean waiting and waiting and hearing horrid, terrible stories from a pack of liars. And being asked more questions by the police. No. I don't think it would be a good idea."

"What's Percy going to do?" They fall silent.

"Oh gosh I feel awful. Is it too late to go? I mean I don't suppose there's actually going to be a class. I imagine Lyle just wanted us to go for you know what's it? Moral support."

"We should go, dears. Lissa's right. We must make an appearance. It's Percy we have to think of."

"Such a British name isn't it? Percy." Lissa signals to Angelo for the check. He smiles and gives a little bow.

"Actually," says Martha, "I think it's German. There was that opera by the one the Nazis loved. Wagner. I know lots of Wagners. They're all over New Haven."

"Parsifal," says Esther. "No wait," she says as Angelo arrives with the check on a tray and discreetly disappears again. "Percy told me. It was a last name in old England that got made into a first name in honour of the last name. I guess it must have belonged to some big-wig barons or something. I'll get this."

"No you absolutely will not my dear. You know the rules. We share. Yes? Or no more little coffee mornings. Isn't that right, Martha?"

"What?"

"We split the bill."

"Oh yes. For sure."

They all search in their bags for their billfolds and count out cash.

"What shall we leave for the tip? The usual percent?"

"Oh a bit more today I think," says Lissa. "I mean he's been on guard as well and kept the room quiet for us. Let's double it."

"Don't spoil the market is what Ike says."

"We should just leave what we think," says Esther.

They place their lire on the table and Angelo comes over. He eyes the lire bills and has done a quick mental calculation for he smiles broadly.

"Le signore sono molto gentile," he says. "Grazie," and he places his right hand gently on his left breast. "Mi diaspice per la vostra perdita," he says. He eyes the tray again but steps back, gives a little cough to clear his throat and starts:

> "'Amor, ch'al cor gentil ratto s'apprende, prese costui de la bella
> personache mi fu tolta; e 'l modo ancor m'offende.
> Amor, ch'a nullo amato amar perdona,mi prese del costui piacer
> sì forte,che, come vedi, ancor non m"abbandona.'"

While he speaks the other waiters come into the room and stand in silence just inside the doorway. The hush is palpable. The heavy red velvet door-curtain falls or is pulled across the doorway and the room dims. Inside the low lights can be seen to flicker and elide the spotted mirrors that give them back paler and softer. The heavy gilding on the frames of mirrors and pictures glows with a dull intensity. Anything dark red appears like liquid blood. Napery, cutlery, glasses, the polished dark floor and the white jackets of the waiters are lit with a pale fire that would not singe a sleeve and as the girls sit and watch and listen, the room seems to be transformed into an antechamber to death where ancient rites are performed that grant the soul a gentle passage into the blackness beyond and dim its eyes by gentle stages so that it will not be disconcerted by the dark.

Angelo finishes and the other waiters begin to applaud followed by the girls. The door-curtain is roughly torn back and against the light that floods in and troubles their eyes they can see a figure blocking it out. It is an elegant shape in a tailored suit and on its head is a beret. It is Lyle.

"I thought I'd find you here," she says. "Come on, we need you. Have you settled? Okay, let's go." She turns around and strides through the front room toward the street door. The girls start to gather their things together.

Lissa goes up to Angelo and places a gloved hand on his shoulder. "Bellissimo," she says and smiles at him. Angelo smiles back. Martha takes his hand and shakes it. "Grazie," she says. The stocky figure of Esther is already out of the room and the other two follow her.

Out in the Via Condotti the sun is blazing and they all reach into their purses for their sunglasses.

Lyle stands immobile waiting for her flock to be ready to move.

Martha looks at Lissa. "What was he saying?" she says.

"He was quoting Dante. It was about love."

"Told you he was a faggot," says Esther.

Lyle and Lissa have started to walk on ahead.

Martha pauses and looks after them along the street. "Oh dear," she says. "Whatever are we going to say to Percy?"

"Good riddance," says Esther as she begins to march forward.

Library of Congress, Washington DC, August 1989

The "discovery" of Mediterranean Cuisine by Anglo Cookery Writers in the Mid Twentieth Century

A Doctoral Dissertation
by Shaney Pettifer
New Atlantic University
August 1989

Chapter Three
"In Bocca di Lupa"
Percival Langrigg

Like Elizabeth David and Julia Child Percival Langrigg also came to writing about cookery by a circuitous route. Quiet and unassuming in character and demeanour unlike the more flamboyant Child and societal David and with but one publication to his name, Langrigg has nevertheless earned, this writer believes, his own distinct place in the history of the "awakening" of white anglophone amateur cooks to the flavours and traditions of the Mediterranean kitchen in the late Twentieth Century through his in-depth understanding of the popular cuisine of Rome.

Percival Langrigg was born in "Tientsin" (Tiian-jin) in China in 1912, the same year as Julia Child's birth in Princeton NJ and a year before that of Elizabeth David in Sussex, England. All three came from upper-class families that were able to count on reserves of property and/or business holdings. While Child was born to an intellectual family David's upbringing in an English country house could be described as "bohemian." Langrigg's mother Gloria was herself born into the Chicago-based Heston Hotels dynasty. As a child she travelled to Europe and Asia with her family receiving little in the way of traditional schooling. Langrigg's father, Hector Langrigg. was born in Helensburgh, Scotland to working-class parents. After excelling at school Langrigg Snr was encouraged to matriculate and with his qualification found employment in the Glasgow-based Scottish & Colonial Trading Bank. Like many young men at that time he was attracted to the potential of, after completing his training, going "out East" with the Bank to work in one of its colonial operations. In 1907 he applied for a position in the Bank's Shanghai office and was successful in obtaining it. In the same year he met his future wife Gloria at a Shanghai social event hosted by mutual friends and they were married as soon as the widely applied rule that forbad employees of European concerns marrying until they had served a minimum of four years in "station" was met. Percival, their first and only child, was born a little over nine months after the marriage.

Percival Langrigg said that his mother's family had been dismayed that their daughter and only child had "married beneath her" but Gloria's business "drive" and Hector's financial acumen led to the couple being given control of Heston Hotel's China portfolio of properties in 1918. Centred on the group's "jewel in the crown", the Atholl Palace Hotel in Shanghai, the couple bought properties in "Tientsin" "Pataho" (Bei-dai-he), Mukden (Shenyang) and Kobe, Japan. Riding out global war, an influenza pandemic and depression in the United States and Europe Heston Hotels Asia became a successful enterprise, so successful in fact that the (as described by Percival) "unmaternal" Gloria swiftly ceded the care of her child to a succession of "ayas" and tutors at the family home in Tian-jin until finally she despatched him to the missionary-run Yantai School in 1920 where he was to stay until 1928. During that period according to Percival he saw his parents not above half-a-dozen times, being left at the school during vacations or sent to stay with "uncles" and "aunts" usually in "Tientsin" but sometimes across China.

In late 1928, when Percival had returned to Scotland to finish his education and "matriculate", the Heston Hotels' fortunes in Asia peaked and then began their slow decline. It appears that the Langriggs Senior over-extended themselves financially, antagonised other hotel operators in the region and, remarkably, did not taken firm enough action to prevent a Triad gang from basing itself at the Atholl Palace Hotel, Shanghai. Percival returned to Shanghai in 1930 to witness that from 1932 onward, harassed and pursued by creditors, competitors and fiscal and civil authorities the Langriggs were forced to sell one hotel after another leaving them with, by 1936, only their Shanghai property. Dismayed by the reversal of the company's fortunes in Asia the board of Heston Hotels recalled the Langriggs to Chicago in the same year. Somehow Gloria and Hector managed to persuade the board (made up largely of cousins) that they could remain in charge of the Asian operation on sufferance. The Atholl Palace saw an uptick in its fortunes in the latter years of the 1930s not least because of the influx of Europeans into Shanghai during periods of unrest in China and during the Japanese-created "emergencies". It was during this period that Percival was, as he put it, "railroaded" into employment at the Atholl Palace where he then lived and acted as Night Manager. By 1940 however the Atholl Palace had been side-lined by other operators in the city. In late 1941 Gloria and Hector decided to abandon the Atholl Palace to its likely fate and took ship for the US, bypassing Hong Kong where Percival had found employment as under-manager at the colonial stalwart Repulse Bay Hotel. The ship in which they were travelling was torpedoed en route to Manila and both senior Langriggs perished.

It will be seen that Percival's upbringing could be described as "cosmopolitan." Fluent in Mandarin Chinese and conversant with Cantonese, well-travelled in China, having enjoyed brief sojourns in Europe, and familiar with the many faces of 1930s Shanghai, Percival nevertheless credited his Yantai missionary schooling, his Scottish ancestry and two years spent mostly in Edinburgh, Scotland (described by Percival as the "coldest" of his life) with the "Calvinist" streak in his character that as he described it "kept him apart" from the hedonistic lifestyles of his European contemporaries in Shanghai. He told this author: "I was the perfect hotel manager. Seeing, hearing but never passing comment. Polite, efficient but never involved. In every way I had been raised as the perfect functionary. An observer with no apparent mind of his own."

Percival's one concession to his senses since early childhood was food. It was his belief that the succession of ayas who cared for him as a child replaced the love of parents with the comforts of food and that this laid down in his life, as he put it speaking humorously but meaningfully, "the joy of cooking," referring of course to the tome by Irma Rombauer (correctly *Joy of Cooking*) first published in 1931 privately and then commercially in 1936. The book has since been through nine editions and sold over 16 million copies. Julia Child credited the book which she referred to when young as "Mrs Joy's cookbook" for teaching her how to cook.

In interviews with this writer Percival described his first remembered taste sensation as a breakfast of leftover rice with warm milk and brown sugar sprinkled on top. Nothing made him happier, he said, than the communal preparation and cooking of "jiao-tzi" (Chinese pot-stickers) boiled in the style of Northern China. In fact it was Northern Chinese food that informed Percival's tastes as a child; the use of both wheat and rice, the use of lamb as well as pork, in fact the rustic home-cooking of his ayas and the domestic staff at his parents' rarely-visited home in Tian-jin. Tian-jon was also home to a large colonial commercial community and here Percival was also exposed to the cooking of Continental European, British and American tastes. In one day he might breakfast on leftover rice, eat British "curry" for lunch, visit a soda fountain in the afternoon and dine on "steak-frites" at the home of a French family in the evening.

At this point it is worth considering the similarities in interest between Langrigg and David and what distinguishes the focus of their interest from that of Child. Child's cooking was essentially bourgeois and reflects the kind of meals made for an affluent household by their cook. Percival told this writer that he had purchased Mrs Child's and Mrs Bertholle's *Mastering the Art of French Cooking: Volume One* on publication in 1961. "I admire Mrs Child and Mrs Bertholle," he told me, "for making the classic dishes of French bourgeois cuisine approachable and practicable for the modern British or American home cook. But," he said, "Mrs David made a better omelette with less fuss and even if I dangled my toes in the Tiber I would likely not be able to catch a pike for quenelles du brochet. Hence they are rarely if ever served at my table." Expanding on the subject of omelettes he confided in this writer that "Timing is all in the making of a perfect omelette a la Child or even David. I would prefer in my kitchen to take a glass of wine or smoke a cigarette and let a frittata take care of itself." Nevertheless, the inference is clear: that Langrigg and David studied and wrote about "every-day" cooking as practised by the less well-off and even the poor who were forced by circumstance to do their own marketing, preparation and cooking and even, in many cases, the growing of vegetables and the raising and slaughtering of their own livestock. Without their cooking the household would have been hungry and likely malnourished. This is essentially the cooking of Provence (David) and Rome (Langrigg) whereas we can glimpse through the pages of Child into the dining-rooms of Paris, Lyon, Bordeaux and Brussels.

Percival told this writer that he saw similarities between the peasant cooking he had experienced as a child and that of post-War Rome. Meat was less consumed in Italy during the late 1940s and early 1950s when Percival arrived in Rome thanks to the effects of continuing post-War rationing and scarcities. Perhaps because of this in Rome Percival found what he described as his "perfect" cuisine: a cuisine that still reflected the centuries during which the citizens of Rome (as in much of Southern Italy) had lived in a state of impoverishment compared to the luxuries enjoyed by their rulers. In Rome this meant essentially the Papal State and Nobility, in the South the Bourbons. The much richer cuisines of the North of Italy especially that of Emilia-Romagna reflect the power of the bourgeoisie in those areas as opposed to Papal and Bourbon near-despotism further South. Still during the mid-Twentieth Century many Roman families were kept from starvation especially during the 1940's by the produce of country small-holdings in the Roman hinterland that supplied them with cheese, eggs, vegetables - and wine. Since the times of the Roman Empire the city of Rome (in common with London, Paris, Chicago, St Louis) had supported a vast cattle-slaughtering industry. Rome itself had gloried in its abattoirs that were situated close to the very centre of the city in their own designated quarter (a practice that the Romans exported to the territories of their Empire) where the markets were extended, improved and even beautified during the period of the Emperor Nero. By the Twentieth Century Rome's chief abattoir area had moved down the Tiber to the area of Monte Testaccio but the established pattern remained the same: the rich consumed the choice cuts of meats while the poor were only able to buy off-cuts and offal. This choice became known in Rome as the Quinto Quarto or Fifth Quarter – the cuts that were either rejected by or simply not offered to the cooks of the nobility: Sweetbreads, tails, hooves, lungs, testicles, tripes, spleens.

Percival had a fascination for such foods and had collected, both on his travels and from friends, a set of recipes that utilised these, to most Europeans and Americans, little-known or frankly repellent ingredients. He spoke of what he called "spleen-burgers" the Pane ca'Meusa of Palermo, the haggis of Scotland, the chitterlings of Southern England, tripe boiled in England and turned into a "fortifying" soup in Turkey, rooster-combs and chicken feet in China, the ultra-fine "fegato" of Venice, the kokorech (cleaned and spit-roasted cows" entrails) and roast sheep's heads of Istanbul and his favourite the Coda alla' Vaccinara of Rome. It could be said, this writer contends, that Percival's interest in food was not as a means of status and display but as a means of survival.

Percival said as much himself when questioned about his experiences in his three-and-a-half-year incarceration in the Stanley prisoner-of-war camp in Hong Kong and, he was keen to add, in the weeks immediately following liberation in September 1945. During those years Percy, like many prisoners of war in the Asian Pacific Theatre, became expert in the preparation of rice and in fact Percival spent at least two years in the rice-kitchen detail at Stanley Camp. Spurred on by the deprivation there much discussion was had on the "goodness" in different types of foods including grasses and other local flora. Percival recalled one "craze" for pine needles in boiling water used to make a beneficial tea. It has since been shown that there is solid evidence for these benefits including supplementing levels of Vitamins A and C in which camp inmates would have been severely lacking. Percival recalled how two women friends of his who he referred to by the initials R and I would regularly walk around the perimeter of the school running track on Stanley Peninsula collecting the needles. It is likely that knowledge of the benefits of pine tea came from the Korean contingent among the camp guards since pine tea is commonly drunk for its perceived health benefits on the Korean peninsula.

To summarise the argument thus far: Experiences and influences of food and eating in childhood and during the Second World War had predisposed Percival Langrigg to preferring "poor" cuisine over "rich." On arrival in Rome where, lacking money initially, he visited the markets, communal restaurants and the butcheries of Testaccio he was informed by his conversations with shop-holders and their customers as to the use of these ingredients and was thereby introduced to and became immersed in "la cucina povera" of Rome.

It will be seen that this experience in Rome, so very different to the introduction to European food experienced by Child and David (who had sometimes to "make do" but did not endure near poverty) was seminal in developing Percival's interests in "authentic" Roman cooking and that it immediately chimed with his latent, interest in "working class" cooking.

The word "latent" is used with some care since, as admitted by Percival himself, he had not until he reached Rome in 1948 "thought through" his interest in food, treating it merely as an "undercurrent" in his life. Although naturally extremely reticent and rarely disposed to talk about himself it is clear that for Percival his interest in food was what could be described as psycho-sexual in that cooking granted him a type of fulfilment that was lacking in his severely restricted social and emotional lives.

The word "cooking" is chosen with care since Percival was more interested in the processes of preparing food than the experience of eating and the enjoyment of eating, hence this author has deliberately avoided the word "food". Percival showed this author a cutting from an American magazine by a reviewer who had attended a series of his classes in which they opined: "Mr Langrigg's classes are much loved by middle-aged women, mostly American, whose figures run from svelte to skinny to malnourished. Of all the food that is prepared in his classes only a few ounces, if that, ever find their way into the mouths of the attendees. All are encouraged to take their finished dishes home with them but who actually consumes them is anyone's guess. Most likely the household Boston bull terrier." This author asked Percival if he were offended by this remark to which the answer was "No. They may live on cigarettes and cocktails. My aim is to try and engender a respect for the native cuisine of the city in which they find themselves. That is all."

From conversations over several weeks it also appears that the enjoyment that Percival found in the various kitchens in which he "worked" from Yantai to Shanghai, Hong Kong to London and then to the South West of France stemmed as much or more from the sensation of being part of something greater: a team, an equipe or a brigade. This sense of belonging clearly, this author believes, gave Percival the "family" he had missed out on throughout his childhood and early adulthood. Boarding school, the school kitchen, hotel kitchens all granted him a place in their processes that he, truly, "relished" as much or more than the dishes that were produced. Moreover, it appears that Percival felt secure in a small, closed, hermeneutic system that gave him status and where interaction followed set procedures and rules. For Percival this brought stability and comfort.

As the world's middle classes become wealthier there is growing disquiet at the "sexualisation" of food. When asked for his views on this Percival laughed. "There's not much sexy about boiled rice and greens of potatoes," he told this writer, referring to his experiences in Stanley Camp. "Food is there to keep us alive," he told this writer, "and to over-sensualise it is just pornography." Percival had made a study of the food of Ancient Rome and was well-informed about the excesses to which the upper classes went in their banquets, often referring to the Feast of Trimalchio in the Satyricon of Titus Petronius Arbiter. It was his opinion that the description is partly at least fantastic and does not refer to a real event. As he explained to this author; "I've been a waiter in many hotels and served very good food to many wealthy people but never did I see the simple enjoyment on their faces that I felt myself the first time I ate a Roman coda alla vaccinara."

Asked by this author why he did not come to cooking much earlier in his life and perhaps have trained as a chef, Percival was at pains to explain that according to the mores of the time when he was growing up this was not an option that he believed was open to him. He compared the profession of restaurant chef to that of the actor, and more particularly actress, in the British Edwardian era. To be an actor was at that time to be looked down upon in society and was not a "respectable" profession. It was a "trade" and to be a cook was no different especially since most middle-class households employed a cook "in service." Percival entered the hotel trade not out of choice but in response to pressure from his parents to "learn the workings" of the business before graduating into a senior management role as would befit a member of the owning family. After moving to Hong Kong from Shanghai in the 1937 Emergency he continued to work in hotels "As the only job I knew," and so continued in London and France after the War. "I didn't ever think of anything else," he told this writer. "After the death of my parents and the loss of the business I simply kept on the treadmill to expiate the guilt I felt. That must have been it."

Gradually, however, Percival was more and more drawn into the kitchens at the establishments where he worked learning more and more techniques as he went along. "I only asked for the most basic tasks," he said. "I was happy to prepare vegetables and wash dishes as long as I could observe how the cooking was done." And so both at the Sherborne Hotel in London's Bloomsbury and at the Mirabelle hotel in South West France with its celebrated restaurant L'Epergne d'Or Percival gradually learned more techniques and was, when there were staff shortages, allowed to join the team of cooks at the most basic level and solely in his down-time when he was not required to perform his management duties. But even this, it seems, did not impel him toward a career in cooking. "You have to learn young," he said, "and I was already old enough to be the parent of most of the boys in the kitchens. The thought of taking up cooking as a career or the thought of opening a restaurant was simply ridiculous. I was learning but I hadn't learnt anything like enough." After his sudden departure from France in Autumn 1948 there arose the possibility that Percival might not return to hotel management but might look to develop a career "in food." Two major factors influenced him to move in this direction; the first was a legacy from an aunt in England that gave him some financial independence and the second was the influence of the American agricultural products heiress Lyle Destrooper.

"I owe my life to Lyle," Percival told this author and since he gave this relationship such significance it is worth briefly digressing into its genesis and development not least because Lyle Destrooper had, when Mme Ferrand, been introduced to the other "lodestar" in Percy's life, the then David Sopley, later Lord Maldon, in Shanghai. David Sopley (died 1953) was credited by Percy with, in conjunction with Lyle Destrooper, encouraging him to translate his interest in Roman cuisine from practice to instruction; in other words, to commence a cookery school. It was David Sopley who in 1950 invited Percy to come and share his extensive apartment on the Piazza Navona and there to "conjoin their kitchens." A full understanding of Percy Langrigg's progress from outsider to amateur to professional (although Percy himself roundly dismissed being viewed as such) would be hard to understand without some explanation of the combined influence of this pair, Destrooper and Maldon, upon his development.

This author has encountered, while researching into Percy

Langrigg's personal history, speculation as to whether he was a) homosexual and b) was lover to David Maldon at various points throughout the latter's life beginning when they were "boarders" at Yantai School. Although Percy himself, when confronted with these topics, refused to answer what he deemed "prurient" questioning, it would, this author believes, be a mistake to ignore speculation of this kind. It is this author's opinion that although Percy Langrigg proclaimed himself totally averse to what he regarded as the post-War "sexualisation" of food that nevertheless he was aware that for himself food and the sharing of food had clearly social and often amatory if not overtly sexual connotations. It is also this author's contention that when David Sopley asked Percy Langrigg to "conjoin our kitchens" that this was the frankest declaration of a relationship that the former could have made to the latter, given his fear of the intimate, short of an offer of marriage. This brief "conjoining", never discussed by Percy Langrigg with this author, can, this author believes, nevertheless be seen as the summation of a romantic and possibly sexual attachment between the two men that dated back to their schooldays. It is perhaps only in this context that Percy's breakdown after the death of David Sopley can be fully understood and, this author contends, not only that but also the subsequent flowering of Percy Langrigg's "latent" interest in food into a full-blown passion.

In the context of Lyle Ferrand-Destrooper's active promotion of L'Antica Tavola Romana and her support for Percy after the death of David Sopley some introduction to her arrival in Percy's life is also germane. The Ferrands had arrived in Shanghai in 1932 to pursue business interests, Sopley Snr, (then the Honourable David Sopley, younger brother of the then Lord Maldon) who had a reputation in Shanghai as a business "fixer" or "broker" positioned himself to introduce this wealthy American to Shanghai businessmen. Sopley Snr, who had frequent bouts of illness brought on by cirrhosis of the liver, charged his son with ensuring that Lyle Ferrand was chaperoned and entertained during her time in Shanghai while Sopley Snr conducted "business" with her husband. Mme Ferrand was clearly taken with David Sopley who, tall and good-looking, had already become known as a young man "about town" and was socially active in the city. Behind the scenes the Sopleys had little money and it was the case that a Ferrand "deal" was for Sopley Snr a "last ditch" attempt to clear a healthy commission and remain "in the game." The "deal" failed to materialise and the Ferrands went home to France while the Sopleys Senior and Junior returned "steerage" [sic] to England where they could live rent-free at Lord Sopley's Essex mansion until such times as their fortunes revived.

By 1934 Sopley Snr was dead of liver disease and after a short career as a stockbroker in the City of London Sopley Jnr was recruited by an acquaintance into a branch of the British Foreign Office that was monitoring affairs in China. David Sopley made visits to Shanghai in 1935 and again in 1937 ostensibly as a trade attaché. During 1938 he made a tour of Southern China with a base in Chengdu, having learnt Cantonese during 1935. In 1941 he returned to China, this time to Hong Kong, as a director of newsreels and was captured and interned there after the Japanese conquest. During this period his uncle in England had also died and David Sopley had inherited the family title becoming David, Lord Maldon in the process. It is not known to what extent, if at all, David Sopley and Percival Langrigg had fraternised during the periods in which they found themselves in Shanghai and Hong Kong at the same time but their school friendship was taken up when they both found themselves in Stanley Interment Camp. What is clear is that David Sopley and Lyle Ferrand-Destrooper also maintained a deep and life-long friendship and re-established contact after 1946. In 1948 after Percival had been working at the Sherborne Hotel, London, for two years he quit for reasons he would not share with this writer and left for France. Through a connection of Lyle Ferrand-Destrooper Percival became manager at the Hotel Mirabelle close to Sarlat-la-Canéda in the Dordogne region. It is not clear whether at the time Percival realised that he was being "set up" in this position by David Sopley not only so that he could earn money but also that he should be close to Lyle Ferrand-Destrooper's French country home. By this time, having lost her third husband, Ferrand, in a motoring accident, Ms (as we would now term it) Destrooper had "retired" to the country home she had shared with Ferrand who had grown up in the region.

Percival was to describe his year and a half sojourn at La Mirabelle as "the happiest of my life". For the first time he found himself respected for his professionalism, he was able to learn the rudiments of French bourgeois cooking in the hotel kitchen and for the first time had a platonic, close, female friend in whom he could confide. It is not clear, therefore, why after less than two years Percival "fled" from La Mirabelle. He did so in the company of Lyle Destrooper with whom he embarked on what he later termed a "culinary pilgrimage" through the South of France, Savoy, Piedmont, Lombardy, Veneto and Venice, Emilia Romagna and Lazio before finally arriving in Rome. Rome was, as Percival described it, "my Jerusalem." Here in this still war-ravaged city he felt for the first time "at home."

Initially Lyle Destrooper rented for him a "monolocale" off the Via Labicana and with the small amount of money he had saved during his employment in France Percival was able for the first time in his life not to have to work but instead to "live off the land." It was during this period that he found his way to the markets of Rome where he questioned stallholders and shoppers on how to cook the produce he saw in front of him. If the results were not satisfactory he would return to the stall and once again through conversation would try to ascertain what had gone wrong. Then he would try the dish once more. He frequented the cantine, the usually church-run communal restaurants that fed Rome's "working poor." Here he would eat spaghetti (or more likely bucatini) all'Amatriciana, pasta cacio e pepe or a soup with bread. "I loved those places," he told this author, "for their simplicity, for the way they filled basic needs adequately and no more, for the fact that they were communal but strictly-run."

In his adopted city he sought out street-vendors and small, family-run restaurants in areas such as Monte Testaccio and Trastevere. Most of all he enjoyed eating at the food-to-go stalls in the markets enjoying suppli, carciofi a la guida, bacchala, porchetta or pinsa. "My favourites," he told this author, "were what I called the Brown Restaurants. The interiors were of that ancient shade of liverish-brown, the tables topped with marble and the windows, usually facing out onto narrow streets of high buildings, almost always shrouded in net curtains." Here it was that Percival first met the cooking that was to become his life-interest; the ox-tail stews, saltimbocce, trippe, abacchio, pujata sauce. "There was in Rome, in the food of Rome," he said, "a strange affinity with the food I'd eaten with the kitchen staff at school and on the streets of Tientsin. Many of the ingredients," he continued, "reminded me of what I'd seen and eaten in the '30s in Edinburgh where luxury and excess were considered mortal sins. It was a cooking of restraint that was based around relatively few ingredients cooked with great skill but without flamboyance." The phrase skill without flamboyance became, it could be argued, the motto for Percival's own cooking and that of his cookery classes.

In the Summer of 1951 Percival was once again re-acquainted in Rome with David Sopley who had come to the city to try and gain entry into the burgeoning Roman movie industry. Later that year David, Lord Maldon, persuaded Percival to "conjoin our kitchens" as he put it according to Percival, at his large Piano Nobile apartment on the Piazza Navona. "I was happy on my own," said Percy, "but I knew I couldn't be a hermit for ever. The offer was too good to refuse." So, Percival vacated his Labicana apartment and moved into his own suite of rooms in the Maldon apartment with the use of the "conjoined" kitchen. Here Percival began to cook in earnest to master the techniques of Roman cooking. He was assisted in this by Lord David's own cook, by the cook employed by Lyle Destrooper and, as word spread, by the local cooks in other wealthy households who claimed to know the secret of one or another speciality. Percival took copious notes at each "lesson" and worked at the dish in his own time until he felt he could reproduce it correctly. The Navona kitchen was large, centred around a simple scrubbed-pine table, with a simple stove, a marble-slabbed larder, basic equipment and only the pots, pans and implements considered necessary by at least two generations of cooks. The one concession to modernity was a large Westinghouse refrigerator "for the champagne," as Percival explained. Not making any concessions to modern kitchen apparatus meant, according to Percival, that the keeping-qualities of ingredients, proper handling and storage, short shelf-lives and ripeness were a completely integral part of choosing what foods to cook and when. One day, he told this author, he came home from marketing to find four women around the kitchen table including Lyle Destrooper. "We've come for lunch," he reported Ms Destrooper as saying, "and we want to watch you cook it." Percival prepared, as he recalled, a simple lunch of bucatinis with a sauce made from sautéed zucchini with rosemary, sauteed pine kernels and a salad of bitter leaves. "They loved it," he told this author. "They were finally eating the food their own cooks made for themselves but never for their employers. It was a revelation." Led by Mrs Destrooper all his guests that day insisted that he not only cooked for them again but that he told them where he bought his ingredients, why he chose them, showed them how he prepared them and let them see how they were cooked. So was born the school of L'Antica Tavola Romana and Percival Langrigg's contribution to the awakening of interest in Mediterranean regional cooking in the US and Great Britain during the next decade.

If it appears that much, or too much, time has been spent relating the personal journey of Percival Langrigg to the commencement of his cookery school and cookery writing it is an approach, as with the early histories of Mrs Child and Mrs David already related, an approach that is dictated, as this writer believes, by the "personal" relationship between these three cooks and their food. "Food is history," as has been said and this can be taken to refer to not only social history but also, at least in this era of choice and of plenty, the personal histories of those who make cookery their career out of choice rather than, as Percival was only too acutely aware, out of necessity. "I've been fortunate," he told this writer, "that I could cook for one or two from the ingredients I chose, when I chose. I tried to replicate as far as possible the conditions under which tens of thousands of Roman women had to cook every day for their family or menfolk and as I cooked I appreciated the skill and dedication with which they went about this most essential of tasks often, indeed usually, without pay or praise."

In 1953 after the sudden and tragic death of Lord Maldon Percival vacated the Piazza Navona apartment and with the assistance and support of Lyle Destrooper began his classes and his writing in earnest from his new and final home on the Celimontana off the Via Santi Quatro Coronati. Although a Presbyterian Christian throughout his life he told this writer, "I wanted to be near that church (Basilica e Monastero Santi Quatro Coronati) from which issued everyday the most divine music as from choirs of angels." The Celimontana (the portion of inner Rome's Centro Storico on the Northern slope of the Monte Celio) became his "turf" as he put it and he was to remain there until his death in 1975. He was often to be seen walking back from the food market close to Termini station, enjoying a pre-dinner Negroni or an evening gelato or eating his favourite food, a simple pizza bianca with stewed onions and rosemary at the local taverna he favoured. Within his apartment his kitchen was the focus of his life; "where the lares and penates live," he said referring to the household gods of Ancient Rome that were believed to guard the spirit of the family, the kitchen pantry and the hearth. As we have seen with Elizabeth David, his kitchen was both aesthetic and utilitarian. On this subject he quoted the English radical thinker and writer and also poet William Morris whose dictum was "Have nothing in your houses that you do not know to be useful or believe to be beautiful."

In 1971 Percival published his one and only book, *A Poor Sort of Meal: The Quotidian Cooking of Rome*, dedicated to both Ms Destrooper and Lord Maldon. Its somewhat off-putting title very much reflects Percival's ambivalence toward any form of recognition. "I covered my book with a bushel" he told this author. However in 1970 his book, having been "discovered" by a friend of Elizabeth David found itself on sale in David's eponymous kitchenalia store in London's Pimlico district. In 1976 the book was republished by London publisher and self-acknowledged "food snob" Guy Glanville at his Forchette Press. It took some years however before it and Percival's "Antica Tavola Romana" cooking school in Rome began to achieve international renown and Percival's accounts of "dour but delicious" Roman food began to have an impact on American and British perceptions of Italian regional cuisine that had up to then been relatively unknown. In the USA "Italian" food generally reflected Neapolitan cuisine while in Great Britain the majority of Italian restaurants known as "Trats" (short for Trattorie) in London were Spanish run with the notable exception of Spaghetti House first opening in 1955. Following Percival's death a small but growing number of cookery afficionados both in the USA and Great Britain began to reference *A Poor Sort of Meal* as an influence. His reputation subsequently grew as in interest in Mediterranean cuisine developed in both countries evidenced by an increase in travel and cookery writing in the national press and magazines.

In 1985 opened the internationally celebrated Quinto Quarto restaurant in London. Quinto Quarto is credited with revolutionising initially British and then American attitudes to the cooking of Rome and Lazio in particular and "cucina povera" in general. In what has been described as "a flight from excess" the pared-back, almost Spartan style of the restaurant and the shortness of a menu that concentrated on Roman "cucina povera" took first London by storm and subsequently New York with the opening of Quinto Quarto in Gramercy, credited with transforming the popularity of the area with queues regularly appearing at the door each night.

The two cooks behind the canteen-style menu and dining experience, Nick Schofield and Debbie Mottola, had "happened upon" *A Poor Sort of Meal* while working at several of London's upmarket and Michelin-system-influenced heavy-hitter establishments. "We'd had enough of French," says Schofield. "We were both looking for something more visceral. Literally." Mottola's own family background had included Neapolitan and Sicilian influences and, she says, "at home we ate the same meal sometimes two or three days. Different bits of it. It was cooking that stretched every ingredient to the limit." It was Mottola who found *A Poor Sort of Meal* while holidaying in the British South Coast town of Bridport. A first edition was on sale in a second-hand bookshop run by well-known cookbook afficionado Stephen Clark among first editions of Child Penguin-published titles. Clark is credited with saying, "the book fell into the right hands."

Back in London Mottola worked with Schofield to recreate Percival's recipes often having to persuade reluctant butchers to supply them with the more obscure cuts of meat and offal (organs). Eventually the two became so enamoured of Roman cucina povera that their enthusiasm persuaded a private investor and frequent diner at Schofield's table to fund them in their passion to open a restaurant. Housed in a converted garage in a run-down area of West London its reputation grew solely by word of mouth until a superlative review in the London Times in 1986 conferred international star-status on its cuisine and its ambience. Acknowledging their debt to A Poor Sort of Meal and to Percy Langrigg the restaurant is closed every 4th July for a feast for family and friends to celebrate Percy Langrigg's birth date on that day in 1912. While achieving fame somewhat later than either Child or David it is still clear that Percival Langrigg's legacy is at least as influential now, even as the "post-war" era gives way to the Modern and that his qualification to be regarded as an influencer on a par with Child and David has, if anything, yet to show its true potential.

Via della Consolazione, Monte Tarpeio, Rome
September 1951

Caffè corretto

Aunt Lena was right. Telephones only ever bring bad news. Hell and damn have I broken the cursed thing? Sit down. No don't sit down. Are you made of jelly? Some kind of mystic flower? Where's your backbone? A glass of water. Yes. Oh bloody hell where's a fucking light switch when you want one? Now. There. Fridge. Ferarrelle. There were two bottles. Oh yes there's still one there it is. Oh god no it's all over. All over the floor. Bloody glass everywhere. Oh you stupid boy. It was my hand Sir my hand wouldn't do what I told it to. No look at it it's shaking like the proverbial. Proverbs. Book of. I will mock when calamity overtakes you. Mock on, melodious mocker. Glass everywhere. Everywhere. I'm stuck. I Can't move. You Can't stay there you'll catch your death of cold. Was I trying to? Oh a death-catcher that's a good one. Positively Struwelpeter. Where's the dustpan? And they shall ring the way to dusty death. I am the dust-catcher with his death-pan. Glass everywhere. If I step backwards it'll be alright the glass will hardly have gone through me. One step, two steps. There now where does she keep it? In the armadio. Yes the armadio. In the corridoio. I'll have to pass the telephone. There is the cupboard. C'e l'armadio. L'armadio e qua. Where's the? There. Here. Now it's in my hand. And the brush. Look they're trying to escape. Bloody stay still you little swines. All right I'll hold you with both hands that'll dish your tricks. Now back to the kitchen past that bloody apparatus. Glass everywhere so down on your hands and knees and let's deal with it. Let's get down to it. Oh hell that knee hurts. Lower away.

Here I am on my knees. Oh Lord receive the soul of David Sopley. Oh David you've left me alone. One is one. Life goes on. Oh madam life's a piece of bloom. No. A piece in bloom. Death goes dagging everywhere. Isn't dagging what you do to sheep? Why would I know that. She's the tenant of the room, he's the ruffian on the stair. W.E.

Henley. Out of the night that covers me. Who used to be able to recite the whole thing? In camp. Someone. Garson. Whatever happened to him? Used to do recitals. People loved it all that Edwardian male bravado. He was good-looking. Was he police? Maybe he stayed on. A lot of them did. If I reach forward. If I cantilever. Is that the right word, cantilever? Look if you could just stop bloody shaking you could get this done. You're making it worse you're pushing the bits everywhere. Darn it. The ball of my thumb. Look it's bright red. Oh and it tastes. It tastes of iron. They say the universe tastes of iron. Just. Look. Reach up and get that cloth that napkin and just, there, wrap it, that'll do for the moment. You're in shock you should have a brandy. This light is very weak. The glass barely picks it up. There's another bit. Glass everywhere. And water. O fons Ferrarellae splendidior vitro. That's most of it. I'd better get a mop and mop it. Put that dustpan down there. Back, back, back out to the corridoio. Oh David did it hurt?

I don't really like brandy. Vecchia Romana. In coffee perhaps. Will the bar be open yet? The one by the Ponte Palatino. No but they told me to go to the Questura. Well bollocks to that. I want to see. Perhaps they won't have taken him to the you know. Don't say it won't say it. Home they brought her warrior dead she nor swooned nor uttered cry. Took the facecloth from the face. No fabulous symbol there. There's the mop. Funny whenever I dream of him he's always on the point. On the point! Of having sex with someone else. On someone else's point about to be skewered. Always. And I've always woken up straight away with that bitter taste in my mouth. Am I awake? Am I dreaming this? Of course you're bloody not don't be so wet. Did he get what he wanted? Did he get fucked first? First the cock and then the knife? Plunged. Plunged, plunged, plunged. Oh the ram in the thicket. The burning bush. The bush aboon Traquair. Don't squeeze it out. Gritty. It's full of glass. Throw it away. Let's sit down a minute.

Don't follow me. I won't follow you. I just want to see where it happened. To know where it happened. I'm not going to be looking for doors to the underworld. Dove andro? Che farro in any case. Senza mio ben. Kathleen Ferrier. Ships in the offing. Sit down. Sit yourself down. Let's sit down a minute. Let's have a look at that thumb. Oh it's just a scratch. It hurts. Shi de buyao! Aya's got hold of my cheek and she's pinching it so hard I can't feel my thumb and now she's let go and it stings so much I still can't feel anything else. Shanghaile wo! Zuo ge nanren! There was always a treat though, afterwards. Leftover rice scraped from the bottom of the dish with warm milk and brown sugar. Malacca sugar? Oh, gula malacca. The food of the gods. If I was half-disappeared down my burrow of death that taste would bring me back. Oh, that's funny. I can just see those long legs of yours sticking up out of a hole in the ground and here's your Scotch terrier trying to dig you up. No but I'll let you go.

They said the Questura. But I'm not going there. Bollocks to that. I'm going to go down to the Lungotevere and I'll have a caffè corretto di brandy at that cafe that stays open all night. Corretto. The first time I asked for a caffe coretto. That was the tiny cafe on the Largo Tritone. Corretto di qua? Corrected with what? Put right with what? They had me there. I didn't know there was more than one way to put a coffee right. At least I was in time to say no to grappa. Filthy stuff. I don't know how you managed to drink it. Brandy. Vecchia Romana. That'll put hairs on your chest. Funny thing to say, really. I always thought it was a funny thing to say put hairs on your chest. Women wouldn't want hairs on their chest surely? I don't remember Mother's chest being hairy. I'm not sure I ever saw her chest at least not after I was a baby I suppose. I saw her dressing once. She was very hairy down there. Very black. Very dark. No, I won't follow you.

I knew what you were doing. What you did. Where you went at night. Right from the moment you disappeared off into the bushes that time at Ostia Antica. I knew what you were looking for. Was it the excitement? Was it some long-suppressed I mean centuries-old hunting instinct? You hunted them out but you were the prey. Don't they tie up goats as tiger-bait in India? So you were the goat and you found a post in a clearing and you tied yourself up to it and waited for the beast to come and mount you. Was that it? Couldn't you make do with a bedroom and a bed like most people? Oh you didn't want to bring them back here. Grazie per la tua squizzita cortesia, condottiere. You Sir Galahad, you knight of the night. Did you circle each other there in the bushes, sizing each other up? Did you pace out the glade before the encounter? Did you come together in a clash of arms? Did you see each other's swords flash in the moonlight? Did you feel the fatal stroke? What did it feel like, David?

I better get dressed.

No, I don't want tea. I hate bloody tea.

So, you know what I'm going to ask. C'era molto sangue? I mean did he bleed to death? How long does that take? Or to put it another way how long till he lost consciousness? Quanto tempo prima che? Prima che lui. Muoia. Or did he die of shock? Could he have died of shock immediately? Did the life just fly out of him? How long can it last after death? Consciousness? Does it come out like a wind, a gust like the wind in the upstairs room? Would it just join the rest of the air? Would it move a leaf, a twig, a branch? Would it still be there just a breath of it trapped among the rocks or a rock or under a bush? Will I be able to breathe him in just a tiny, tiny particle of him if I go there now?

A flower sprang up where Hyacinthus died. Now how did he die? Wasn't he hit by some kind of rock or a discus or something? What was that boy's name? I don't remember. But there was the plaque on the wall of school chapel. Killed by a cricket ball. Did a flower spring up? If it had the groundsmen would have mowed it to death in minutes. Any wonder I hated cricket? The thought of standing there until some object hurtled down at you fast enough to kill you. Was it Jenkins?

You often read that, don't you? Livy. Lots of it in Livy. About blood soaking into the ground. The blood-soaked ground.

Should I shave?

It must have been a familiar enough sight at one time. To a lot of people. The survivors of course. The ones who told the ones who wrote about it. I mean those gory Roman battles. How many gallons do you think are shed from one end of Livy to the other? One person one gallon. So, in the average Punic Wars encounter what do you think? Ten thousand gallons? Assuming they exsanguinate completely which probably most don't so let's say... let's say one gallon per four people so two pints per person so back to thirty thousand dead that's thirty thousand divided by four bugger no never could do twos into noughts so let's say twenty eight thousand dead that's seven it's odd how a seven fits into ones and fours and eights and twos you would think it would be ones and threes and fives and nines sort of harder more masculine as my mother would say: why can't you be more masculine like your father. I like seven. Seven's a sort of closet even.

Even though it's odd. Evens are odd but odd is even. If you see what I mean. So that makes four thousand gallons of blood per encounter so how many swimming pools is that? Now if I remember rightly that's about one swimming pool and how would I know that. At the Repulse. So, over the course of the Punic Wars that's let say… oh goodness at least a hundred swimming pools of blood and from urbe conditum to the sack of Rome by Alaric let's call it the end which it was more or less then how many swimming pools? A thousand? Well, it gives you the idea. Do you think it made the ground more fertile? I mean if you were a farmer and there was a battle over your land, and you managed to survive it which would be unlikely but let's say you did then would you think let's get the leeks in early bound to be a good crop? Or would there be so many bones and bits and pieces and teeth scattered about you'd have to give up the land and move somewhere else? And would it be squidgy like a swamp like Flanders and the Somme and what went on in Europe? All that land went back to farmland, didn't it? Like the Plain of Waterloo. I wonder if they got better crops afterwards than before. Do you think a seed might fall where David was killed? Maybe a bird will shit there and there'll be a seed in the shit all nicely fertilised and the seed will put down a root and find all that blood and grow up ever so strong and tall just like its father. What shall I look for next year? Stonecrop? Valerian? Asphodel? I hope it's an Asphodel. Who said they wanted to see an asphodel so much they thought they'd die when they did? Kitty. It was Kitty in camp. She was mending something or other and we were talking about tapestry because camp conversations could be quite free-ranging and it turned out we both loved the Burne-Jones tapestries and all those asphodels. Asphodel. We were going to go South next year to see Paestum and Selinunte and Segesta and I said please can we go when the asphodels are in bloom they grow in rocky places.

So my face is shaved. That's what we were told at school. Not to neglect ourselves. Don't let yourself go.

Is it getting light out there? Not much.

From age fifteen to age what eighty scraping your face with a razor every day. Even in camp I did it. No that's not true I grew a beard once or twice. Once when I was eighteen to look manly for my mother and in camp for a bit but getting it off hurt like hell. Sae rantingly, sae roaringly, sae wantonly ga'ed he. He played a spring and da-ha-ha-hanced it roun' beneath the-he gaaaaloows tree. Oh what is death but parting breath?

Shit, shower, shave. Get dressed.

You know I don't care what I wear. David would. David does. Always so dapper, our David. Never know when you're going to be called to Government House he used to say. Like knowing how to eat an orange with a knife and fork. He was what my mother would have called a clotheshorse. Almost anything looked good on David. Or David made anything he wore look good. Slim hips. Snake hips. Bedroom eyes. NSIT. MTF. To have and to hold. Well, you could hold him, but you couldn't have him. Or you could have him and hold him, but you still couldn't have him. Oh, these bloody buttons why won't they do up? I mean he liked being had. I wonder how many men had him over the years? Enough to fill a swimming pool? Soldiers and sailors and tinkers and tailors and rich men and poor men and bloody old thieves. They had to look nice, dress well. He was like a deb or one of the fishing-fleet girls. So, he did discriminate. To an extent. At least I think he did. Not that I ever caught him with anyone. He was very discreet. The soul of discretion. But you could tell sometimes. At a party. Or even in the street once or twice. Just that shadow of a look that passed between them and you knew he'd had him. You knew he'd parted his cheeks and stuck it in and banged away until he was done and you know it wasn't to my taste at all. Really. Fucking David was like fucking a waxwork.

How did my teeth get through camp intact? That one Wisdom toothbrush lasted me all that time. They must run in the family, good teeth. Now they're beginning to look a little worn, aren't they? And the gums. Must stop drinking that cheap Frascati. It probably dissolves them. Last time round. Spit and rinse. There we are. Now. Yes. That Creed David gave me for Christmas. Just a little. Nature needs not what thou gorgeous wearest. Yes, it is gorgeous. Unlike me. I'd love to be playing Lear I'd say it Nature needs not what thou, gorgeous, wearest. But that would be silly. Silly, silly, silly.

That cherry-coloured tie with the white dots. You know there are two kinds of cherry in Turkey; keraz and vishne; sweet and sour. And my dark grey suit and my Ferragamo shoes. My one luxury. But they fit me so well. Why dress up for death, you ask. Why not? I say. Am I to go down there in my pyjama suit? Or a pair of slacks and a moth-eaten sweater? If I had a corset I'd put it on. Anything to hold this bag of emotional pus together and stop it bursting and spilling out into the street. Breathe in. Must go on a slimming diet. But at least I'm cinched. Cinched around the waist. That'll stop me from drooping. Should I take a shooting-stick? Wouldn't that be too English? The Italians would love it. But I don't think I should, somehow.

Testicles, spectacles, wallet and watch.

Watch. That gold Cyma that David gave me. He was lavish with his gifts like an oriental potentate. Like a maha-rajah. Wouldn't it be funny if it's stopped at the time he died? What time is it? Five-thirty. That looks right to me. All the things that just go on after your death. Your watch, your gas supply, your post, your hairs, your toe-nails. Until they're stopped. The watch is automatic. I suppose I'll carry on wearing it. What a carry-on. What a carry-on over carrion. The silver earth rilled with his golden blood. And bright enamelled flowers everywhere. Wouldn't that be nice? Soul clap your hands and sing. Blow, blow, blow the man down. Some talk of Alexander and some of Hercules, of Hector and Lysander and such great nay-hames as these, but of all the world's great herehereoes there's none that can comparehareharehare with a tarr-rarra-ra-rarra-ra-rarrra-rah for the British Grenadier. Oh early one morning just as the sun was ryehyesing I heard a young maid in the vahalley below; oh never leave me. Oh god I'm going to blub. Oh god. Oh god. Sit down on the bog. God won't mind the bog. Oh god David did it hurt? Did you fight? Or were you all adrenaline and not feeling or thinking just acting yes that would be it; you look down or across or over at yourself from just not far away and you see it all happening but you don't feel it, it's all happening to someone else and then the spectator is all that's left and then you float away you dissolve and you just melt away into thin air but the air must be quite thick really mustn't it with all those souls drifting around like amoebas in water under a microscope and perhaps they get stuck on things like that slippery weed on rocks by the sea or on twigs like those prayer-scraps tied to trees.

Oh David where have you gone? Are you stuck or are you free? I hope you haven't been caught on wire like a piece of rubbish paper but who's to say that what happens after death has dignity? It could be like Belsen but souls all left lying around. I need to sit down. I'm sweating. Dripping. Oh, let's cool down. These thoughts are no good. No good. Revenge kills the revenger too that's the tragedy. Oh, I think I'm going to. Head between the knees; god I'm clammy all over no I'm never sick. Oh breathe. In. Out. In. Out. No stay here on the chair yes terrazzo can look wildly inviting sometimes but don't lie down it's cold and you'll catch your death. Oh, and here it comes whoop it's like a foetus inside me doing a somersault whoop it wants to come out of my mouth no hold your belly together and blow it out there we go then you can breathe. The incubus is outyubus. Feel a bit better. Cold. A bit cold. Steady. Sit. Stand up, stand up for Jesus. Here, let me. Oh. No. That isn't it. I should be the other way round looking at the door but oh help I'm trapped. Oh. Am I on the floor feels like. Knees. Kneeling. Hands on the loo seat. Thy mercy seat in somethings of something light. Depths of burning. Oh seat be merciful. Push. Oh. I can still be sick then no it's just bile. Do you remember at school when we all came down with something and twenty of us were sent to the infirmary and we were made to stand in the corridor we weren't even supposed to lean on the wall and the floor was terrazzo too and all the shit just flowed out of our shorts and onto the floor all water with bits in it. Like the dysentery. Just like the dysentery. Those bastards who wouldn't help clear out the latrines or the ones who refused to drink the rice water they were all British you know they'd rather have got dysentery than do any work. The Dutch were much better. Shame the Americans went so soon. They were the best. Us bloody British were terrible complaining all the bloody time and never lifting a finger. Still complaining all the way to Australia or Aden or wherever no wonder the Nips despised us. Can you stand? Yes. Legs a bit shaky but yes, I can stand. There I've stopped sweating. Let's have a wash and rinse out my mouth. There. The door. Open it. Crikey I dreamt I shat in marble halls. Opulent, this place. Never fails to impress. A little water clears us of this deed. There we are. Ready for the fray? Shall we try again?

Coat. I'll just take the blue gabardine. And a scarf. That paisley that's wool on the other side. And a hat. That one. Stick. Stick? Oh for goodness sake they'll think you're his father. No stick. Gloves. Yes. Front door keys. Yes. Deep breath. Don't look around there's no one there. Uproot yourself. You've grown too comfortable here. Not for ever by still waters. Pull up your roots. They're not that deep, really. What screams when you pull it up? A mandrake. Tomorrow to fresh woods and pastures new. Today. The Piazza Navona. See that light in the sky that's dawn and smell that smell of the city when they're all asleep bar a few souls and the light cracks the darkness open and it's all begun again. That feeling of something extraordinary – what is it? Rapture. First day of holidays, that's it. Awake at dawn in December. Going home going somewhere. Goodbyeee don't cryeee. The mad excitement. Mens praetripidans avet vagare, come on Percy, linquantur Phyrgii campi, damn you, oh there's joy down this path, there's a new life down this road, oh I love roads, the roads that go on and on, those silk roads leading to the dawn all the way han by han to Bokhara and beyond. It's there there's a joy. I love the smell of a morning road as you leave the city early when it's a frost on the gardens and shell-pink at the edge of the sky. There is a dearest freshness deep down things. It's fresh today, isn't it? And all flesh shall feel it together. Oh and today we will see such things! We will feel the cold on our faces, we will gather in an upper room to listen to the tax-gatherer and we will know newness. We will be born again and we will breathe the undisturbed air see the unlaborious earth and swim the oarless sea. We will hear the casual shout that rends the frosty air and all flesh shall hear it together. Sons of the morning so gloriously bright. Here now it's here that smell of the cold curling off the earth before the day begins. Here in the long unlovely street doors where my heart was used to beat on the bald street breaks the blank day, no it's the beginning, couldn't he see? My heart becomes an April violet and buds and blossoms like the rest. Now fades the last long streak of snow. He had a thing about being buried. Old yew that graspest at the stones. Had I lain for a century dead. Now rings the woodland loud and long. Come on, David. Ring out wild bells? Bit grandiose. Here I go turning left into Campo dei Fiori. A second birth. A rebirth. New every morning is the love. No. As oe'r each continent and island. No. Tennyson I'm sure it's Tennyson. Not Keats. David, what is it? Oh yes of course oh love they die on yon rich sky they faint on hill and field and river our echoes roll from soul to soul and grow. For ever and for ever. I shall always echo you. You will always echo me. We will always echo each other. We'll be the famous fabulous flying echo brothers on at the Palais this very evening. Oh near and far from cliff and scar. Set the wild echoes flying. Oh the running of the deer I asked you do you remember had you ever seen the running of the deer? That's all I miss about England. I'm happy with the gaudy melon flower but I'd love to hear the sweet singing in the choir past three o'clock on a cold frosty morning. Give you good morrow. Let nothing you dismay. Coming out of the night into the light in the bleak midwinter. The virgin birth. Here we go Gubbionari.

But we get snow. We've had snow here. Much colder than you think, Rome. In Winter. Proper four-coat weather sometimes. If I complained about the cold in Tientsin Dad used to say take you to Peking my lad then you'll really feel it. That's what the aya used to say; four-coat weather and what did we eat you know I Can't remember. Mutton of some kind I expect. Now Turkey, there's a country that does cold-weather food well. Those soups; tripe and lentil. Tripe or lentil. Not together. Two different soups. Those dishes of beans with bits of meat mutton again. Perhaps I should just go to Turkey and learn how to do their cooking. Not an easy language though. Largo dei Librari. Click, click I can hear my footsteps. It's funny it feels as though it's going to snow. I know it's nonsense but it feels like that moment before the snow starts when there's a hush. Snow at Yantai. Tobogganing. Cocoa. Lo he comes with clouds descending now who's being silly but better snow clouds than fog to descend in. No before that. I love to hear the snowstorm hing, 'tis but the Winter garb of Spring. John Clare. Standing there feeling the chill on my skin feeling the contrast. Feeling. Reeling. Feeling it real. Morris now he was our favourite, the master enameller; he made himself into those knights, he simply crossed through time westward the banner rolls over my wrong you could feel the cold walls and hear the flick and flap of the flag straining out we were there. There. You were there. Pompiere. Desolate he had a feeling for desolation; strange when you think he was brought up in a nice big suburban villa with an island in the garden. With a boathouse for the summer heat. We used to act them out, didn't we. Give us Jehane to burn or drown. You put a tea-towel over your head and twisted it round over your face so you couldn't see. And you made me be Godmar. In the end we had to take it in turns to be Jehanes. Didn't we do a performance once? Yes of course we did. Mr Dunlop that was it. He read it and we did the actions and mimed the direct speech. Only I was Jehane that time and you made a very wicked Godmar. Who played Roger? No one. I think we just conjured him like Banquo. I felt that desolation that loss of hope in camp. Just the same feeling. The very same. Verily. Before camp when we knew they were coming. On the cliff with those poor devils. Leaving the dogs. Loss of everything. Loss of our lives. Losing our freedom. I felt it. What he described. Morris. He was good at that. How was he so good at that? Some sort of clairvoyance? Like a seer in a trance seeing all his own mischance. Every comfort stripped away. Raw. What happens next? We don't know. What are they going to do to us? We don't know. Are they going to kill us? We. Don't. Know.

My soul is shivering. And I saw above me the cold and rook-delighting heaven that seemed as though ice burned and was but the more ice. San Salvatore in Campo. The holy saviour in the field. The Campus Martius? That was around here somewhere, wasn't it? All those Romans in their voting pens. The Gracchi and all that. And even love froze for a little while and there wasn't fear or pain or grief because they need warmth to survive and perhaps that's what hell really is just freezing cold there are no fires in hell no roaring bonfires there. But colour, there's still colour, and sounds are very sharp and pointed and precise and perhaps that's what we find when we step outside the door. Earth stands hard as iron. The universe tastes of iron. Water like a stone. I saw it once through a doorway where was it? I looked through the door and on the other side it was immense and cold and there were stars and it had a little ringing noise that was just one fraction above silence and it was cold and it was death but it was also life and I knew it. I knew what it was. Fled is that vision do I sleep or wake? Seggiola. Sun's coming up. Don't want to walk the whole way down the Lungotevere. Think of a back-road.

First you have to go cold. If you don't go cold you won't warm up again. The cold you catch your death of. With. Where was it? Not Morningside. It must have been near the Meadows that cemetery. Grange Road. And what on earth was I doing there? I didn't live there. Was I visiting someone? I really don't remember. What prompted me to go in and watch the snow falling on the graves? Bit grotesque really and I've never I mean I haven't ever told anyone. That I felt I had to go in. That I just stood there in that sort of gardeners'' niche that was cut back into a slope and lined with stone like a sort of cave. With some sort of gothickery going on around the entrance. The floor was earth and there were bunches of dead flowers in the corner. It was so very cold and I think I must have been a bit low at that time I often was low in Edinburgh and I just stood there and watched the snow come down

and looked at all those graves and his weak spirit fails to think how.
Think how. Think how they must freeze. No that's not the right order.
But I just stood there and got colder and colder until I had to move or
not move again then I walked out of there and I felt better not warm
at all not at all but better somehow. Changed. Utterly. Reborn.

Iam laeti studio pedes vigescunt. Iam ver egelidos refert tepores.
Linquantur Phyrgii Catulle campi. Oh David the claras asia urbes I
swear I can see you in your Phrygian cap leading the rout with your
glass of wine in hand yelling at your panthers to move on. The king
sat in Dunfermline toun. And we said it together Carmen 46 didn't
we the whole thing together that was one we always had word perfect
and it made us sad and it made us happy and it's a metaphor for life
you said and how right you were you always were. O dulces comitum.
Will you wait for me for a bit before you walk away diversae variae
viae reportanting? Will I get a glimpse of you on the frontier, on the
road to Koko Nor? A Tartar horn tugs at the North wind, Thistle
Gate shines whiter than the stream. The sky swallows the road to
Koko Nor. On the Great Wall, a thousand miles of moonlight. These
times a traveller's heart is a flag a hundred feet high in the wind.

But the Tarpeain? That's a new one on me. I know about the
Borghese Gardens I thought that's where you used to go. That has
its moments every now and then but the Tarpeain? At night? The
height of stupidity in every sense. But you know no one really notable
was ever done in there. It was ignominious. The height of ignominy
to be chucked off a cliff. So why did you go there? Was there a higher
level of thrill? Were the gardens just too tame? Too smooth, too
predictable? Had the regulars all had you already? Were you bored? Is
there a different type on the Tarpeian? More authentic? Lower class?
The lorry drivers and the abattoir-workers and the sewer-cleaners?
Borghese just too middle-class? Plenty of dissolute types up there,
though, even in the gardens. Lots of boys for hire. Perhaps that was
it? Yes of course that was it. You were beginning to feel too old and
when you felt the boys, they were too young. You couldn't compete
for the married men. So change your groves. Hunt where they boys
are older and stronger and the married men are more dangerous. You
still had the body of a youth, and you could pass for one in the dusk
with the light behind you. You still had the arse of a nineteen-year-
old. You said it yourself. Smooth and sweet.

Cross the road here. Arenula then down Catalana past the Palazzo Cenci.

You know when we were at school I had such a crush on you from the beginning. You recognised it. I tried to get as close to you as I could but you were Senior so that wasn't allowed. We might as well have been in a leper colony for the amount of touching that went on. In public. Except during games. You were so untouchable you might have been a god. I didn't know why you were so aloof. Until you told me. Did they corrupt you, David? Is that the right word? Goodness didn't see that car. Alright, alright! Calm down! Keep walking. Corrupt you, did they? Infect you with mortality did they? You so perfect so pure looking. That was your secret, wasn't it? No amount of spunk inside you could ever make you human. So free from mortal taint. I wanted to be you. No not be you. I wanted to inhabit you to have your grace your looks your mouth your arse I wanted to feel everything you felt but still have my own thoughts I had such a desire for you to be you it used to make me sick. Until we were finally there together in the vac but you still didn't let me know where you went at night. Those bad dreams, I used to invent them so you'd come and sleep in the bed next to me then we'd stay awake for ages making up our game. Latin, Greek, English, French it didn't matter; they just had to fit together and if we'd carried on and written it all down like we said we would, we would have had what would we have had? Palazzo Cenci. An epic? An Idyll stitched together from lines and verses? A play? Yes, it could have been a play they had to bear speaking aloud of course because that's what we did, we said them, because you couldn't prove they matched unless you said them. And it diverted me. You Ganymede. You flirt. Even when you were what? Eight, nine? You wanted sex. Congress. Even before you knew what got done and who did it. I know I didn't. Until that evening on that last day of term after the party on the beach. I did want to lie with you of course I did but even when I understood I didn't know who would put it in to who. I mean I couldn't choose and we didn't choose did we when it finally happened we weren't a man and a woman were we I mean we were both men and we did what men wanted and we got what men wanted and I think you liked it. It was a union wasn't it I mean as far as it can be between two separate individuals it was a union. And I loved you. I couldn't live with you. Not as a couple not in the same bed each night I'm sorry. Would that have made a difference? Would you have come back to earth? Would you have hearkened to your terrier barking and come back?

No but you were gone, long gone before I ever met you. And I won't follow you. I can't follow you. I'm not a golden boy or girl to mingle my ashes with yours. I'm more in the chimney-sweeping line myself. Now I'm going to break the rules and no scorn or ridicule please, but this is a Shakespeare quotation warning – no you had the last one I think I'm right in saying – so so oh let me not to the marriage of true minds provide impediment nor bend with the remover to remove. Your turn. Twice or thrice, yes that's good. Had I loved thee before I knew thy face or name. So in a voice so in a shapeless flame Angels affect us oft and worshipped be well I worshipped thee so you can have the rest go on Still when to where thou wert I came some lovely glorious nothing did I see. That it assume thy body I allow. What is "it"? Well David, it's the entire whole of fucking creation you fucking stupid bastard; there was nothing I ever admired or wanted that wasn't you and now where have you fucking gone and left me? I mean who is Sylvia, what is she that all her swains commend her? The heavens such grace do lend her. You were my heaven, you absolute piece of shit. It's only an alleyway I've been down here before. Via del Tempio. Here we are. This'll take me to the river.

I love these pre-War shop signs with the belle epoque curls and flourishes. And the gilding that catches the streetlamps. I love the glow from sodium lamps it's so golden and warm. Like gold to aery thinness beat. But you're gone. My sacrifices offend you. The smoke will not rise. Auspices and Haruspices. You didn't want my confession. That's what makes gods gods. They don't care about us and our petty whinings offend them: like a parent with too many children they've heard it all before. Those are your white marble gods of course not the painted deities of actual Rome. And Greece. They were like us or like aspects of us as the Hindu gods are. I believe. They weren't really all that classical they were really rather modern. The eyes were painted in so they looked as though they were looking at you. Now if you want a proper deity something so removed it could be from another planet go to the Vatican Museum and see the black statues of those Egyptian cults. Quite a shock after all that marble. Those are stones you could get down and worship. Perhaps I could get a job as a cicerone. I could go to the tourist offices and dress up and speak nicely and regale them with my knowledge and I'm sure they'd recommend me. Perhaps I'd get some film stars. Probably I'd just talk too much and lose them in facts which tourists rarely want they'd rather have the fiction, what they'd call romance: oh Iddley was sooo romantic if you throw a coin in the fountain and wish it will come true and we were taken to the place where that English poet Keats said his last goodbye to his girlfriend before he died, they were going to be married the next day, I know so tragic. Some of my class are wet from the slough of romance, should one throw them a lifeline before they're sucked back in? I'd love to counter some of the things they come up with but it's just as good to share them with Lyle over a negroni. Does Lyle know? I'd like to get some flowers. But where?

Bring me a gentian.

Bring me a torch.

That's what I need. Gentians. Big ones.

Where do you get Bavarian gentians in the centro storico at six in the morning?

The Hades Florist? They have to be big and dark, mind, I'd tell him, jolly right I would, only the dark ones, thank you, no ordinary gentians, you know; I want torch flowers of the blue smoking darkness and they have to have that smoking blueness of Pluto's gloom, ribbed and torch like you see, with their blaze of darkness spread blue down flattening into points. No, thank you amaryllis will not do. Not at all. I want those black lamps from the halls of Dis, the ones that burn dark blue the ones that give off darkness, blue darkness. No not those. Those are too like Demeter's pale lamps.

Reach me a gentian, give me a torch.

I'm off to find my way into the arms Plutonic. Into the sightless realm where Persephone herself is but a voice. Let me guide myself down the darker and darker stairs until I'm pierced with passion. I know I said I wouldn't but David where else would I andro?

Turn left. Lungotevere Cenci. Oh god there it is you can begin to see it up there the back of the Campidoglio. It must have been like throwing people out with the rubbish. The whole cliff was probably a mass of offal and peelings and shit and god knows what and crawling with rats. Probably if you didn't die and were badly injured you were just eaten by them anyway lying there longing for a sword to chop off your head and end it all even if they had to chop twice. Should I have called Lyle? Yes, I should have called Lyle. But I wasn't quite myself back there in the flat, I mean falling on the lavvy floor and dropping the bottle and cutting my hand – where is it? – can't be bothered to take my glove off. Won't die of it. Lyle will know soon. If not already. She has friends everywhere including the Questura and it's not everyday that a Milor Inglese gets murdered on the Tarpeain and him a well-know omosessuale and froccio and probably una spia Inglese while you're about it. She'll want to get there before the press and she's probably on the phone right now persuading some Commissario to keep it quiet for another hour.

Lyle, I can't talk to you. I have nothing to say I mean that is there's nothing that I can spew out; my stomach is empty. Oh I should have listened to you and gone out on my own and not gone to live with him or he with me. You said we shouldn't go below the moon and you were right. Wrong realm. And I couldn't really do it with him I just felt I had to get a ticket and join the queue. Was that unfair was it my mad jealousy? Six of one I expect. But he was right about the classes and everyone wanting to see where Lord David and his catamite lived. Did you know that Catamito was the Roman equivalent of Ganymede? Yes of course you did. Hardly me the Ganymede. And they stole spoons do you remember? And napkin rings and tea-towels and all kinds of stuff for souvenirs and there are their walls, high, high with no ceilings heading up into the grey sky and there's your tea-towel among their cloudy trophies hung. Well now we'll see. We'll just have to see if they'll still come when I've moved out. Of course, I'll have to move out. I'll do this class today and no more until I move. I can trust this lot today more or less but there'll be scores of them next week just there to look around and imagine us at it together "what do they do?" hoping for some kind of powder-puff Mayerling I shouldn't wonder.

Where shall I go? Whither goest thou? Who said that whither goest thou. Have I blasphemed? What happens if you say the same words in a different context just a simple selfish context? I mean knowingly or more-or-less knowingly? They just sort of rushed into my head. I mean it's not as though I'm expecting to find a gardener on the side of that cliff sitting on a rock and asking me where I'm going. Is it? I didn't visualise that. But now I can't get it out of my head. There's a bank of acanthus down at the bottom like the one by the tram stop on the Labicana.

What is it this afternoon? Involtini di Manzo. Everything's ready. I'm going to do it. They'll all be looking at me eyes full of moisture, the poor tragic little terrier, he'll be the Greyfriars Bobby of Rome down there by the Piramide maybe bang up against Keats. Imagine having a dog and calling it Bobby, you'd look at it every day and wonder what it would do if you died first. Eat you if no one came looking. Is that the booth over there? I love the word booth. Was it Aunt Rachel who spoke the Gaelic? Yes it was. Such a soft-sounding language like rain on peat. Lang may your lumm reeek. No that's Scots. Booth she would say booooth and that meant shop. Booooothe. Who was it said poc ma hon in front of her and she was so embarrassed? Mortally embarrassed. Poor Aunt Rachel. She hung on until we knew they'd been lost and then she upped and died. Or downed and died. It's funny how hidden love can be how simmering and slow it isn't all Crepes Suzette at your table. Most often it's a simple stew. But there it is hoving into view. Is it open? Yes it is. Who's there? Anyone with a camera? Anyone in a flashy suit and a homburg? Wish I'd cleaned my glasses. No, doesn't look like it. Just the usual coffee stall with the market porters and the taxi drivers. Giorno, giorno. Posso? Grazie. Buon giorno. Caffè coretto di brandy. Eccoti. Si una bella giornata. No, Scozzese. Si da tre anni ormai. Puo fare freddo anche a Roma. Hai? Gli Scozzese amano il gelato. Anche in inverno, si. Si, il migliore del mondo. Si. A lei! Buon giorno! Giorno. Giorno. A lei.

Mens praetrepidans. Feel better for that coffee and brandy. Nearly there. Almost there. I could turn round and go to the Questura later and not see anything at all. Not look. Don't look! All the time we used to say that in camp. Everything was on view. Don't look. Don't look at birth or life or death hang a curtain up in front of it. Shame we didn't get to do that final Revue. The Yanks rather put the kybosh on it dropping that bomb on opening night. What was her name? She was good. We were going to do that Noel and Gertie routine weren't we. Tonight at Eight-Thirty. And you came into the rehearsal the day before and told me what was going to happen and you warned me it wouldn't all come out pat as if we'd just walk out and go back to who we were. Those were some of the worst weeks of all. People kept on dying. You began to find out who was coming back from the other camps and who wasn't. The Nips didn't shift. We thought they'd come from town and massacre the lot of us. Sorry I've got bad news for you. And you. And you. Oh but there was good news of course there was good news, the war was over but there was that drag as if you were caught in a strong current and you could see the beach but you didn't think you'd have the strength to get there. And we were all so ill we didn't know how ill we were. So they kept on dying. Even when the food came in. Such an odd assortment. Tinned mutton, butter, chocolate, Spam, dried milk powder. Fruit is what we wanted. I used to dream about mangoes and pineapple and guava and lychees and oranges and yes, I do know how to eat one with a knife and fork just in case.

They still have it at home. The death penalty. Here the fascists brought it back but it was repealed in '48. Who told me that? Firing squad. They used firing squads. So if they catch him he won't get the death penalty. Or them. What if he's there? They're there. What if they've caught him and brought him there to make him confess? What then? Well no different to after the war I suppose when they arrested the guards and the commandant and co. They took them away for a trial. I mean what point was there in killing any of them? I know they did in some camps. Or at least I heard they did. Or read they did. But you can only die once however long you can make it last. So what's the point in taking one life for a thousand or two thousand? There's only so many times someone can scream, and they'll never make up for all the screams together. Pat like the revenger in the old tragedy. Let justice be done. Fiat iustitia. Et ruent.

It's morning now almost. As o'er each continent and island. Oh, the papers. It'll be all over the papers. I wonder what they'll say about the place? Will anyone dare say it's a haunt for homosexuals? Not L'Osservatore I don't suppose. I wonder what stories they'll make up? They'll bring up the spy stuff you can bet your bottom dollar. Well that would be true after a fashion. All that message-passing you were mixed up in in camp. That David Louie on the outside, I wonder how many of his people were bumped off by the Japs? The loyal Chinese. The loyal Indians. The ones who hated us were some of the worst bastards of all. Here I go same old newsreels playing. Newsreels. Tennyson. Morris. Involtini. Will I ever think an original thought, speak an original line or cook an original thing? Originality's overrated. Who said that? Me? My one original thought is that there's no point in being original. Very good. A palpable hit. There you go. But really what's the point? Don't we just fire out words in some kind of order to make order and if we can't make order ourselves we make order out of the words of someone who did make order with words but it just looks like order; does it mean that reality has an order or do we just order our words to make it look real? Loquor ergo sum? In camp we just bitched most of the time. It made some kind of order out of our lives. Words are merely labels. Tree. Pine tree. Tall pine tree. Thank God for adjectives. Thank God for poetry frankly I don't know what I'd have done without out it all my life; it's more real than reality. And what's poetry? An original ordering of words. Nobody's ever written the same poem as someone else as far as I know. I mean how many Homers were there before it all got written down? Each one a word or two different. Or how many versions of Greensleeves from the sublime to the ridiculous?

The Tiber Island is always a bit of a let-down. Probably you need to see it when the river's in flood so that rostrum looks as though it's cleaving the waters. Not a cleaver I hope. Or a hatchet. Please let it have been the right kind of knife for the job. And keen. Not a dull old blade. And quick. He'll have choked on his own blood. They say drowning's peaceful. Me? Suttee by water? I'm much too dull for that. The main thing is to stay out of the way. Keep your head down. No interviews with "the close friend", "the constant companion". Lyle'll manage something. She'll know what to do. She must know by now.

Am I slowing down? I think I am. Iam laeti studio pedes vigescunt I don't think. Why am I wearing the shoes with lead in them? I think I want to be sick. I should have just gone to the Questura as I was told. Stupid boy. Better not sit down – I might not want to get up, let's just lean against the parapet a minute here by the footbridge. I'm glad I came down the river. Time like an ever-rolling stream and all that. A meditation, that's what you call it. They fly forgotten. Well, they get washed away really. Life flushes out its drains. Life goes on. That's what we say. Well, our lives go on anyway not yours. You're not alive any more. At least not in the sense you can order a caffe coretto and drink it. Eheu frater. That's done now I'll build a boat and sail it back to Italy and up the Po and have it dragged across to the Garda Lake. There they rowed and there we landed. O venusta Sirmio! The poet's hopeless woe. Typical Tennyson to see woe in everything. He was a bit blackward in his thinking. A bit death obsessed. The under-lying dead underlay the whole edifice. But you can't have a resurrection without death can you? Please I don't want to see a shade waiting for me. No thank you. I want him to be gone. Gone home to his cubile lecto. I'm not taking his body back to English earth and tracking the ship each nautical mile. Where will he be buried? It'll say in the Will no doubt. He won't have dragged me in to that? He said he wouldn't. There must be solicitors in London. Lyle will know.

Oh glory, I'll have to get going. I feel as though I want to shit. My bowels are falling out. Just like they do when you get bad news. I'm being drawn. God the stench when your own innards came out if you survived the hanging and presumably some did. But then you'd have died of shock, surely. Burning must have been worse if you couldn't pay someone to strangle you first. Presumably the crowd would have wanted the screams. The two books of my childhood kindly sent from Scotland: *Fox's Book of Martyrs* illustrated and *Struwelpeter*. All those men in black with the funny hats standing in a pile of wood clutching their rosaries while the fires were lit. Nightmares? And the man with the tailor's shears who came to cut off your thumbs and the stumps sprouted blood while he ran away on those long legs wearing the bottle-green coat. Words in a certain order can have power beyond measure. Not enough to bring people back to life at least in the coffee-consuming sense because when your time's up it's up. Clotho or Lachesis? I can never remember. Does that matter? Your time. The time that stops and ends in you. With you. My time intersects your time and your time intersects mine but yours is yours and mine is still mine and you take the high road and I take the low road and one of us will be in Scotland before the other and it looks as though it's you my darling David. I'm sorry. I'm so sorry. Not in the sense of apologising. I'm simply sick to my stomach with a profound sorrow. In the fundament. A fundamental sorrow. I wish I could remember that German song we all must part – muss scheiden was it? Und aller mensch in aus der Welt? It's our condition and thank god we don't think about it all the time though Tennyson seems to have thought about it most of the time. What was breakfast like in his house? Remember toast is just dead bread? Think how many oranges died to make that pot of marmalade? He knew the answer in his own funny Scandinavian Lincolnshire way: words.

Words, words, words; people say it's only words; actions speak louder than words, words can never hurt me but that's all a bit jejune, isn't it? A bit lazy so you cut my throat and that counts for more than all the words I've ever spoken because it's real. Inescapably real. It's an event. It's real. Words are not an event. That's what you say. But you said them or even just thought them and isn't that an event too? So there are grades of event? Are there? Murder or drinking coffee are truer events than saying, "un caffe"? Truer. And truth is relative and there are grades of truth? So only material things are true? Isn't that Mechanism? So what about that reredos in Venice in Saint Mark's? The only things that are real are the metal and the stones. Is that right? Did Yeats see it? You'd think he must have done. It's the kind of thing the smithies of the Emperor would have made. So the truth lies only in the things and not what they point to. In which case we might have left the gold in the ground and saved a lot of labour and concentrated on operating espresso machines and murdering each other. Let's cut to the chase then I must stand up and walk up that road. God is a poet and poetry is all that really matters. In the beginning was the Word and then there was line two. See I wasn't sick. But I could still really do with a shit.

The Vico Jugario. They say it's ancient. Very ancient. Older than Rome. The street of the yoke-makers. Or the street of the yoke. Yoga Street. The street that links. The Way Between. I like that. The way between things. Crossing the Via Flavia now. The Vico Jugario. If I'm right it ends in the Piazza della Consolazione. How very nice. The link between the broad son-sweeping river of death and the place of consolation. Practically Dantean. And I must do something but what? Soldier on. That's it. Soldier on. Some talk of Alexander and some of Hercules. Of Hector and Lysander and such great names as these. Ta-ra-ra. Hearts of oak are our ships, hearts of oak are our men. Ready boys, ready. Steady, boys, steady. I'm neither ready nor steady. Steady nor ready. Now, unready. It didn't mean he was unprepared, it meant he wouldn't listen to advice. Sellars and Yeatman. How we loved it all, that de-bunking. You couldn't even mention that book in camp it was unpatriotic. Unpatriotic to say we got our come-uppance. Traitorous. Some people wouldn't mention Noel Coward and as for Maugham. Venom. All those hearts of oak in the Prince of Wales and Repulse. And did the Grenadiers manage to save Singapore? Why does it always come back to that? What did that war do to me that I can't think forward anymore? I'm pinned by it like a moth on a tray. It didn't get everyone like that, not the selfish ones, they did better. I wonder what it's like to be self-centred. That's rather stupid. We all are. It's the way we're made. Look at David. He didn't lose faith in himself or the Empire or if he did he kept a tight lid on it. But I couldn't stand all that pain. All that death and not just us but all of them all the Chinese and not even the death but the killing. All that killing. Even without the screaming. That's my own newsreel. It's always playing. In fact, come to think of it, it goes on so long we haven't even got to the first picture let alone the main event. That would be *Gone with the Wind*. Obviously. That was on at the Palace wasn't it? Nathan Road.

Bit of a breeze coming up. A nice morning breeze to sweep the streets before the day begins. Is it a little fresh or is that my imagination? Does it come from fields of snow and ice with a bit of a chill to wake us up? Or are they blown softly from the fields of sleep no that's the evening wind. Was that Keats? There's the one by Housman, the winds that out the westland blow, not that one. I think it's Keats. I'll look when I get home. The dawn with rosy fingers. The Rione Campitelli. Not very savoury. Through the gate. Up among the trees. This isn't very picturesque, David. Not Dodona exactly, at least it didn't speak to you and say don't come in here, or if it did you must have been so keen on the chase so doped up with it you couldn't hear what they said. The breast of the nymph in the brake. Or a flash of arse-cheek among the foliage. Stinks of piss. Why must people leave their rubbish just anywhere? David, was this really some kind of paradise for you with all those cigarette packets and human shit and empty tin cans? It makes me think you must have been like a dog getting scent of something we humans can't get. That smell of sex those glands and membranes gently excreting lust into the air and smearing it onto the leaves like invisible slug-trails. Those glances at midnight in the wine-dark wood. Those torches of desire that cannot singe a sleeve. Lamps from the halls of Dis. Is it Michaelmas? Someone will want there to be a mass for you for your soul. Maybe I shall go and see the candles shedding darkness. On the. On the. Not even lost, David. Never found. Such a thing is never to be found in this world and our passions are lost in the dense gloom. How very baroque. Are you still here? Lead me then, lead me the way down the darker and darker stairs and I will follow you. You can't stop me. I'm going to bring you back with music. What shall I sing? Lor lumme. Whistle a little tune. Ta-da dah-dah-dah-dah dah. Oh early one morning just as the sun was ri-i-sing I. What was that? Someone shouted. Oh heck. Someone yelled silenzio. How embarrassing. It must be over there. They must be over there. How do I get there? It's just random shrubbery no hold on there are little paths everywhere they look grey. Just a fence ahead and a kind of cave behind it. Up there looks like the highest point. No, but that yell came from over on the left. Find a path. Follow a path. There's a light, someone must have brought a battery-torch. All these twigs and I must sound like an elephant crashing through the undergrowth. Va tacito, Percy. Nascosto. Too late, they've seen me. Best foot forward. Two carabiniere, three? And two men with hats and raincoats. One of them's coming toward me.

What's the inspector's name? Commissario. I can't remember, Bugger. Si buon giorno a lei Commissario mi dispiace Ispettore Percy Langrigg sono l'amico dell' Lord Maldon. La Questura mi ha chiamato. Al telefono. Si alla Questura ma. Si. Mi dispiace. Io volevo vedere. Per favore. Si io sono la sua famiglia. No non mi muovo. Non tocchero niente rimano qui. Certo.

E lui? Is it that lump on the grass? It looks as though he was heading upward then; trying to touch the wall. Safety? Like the games we played at school. The wall was neutral. Touch the wall and he couldn't touch you. Was that it? What's he doing? Did he see the blinking grail after all. Covering you up. I must ask. I have to ask don't I?

Com'e morto? Perche non puoi dirmelo? E un segreto di stato? Non, mi dispiace. Sorry. Per favore puoi dimerlo. Let go of my fucking arm. Let fucking go. Shoved away under the trees out of the way. He will talk to me. Senta, scusi, Ispettore. Com'e morto? Quando e morto? Di cosa e morto? Si certo io sono sua famiglia. Era mia marito. Abbiato vissuto insieme.

He's looking at me in that way. Not disapproval. Interest. He's imagining us naked together. Me and David. Or me and him? Is it true what they say that proximity to death gives a sexual charge to the living? Didn't happen much in camp but then we weren't really alive or only just. But yes, look down there down to his flies; there's something stirring, old Pan perhaps living in this glade giving men hard-ons for each other. Yes, I would. I would get down on my knees if it was just the two of us and I'd drink it up and lick my lips or I'd even bend over for him and let him have his way. This is right, it's right to feel this way, you have to find a way to feel alive when you're with death and this is the most basic isn't it or having a cup of sweet tea and a biscuit in the next room, it's the same: we need food after a shock, we need something inside us. That's what they say. Now he's looking at David. Beckoning. Si sto arrivando. That one's really good looking that one it's just the uniform. Now he's looking at me again. Sei sicuro? Si. Yes I am. He's saying something to the other carabiniere he's leaning forward. Where did they get that coat? Is it a coat or a blanket? It's not a horse blanket, is it? There he is. Gosh he's tall isn't he, and such long legs; people always said what lovely legs he had and his great big feet, they look a bit awkward now like a dead albatross. Hanno preso il suo orologio. Not that it would take a great detective to work that out, you can see the mark on his wrist the pale stripe. Altro? Aveva un anello con sigillo. Mano sinistra. They're pulling out his arm from underneath him, should they be doing that? I mean have they taken photographs yet? Shaking his head. Ring's not there then. Aveva un portafoglio con se? Non lo so. Dovrei guardare a case. A volte prendeva solo banconote. They're looking at each other. Veniva qui spesso? Non lo so davvero. Non mi ha detto dove stave andando. La notte. Si la notte. Ma aveve vissuto insieme. Avevamo suite separate. That look again. I must shut up now mustn't say anything more than people already know or it'll all get twisted around well it will anyway but no fuel for the fire from me. Look he's wearing that sweater I gave him.

Lovat.

David must still be warm. The Inspector is looking at me. The other one is lifting David's head by the hair. Oh lord, lord, lord that really is the end now he's really dead really gone. Really gone. Now I Can't see him alive anymore so he's really dead. He was standing there looking at me I know he was he was wanting to see that I saw him like he was but I can't David. I can't. That's you now. A man with a cut throat. I'm sorry David I'm sorry. You're a man with a cut throat and I'm going to spew.

Grazie, grazie. A handkerchief how gallant. And an arm around the shoulders. Very strong. And my height too. He's quite close and he has a nice moustache and nice lips and a nice cologne.

"Mi dispiace per la tua perdita. Amico. Certo. Grazie. Sediamoci. Laggiu sull'erba. Posso aiutarla?

"Non, grazie.

We sit together on the grass. He has kind eyes and he says:

"Hai qualcuno a casa? Un amico? C'e qualcuno che puoi telefonare? Bene. Piu tardi dovrai venire alla Questura. Ti inveriemo una macchina. Guarda, ecco la mia carta. Puoi chiamarmi. In ogni momento. Vivo per conto mio. Okay? Sigarette? Mi dispiace che sia solo Nazionale. Lucky Strikes. Camels. Le sigarette americane sono migliori. " That lean into the flame. "Non vuoi farmi domande? Dopo. Dopo. Stai tremando. E naturale. Ecco la mia sciarpa. Non. Veramente. Puoi portarle con te. Oppure posso." A rather sweet pause. "Posso ritarlo. Quando ti senti meglio. Si. Si. Dopo. Bene. He stopped. Now he's saying, "Sergente fermi quella persona."

He's looking past me. He's getting to his feet:

"Questa e una scena del crimina, signora, non puoi essere qui. "

He has nice shoes. Signora? Lyle.

"Don't look."

"I didn't come to look I came for you. No, I don't want to know. How are they treating you?"

"Very well."

"You can't stay here. Percy, don't look back, you have to come with me."

"I'm coming with you."

"He told me not to try to follow him."

"That was good advice. Commissario posso portare via il mio amico? Lyle Destrooper sono. Si certo a la vostra disposizione. Alle undice. Piazza Navona 78 piano nobile. Alle undice. Grazie. Fino a piu tardi allora. He has sad eyes. Grazie per la vostra gentilezza. Percy. Andiamo. Oh. Momento. Commissario posso lasciarli qui. Solo da un lato. Ah. Grazie. Grazie."

She's putting a buch of flowers on the ground.

"That scarf doesn't suit you."

"It's his, the inspector's. Don't say anything about it."

"Very well. Can you walk?"

"Of course I can walk. Can you walk on those heels? How did you know I was here. I mean I knew you would know I was here."

"What have you done to your hand?"

"My hand?"

"It's bleeding."

"Bleeding? Oh yes, I dropped a bottle on the floor I was just trying to pick it up."

"This morning?"

"Yes. Earlier."

"Do you want to go home?"

"I have to, don't I? The police are going to come and pick me up."

"I can always call someone."

"Of course you can."

"Don't be waspish. Please."

"I'm sorry. I wasn't thinking about you. I'm sorry."

"It's natural, Percy. Perfectly natural."

"He's gone you know. I mean he isn't there or it isn't there whatever comes out of us when we die, our ectoplasm or our spirit or our soul or whatever. It was there when I arrived but when I looked at what they'd done to him it went."

"Good."

"Good?"

"He always knew when to leave a party."

"Is that a Schiaparelli?"

"Yes."

"Is it black?"

"No, it's a very dark blue."

"Lyle..."

"Yes?"

"Where did you get those flowers?"

Lightning Source UK Ltd.
Milton Keynes UK
UKHW020804031022
409835UK00012B/1610